NOON

About the Author

Nancy Learned Haines decided in ninth grade to become an engineer, to use her love of math in practical applications. She received a master's degree in industrial engineering and worked for almost seventeen years as an engineer before she decided that she didn't have to continue in a career choice made while she was barely in high school.

Her husband, David, had been collecting books by and about Quakers for many years and had introduced her to the lure of used bookstores. So, when she "retired" as an engineer, she became a bookseller. Her bookstore, Vintage Books, offered general used books and wonderful antiquarian books in a renovated barn in Massachusetts, with a specialty in used and rare Quaker books and manuscripts; at that time, Vintage Quaker Books was the largest source of out-of-print Quaker books in the world. Nancy closed the shop after twenty-five years in business.

In 2000, they acquired a collection of letters written between a pacifist who went to France with the Quakers during World War I and his activist girlfriend at home in Cambridge, Massachusetts. This collection is the basis for Nancy's first book, *We Answered With Love: Pacifist Service in World War I*. She also wrote a children's book, *Approved! A Story About Quaker Meeting for Business*, which introduces children to the Quaker process of communal decision-making. Currently, all her projects have something to do with Quakers.

Nancy and David now live in Hillsborough, North

Carolina, on land granted to Quakers on the ancestral grounds of the Occaneechi and Eno Tribes of Native Americans along the Eno River. Their property was originally deeded to the Quaker Fincher family. Discovering that tidbit piqued their interest in learning more about the Friends who settled along the Eno River.

The original Eno Friends Meeting was laid down in 1843. All that remains now is the Friends cemetery, which is on private land. Nancy is a member of the new Eno Friends Meeting in Hillsborough, which was established in 2013.

For more information, visit her website—https://nancy-haines.wordpress.com.

MY CHILDREN FROM

ANOTHER WORLD

BOOK 2: NOON

PAYTON FLETCHER
aka _GLASSES

Podium

In dedication to my friends and family,
whose support kept me putting pen to paper.

Published in 2023 by Podium Publishing, ULC
www.podiumaudio.com

Podium

NOON

1

I kept my stance solid, blocking the blow that went straight for my sternum and throwing it off, before spinning and throwing a kick out that disturbed the air.

My target bent her knees, her eyes flashing with energy, "**Fang Pounce Technique!**"

I quickly flipped through the air as she dove through empty space, her nails outstretched into the facsimile of wolf claws, her Vitae sharpening the air around her fingertips as she tried to rend me.

"Good form." I dropped my **Grace Stance** as I landed on the ground. "I think it's time we take a break."

Daka's eyes crinkled as she breathed heavily and wiped her brow of sweat, smiling. "Sounds good, Dad! Is it time for nosh?"

I wasn't sure how Daka had gotten it in her head that *nosh* was a word for food, but with how many travelers came through Gelvurt these days, I didn't doubt she'd picked up her strange words from somewhere.

I looked up at the sun; it was getting later into the day for sure. "Maybe. Zao said he was making a specialty from his hometown, so I can't quite say."

"Nice. Zao's food's always proper good." Daka smiled, looking ready to dash away from the training ground toward the keep before I reached out.

I grabbed her arm. "Daka, don't forget your stretches."

"Oh yeah, oops."

We set up across from each other, and I began to slowly go through the motions of stretching, Daka mirroring me as we began to slowly wind our bodies down from the stresses of the spar.

Daka had grown a lot over the years since I'd first held her as a youngling. No longer quite as little, my little warrior was. She'd grown a full head of black, curly hair, much like my own, that came down short.

I smiled at the memory of how adamant she'd been to cut her hair when she had the chance, something Natakia had almost tackled her over. It was rare to see such a reaction from my gentlest child, but she certainly had tender spots, hair being one of them.

A prodigy of Vitae and with a lean, trained body, Daka was always moving, never letting anything stop her. She had such a fierce heart for our family. It was comforting to watch it grow larger every day.

The warmth in my heart grew as we stretched, my mind going to the big event coming up. "So, Daka, are you excited for your birthday?"

Daka blinked before smiling. "Definitely, Dad. I'm still trying to figure out what to get Dalton though. He's always so picky about what you get him! And I can never top Aunt Penny!"

"She certainly has you all figured out," I agreed. Penelope couldn't always join us for the celebrations, but she made up for it in the fascinating toys she would send.

I had even found them quite entertaining myself, although they were often difficult to top with normal gifts that were available.

Daka stuck out her tongue before giggling. "I'm really excited though. I'm going to be ten! And I'm looking forward to the next technique you teach me."

She was fluttering her eyelashes, like her sister always did to get something she wanted; an amusing imitation, but I shook my head back and forth as I stretched my legs. "I've been considering what to teach you."

"Yeah!" Daka broke off from her stretches to cheer. "I'll learn it so fast, you're gonna have to teach me another one!"

I smiled, but even in jest, there was a speck of truth in her words. Calling Daka a prodigy was almost a disservice to the sheer potential she possessed. She'd once learned a technique I was trying to teach her within moments of just watching me perform it.

of a topic in Rusk, where women had other things to worry about, like giant scorpions.

Natakia stared at me, as if searching for any speck of dishonesty, before she bowed her head in defeat. "Lunch is ready?"

I smiled at the small win. I knew this wasn't the first or the last time I'd comfort my daughter about her appearance. For one so strong and wise, she was still so vulnerable.

A notion that rang true for all my children.

"It is." I nodded, standing up and heading toward the door before looking back at the two close friends. "And Zao set aside some sweet cake for dessert."

That got both of the young girls' attention.

I stood outside my personal office, taking a moment to collect myself. Gelvurt had grown in such robust ways that it was hard for me to think about them in detail.

After the establishment of Tribus Academy, many of those who had helped construct it stayed in the area, moving their families out to take advantage of the opportunity provided by the academy. Cheap, new, and supported by the heroes of the empire, the academy drew many who wanted to be a part of the history that would grow from its halls.

Gelvurt, Niers, and Alwur had become known collectively as Tribus, almost considered a separate land from House Velbrun's influence.

And the area had become flush with trade, commerce, and development far and beyond what I had planned. Far beyond what I could handle as a sole individual. Orion helped, when he could, but he was an opportunistic merchant at heart and had busied himself with growing with the success of Gelvurt.

I had needed help, but I wasn't sure how comfortable I was with where that help had come from. I knocked on the door. "Dalton? Can I come in?"

"It's your office, Father. You can come in as you wish." Of all my children, Dalton spoke the least like a child of his age.

I stepped inside, smiling at my son sitting behind my desk, looking far more comfortable there than I ever had. His long silver hair, a perfect match for Lydia's, was tied up in a ponytail to keep it out of his eyes as he poured over the documents I'd gotten out for him this morning.

"How are you doing, Dalton?" I came over to look at some of the documents he had put aside.

"The Varnedoe family is making trouble with property lines again, as they always do every year when it comes to planting season," Dalton said with utter boredom that belied his ravenous gaze. "I have a few documents I need your signature for, to approve the purchasing of new plots of land for some new construction, but otherwise everything is fine. I triple-checked our quotas, and we're in the black."

I laid a hand on his shoulder. "You've done a great job. Thank you for your help, Dalton."

"It's nothing, Father. Just numbers and laws," Dalton said with indifference. It was amazing how simplistic and average he viewed his mastery over the economic and judicial regulations of the empire.

If anyone asked, and I trusted them, I would tell them that Gelvurt had truly begun to grow when Dalton had learned to speak and began to learn the ways of the empire. He had seen loopholes and opportunities that were far beyond what I would have ever noticed.

I knelt to be eye level with him. "This isn't nothing, Dalton."

He glanced at me, not looking particularly impressed by my sentiment, but I meant it anyway. The coldest of my children, Dalton was not loved any less.

Checking over some of the documents, the ones that needed my signature, I frowned at one of the names. "This is Lord Barbrook Velbrun of Warnok. I've heard from Jorge that his practices are vicious and predatory against commoners."

"He's one of the largest investors in House Velbrun," Dalton assured me with confidence, "Having his business here will only be a benefit to us."

"And to the people of Gelvurt?"

He shrugged. "Barbrook's predatory nature has been overestimated. There's nothing wrong about getting the proper return for your product."

He said it with such indifference. My son did not care for the people of his village as much as I would like. Numbers and laws, he had mastered, but a genuine care for those beyond him and his?

I did not blindly sign the documents he prepared for a reason.

"I'll need to take a hard look at Lord Velbrun of Warnok's business practices before I sign off on this." I ignored the offense in Dalton's gaze. "Thank you again, Dalton. Zao's prepared lunch."

Letting out a sigh of frustration, Dalton leaped up from his chair. "Yes, Father. By the way, I finished translating that book he gave you last month. I put the translated copy in your library."

And with that, he walked out, leaving me with mostly finished work in a handwriting far beyond mine and a spark of admiration for how skilled and amazing my children were.

Even if they still had much to learn.

2

Hey, Rakta, what's up?" Doh was in the middle of sewing one of Macy's toys up after a brief snag had shaken some of its stuffing loose.

I nodded. "Lunch is ready. I already told the children. Will Dresden be joining us?"

"Maybe." She shrugged. "The captain wanted him to help out with some of the training for the new guards from the capital."

That made sense. With Gelvurt growing larger, more man power was needed to keep it safe. I didn't regret making Kingsley the captain after it was clear Captain Barker wouldn't be returning, for better or worse. I hoped I'd one day hear word of the man out there in the world somewhere.

Regardless, Captain Kingsley Arnet had been doing a fine job of keeping things safe and secure within the growing town. Certainly nothing that I could complain about, what with the nearby bandits having been cleared out years ago.

"And . . . done!" Doh hopped out of her seat and dusted off her dress. "Let's not keep the kiddies waiting any longer, my lord!"

She wiggled her eyebrows teasingly before passing me into the hallway, heading toward the dining room with a skip in her step.

I shook my head as I followed. Even as a mother, Doh had matured very little. Not to say that she wasn't a good parent, of course, but she'd certainly not allowed herself to be convinced by time to become a bit more adult.

Even her appearance was the same, which I assumed was by virtue of her simply shape-shifting into a younger form, of which I'm sure there were no complaints from Dresden. Of course, that was not something I could entirely say the same for me. It hadn't escaped my notice that I had a few stray gray hairs, perhaps from all the stress of my life.

"Yes, yes." I put my stray thoughts of age aside and followed Doh. Zao wouldn't let anyone eat until everyone was at the table, and I knew the longer I waited the more I tested my children's patience.

"Daka, you stink." Natakia wiped her mouth primly as she shot her sister a look.

"Oh yeah." Daka sniffed herself, grinning. "I was out training with Dad. We worked up a huge sweat!"

Sitting down to Zao's delicious meal of sauced meatballs, a specialty from his home in Katung, it didn't take long for my daughter to distract herself from her meal to snipe at her sister.

"I'm sure you did." Natakia seemed unimpressed. "Maybe you should have sprinted to the bath before coming to the table?"

Daka looked confused. "Dad smells too."

Natakia glanced at me, my fork of meatball paused an inch away from my mouth. "I noticed, but he's a man; you're a lady. You should be more concerned about how you smell."

"Why?" Daka asked, chewing on food. "I'll just get stinky again training this afternoon."

I spoke up, swallowing my food. "Daka will take a bath after lunch, I'm sure. And so will I."

Daka nodded, Natakia not looking quite pleased, but I'd heard this song and dance before. I wasn't going to stop light teasing between the sisters, but Natakia sometimes got . . . carried away with her words. They were her greatest strength, but she sometimes exercised them too liberally.

Doh spoke up, cleaning Macy's mouth of sauce. "So, what did you and your dad do while training?"

Usually, a question that Daka would love to answer, from the stretches we began with to the spars, but my little warrior gave the maid an uncomfortable look.

"Uh, you know, fighting." She picked at her food, not seeming enthused to talk about it all of a sudden. She'd never been the fondest of Doh, not like Natakia, who had latched on to the maid and her daughter.

I smiled, picking up my daughter's slack. "Daka's Vitae has been building steadily over the last few months, larger than even I had at her age."

Doh blinked. "Wow, that's pretty amazing. I mean, you were above the average too, right?"

"Yes, I . . . trained a lot when I was young," I said. "It's all you have to occupy yourself on some days in Rusk."

Dalton was eating his food silently, his eyes watching the conversation at my side but otherwise occupied with his thoughts, from what I could tell.

Natakia's eyes sharpened at my mention of my homeland. "Rusk? Dad, when are we going to visit Rusk? You've talked about it so much; the stories made it sound amazing."

Daka nodded, agreeing with her sister. Gelvurt was so close to the border that the idea of an international trip had always been at the tip of my daughters' tongues.

"Well, perhaps one day, when you're all older and I've got less work on my plate." I took another bite of Zao's delicious food, once again thankful that I'd gotten the chance to steal the man up for my own keep rather than let him slip through my fingers.

Dalton wiped his mouth before he raised an eyebrow in his sisters' direction. "What would we even go see? I'm sure Father's stories have done the wonders of Rusk far more justice than actually seeing them would."

"No!" Daka humphed. "I mean, yeah, Dad's stories are great, but I wanna see Brota's Plateau with my own eyes! I wanna stand where he stood! Move with the wind, speak with the sun!"

"And I would not discount Garrok's Archives, Dalton," Natakia spoke up. "It's said his voice has lived on within its ancient halls, continuing to tell the stories of the ages . . . It sounds magical."

My heart warmed at how enthused my daughters were with my land, but a part of me agreed with Dalton. My homeland was rich with history, but that did not mean the people there had taken every lesson of our past to heart.

I chuckled, turning to Doh. "Speaking of training, how has Macy's come along?"

"Oh, she's doing great! She's got her mama's talent, that's for sure." Doh ruffled her quiet daughter's hair. The girl squirmed a little, Doh's smile turning slightly somber. "She'll remember things I didn't."

"I'm sure she will." I nodded, turning back to my meal. I knew Doh was worried about her daughter's bloodline eventually awakening. It was comforting to know that she was preparing her for it.

The lunch went on, Daka and Natakia squabbling a bit more, with Macy oftentimes agreeing with Natakia when the young girl motioned her to. Dalton silently observed, looking at least somewhat entertained.

It was a shame Dresden couldn't be here. These meatballs were delicious.

As we finished up and let our meal settle, I called my children to my side for a walk around the keep. It was important that we spent time together, I thought. My work could take my time from them for hours, and I knew I did not share as many interests with Natakia and Dalton as I did with Daka.

"Children," I said, "I'd like to play a game."

Daka immediately looked enthused. "A game! What game?"

I smiled, noticing that Natakia and Dalton were nowhere near as enthused as their sister. Dalton was fonder of puzzles or reading, and Natakia, well, she'd much rather spend her time speaking with the various servants and Macy.

Luckily, I had some incentive handy.

"Well," I said, kneeling to all of them. "As you all know, we're celebrating your birthday in a few days. Aunt Penny and Uncle Shawn are both coming."

Dalton blinked. "Uncle Shawn is coming?"

"He had some time away from work," I said. Although he had been quite adamant that he'd wanted to speak to me about work-related things as well. "Winfred will be coming too."

"Yeah!" Daka pumped her arms. "Winfred!"

Natakia wasn't one to get distracted. "And what does this have to do with a game, Dad?"

"Because I've already got your birthday presents picked out and ready for the day," I said. That got all their attention, three pairs of interested eyes now at my disposal.

I chuckled. "We're going to play a game of hide-and-seek. You all have fifteen minutes to find places to hide around Gelvurt. I'll be searching for you."

I trusted Gelvurt enough, with Captain Arnet's measures, to allow my children to roam about the town. At least while the sun was so high in the sky.

"I'll have thirty minutes to find you. If I don't, you win," I finished my explanation with a nod.

"What do we win?" Dalton's eye was on the prize, this whole game a problem he had to solve now.

"Anyone whom I can't find before the thirty minutes are up gets their birthday present early."

My three adorable younglings tensed with excitement before looking at one another with competition in their eyes. It was adorable, how much they acted like their age sometimes.

I hoped they understood the lesson here. I absently noticed Natakia glance at me, a new glint of something in her eyes.

"The game begins . . . now." I sat down on the grass, watching the three split up and begin to run as fast as they could, Daka easily leaving the other two in the dust.

This was going to be a nice day.

3

Wind rushed around me as I sprinted through Gelvurt, only stopping at times to keep some of the unsuspecting guards or townspeople from panicking at my haste. Most had gotten used to the sight of my techniques, thankfully.

Dancing across the rooftops of Gelvurt, my sight sharpened as I channeled Vitae through my eyes, looking throughout the town to search for places that my most active of children would have hidden.

Daka was a straightforward girl. She would have hidden somewhere conventional, if not beyond the limitations of a normal child.

I landed near the outskirts of Gelvurt, bending down as my **Scourger Bloodhound Technique** blossomed, my senses fading as the scents of the world flared around me.

Hundreds of people had come this way, but finding the strong scent of my daughter was an easy task. Opening my eyes and letting the technique fade, I stroked my chin. "She's probably hiding in the forest somewhere."

Following her scent, activating my technique regularly to keep on track, I eventually came to the end of the trail, but with no Daka to be seen.

"Her scent ends here." I looked around, in the middle of a meadow. It was a familiar one, one that Daka and I sometimes trained in, so there were older scents of ours intermingled here.

Sharpening my sight with Vitae, I examined the trees, trying to see any movement, but . . . I could not see her anywhere among them.

Walking out into the center of the meadow, I kept my eyes up. "Perhaps she isn't here? Did Daka manage to mask her scent? She's certainly seen how I track people in the past."

I continued to walk through the meadow until my foot stepped onto soft earth, plunging an inch or two into the overturned soil.

I looked down. "That's interesting."

Sticking out from the grassy landscape, there was a sizable area where the ground had been displaced. I stared at it for a moment before remembering where I'd seen this before.

The **Burrowing Mole Technique**, one of Daka's favorites.

Kneeling down, I felt for the barest of remnants of Vitae within the soil and found what I was looking for. Shaking my head, I readied my own Vitae. "Daka, you're definitely taking a bath after this."

Letting the Vitae vibrate through my body, focused on my hands and feet, I whispered, "**Burrowing Mole Technique.**"

Taking a deep breath, I dove in, beginning to dig through the ground myself.

Following Daka's trail underground was not as easy as it was aboveground. Her scent was still masked, and all I had to go off of was whether the soil I had dug through felt recently disturbed.

A few minutes later, however, I felt something shift in the earth ahead of me. I began to dig toward it, feeling vindicated as the shifting suddenly became more active and moved away from me.

Picking up my speed, I ripped through earth toward my daughter and reached out through the soil as I caught up to her, grabbing onto her ankle.

I heard a dull scream of surprise through the dirt before I reaffirmed my grip and began to head toward the surface, dragging my daughter out with me in an eruption of soil.

"Phhbt!" Daka was hanging upside down, her foot in my grip as she spit out dirt. "Dad! I swallowed some! That's a load of tosh!"

I playfully shook her a little bit, specks of dirt falling from her clothes and hair. "Did it taste good?"

"Zao's cooking is better." She grinned at me before she easily flipped to her feet as I let her go. She shook her hair, sending even more dirt flying through the air. Straightforward and never afraid of mess, my little warrior was.

I shook the dirt off of my own clothing, knocking remnants of turf from my hair. "The maids are going to be cross with us."

"Not as cross as Natakia." Daka looked at the hole we had left in the meadow. Thankfully, I doubted anyone owned this land, so I was sure there'd be little complaint.

I rubbed her head. "Were you really going to stay down there for thirty minutes? I know you've been working on your breathing, but . . ."

She looked up at me, smiling toothily. "I'm up to forty-five minutes!"

My children were truly incredible.

"That's great, Daka." I knelt and gave her a big hug before standing up. "I need to go find your siblings now."

"Can I help?" Daka danced on her toes, ready to rush out and find her siblings for me at the drop of a hat.

I gave her a smile before making a show of sniffing her. "How about you go take a bath instead, my little warrior?"

Her pout was adorable, but I held strong.

Still dirty from my search for Daka, I wandered into the first place I'd expect Natakia to head to in order to hide.

"Welcome to Irelia's Threads, my lord." The girl behind the desk, I remembered her name was Eris, was a staple of the dress shop. Natakia always enjoyed Irelia's needlework, so she'd built a rapport with the store owner.

I smiled. "Yes, thank you, Eris. Have you seen Natakia around lately?"

"I'm sorry, my lord." Eris shook her head. "She hasn't come by lately, although I did hear she was in a rush from some others a few minutes ago. I believe they saw her heading toward Orion's general store?"

She was a good liar, of course. A lie, followed by a bit of misdirection.

I nodded. "Could I perhaps check in the back?"

The girl flushed, looking caught. "Ah, well, perhaps? Irelia doesn't really . . ."

Moving before she could begin to really complain, I stepped into the back hallways of the dress shop, feeling my time ticking with every step taken.

"Natakia? My desert flower?" I opened up the doors as I passed by them, until I came to the dressing room. "Natakia?"

There was a soft sigh behind the door. "Come in, Dad."

Smiling, I opened up the door, revealing Natakia taking a sullen sip of tea from a nice porcelain teacup of Irelia's collection. The room had a large full-body mirror set up, but my daughter sat a distance away from it in a comfy chair.

"I see you got comfortable." I came over to kneel next to her.

Looking away toward the wall, Natakia took another sip of her tea. "I thought Eris would be a better liar. I guess I should have been more careful."

"She's not quite as experienced as you, Doh." I gently took the teacup and plate from her and put it aside.

My "daughter" nodded before she paused. "Uh, what was that, Dad?"

I pointed over to the mirror. "When Natakia's disappointed in herself, she looks toward the closest mirror, not the wall."

"Natakia" blinked before she frowned. "That can't be healthy, you know? I'm worried Macy's going to be spending half of her time as a shape-shifting mirror for the girl when she grows up."

The concern was legitimate, my daughter certainly well acquainted with vanity, but I was suitably unimpressed by Doh's concern.

"And yet, you still took her form to help her hide?" I'd considered the option—Natakia and Doh were close, no matter what my friend had to say about her self-centered interests.

She blushed, gesticulating with her arms wildly, "She's persuasive, okay!? Besides, she knew I liked trying to get one over on you sometimes."

I chuckled, shaking my head. "Get back to the keep, Doh. I need to go find my daughter."

As she grumbled, taking one last gulp of her tea and stomping off with her head held high, I began my search anew. Unsuccessful as it was, the trickery had been time-consuming.

"I know she's here, Joseph," I said, coming up to the bar of Gelvurt's old tavern. I'd rushed around the town, talking to Orion and anyone I'd thought I could trust information from.

A few misleading accomplices were understandable, but I was

beginning to wonder how Natakia had managed to bribe everyone so quickly to work with her.

Lydia would have loved how capable her daughter was at knowing how people ticked.

Joseph grunted. "Took you long enough. Charlotte got talked into keeping her company in the back until your time ran out."

Curiosity pushed at me. "And how exactly did she convince your wife?"

He shrugged. "She congratulated her about our wedding anniversary next week. Frankly, I'm not even sure how she knew about it, but she certainly bought my silence with the reminder."

I nodded, "My daughter must have talked to your wife about it before."

Not wasting any more time, down to my last seven minutes for this little game according to my sand timer, I wandered into the back and found my daughter frowning as I came in.

"It's not fair," Natakia huffed. She'd never been fond of the smell of this old tavern, the last place I'd ever look for her if Orion hadn't mentioned it as an option. "I tried to get Daka and Dalton to work with me, but she ran off, and Dalton . . ."

I gave her a hug. "You did wonderfully, Natakia. Now I need to go find your brother."

Dashing across Gelvurt, I thought quickly about Dalton's tactics. I almost considered that he would pursue Natakia's route, convincing others to aid him, but he wasn't quite the social spirit that his sister was.

No, he was clever and thought outside of the box. I'd told my children to stay around Gelvurt for the game, but I had never outlined what those words truly meant.

In hindsight, I could see Dalton salivating over the vagueness of that rule.

I started back toward the keep, catching his scent with my technique, before beginning to head in his direction as quickly as I could. Dalton was certainly the stealthiest of my children but purely in a conventional way.

He had never trained much with Daka and me, which would always be his choice.

And then, having followed his trail far beyond the line I would have said "around Gelvurt" ends, the trail suddenly split. Two distinct scents that were both Dalton's and yet went entirely different ways.

"Interesting." I followed one of the trails before it also split again, this time into three separate scents. Taken aback, I looked around. "Dalton, how did you manage this?"

Putting my son's hidden skills aside, I let my Vitae begin to vibrate. I only had five minutes left before Dalton would win this game.

It was time to make this a little more difficult for my clever child.

4

I settled into my **Grace Stance** and began gathering Vitae into my limbs, the wind around me beginning to push me forward in the familiar rush of the **Great Wind Sprint Technique**, the trees blurring around me as I began to follow the various scent trails that Dalton had left.

And yet, almost disappointingly, I came to a stop quite soon, halting my rush at the end of the third trail I had followed. In front of me, squatting with his back to me, was my son, his form unmoving.

"Dalton," I called out, approaching leisurely. The game was over, but I was a bit disappointed. Had my son thought the scent trails would keep me occupied for longer? Perhaps I'd just gotten lucky?

He did not turn to greet me; in fact, he did not greet me at all. Perhaps he was frustrated by being found? I suppose that he thought he would be able to evade me more easily than he had.

I came over, gently reaching out to him. "Dalton, you surprised me with the trickery with the scents—"

My voice stopped as my attempt to pat him on the shoulder, grab his attention, failed as my hand went straight through the form of my son. The illusion popped at my touch, bursting into a faint mist that tickled at my frozen fingers.

I blinked. "What?"

Of all the things I had been expecting, a spell had not been one of them. Taking a look around the area, at the scent trails, now looking for it, I could plainly see the Mana soaking these scent trails.

When did Dalton become a magician? Was this an attempt to kidnap my child? I shook the thought from my head.

No matter the game I played, I would find my son.

Pulsing my Vitae outward, I disrupted the Mana empowering the false scents around me, my sight and hearing fading as my **Scourger Bloodhound Technique** activated once more. Dalton's scent was alone, but that did little to calm my heart.

With no more false trails of fake scents to mislead me, I quickly gripped onto his scent, my senses reawakening as I pushed my body forward, following it.

I dodged tree after tree, only three minutes left to find my son at the end of this trail, when my senses, now looking for signs of Mana, suddenly flared in alarm.

A large oak that I tried to dash by suddenly erupted in a loud thunderclap of noise, my sight going white for a brief moment as the triggered spell flashed with a bright light alongside the discordant bang.

Thrown off, I staggered off to the side, quickly recovering from the noise and light, but not from the shock of the trap. I took a deep breath, looking at the minor scorch mark on the oak.

"Dalton . . . How did you hide these tricks?" I shook my head, a frown forming. "Or perhaps you truly have been taken."

Spending no more time on the idea, I followed the scent trail again in a blur, quickly dashing and darting away from the trees as two more triggered spells went off. And yet, with two minutes left, I realized with a sudden clarity that the slight curve of Dalton's trail was leading me in one big curve.

A curve that led right back to our home, Velbrun Keep.

"What!? How did you do that?" Daka's voice was loud and clear as I stepped into the keep, my form no longer rushed.

My quarry replied, "Good investments. Father has been saying that our birthday this year will mark our first steps into adulthood, so I assume they'll pay off."

I had a minute left as I crept around the bend, the last few grains of sand beginning to fall from my sand timer.

"It's impressive, but will they really stop Dad for long? I'm sure his nose has been tricked before." Natakia sounded politely cross, delicately poking holes in her brother's plan.

I stopped, my last few seconds beginning to tick down. My children were just around the next bend, my hidden son just inches from being found. It would be invaluable to hear what they had to say in such privacy.

"I'm certain. He chased after both of you first."

"Ha! So you did need our help!" Daka sounded victorious, I could even imagine her pointing at her brother in triumph.

My son humphed at the very idea. "In the same way I'd need help slowing down a bear. You just bought me time."

"If we had worked together, like I'd said, then we could have all played to our strengths and gotten our birthday presents early." I honestly agreed with my daughter after seeing all my children's efforts.

"Huh? You said that?"

"I tried to before you ran off."

"Regardless"—the smugness was palpable in my son's quiet voice—"the game ends in my favor in five . . . four . . . three . . ."

I rounded the corner. "Hello, Dalton."

"Fuck."

I was going to have to speak with Doh about the language my children were picking up. They really shouldn't know such words at such a young age.

My three children sat on the couch in front of me, each of them having failed to win our little game and taking it quite differently from one another.

Smelling of fresh bathwater and cleanliness, Daka was in the middle, her eyes on her siblings as she tried to cheer both of them up. The first to lose and yet taking it the best, she was smiling and comforting them in her own unique way.

"You had everyone to help you out this time, Natakia, but I'll show you all the awesome places you could have really hidden from Dad! He'll never find you! We'll convince him you moved away!"

Natakia lightly huffed, looking away from Daka's attempt to comfort her. I'm sure she would be upset for quite some time, but perhaps I could speak to Zao about fixing her something special.

Daka swerved toward her brother. "And just think about next time, Dalton! Like the bear, remember? I'll hold Dad back for a few more seconds, and you'll get to win next time!"

Dalton's head was down, his gaze at his feet, but I could feel the anger roiling off of him. A familiar cold anger that I felt from him every time he failed or was deprived of some reward.

Taking them in for a moment, I spoke. "Children, look at me."

Upset as they were, besides Daka, they turned to look at me. My little warrior quieted, her attention firmly on me. I met each gaze slowly and surely, making sure that each one felt connected with.

I could see Natakia's frustration with her siblings, Daka's lack of disappointment, and the cold glint of Dalton's ire. All three of them responded differently to the test but had played to their strengths well.

"You all did wonderfully," I said. "Every last one of you went above and beyond what I expected of you individually."

Natakia spoke up, a light tremor of accusation in her words. "You wanted us to work together."

I nodded. My children were fiercely independent. Yes, we spent much of our time together, but they did not often lean on me like other children might with their parents.

While I was unafraid of independence, I did find their distance from one another concerning. Perhaps born of my own sibling troubles, I worried about how little they supported one another. There would come a time, I'm sure, I would not be around to support them myself.

It spoke of Natakia's usual insights into people that she had noticed so readily.

"I did. I was unsurprised that you didn't, but that doesn't take away from the clear fact that I am proud of what all you achieved on your own." It was hard to put into words how amazing my children were.

"We wouldn't have won even if we had worked together," Dalton said, his gaze like an iceberg off the Fjordic coasts. Hard and unmoving.

I smiled warmly. "Few know the future. And yet, in my experience, being alone . . . is hard. Even if you had failed, you would still have the warmth of one another to share that failure with."

My son did not look convinced, but some lessons took time. He was but a child, and his circumstances made him unique in ways that I was not adept in.

Gesturing to them all with a hand, I said, "You're all turning ten in a few days. In Rusk, ten is the age when a child is considered capable enough to begin learning the responsibilities of adulthood."

The children of hunters would have their first kills, the child of the Storyteller would tell their first tale, the beginnings of taking up the roles of their parents would be in motion. Now, they wouldn't truly be considered adults until they made great strides within those responsibilities, but that was neither here nor there.

I trusted my children to make great strides in everything they did, no matter what age or what the subject matter was. All I needed to teach them was the importance of, well, one another.

"As you begin this journey to adulthood," I said, bending down to lay a soft, comforting hand on each of their heads, one by one, "I want you to remember that you have one another, that you have me. Nothing can change that."

Natakia's eyes watered, Daka's smile growing. Dalton's gaze warmed a fraction so small I doubted even he was aware of it. I gave them all a smile, one I hoped they could lean on if I were ever not by their sides.

After a moment, I stood up. "Now, I believe it's time for early birthday presents."

I almost laughed at the looks on their faces. Was this how Doh felt when she messed with someone?

5

B ut we lost!" Dalton did not look as happy as his sisters, never enjoying being handed something without having a sense of earning it. Birthdays, after years of negotiating, were an exception that he allowed.

Natakia shushed him, a finger to her lips, as if her brother might convince me to take back my offer. Dalton shot her a dirty look but simply crossed his arms, looking vaguely unhappy. I shook my head, stepping into a small closet to remove the box I'd hidden inside as they argued.

After Daka had found last year's birthday presents, a set of magical training weights I had commissioned, I'd found many places where my most rambunctious would not think to look.

"Yay! Presents!" Daka called out as I came back into the room, the oaken box in my arms. It was a sturdy and hefty box, made to keep but the most dedicated of younglings out of it.

Natakia looked a tad suspicious. "One box, three of us."

Dalton crossed his arms, looking away. He obviously was still quite unhappy at the nature of my little game but seemed willing to not mention it for the moment.

Kneeling down, I placed the box on the ground between my children and I said, "You're getting these now because you all proved yourselves capable and . . . perhaps, I want some time for you all to enjoy my gifts before Aunt Penny arrives and once again humbles me."

Natakia hid a smile behind her daintily raised hand, and Daka giggled. Dalton seemed unconvinced, but he was looking at me again with a tiny frown. I'm sure he would be happy he'd paid attention in a moment.

"First," I said, "Daka, open the box."

Stars shining in her eyes, Daka dove onto the box, Natakia and Dalton looking on in curiosity. She tore the wooden top off and looked inside, her entire body freezing as she saw her gift.

"Is this . . . ?" With as much gentleness as my little warrior could muster, Daka slowly removed her gift from the box, the metal of its tan blade glinting as it reflected the sunlight from the nearby window.

A throwing axe, properly weighted for both throwing and close combat, with strong black wood bound in metal for its handle. It was smaller than my own collection, perfect for my daughter.

I leaned over, helping her keep the axe aloft as I glided my finger over the tan metal of the blade. "It's crafted from ramlian, found under the plateaus of Rusk. Poor material for enchanting, but . . . it is considered one of the finest materials for conducting Vitae."

Daka looked up at me, tears in her bright blue eyes. "My own axe?"

"Yes." I wiped her tears. "One that I will be properly teaching you to wield, in the same way that I do. Our training will be much harder now, and I will no longer be teaching you idle techniques. You will learn those of our ancestors."

"That . . . sounds amazing, Dad." There was a mystified undertone in her voice as she held her axe with reverence.

I let her digest her excitement before I burdened it with my expectations for this training. The time would come for me to speak of the responsibilities and the history of our techniques. Daka could learn things so quickly, I knew I would have to slow her down for her to understand the gravity of what I taught her.

"Ahem." A small voice got my attention, my eyes going over to Natakia with her arms crossed, looking somewhat peeved.

Smiling, I went to sit with Natakia and Dalton on the couch, letting Daka enjoy the weight of her gift. Dalton was looking at the blade with a calculating glint in his eyes.

It was always difficult to purchase things without him finding the records for them, but I'd managed to pull it off for now.

"I don't suppose there is a nice dress in that box, as well?" Natakia was looking up at me expectantly, making me chuckle at her tone.

I motioned to the box. "No, there is no dress in the box. Instead, I have this for you."

Reaching into my pocket, I pulled out a letter that smelled faintly of roses, the perfume having persisted weeks after I'd received it.

She took it from my hands, haste coloring her usual properness, and opened it with a look in her eyes that was remarkably similar to Daka's.

Natakia opened the letter up and read aloud as her eyes coasted across the words, "Dear Lady Natakia Velbrun, you are hereby invited . . . Rose Gala . . . and the capital estate of High Lord Gren Iriend for . . . for the annual ladies gathering."

There was a silence for a moment as she read over the various details more quickly, the dress code, the proper times, the agenda, and other ladies of her age that would be in attendance.

"I never had a debut before . . ." Tears ran down her cheeks, her bright, unrestrained smile a salve on my soul at having made my daughter cry, even in joy.

Hugging her close, I smiled. "I know you haven't had much chance to speak to many of your age. After your birthday, we'll all be going to the capital."

"I don't, but, I, I—" Natakia struggled with the letter. "I don't have a dress for this. I need . . . I need the perfect dress."

"We'll buy you one in the capital, as fine as we can find." I'd been setting aside money for this since my children uttered their first words.

"And . . . And Macy . . ."

"Macy can come, as well, pending her mother's approval." Doh had said yes a week ago, on the condition that she and Dresden come with as well.

She hugged me, her crying face smothered into my chest, and I wrapped my arms around her, tightly pulling her against me as she privately thanked me over and over. Another pair of arms, Daka's, crashed into me.

"This is the best birthday ever!" Daka's grip was strong and filled with love as she held her sister and me in her embrace.

And yet, I opened my eyes to look at the last of my children. Dalton, his gaze suspicious and yet eager, seemed reluctant to join in on the family hug.

Gently pulling away from Natakia and Daka, and letting them continue hugging each other, I said, "I have one more gift to hand out."

Standing up and moving over to my son, I held out my hand to stand him up as well. He acquiesced, his features tight as I made no motion, yet, to bring out his gift.

"Dalton, you possess ambition that reminds me of so many that came before you," I said, holding his gaze with my own. "Sometimes, I am concerned about the way you see people, that you confuse them with the numbers you cling to."

Dalton frowned, "Father . . ."

I held up a hand. "And yet, I know that you have, much like your sister, felt constrained by Gelvurt. What you seek, the opportunities to learn important lessons, cannot be granted here in full."

Pulling out the second letter I had in my back pocket, I handed it over to my son. He took it from me, opening the letter to read, but said nothing aloud as his eyes skimmed over the contents.

And yet, his eyes widening was enough for me to know he recognized what was in his hands. Daka and Natakia watched on with interest, neither accustomed to Dalton looking so emotive.

"While the ownership is legally within my hands," I said, taking my son by the shoulder, "this property belongs to you, with both the business decisions and profit solely within your hands."

I looked at all of them, turning slightly from facing solely Dalton.

"While we are in the capital, and you are all exempt from your lessons at the academy, I will support all of you as you take the first steps in your journey to adulthood," I said, my eyes burning, "I . . . You will have to be kind to my heart. It isn't . . . Watching all of you grow up will not be easy for m—"

Daka's form hit me forcefully, throwing me into a hug again that I welcomed gratefully as I wrapped my arms around her, Natakia swiftly coming over to join in on the family embrace. A few moments later, I even felt the arms of my son join us.

"Thank you." Dalton's voice sounded strained, almost unfamiliar with emotion. "Father."

My thoughts went to his hidden skills, the spells I'd never noticed him practice or learn, but I decided those questions could wait for another time, another day.

* * *

A day later, my children were eagerly waiting beside me on the balcony of our keep, looking out onto the horizon as the sun began to set.

"Do you see them, Daka?" Natakia was squinting her eyes.

Daka's eyes flared with Vitae. "Uh, not yet. Maybe they got los— Wait! I totally see them!"

"Really!?"

"Oh wait, that was a deer."

Dalton steepled his fingers over the edge of the balcony. "I don't see why we have to wait for them every year. They'll knock on the door when they arrive."

"Uncle Shawn loves it when we wave at them," I reminded my son. Shawn said it made him feel like he was really being welcomed to the family, so I was happy to oblige him.

"Wait," Daka screamed, pointing out toward the forest line, "now I totally see them!"

And sure enough, breaking through the tree line, was a carriage pulled by brilliant green horses, riding toward the keep faster and smoother than any normal horse could have managed.

I held up my hand. "Alright, kids, wave!"

Daka danced on the balcony, both of her arms wildly waving in the air, as her sister waved at the approaching carriage with a prim and proper raise of her hand. Dalton managed a weak wave, not looking interested.

"I'm gonna go greet 'em!" Daka jumped up onto the balcony rail before leaping off toward the ground below, sending my heart through my chest even if I'd seen her do it a thousand times before.

I chuckled, calming my pulse. "Your sister has the right idea. Let's go greet them."

Natakia nodded, walking inside the keep to head downstairs. Dalton followed, sending a glance back toward where Daka had jumped off of.

"She's going to break her neck one day," he said.

I took a deep breath, still calming myself, as I glanced over the balcony rail. "Not from this height."

It was only a small relief, but one that I had learned to hold on to tightly so as not to gain too many gray hairs too soon.

6

The carriage came up to the keep, Daka running after it with a smile on her face, trying to chase it down. The cloaked driver of the carriage pulled on the reins of the horses, slowing them down as the carriage came to a rest.

I walked up with Natakia and Dalton behind me as Daka jumped on top of the carriage, frowning. "Does CAD know you take these horses out for leisurely visits?"

"Humph." The cloaked driver snorted, thumbing back to my daughter stomping their carriage's roof. "Nothing's leisurely when the Velbrun spawn are about."

My faux frown melted into a smile. "I'm glad you made it here safely, Penelope."

Pulling back her hood, Penelope ran her gloved hand through her short brown hair, smiling at me. "You won't be so glad when I bust out my awesome presents."

Natakia came up, curtsying. "It's a pleasure to see you again, Aunt Penny."

Dalton joined her, bowing silently. And yet, my attention wandered over to Daka on the roof of the fanciful carriage, her face lit up with excitement as she knocked on the wood of the roof.

"Winfred!" She banged on the carriage. "Wake up! You're here!"

There was a rumbling in the carriage for a moment, before the side door opened and the tangle of strawberry blond hair that was Shawn's son tumbled out, almost tripping on the steps of the carriage.

"Save me, Daka!" He came out a few paces before an arm struck out and grabbed him by the shoulder and pulled him back into the carriage.

"Hair first, young man," Tracy's disembodied voice echoed from the carriage. "I swear . . ."

Daka flipped off of the carriage, pouting as the common sound of Winfred's struggles with his mother's combing began in full.

I left Natakia and Dalton to speak with their aunt, walking up to Daka as a figure finally made their way properly out of the carriage.

"Daka! Rakta!" Shawn smiled, his dimples shining as he came out with his arms raised in celebration. "It's been so long!"

"Uncle Shawn!" Daka skipped up and jumped into his arms, Shawn easily returning the powerful hug she gave him.

My friend made a show of staggering under her weight. "Oh! By the gods, Rakta, what are you feeding this girl!? She's gotten so big!"

I chuckled as I came up, my daughter giggling in his arms.

"Don't go saying that to Natakia," I said as I came up to clasp him by the shoulder, Daka swinging over to hang off of my arm and climbing up onto my shoulder.

Shawn laughed. "I know, I know. How have you been, buddy?"

"Busy. Gelvurt is growing faster than I ever really imagined. Means a lot more work for Dalton and me." I looked back to see Penelope in a conversation with Dalton, Natakia politely listening to them.

Shawn smirked. "The offer still stands to have an actual financial advisor brought down here, you know? I know people."

"Yeah, Dad, Uncle Shawn knows people!" Daka giggled, sounding high on the day's excitement.

Even if I had not outright told my children that their uncle was the king of the entire empire, they were insightful enough to know he was influential. Although, I suspected Dalton and Natakia had a far more precise idea of who he was than Daka did.

"Thank you, but"—I glanced over to Dalton—"my son is a natural with financ—"

"Daka! I'm free!" Winfred sprinted out of the carriage, his long, combed hair trailing in the wind behind him as he ran past Shawn and me and into the open yard in front of the keep. "Beat you to the trees!"

And he was off, quickly joined by my daughter as she squawked at the challenge, kicking off from me into the air after him. They screamed at each other, rushing toward the tree line. It was like two dogs that hadn't seen another dog in months.

"Winfred's certainly gotten faster," I said, watching the royal scion managing to momentarily outpace my daughter, an impressive feat for one his age.

Shawn watched them go with a glint of pride. "He's been training with my personal squadron. Honestly, it's even more amazing how fast Daka is catching up with him."

I watched the two young blurs collide as my daughter caught up, both of them tumbling into the grass and wrestling, their race to the trees forgotten.

"It's . . . nice that he gets to come here every now and then," Shawn said. "No one in the capital really lets him feel like a kid, you know?"

I nodded. "I think it's healthy for Daka to have an equal at her age."

Although, with my own plans to train Daka seriously now, I doubted Winfred would be able to match up with her for long. Not to downplay Shawn's own capabilities as a teacher, but Daka was just a naturally good student.

"Daka's hair is a mess just like Winfred's." Tracy came out of the carriage. "I swear, it was easier to get him to sit down and listen before he met your little rascal."

"Her joy for life is infectious," I said, before noticing another shift of weight within the carriage.

Another figure came out of the carriage, one that I did not recognize but instantly put me on edge. With shaved black hair and a jagged scar on his cheek, the armored young man held himself with the duty of a guard.

I recognized the colors of his attire, Shawn's personally trained squadron of Protectors, but my eyes lingered on the hints of shiny black scales that were scattered across the edge of his hairline.

Shawn smiled. "Rakta, this is Tanner. He's one of my newest Protectors, and well, the king can't leave the capital without some sort of protection."

He shrugged, looking mildly resigned as he often did when it came to tradition.

I extended a hand. "It's good to meet you, Tanner. I'm Rakta Velbrun."

"I've heard much, Lord Velbrun." Tanner shook my hand. "I'm sorry if I make you feel uneasy. I'm afraid little can be done about it."

"Tanner has some dragon in his bloodline, but he's a good man who has had to prove that more than most do," Shawn explained gently.

And with the tint of his scales, there was little wonder about the specific breed of dragon. An onyx dragon was a terrifying beast but a rare one on this continent. I was more familiar with the pit-making agate dragons of Rusk or the solitary quartz dragons of the empire's mountains.

Still, those with dragon blood in them were often territorial and had bouts of obsessive hoarding mania for the precious gems of their heritage. Not to mention the auras that percolated the air around them, warning off others from their presence.

"I understand." I nodded. "Like I said, it's good to meet you. Thank you for keeping my friend here safe."

Tanner shook his head. "It's the least I can do. Shawn has done a lot for me."

With that, we settled into a comfortable conversation, catching up on the finer details of life until Penelope came over with Natakia and Dalton at her heel.

"So." Penelope smiled. "What's Zao cooking?"

I smiled, calling Daka and Winfred back from the tree line to come and prepare for dinner.

Tanner had excused himself from having a meal with us, which was unfortunate as much as it was relieving. While I certainly had sympathy for the man, his aura was not as easily ignored by the younger children, besides Winfred, who seemed far more used to it.

Daka, in particular, did not look particularly pleased while he was around and opened up from her uncomfortable silence soon after he'd taken his plate to his guest room.

"So," Penelope said after swallowing some of Zao's stew, "Daka, I heard about your dad's gifts."

"Yeah!" She nodded, mouth full of food. "He gave me my own axe! I'm gonna name it something really cool . . . Maybe after a bird like Dad did!"

The artificer scoffed. "Well, if you ever need help with a name, just let me know. I've become quite good at them over the years."

Shawn and I shared a glance. She'd certainly named many things, but Penelope was not exactly one I would lean on for such a task.

"Don't let her fool you," Doh spoke up, rubbing Macy's mouth clean of stew. "She's terrible at naming. Those horses outside are called Green One and Green Two."

Penelope glared at the maid. "Those names are efficient and roll off the tongue!"

Doh stuck out her tongue at her, her daughter following suit. Penelope's face went bright red at the double assault, and she glared at Dresden, who'd been silent and barely paying attention, as if daring him to join in on his family's antics.

The table calmed down after a moment, with Daka enjoying her meal, before she swallowed and looked back up at Penelope.

"Oh yeah, and he's gonna train me!" Daka pumped her fist.

My friends' eyes suddenly turned to me, interested.

"Really, Rakta? You're gonna teach Daka everything you know?" Shawn asked.

I ruffled my daughter's hair warmly. "Everything I know will just be a drop in the bucket for her. Of course, we'll be pacing the training properly."

Penelope hummed. "Not gonna teach her the **First Dance Stance** right off the bat?"

"**First Dance Stance**?" Daka's eyes lit up. "Like Brota? Brota's first dance!? It's a stance!? Dad, can you teach me Brota's first dance? I really want to learn that!"

Natakia and Dalton were also looking at me with interest, their meals forgotten. I gave Penelope a somewhat dry look that she shrugged at. I'd not spoken much about my most powerful stance . . . mostly because showing it off to Daka would be dangerous. If she attempted it recklessly . . .

"There will be plenty of time to learn such things, but first, eat your food. You, too, Natakia." I gave my desert flower a look as she began to slowly nibble at her food again.

Doh nudged her. "Yeah, the sooner you finish, the sooner you and Macy can get back to practicing for that big party in the capital."

"Oh yeah." Shawn smiled. "I'd heard about that. You actually managed to get invitations, Rakta?"

I scratched the back of my head. The Rose Gala was a very big event, one that all young ladies of nobility sought invitations to. It was the perfect time to make connections and friends and introduce yourself to very important pillars of the empire.

Natakia smiled, speaking up. "He did. Macy and I are going to make our debuts, and it will be glorious."

Macy nodded, agreeing with her friend while silently eating her food.

"We, well," I muttered, "an old friend from our adventuring days was happy to help. She seemed delighted to have Natakia and Macy attend after I asked."

Penelope furrowed her brow. "Really? Who?"

"Harriet Pillops," I said, taking a bite and swallowing. Looking up, I noticed Shawn and Penelope were staring at me in shock. I'd known they weren't too fond of Harriet, but I was never sure of why.

Lydia had also never spoken very kindly of her. I really had tried to figure out the distaste for the woman, but she always seemed very polite and earnest to me.

Shawn spoke up first. "Harriet? The merchant girl? The same Harriet that used to watch you train all the time? The one that asked you to show her around the capital?"

"Well, yes, I believe I remember her being unfamiliar with the area."

"She was born there! You weren't! Why would she ask you to show her around!?" Penelope was waving her arms in the air.

It'd been years, but looking back on it now, it did seem a little strange. Perhaps she truly did have some kind of ill intentions toward me? Lydia had never let me show her around, instead offering her magic to show the up-and-coming merchant the shortest route back to her shop.

Doh blinked, looking at me. "Oh my god, Rakta, you never told me you had a stalker!"

"Father." Winfred looked up from his meal. "What's a stalker?"

And the conversation, which I'd had very little control over to begin with, became complete chaos as stories began to be flung around about other interesting individuals we'd met in the capital, food was slowly consumed, and my heart ached a little at the thought of what Lydia would have to say right now.

7

After putting the children to bed, giving them all—Winfred and Macy included—a story to enjoy before they slept, I was alone with my thoughts and the gentle noises of the night. I was grateful that even Dalton enjoyed listening to my stories, giving me hope for his life outside of his interest in commerce.

Out on the balcony, I sipped on some of the remaining wine that I had gotten out for my guests, but my thoughts lingered on something I had not thought about in quite some time.

Lydia's prophecy, or rather, the prophecy made through the lips of my wife, one she had not shared with me in all our time together before her passing. The prophecy that had foretold that my children would be the forefront of a grand destiny.

"How will I fight that battle for them?" I wondered aloud. Simply leaving them to fate's whims did not sit well with me. In Rusk, a man's life was a story for him to tell with his own hands, not one for the gods to intrude upon.

They were growing up so quickly. Their souls from another world . . . It was a hard concept to grasp. Reincarnation wasn't a common spiritual idea in Rusk, but in far-off lands, there were inklings of monsters that could never truly be killed, only ended for a time.

How much did they remember of their past lives? How much did it affect them? What was this world that was beyond the veil of my understanding? I'd often been tempted to simply ask them, but I would have to reveal the reason behind my questions, the prophecy that they were intertwined with.

I sighed. "Children should not be burdened with such knowledge."

And yet, they were beginning their journeys to adulthood, weren't they? I could not let them begin this journey ignorantly.

A knock came at the balcony door behind me. "Hey, buddy."

"Shawn." I did not turn around, but I could feel him join my side. I glanced at him and frowned at the dark look on his face, one that had grown to suit him after years of being king. "You needed to speak with me?"

He said nothing for a moment, before he sighed. "The night sky really is beautiful here, you know?"

"It is," I agreed, pointing to the bright sparkles in the sky above. "The stars inspired the first stories of Rusk; it is said that the first ancient Storyteller spoke of them dancing through the air to stitch our world together."

"You don't see this kind of view from where I come from." Shawn's voice was filled with yearning, as though even if there were not a beautiful view there, he missed his home.

"Beauty cannot make up for the warmth of home." Rusk called out to me sometimes, wanting me to return, but I was not sure what I would even return to.

Shawn grabbed my wine bottle, taking a sip. "Rakta, I've got a lot of things to talk about, and I don't know where to even start. Zactrik, the future, my home . . ."

I let my Vitae vibrate a bit, clearing out the vague sluggishness of tonight's drinks. "Start wherever you'd like, Shawn. I'll listen well."

"I . . . I know you will, buddy." Shawn chuckled. "That's why I gotta be careful with what I say, you know? Because you'll hear it, and sometimes I don't . . . I don't know how much I want some things to be heard."

I said nothing, did nothing, and simply watched him carefully. Shawn was not a very heavy drinker, and I could see the slight blush of his cheeks after tonight's warm welcome.

He could do the same as I, flush out the liquid courage, but perhaps that was what he needed right now?

"Your kids, Rakta," Shawn said, instantly sharpening my attention to a fine point. "I can't be a hundred percent sure, but . . . I'm pretty sure we came from the same place."

He turned to me.

"I'm from another world too."

Over the years, I'd mentioned little to Shawn about the particulars of the prophecy. Yet now, on this balcony, I could see a familiar glint of knowing in his eyes.

However, any suspicion or questions I had were thrown by the revelation of Shawn's origins, a question that I and the others had debated for years, Penelope biting at any little tidbits of information.

"You are from another world?" I asked, a part of me not quite accepting the statement as fact just yet.

He nodded. "A few months before we met, I was just a student at a school in a place called Earth. It's different, Rakta. No monsters, no energy manipulation, nothing like that."

"No energy manipulation?" That was a dear price to pay for no monsters. "Have there been no attempts to build Vitae or Mana?"

He shook his head. "There isn't anything like Vitae or Mana. We don't have that on Earth."

My mind went to the Deadlands, a horrific wasteland that existed within the pages of fairy tales where Vitae was drained away and consumed by the vegetation itself.

My throat suddenly dried. I took the wine from him, taking a swallow, before handing it back. We would both need some liquid courage tonight. "That is . . . quite the revelation, Shawn."

"I know." He took another swallow. "I'm not trying to scare you or anything like that. I just feel like . . . I needed to tell someone, okay? Zactrik is preparing something, Derra keeps turning, and . . . I think your kids are at the root of it all."

It was an unfortunate truth that I liked even less leaving the lips of another. "And they come from the same world as you? How can you be sure?"

"Honestly," he said, "it's because of two things. Daka uses slang from our world every once in a while."

"And the second?" I asked. I certainly wouldn't want to give this away to others I did not trust.

He took another swig of wine. "Oracle told me. It's this voice I hear, a gift from the Overseer. It tells me things, helps me out from time to time, but it's been . . . quiet recently."

It felt like he wasn't saying something, but I was internally reeling. An oracle within his head? It made some things make much more sense, his intermittent sense of knowing. And yet, my mind caught on a different detail.

"Overseer?" I felt light-headed, like I was moments from falling through the ground below me into empty, open skies.

Shawn paused. "Are you okay, Rakta? Fuck, I'm going to fast, aren't I? This . . . I'm so sorry, buddy. I'm not trying to scare you or . . . or make you rethink everything. I just have to get this off my chest, okay?"

"I'm fine." I took a deep breath, in and out. "Have you not told Penelope or Ulric?"

"I . . . I will. Hopefully." Shawn looked away. "I just needed to tell someone, you know? And if I'm right about your kids, then . . . it's best that you know now."

"You should tell them, Shawn. They'll listen to you, just as I will." Resting up against the rails of the balcony, I nodded to him, feeling slightly more prepared for this conversation. "Tell me everything."

Shawn swallowed. "Alright."

"Tag, you're it!" Winfred flipped through the air as Daka smacked him in the chest, sending him flying a few feet back.

Winfred laughed, landing on his feet. "Not for long!"

He rushed after my daughter, both of them having used the keep's grounds as the site of their latest game, both of them swiping at each other faster than any child really should.

Natakia and Macy were watching them play from the steps of the keep, both of them enjoying a small plate of biscuits. With them was a dark-haired boy, looking a little lost and maybe just a bit scared at the Vitae-enhanced roughhousing of my daughter and her friend.

"Alan has gotten big, Orion," I said, glancing at the man beside me.

Orion chuckled. "He's not the only one. Marisha has me watching my weight more and more these days. She's quite taken with Natakia's diet tips."

I smiled. I wasn't initially sure if Natakia should really be considered counsel on proper eating, but I had not seen anything improper about her advice. Some of the ladies who had taken to her guidance certainly weren't wasting away like I'd initially feared.

"How is he doing at the academy?" With the education it provided, supported financially by the funding of the king and some of my own coin, the townspeople were free to send their children for a pittance. I'd initially been surprised at how proud Jorge had been that even his poorest townspeople were getting educations fit for noble children.

After a few years of being a noble, investing myself into this town, I understood a bit more.

He smiled, looking down at the ground through the window. "Quite good. Even has a bit of talent for magic that he'll be developing soon. I hear from Al that Dalton is quite the rival."

"Yes, Dalton excels in his classwork." I was quite proud of him being top of his class, even excelling past the study work of kids years above him. "Daka, however, rarely sits down long enough to do her classwork before she's off running around again."

Of course, she dominated when it came to practical, physical courses at Tribus Academy.

"And magic? You once said that their mother was quite talented."

I looked down at Dalton and Natakia, my eyes lingering on my son. "They both have the potential for it, but neither have really pushed for it yet. Although . . . Natakia has asked about the Velbrun magical traditions a few times, especially after hearing about her mother."

I still needed to speak to Dalton about his own hidden talents.

"Well, I wish you well. Let me know if you need any help with the Velbruns." Orion chuckled. "Just like old times."

I nodded, smiling slightly. Orion had certainly been a boon to my opposition to House Velbrun. He was persistent and meticulous in his work, which had put him in a good position when Gelvurt had begun to grow. His investments and worth as a merchant had grown right alongside it.

Of course, we rarely got to speak as often as we once did. Our children interacted more with one another than we did with how busy each of us had gotten in recent years.

"Where's Emily? I'm sure Natakia wouldn't have minded her tagging along." Orion's daughter was a few years younger than my desert flower, but they got along well enough.

Orion chuckled. "With her mother getting ready for tomorrow's big day. She wants to find something for Natakia and, well, impress her with a new dress."

"I'm sure my daughter will be excited to receive a gift from her." She loved gifts to the point of demanding them at times.

Gazing at Alan, the boy making idle conversation with my prim and proper daughter and her friend, I thought to my own son again.

"If you'll excuse me, Orion." I nodded to him in thanks for the conversation. "I need to go speak to my son."

8

I knocked on Dalton's door, giving him a few moments before stepping inside. Dalton's room was clean, but *sparse* was a more appropriate word to use. He had a bed, a desk, and a wardrobe of outfits, but nothing personal beyond a few books on a shelf above his desk.

Where had all his toys gone? Where did he keep the gifts from past birthdays? I couldn't imagine he'd thrown out some of the marvelous magical gadgets that Penelope had given him in past years.

My son was currently lying on his bed, over the covers, with a book in hand. The bold letterings of the book's cover read *The Routes of Neve*, a book I recognized as a collection of maps that detailed the travel patterns of the Donns, powerful, world-shaking merchants.

"Are you busy, Dalton?" I did not want to disturb him, but after last night's conversation with Shawn there was a pressing need within me for answers.

I had far too many questions to handle at the moment. It was important that I not pressure my son just so I could appease some of these burning curiosities within me.

Dalton marked his page, closing his book. "Not particularly, Father. Is Winfred still outside playing with Daka?"

"Yes, they're having quite a good time, if you wish to join them." I came over to sit on his bed, my son watching me with his placid, expressionless gaze.

He shrugged. "No, I just wanted to know. I wanted to talk to him about the capital for a bit. Besides, I can't exactly keep up with them."

"About that." I kept my gaze steady on him. "I'd like to know about the magic you used during our game the other day."

Dalton's body stilled for a moment before it relaxed, his eyes flickering with frustration before it was snuffed out and he was once again watching me with little emotion in his eyes.

"Our game?" My son shrugged. "I picked up a few tricks, Father. Daka picks up new tricks all the time."

Unless Dalton was implying that he could pick up spells by sight like Daka could, then I doubted it was an exact equivalence. Even Daka needed some training in the fundamentals.

"Spells are complicated, Dalton," I said, hoping to get straight to the point before he could dodge my question. "I don't expect to know everything about what you can do, but know that I'll support you. Is someone teaching you? Do you trust them?"

He sniffed, much like his sister might when annoyed. "No one is teaching me. And I only know a few spells."

Silently, I looked at him expectantly.

"I only know **Fog of Self** and **Concussive Flash**, nothing that taxing." He did not look happy at having the answers pulled from him. "I . . . also know a cleaning spell for when I don't want to take a bath."

"And how are your reserves? Casting as much magic as you did in the time you had speaks volumes of your Mana." I was happy to hear the truth from him, but I couldn't tell if those spells were impressive or not. They'd certainly seemed beyond a basic level of skill.

He looked away from me. "It's fine. I don't cast more than I can handle."

For a moment, I remembered I was speaking to a child, no matter what soul or mind he possessed. Perhaps he did not truly understand Mana and the exhaustion its overuse came with?

"You never said you were interested in magic," I began. "Why didn't you tell me?"

"I'm not," he said plainly. "I'm just interested in what magic can do for me, Father. It's a tool to be used, nothing else."

A decidedly less spiritual take on spiritual energy, but he was certainly not the only one to have such thoughts. Perhaps his aunt had rubbed off on him with her decidedly meticulous methodology of practicing magic?

"And why haven't you pursued the courses at the academy? They offer the basics of magic; you might even be considered for an apprenticeship."

Dalton was silent for a moment, gazing toward the wall with a small frown. There was frustration in his eyes once more.

"I don't like learning with others." He said it quietly, but I could hear him easily. "Admitting weakness of any kind, like acknowledging you have more to learn in front of others, is the first step to being trod upon for the rest of your life."

The underlying anger and distaste and wholehearted belief in his own words stunned me. Shawn had never mentioned his world, possibly Dalton's as well, was so cutthroat.

I fought the urge to hug my son just yet, but I sought to comfort him gently, moving next to lie beside him on the bed. "You're fine with learning things with me, your sisters."

His jaw tensed, his eyes closing. "It's not the same."

There was a tension in his voice that I didn't want to break; it didn't feel quite right at the moment. Instead, I simply wrapped an arm around him and pulled him into a small embrace.

"Then perhaps, when we're in the capital," I said, "we can find a private tutor for you. One for you and your sister, since I'm sure she has the potential."

"Daka should sit in on it as well." My son's voice was quiet, but his request was amusing.

I chuckled. "Do you really think she'll enjoy the long lectures?"

"Not at all, but she'll ask tons of questions and save Natakia and me the breath."

I laughed, hugging my son. He was still tense, his clipped words hinting at things left unsaid, but we had relaxed together. My son had one less secret he felt he needed to hide from me, and I understood him and his capabilities a little bit more.

"I hope one day you will tell me how you learned the spells, Dalton, but I will not pry. I doubt you would take risks, but as your father, it's my duty to worry and help you." I said it somewhat slowly, letting each word roll off my tongue carefully. "Your mother would be proud to see what you've achieved at your age."

He froze for a moment before relaxing. "Well, thank you, Father. If there's nothing else, I really want to get back to my book."

Nodding, I left him to his private study. I'd gotten a few questions answered, letting me worry about the others I had with more focus.

For one, if what Shawn had told me was true, why was Zactrik so interested in those with the blood of monsters?

In a private room, Penelope, Shawn, Tanner, and I sat around a small table, the children being watched over by Tracy and Doh.

They watched as I read over documents that Penelope had passed over to me, waiting as I slowly digested the reports of disappearances and kidnappings going on throughout the Certillian Empire.

"How?" I slowly asked. "How is he behind this? I thought that your investigations had rooted out those loyal to him from the nobility. He shouldn't have these kinds of widespread resources, should he?"

Shawn frowned. "He shouldn't. I'd like to say we got rid of a number of nobility, but we couldn't put much pressure on the higher lords of the royal houses."

"You think that he has some of the higher lords in his pocket?" The idea was unfortunately not very surprising, but frustrating.

Penelope nodded. "Less think, more know. The local CADs have been investigating things off the records from a few 'mysterious' benefactors. We know of at least three that are supporting him on the side, but we're slowly doing what we can to corner them and put an end to that."

That was relieving.

"The real problem," Tanner spoke up, having been quiet up until now, "is outside of the Certillian Empire."

He tossed over another set of documents, which I read with a careful gaze. I wasn't a great skimmer, and this was far too important of a topic to be missing details.

"Reconnaissance from Rusk, Kafang, and Prayers? We're not sure if Zactrik's even in the empire right now?" I asked. "Who is running everything if not him?"

"Followers, researchers, rallied bandits," Tanner said. "I think the devotees of the Depth of Death are also involved, but that's only based on one eyewitness."

I raised an eyebrow. "Who?"

"Me," he said back, looking grave. I fought down my unnatural revulsion at the man, his aura spiking as his eyes glinted with the hardness of memories.

Nodding, I turned back to Shawn and Penelope. "If Zactrik's influence is spreading beyond the border, what can we do? The problem has spread beyond the empire at this point."

"I've put CAD on high alert. They'll get an international response ready, but we still have to focus on the empire's concerns while they do that," Penelope said.

I pushed the documents away. "Do we know his goals? Anything about this man?"

"He's not a man anymore," Tanner said. "He's a monster. He kidnaps those with any monster in their blood to poke and prod at them, learn about how their bodies create and manipulate Primus."

Primus, the wild primal energy that was only fostered and used by monsters and those with their lineage. Was Doh in danger? Was Macy? I'd have to keep an eye on them in the capital.

"We managed to pry out more details from the Velbruns about Zactrik's history. He's always been distant, but a few anonymous sources have confirmed that he never sided with the Warlock King," Shawn said. "Speaking of which, you can rest easy about one thing. House Velbrun doesn't seem to be involved with Zactrik, or at least, none of their high lords are."

Tanner scoffed. "Yet."

If I'd had any real loyalty to my house, I may have taken offense to his dismissive tone, but I was frankly quite bankrupt in that regard. The few Lords Velbrun I cared about would not tolerate the likes of Zactrik.

"It's a relief, a small one," I admitted. "But why tell me all of this? I appreciate it, I do, but unless you wish me to pick up my axe once more, there isn't much my influence can do."

"I actually have a plan," Shawn said with a sly smile. "But I need to confirm some things back in the capital before I can really say anything about it."

Then his smile dropped, and he just looked tired for a moment.

"And honestly? I just need to make sure everyone is on the same page and ready. Situations like this only get worse when people don't communicate properly," he said, his forlorn sentiment stained in experience.

I nodded. "I understand. If there is anything I can do, let me know."

"Good. I'm sure we'll have something for you to do eventually," Penelope smiled deviously.

Shawn laughed, and I smiled, all of us enjoying a speck of levity among ourselves in private as my thoughts slowly turned toward tomorrow. The big day was closing in fast.

My children's birthday.

9

There was an energy in the air, spread and shared by every gaze hanging off of my words. I sat with my arms out, gesticulating slowly as I drew out the meaning of my words into the air.

A true Storyteller would have been able to truly impart the visage of his tales into the world, but I still managed to enchant my audience.

"And so, Tacta was so happy at the birth of his son that every year he would dance the entire day, every member of the tribe giving his son a new gift to aid him in the coming year."

Daka, Natakia, and Dalton were all sitting before me, their friends and family off to the side watching. The wondrous smell of Zao's celebration cooking was heavy in the air, drifting in from the nearby kitchen.

My younglings were all dressed in their finest clothing, each of them properly attired for this wondrous occasion of their first steps on their journey to adulthood.

Natakia had one of her finest dresses on, the pink tassels of her light-blue dress dancing as she lightly swayed back and forth, her eyes watching me closely.

My son wore a gray silken tunic with soft yellow highlights on the shoulders and pants, with proper cuff and shoulder adornments. He lightly pulled on the soft yellow scarf around his neck as he listened.

And Daka, my little warrior, hung off every word of my familiar annual tale, her own soft blue tunic a far cry from the dress that Marisha had wanted her to wear, but I was not going to force my children to wear something they did not want to.

Besides, dresses weren't as common in Rusk as they were in the empire.

"Word traveled," I continued the tale. "And soon every child of Rusk was celebrated after the dust plague passed, with each step of their journey of life a valued and beloved time."

I took a step forward and gave them each a kiss on the forehead.

"You three are the stars in my sky," I said, feeling my heart ache at watching them grow up so quickly. "If your mother . . . She would be so proud of how exceptional each of you are."

I knelt down and gathered them all up into a hug.

"Happy birthday, my children."

And the solemn spell of ceremony around us was broken as a great cheer went out through the room, every guest to my children's birthday party yelling together.

"Happy birthday!" From Shawn and his son to Doh and Macy, to Orion's family and even some of the other children from the academy that I didn't recognize, everyone here honored my children with their celebration.

Daka pulled away from me, looking up with stars in her eyes. "We get to nosh and open our presents now, right!?"

The same question bubbled in her siblings' eyes, but neither openly said it so brazenly as their sister. They used her as a mouthpiece far too often, to my amusement.

"Well," I said, looking at all the other eager and hungry eyes. "I think we've kept Zao waiting for long enough. Everyone, let's head outside to enjoy a nice meal in the sun!"

Another round of cheers went out through the room as everyone began to move outside, my servants bringing out delicious platters of stew and Katung meatballs for all to enjoy on the wooden tables I'd set up.

"Are you excited about the capital party, Natty?" Emily, Marisha's young daughter, asked my desert flower. "I heard it's gonna be real fun."

Natakia smiled, taking a small bite of her birthday meal. "It's going to be wonderful. Dad said he'll buy me any dress I want for it."

She eyed me, as if my child was daring me to go back on my word. It was a threat that held no heat, not like those she gave Daka sometimes.

"Aw, I wish I could go!" Emily kicked her legs a bit. "But Mommy got me a cute dress for the party. Do you like it?"

My daughter looked down at her flowery teal dress, admiring it for a moment. "It suits you, Emmy. I love the way it goes with your eyes."

Macy nodded, agreeing with the assessment.

The young girl gasped. "It goes with my eyes? Really?"

I turned away from the conversation of young girls, watching Daka running away from Winfred and a smattering of other academy children trying to chase her down and tag her.

Winfred, a king's son at heart, was much better at helping the other children play with them, helping them get into position or getting them involved. Daka was flipping over team efforts to trip her, hopping over the heads of her friends, and it was really only luck that had one of the kids finally jump up and tag her shin as she flew by.

"Got her! She's it!"

The kid who'd done it, a small brunette boy, looked happy for a moment before what he'd done registered.

Something changed among the kids as Daka landed, and I could see the air around her vibrating with her Vitae. She looked back over her shoulder at them all with a big smile and shiny blue eyes. "Alright! You all get ten seconds!"

Winfred called out to the other kids, "Scatter!"

He ran off with a playful fear in his eyes, but the other kids looked a little more genuinely afraid as they ran away from my daughter, but it all still seemed like good fun. I'd step in if Daka got a little too carried away.

"Are you sure they should be running around like that so soon after eating?" Marisha was frowning worriedly at all the children playing. "It won't be good if they push themselves."

I considered it for a moment. "Let them have their fun. I'm sure they'll rest before they get to that point."

Or never have such limitations in the first place. Daka had long broken the barrier of rest between meals and playtime.

Off to the side, at a nearby wooden table, was Dalton as he watched the other children play, speaking idly with Alan, who seemed comfortable to simply listen and respond. They weren't the closest, but Dalton gave very little of his time and attention to others unless they impressed him somehow.

Penelope came over from a different table. "Alright, alright, when are we getting to presents? I'm dying to knock you out of the water."

"I'd expected the children to ask first, Penelope," I said, smiling at her frustrated look.

She sniffed. "Don't drag your feet because you're scared, Rakta. It's a bad look."

Taking the playful sting in stride, I called out, "Present time!"

All the children turned their eyes to me, Daka's hand disturbing the air with how fast it came to stop a few inches from the sternum of one of the kids she had been rushing after.

"Presents?" Daka blinked. "Presents!"

And so ensued a rush of motion my way. Despite her claims, I was confident that Penelope couldn't have designed gifts better than mine this year.

How had Penelope designed such amazing gifts for my children? Truthfully, it warmed my heart that she spent so much time and care on the magical items, but wasn't this a tad excessive?

Dalton was looking at his sturdy-looking gray satchel in wonder, putting his arm into it far deeper than it should have truly managed to go down. "And it can hold how many pounds of weight?"

"Exactly nine hundred and eight kilograms," Penelope said, shooting me a triumphant look. "I'd say it's a pretty amazing gift."

My son nodded. "It's far more useful than the Color Cube. Thank you, Aunt Penny."

Penelope's face fell at the mention of the Color Cube. A strange toy she'd made for Dalton based on one of Shawn's ideas. Dalton had solved it in moments, getting the sporadic and random multicolored cube into six different sides of solid colors.

I had never managed to figure out how you got the multicolored squares on the cube to all shift to the same side before Daka accidentally broke it trying to figure it out herself.

Apparently, it was quite popular in the capital, but Penelope had expected it to be a bit more difficult for my son than it ended up being.

"Yeah, well," Penelope struggled for a moment. "I call it the Big Inside Bag, but you can come up with your own name for it if you want."

Dalton nodded, and I dared not ask him to compare the gift to mine. My heart did not want to hear the answer.

"Yes, thank you, Aunt Penny." I looked over to my desert flower who was currently slightly lost in wonder at her own gift, a floating mirror of impeccable design that shifted in size as Natakia gazed at it, moving to allow her to see anything as she wished.

Penelope came over, staring into the mirror. "Mm-hmm, I knew you'd like it. I call it the Shifting Attendant Mirror. Remember, you need this brooch on your person to align yourself with the magic. It'll do as you think as long as you have it."

The brooch in question was a silver stem with glistening emerald petals fashioned into a beautiful natakia, the flower that my daughter was named after. The only Certillian equivalent would be that of a rose, but with jagged petals and spiny needles similar to a cactus.

Daka was jumping up and down, waiting for her own gift. She was practically bursting with excitement after receiving a beautiful necklace from a blushing Winfred, enchanted sparring clothes from Shawn, and tons of candy and sweets from the other children.

Penelope came over, smiling. "I bet you're ready for your gift, huh?"

"I'm so bloody ready!" Daka almost looked like she was going to pulse out her Vitae if she wasn't careful. Only now, she could survive such an expensive use of her life energy.

"Well," Penelope said, pulling out a box from her belt, "I know you're quite the fighter."

"Yeah!"

"Like to jump around."

"Yeah! Yeah!"

"Stop screaming at me."

"Okay!"

Taking a deep breath as Daka nodded, Penelope opened the box and took out a helmet. Made of leather, the fine craftsmanship of the gift could not be understated. The small hints of runic imprints on the leather could only be the glacier hiding the larger magical enchantments engraved within.

"This is your Armored Helmet." She bent over and gently placed the helmet onto my daughter, making adjustments to the straps. "Don't let it fool you; it's better than a lot of the metal stuff the guards in the capital wear. Comfortable, magically warm, and it'll help you out if you do manage to get hurt."

Daka's eyes were bright underneath the lip of the leather helmet's eye slots. "Wow, this is bloody amazing, Aunt Penny."

"Well, the point is to keep you less bloody, but yeah." Penelope giggled before giving her a hug "Just be careful out there, okay? It can be a rough world."

I remembered my wife's last words to my children. I wondered if they remembered them.

"Dad, Dad, do I look cool?" Daka turned to me, showing off her gift. "I look really cool, don't I?"

Her dark hair, much like mine, was pressed down by the helmet, making her look like the small warrior she had always been in my heart.

"You look cool, Daka." I smiled before looking over at Penelope, who'd gotten quite smug over the last few seconds. "Thank you, Penelope. They'll cherish them forever."

For once, I even included Dalton in this. I'm sure he'd find plenty of uses for his new magical bag.

Penelope's smug grin settled into a soft smile, before she shrugged. "Well, gotta do something for them, don't I? I don't get to invent for fun much these days, so, sorry if I go a bit overboard."

"I'm sure they can enjoy both of our gifts equally." I rested a hand on her shoulder and watched as the next guest came up to my children with a present.

With that, the rest of the day continued, and many gifts were given. Natakia was gently torn from her mirror by Macy, and they continued their conversation with Emily, while Alan helped Dalton begin to pack his things into his new bag.

And Daka ran around even more recklessly, her head now truly protected.

10

In the late night after the party ended, I awoke to familiar sounds of sniffles shuffling into my room. I pushed myself up, looking at my daughter. "Daka?"

My fearless, reckless daughter looked pale and distraught, her form shivering and her eyes wide. "I . . . I had a nightmare again . . ."

Without another word, I was at her side, gently picking her up and hoisting her into my lap and hugging her. She clung to me with all her might, her body shaking.

Unfortunately, this was familiar. No matter how bright my daughter was, like the sun, there were times when even the moon balked at the darkness inside of her. Daka never explained her nightmares to me.

Was it because they were too frightening? Or were they terrors from another world? The world that Shawn had told me so much about. If so, I could understand her fear. They came from an alien and cruel place from what Shawn had spoken of.

And yet, did my own world not have its own horrors? Perhaps, if I revealed to my daughter what I knew . . . she could open up to me? And yet, what if she was not ready? What if she had not told me for a reason?

Struck with the fear of making it worse for my child, I simply let her rest in my arms quietly. Moments passed, perhaps even an hour, and she slowly began to calm, no longer shaking in my arms.

Daka slowly pulled away from me, as if hesitant to lose my warmth, before looking up to me with her glistening blue eyes, shining with horrors behind them I wish I could understand.

"I'm Daka." She said it as she always did, with a resolution to it and yet an undertone of deep need for affirmation.

I nodded, "You are Daka. You are my daughter whom I love with all of my heart, and nothing would ever change that."

I'd said these words many times, and yet now I said them with new meaning, new understanding seeping in. Was she scared of who she'd been?

She hugged me again, tightly. "I love you, Dad."

"I love you too, my little warrior."

We sat in the familiar silence of our unfortunate tradition. And yet, just as I thought it was time to begin to carry her off back to bed, or perhaps allow her to sleep in mine tonight if she was truly shaken, she surprised me.

"Dad, am I going to have to kill people one day?" The sobering question struck me dumb.

I defaulted to a familiar question to buy me time. "Why do you ask, Daka?"

"I don't want to kill people . . ." While the sentiment should have warmed my heart—no father wished to raise a bloodthirsty butcher— something about the statement sent a chill through me.

It was said with so much experience. Less like that of a child wishing to do no harm and more like that of a retired veteran of war, his Vitae stained by the life he'd ended en masse.

Taking a deep breath, I played with my daughter's hair, running my fingers through her dark locks, before murmuring to her with sincerity, "The choice of whether you take life is always in your hands, Daka. No matter what anyone ever tells you or has you believe."

"I'll never take a life. I'll never be a killer."

It sounded less like a statement and more like a mantra. One I hoped would ring true throughout the universe.

"I believe you." I kissed her forehead. "Do you wish to go back to your room?"

She shook her head, and I settled her beside me as we laid down once more, her breath slowly evening out into a peaceful slumber.

"So you won't be heading back with us?" Shawn asked. "It'd be a whole lot safer, you know?"

I nodded. "Yes, but we plan to take a few detours. My children have heard much of Lydia's and my adventures, and they're excited to see where they took us in person."

Not to mention, I felt a tad guilty for not raising them as Lydia had wanted. She'd always talked about raising the children on the road, nomadically, not confined to a keep of her family.

Penelope sniffed. "Well, you have some galewinds, so if you keep us waiting too long, we'll have to assume you got lost or hurt. Don't make us come looking for you."

"Well." I chuckled. "We shouldn't be too far behind you. Although we are traveling a little heavier than you all."

With Doh, Dresden, and Macy coming with us, we'd have to bring more supplies, and that'd weigh down Jeta and Johnson somewhat. We'd have to take more breaks, as well.

Getting our own galewind horses from CAD had been quite the surprise a few years back. A belated gift for all I had done during my time as a member? Something Penelope had organized?

Regardless, the two steeds were worth their weight in gold, and they certainly were not light. Although, you'd think that with how fast they were.

Tracy walked over from saying goodbye to Natakia, both of them having a private morning together talking about the upcoming party. "Just be careful. I'm sure Shawn has let you know the state of things."

"He has." I wouldn't be letting my guard down. I'd discussed with Dresden and Doh the current dangers, and they would be on their own high alert.

Doh had gotten reasonably good with a dagger in the past few years, but more so, she was much faster at casting her magic. And Dresden could certainly hold his own.

I nodded to them all as they began to get into their carriage, my children coming to my side. "Thank you for coming; it's always a pleasure having you around."

Penelope smirked. "When you get to the capital, don't be a stranger. If you have any time outside of your kids and Harriet bothering you."

"Harriet doesn't bother me," I said, furrowing my brow. She had done me a great favor. Why would her presence bother me?

Shawn poked his head out from the window. "You should tell her that, buddy. She'll love it. Come on, Winfred!"

He called to his son who was currently lingering next to Daka, his gaze begging up at his father. "Father, can't I just ride back to the capital with them?"

The two gifted children had spent the last few days having the time of their lives with each other, both of them enjoying their time tremendously.

"Sorry, son." Shawn shook his head. "I'd rather have you with me."

Winfred kicked a rock. "Okay."

"Don't worry, Winfred!" Daka shook his shoulder a bit. "When I get there, Dad'll have taught me all sorts of cool techniques for me to show off to you! We'll have tons of fun!"

Winfred puffed up his cheeks. "I'll learn some techniques, too! We'll trade!"

"Sounds bloody awesome!"

With that, Winfred tore himself away from my daughter and went back to the carriage. It was nice that Daka had such a close friend in Winfred, and yet . . . something paternal welled up inside of me.

"It was wonderful having you all here." Natakia did a curtsy to the carriage riders.

Dalton bowed. "Please come again."

Shawn stuck his head out the carriage window again, his wife and son waving goodbye behind him. "Rakta, I'll see you at the capital, okay? We have a lot to talk about!"

"See you then, Shawn." I waved goodbye to my friend, my children waving the party off, as well.

And then they set off down the path, Green One and Green Two pulling them down the trail faster and smoother than any normal horse could aspire to.

As my family prepared themselves for a trip to the capital, I had to make my own preparations. Walking into Gelvurt, I walked to the outskirts, or at least, what once had been the outskirts of Gelvurt when it was small.

Now, I walked through developing streets of budding cobblestone up to the stone stairway to the large oaken doors of Tribus Academy.

The culmination of years of effort from me, Jorge, and Caitlyn, Tribus Academy was home to the youth of tomorrow. Staffed by scholars, magicians, and cultivators from across the empire, it attended to every need a child could have as they grew into their own destiny.

And while Jorge was busy in Niers, spending much of his time tending to the local economy like a gardener would tend to a flower, Lordess Caitlyn Velbrun of Alwur was much more present.

"Good morning, my lord!"

"How are you doing, my lord?"

"Ah, uh, my lord!"

I nodded respectfully to the teachers and children as I passed, some of them unused to seeing me even after all these years. I did not manage the academy myself, leaving that to Headmaster Gotswain, but I still kept a close eye on things, to make sure that nothing dishonorable happened to my children.

"Oh, Rakta."

I stopped, recognizing this teacher and smiling. "Marge, how have you been?"

The alchemist smiled, tucking some hair behind her ear as she spoke to me. "I've been doing well. The children have been practically inhaling the coursework for this semester."

"That's good. And Daka hasn't given you any trouble?" Daka did not excel in subjects outside of her own Vitae and fighting.

"No, no, she's a sweetheart. Always asking questions," Marge said. "In fact, I'm more concerned about Natakia. She has a dreadful time with the . . . more particular ingredients that alchemy requires."

Ah, yes, Natakia did have a dislike for slimy things.

"I'm sure she'll manage somehow."

Marge giggled. "And of course, Dalton has been excellent. Well, I need to head to my next class, so I'll talk with you later. Oh, your children will be going to the capital with you for the next few weeks, yes?"

"Yes, they will be. It's a part of the birthday present." I nodded.

"Well," she said, "tell them I said happy birthday."

With that, she walked off. It was truly amazing what the support from the community and her role as a teacher had done for the poor alchemist after the death of her boys. It was a bright spot, really, to know that not all tragedy led to Vera's brand of darkness.

However, I put such thoughts aside for now. I needed to go speak with Caitlyn.

11

Assaulted by a hag after being unwilling to betray her people, Caitlyn Velbrun had been afflicted with a curse that transformed her, body and mind, throughout the day.

A child at dawn, a crone at dusk. At noon, the lordess was at her true age, her prime. And yet, when we had first met, I had promised her my aid in removing this curse, but that was easier said than done.

"Good morning, Caitlyn." I walked through the open door into the lordess's private room at the academy, lightly knocking to announce my arrival.

"Good morning."

The teenage Caitlyn was currently stretching, going through the various poses and movements that we had long devised to aid her Vitae.

She seemed mildly annoyed at my disruption, but at this time in the day, she was likely to be annoyed by most things. Not that she could help it, of course.

"How have things been?" I'd last talked with her a week ago, my preparations for the party and my guests having kept me busy since.

Letting her stance drop, Caitlyn looked over her shoulder at me. "Stressful and boring. No, just stressful. I have a meeting this afternoon, so I'm preparing."

I nodded. "Anything I should be aware of?"

"No, just some merchant debacle. They were directed here from Alwur to meet with me because of how impatient they were. Nothing I can't handle."

I was sure she could. While finding the hag responsible for her curse was unlikely unless she turned up again, Caitlyn and I had decided to instead focus on developing a way to combat the curse with her Vitae.

Truly, Caitlyn had already done most of the work, having laid the groundwork for the method by using her Vitae to lengthen her time as an adult.

Working together, we had built upon her groundwork and produced something new for the lordess that, while not a cure, was far more beneficial.

A new stance, one wholly unique to Caitlyn, called the **Threefold Stance**.

It was less of a physical stance and more of one that required a specific state of mind and self-awareness of her Vitae and her curse, but it refined each transformation that plagued her into its purest form, allowing her to bring them forward as required.

The child was infinitely gullible but unpredictable and charming. The crone was remarkably unpleasant but clever and unfailingly insightful in her cynicism.

"How are things with your Vitae?" Primal energy was chaotic, and I knew that Caitlyn's morning stretches and exercises to calm it could only do so much.

Saying no words, Caitlyn dropped into her **Threefold Stance**, her arms at her side and her poise impeccable, her eyes closed as she concentrated. I could feel the thrum as her Vitae began to blend with the esoteric primal energy of her curse.

The teenage Caitlyn aged, her flexible clothing shifting slightly as she grew a few inches, her arms becoming muscular and well toned. Her skin darkening into a brilliant tan, almost golden, Caitlyn Velbrun breathed a sigh filled with power as she finished shifting.

"Everything's working well today." Her words were full of power.

The prime, a form that had refined every aspect of Caitlyn's original adult form. Once she began to use these forms in tandem with actual techniques and the chaos of battle, she would be a remarkable combatant.

Relaxing her control, Caitlyn quickly de-aged, her Vitae returning to normal as her skin lost its golden sheen and her body returned to its current cursed appearance of the hour.

"You've come far." It was a great relief that I had managed to help her with this curse in some way after she had helped me so much with my children.

Glancing at me with an instinctive glint of annoyance, Caitlyn blinked the glint away and smiled at me fondly. "Well, I've not been alone in all of this. I assume you're getting ready to leave?"

I nodded. "Yes, we'll be gone for at least a month. I'm sure you and Jorge can keep things in order while I'm gone, but I apologize for the extra work."

Luckily, nothing strenuous was planned for quite some time. The local quotas had already been met, and taxing could be handled easily enough by Caitlyn or Jorge in my place.

"Nothing we can't handle. I'll make sure things are handled here before I run to Alwur for a day or two." She spoke to herself, detailing out her own plans under her breath. "Let the kids know I said happy birthday. I didn't have the time to come up and say it myself."

"I'll let them know." Natakia and Daka were fond of Caitlyn, although for different reasons. Natakia enjoyed her elegance, as she put it, while Daka liked to play with her when she was a kid.

With everything said, and Caitlyn properly informed, I made my way to leave.

"Wait." Caitlyn stopped me in my tracks, her tone suddenly serious. "I know you've seen the reports. Bandit movement on the Ruskan border is rising."

I sighed. "Yes, I have."

It was an unfortunate truth that I'd had to deal with my own people making attempts on the lives of traveling merchants in the area. The derision I had faced from Ruskan vagabonds due to my position was palpable.

"You've been quiet about how you want to respond. Are you really going to have me make a decision for Gelvurt while you're gone?" Caitlyn's tone made it clear what she thought of me leaving it in her hands.

I did not want to think of this right now. I was supposed to be preparing for a family trip, and yet, I could not shirk my responsibility as a noble. Caitlyn would have my hide.

I looked away. "Additional patrols, but interrogating Ruskan travelers for simply being in the area should be done gently."

News of banditry always inflamed the hatred some carried in their hearts for those of Rusk. I did not need the blood of innocent travelers spilled on Gelvurt's land because of overzealous guards.

Especially not the blood of my people.

"I'll pass along the word to the captain." Caitlyn seemed satisfied.

I left without another word, wanting to return to my children as soon as possible. My thoughts were uneasy, my mind going to my sister.

Would she ever step foot into the empire? What would she push me to do?

Come the next day and everything had been prepared. Natakia's dresses were accounted for, Daka had brought extra bandages, and Dalton had made it clear that everything he needed was in his extradimensional bag.

Doh had gotten Dresden and Macy ready as well, my friend having made sure that her husband and daughter were properly awake this early in the morning.

Dresden carried Macy in his arms, my fellow father looking barely aware of the world around him. "Why so early?"

His daughter hummed in agreement.

I walked over, grabbing Macy's bag along the way and placing it in the storage compartment of the carriage. "We want to make good time before nightfall. I'd like to avoid traveling by moonlight."

"Nighttime is when the monsters come out!" Daka ran by, her helmet firmly on.

Smiling, I looked around for her brother. "Well, perhaps, but I also happen to like seeing the road when traveling in a carriage as quickly as we will."

I was no expert driver, and the galewind horses could be temperamental.

Natakia, yawning, offered a weak hello as she walked by me and into the carriage, barely saying a word. Her brother, whom I eventually found napping against the stable, was gently woken up and led into the carriage.

Daka, already sitting down, did not look the most pleased that Doh had taken the seat right beside her and seemed a little uncomfortable.

"Dad, can I sit up in the driver's seat with you?" She fiddled around with her hands.

Dresden and I shared a look. I'd planned on him being up there with me just in case we ran into trouble, but perhaps it was good to have a fighter in the carriage with everyone else?

Turning back to Daka, I asked, "Are you sure, my little warrior? I'd thought you'd enjoy some extra sleep."

"I'm awake! Full of energy!" I didn't doubt her words, but maybe this was a good chance to ask her a question I'd been curious about.

I nodded to Dresden, and the two of them switched, Daka clinging onto my arms as I carried her to the front and Dresden sat beside his wife.

Eventually the entirety of both families were loaded into the back of the carriage, Daka untangling herself from my arm and sitting in the passenger seat next to me.

"All good to go!" Daka grinned.

Nodding, I whipped the reins lightly against the supernatural stallions, and we were off. Our first destination was a day of travel away.

And yet, as the carriage picked up speed, I looked over to my daughter. A question that had long plagued me bubbled up once more.

Why did Daka dislike Doh so much?

12

It was an hour into our journey before I broached the question. I was unsure of what her response would be, what mysteries I would uncover. Shawn had raised so many questions about my children, and I was doubtful I would like every answer.

Perhaps, had Doh done something to Daka? Or Daka's previous life had set her against those who could change their shapes? I garnered nothing from idle ideas of what her answer would be, so I finally spoke.

"Daka," I tried for her attention, her eyes having been wide and following the blur of the trees around us. The temperate forests of the Certillian Empire were beautiful, but there were other things to discuss.

She turned toward me. "Yeah, Dad?"

"Why are you so uncomfortable around Doh?" Straight to the point, gentle. There was no need to push harshly. I trusted my daughter would open up to me eventually, even if she did not speak with me today.

Daka blinked before she shifted uncomfortably around in her seat. "What? I, uh, I'm not . . ."

"You can trust me with your words, Daka," I said. "Everyone else is asleep."

My daughter chewed on that for a moment, her eyes filled with a fear reminiscent of the nights she woke in terror. It made my heart feel a little heavier, asking her this, but the most difficult questions were oftentimes the most important.

"I just," Daka began. "Why is she here?"

"Did you not want her to come on our trip?" It was a reasonable complaint, seeing as this was meant to be a personal journey for our family. I had considered that myself, honestly, but the Bookers had simply grown into our own lives seamlessly.

Daka frowned. "Well, uh, I mean . . . not really. I meant, though, why is she . . . here? At the keep, with us. Didn't she . . . Didn't she steal from you? And she messes with memories . . ."

I thought about that for a moment. It was true. I had told the story of how I'd met Doh many times, although not for a while. And yet, it had seemed to stick with my young daughter.

Still, the topic of memories was more pressing. I had never considered that my daughter would dwell so deeply on the implications of Doh's magic.

"Are you worried that she bewitched me?" I put an arm around her, comforting her as she put her knees up to her chest and thought. That had certainly been a concern of mine once upon a time, that Doh would subvert me when I least expected it.

"Is that possible?" Daka looked up at me.

I thought about it for a moment. "Doh's manipulation of memories is a powerful magic, but not a particularly swift one. And it isn't infallible. You'll learn this in time, but Vitae can disrupt the fine manipulations of Mana."

"So she wouldn't be able to mess with your memories?"

"Only if I allowed her to do so."

Daka stuck out a tongue like she tasted something bitter. "Don't do that, Dad. You don't want her anywhere near you."

My thoughts had begun to linger on the moments I had, in fact, allowed Doh within my mind, when I felt the almost palpable disgust in Daka's words.

"My little warrior, is there something else that bothers you about her?" It couldn't simply be her past, could it? Doh had only stolen from me, something far easier to forgive compared to what others had done.

And if all it took for Daka to distrust someone was a history is thievery, then perhaps there was a longer conversation to be had at some point.

She was silent for a moment, looking away from me, before almost growling, "I don't like how she looks."

I blinked, never having considered that particular sentiment from a child of mine. Had I truly heard her correctly?

"Everything about her looks wrong." She continued, "I don't like her getting near me with her disgusting Vitae. I . . . I hate it! She's an abomina—"

"Daka, stop." Vitae had slipped into my command.

She froze. I'd spoken with more heat in my voice than I'd meant to, but it was better than allowing my daughter to fall deeper into her disgust-filled rant toward a close family friend and wake everyone up.

"Daka." I tried to ease my voice back into warmth, but it was difficult after hearing such words from my daughter. "How long have you felt like this?"

"As long as I can remember." Daka was quiet, like she was admitting a great wrong. "Tanner, that dragon guy, was the same, and . . . and Macy has started looking more . . . wrong, too."

I considered that for a moment, gathering my thoughts, before a small epiphany lit up inside of me. "You're speaking of those with monster blood."

She was silent, but if she was having the same revelation, I could not know.

Daka's unique vision, able to see the Vitae of others, had pushed my child to grow up disturbed by the unfamiliar sights of those with monster-stained Vitae.

Seeing my daughter so still, I held her hand. "Do you think these thoughts are right? Do you think that Doh means any of us harm just because of how she looks?"

"I don't know." Daka gripped my hand tighter. "I'm sorry, Dad. I just . . . It feels like when . . . back when . . ."

She was struggling, I could tell. "What does it feel like, Daka? You can tell me anything."

I had to start vibrating my own Vitae through my grip as Daka's became impossibly tight, threatening to break the hand of a lesser man, Daka's gaze staring out past the trail we traveled on and toward the horizon.

For a moment, I wondered if she wouldn't answer before she spoke as if her voice were the wind.

"They feel like the enemy." The words were dispassionate, so unlike my little warrior scared of killing. They were the words of those that had not only seen war, but had been involved in the worst parts of it.

I put the reins to the side and hugged my daughter, feeling her arms wrap around me as I wrangled with the thoughts and feelings inside of me.

"Daka," I said with as much vehemence I could put into my whispered words, "I promise you. You have no enemies here."

We stayed like that until the horses needed guiding once more.

"Seems like a good place to camp."

I smiled at Dresden. "Yes, well, it's a familiar camping area. My adventuring group used to camp here when we were in the area. It's quite well used."

The clearing was surrounded by larger standing stones, carved over time by the weather into smooth pillar-like rocks sticking up out of the ground. Many of them were marked by sharp cracks and scars where my friends and I had trained.

The kids were currently playing; well, Daka was running around trying to find Natakia and Macy hiding behind the stones. She had pushed aside the conversation we'd had, almost like we hadn't ever had it.

It was relieving, and yet, I could not help but worry. Daka's issue, her concerns, could not be resolved in a single day, and I . . . I felt out of my depth.

Dalton was walking around, examining the standing stones and looking at the deep marks left by old techniques and spells.

Whistling casually, Doh came over. "So, you ever name this place? Since you liked it so much?

"Shawn called it Camp Standing Stone." Penelope had wanted to call it Camp Seventeen Smooth Standing Boulders, but Shawn had refined it down to a less bulky name with similar alliteration.

"And it's safe?" Dresden kept an eye on the forest around us.

I nodded. "We never had many problems with monsters here, but it's been quite some time since it's been used. Something could have moved in, but we'll only be here for one night."

"I'll keep watch tonight, since you drove all day." Dresden walked off on patrol.

I was grateful for the reprieve. When traveling with my children to Velbrun for their yearly visits to their noble family, I spent much of my time on watch. It was nice to have a second set of eyes.

Doh gave him a kiss on the cheek. "Don't go too far."

"I won't." Dresden smiled at his wife.

Watching him go, Doh crept closer to my side. "So, how'd the talk with Daka go?"

"I'm sorry?" I'd been so involved with my thoughts on the matter that I hadn't entertained the notion of someone asking about it.

The maid smiled. "I kind of thought you might ask. I'd wondered for a while what she disliked about me so much. Maybe it's because I shape-shifted too much when she was a baby?"

That probably didn't help, but Daka's issues felt much deeper seated.

"We talked, but it isn't something I want to discuss so readily until I've . . . considered it more." Daka had trusted me with her thoughts and feelings. It wasn't my place to go share them so readily. "I apologize for her distrust; the circumstances are out of your control."

Doh relaxed. "That's good to hear. I really thought I'd done something, uh, I don't know . . . bad? It seems like she gets along . . . okay with Macy, at least. That's what really matters."

And yet, that might change when Macy awakened her doppelgänger blood. I blinked, remembering a part of the conversation that had not crossed my mind yet.

"Daka . . ." I considered my words for a moment. "Daka mentioned that Macy was beginning to look different, her Vitae. I think . . ."

"She'll awaken soon?" Doh frowned. "Yeah, yeah, I . . . I think I was probably around her age when mine did. Daka can see that kind of stuff?"

I had not discussed with Doh the full extent of Daka's capabilities, but she knew that my daughter could see Vitae.

"Apparently, yes." An unfortunate aspect of her ability.

"Well, I'll just have to watch out for it." Doh reaffirmed herself, looking to be a mother for a moment, before she grinned at me like the same maid that had traded her way into my keep so long ago. "Are you excited to see Harriet at the capital?"

"Well, I'll be visiting many old friends, Harriet being one of them." My thoughts went to a little street restaurant that hopefully still sold Ruskan delights. My children would love the food there, I was sure.

Any further conversation between Doh and me was halted as Dalton came up, putting away a book into his magical bag.

I nodded. "How are you, Dalton?"

"I'm fine, Father." Dalton brushed off a bit of dirt from his traveling clothes. "Where are we going? I know you mean to surprise us, but I am curious."

I smiled. "Well, don't ruin the surprise for your sisters, but we're going to a very special place."

Seeing my son's interest refuse to fade, and Doh's own interest growing, I smiled.

I brought out my map and showed him the destination. "A hidden Mana-rich pond where the fish have learned to sing the songs an old traveling bard taught them long ago."

"Singing fish." Dalton didn't seem quite as impressed. "That's our first destination?"

I gave him a side hug, putting the map away. "It's a very special place, Dalton."

It had been years since I had last visited the pond. I couldn't wait to have my children listen to the same songs that Lydia and I had danced to so many years ago.

"It's where I first proposed to your mother."

13

Once again traveling early in the morning, my son sat next to me today. Daka had tuckered herself out testing a new technique I was teaching her and had passed out in the carriage soon after.

With privacy between us, Dalton eventually broke the silence. "How many fish are there?"

"Hmm?" I looked over to him, a bit surprised at his topic of choice. "At the hidden pond?"

He nodded, not opting to explain himself any further. I leaned back, keeping the horses moving forward at a swift pace, but allowing myself to consider the question.

"Last I saw, there were many fish, a whole choir," I said, my thoughts going back to the wondrous sights of the pond. It was a beautiful oasis in an often dangerous world.

Dalton nodded. I noticed he was making notes in a small journal he had pulled from his bag, but he kept the contents covered with the flap of the book.

I smiled. "Are you making plans for your store?"

We had talked little about his new business, but I could tell that Dalton had thought of little else than his own storefront these past few days. He was always making notes and speaking with traveling merchants.

"Yes, Father." For a moment, I thought he was going to leave it at that, but he eventually continued, "Capital is my biggest problem. I either need to find a new niche to monopolize or have the starting wealth to sell similar commodities as my competitors at a lower price."

I nodded, long conversations with Orion having taught me the basic principles of business and running such a store. "A niche sounds more doable; the capital merchants won't be lacking in their coin purses."

"And to do that, I need to understand the local market, the needs of the capital." Dalton had no trepidation in his voice as he outlined his problems, merely stating them matter-of-factly.

Still, even as my child seemingly had no fear of the obstacles he faced, I considered how I could help. I did not know the needs of the common folk of the capital, nor did I have a very close relationship with many of the merchants there.

Harriet may know more, but I was reluctant to press her for any more help. She had already done so much for me, and I truly had little to give her in return that I felt was of equal value. Of course, I'd already made plans to give her favorable trade deals moving forward.

"What have the merchants mentioned?" I was sure he'd gathered some sort of insight.

Dalton closed his journal and looked out into the passing forest. "Simple commodities are all sold and have cutthroat competition. One merchant suggested expanding into more magical commodities."

"Ah, yes." I nodded. "Your aunt Penny sells magical items and devices to some of the shops in town. I'm sure she'd have some insight into that."

"Would she be willing to sell to me exclusively at a discount?" My son's question was dry, like he knew how unlikely that was.

And yet, I considered the idea for a moment. Penelope didn't really sell to the stores to make money—she made plenty with the contracts she had with the empire and CAD. A number of the magical items she sold to stores were just the excess she had beyond her usual quotas, her mass-construction process still being refined.

Although, a conversation did come to mind from a few years ago when she had complained about how shy the market was in regard to her more bizarre designs. Perhaps that was a route to take? It would be irresponsible of me to promise anything to my son, however.

"You'd need to speak with her, I'm afraid," I said. "I'm not sure of the exact details of her relationships with those stores, but I'd be surprised if House Iriend didn't own some."

"Ah, yes. She couldn't stop selling to her family," Dalton sighed. "The alternative is selling rare materials for magical products, but that's adventuring work if I want to actually profit from it."

Dalton had never spoken fondly of having to go out into the field as an adventurer. Although, I wasn't quite sure what the implied alternative to adventuring was. Perhaps he meant buying cheap and selling at a higher cost?

I nodded. "Hopefully, she can at least give you an overview of the market. Orion has done quite well with his humble beginnings."

"Orion, of course." Dalton's smile was sharp. "While the people of Gelvurt have propped up a familiar face, it's only because Niers is more economical that a real competitor hasn't come to knock him out of the ring."

I blinked. My son had never been so loose with his tongue in regard to my friend's business before. This opportunity in the capital must have given him confidence that I'd never thought he lacked.

"What do you mean, Dalton?" I'd never thought Orion was so close to the edge.

"Say you have a strong enough capital." Dalton held up a hand, counting out his points. "You can afford lower-priced goods than any local business, weather the lack of profits, bankrupt your competitors, and then make up any losses with higher prices based on your new monopoly."

I had never heard such callous merchantry spoken with such casualness before and certainly not from my own son. And what did he mean by bankrupt? Was this a term from Shawn's world? My son had always cared more for monetary gain than his fellow man, but to hear him speak like this . . .

I thought of Lord Velbrun of Warnok, the noble that Dalton had sought to introduce to my town. Had he thought so little of his vicious methods because my son knew far worse?

At my contemplative silence, Dalton spoke up once more. "It's just a business practice, Father. I'm not in a position to do anything like that."

"Of course, son," I said, taking a moment to relax. He was only a child, even with his worldly experience. "These are simply ideas I'm . . . unfamiliar with. Did you have any more ideas regarding your business?"

We settled into a comfortable conversation, listening as my son, somewhat hesitant at first, spoke about his plans regarding the capital.

He spoke of profit, economy, and building his business like a commercial tactician, something I'd have expected from the legends of the Donns of Neve, the merchants that had united most of Derra under one language and one coin.

It was fascinating, although somewhat terrifying, but I still couldn't help myself from smiling fondly at the undercurrent of passion in my son's usually clipped, cold voice.

I stopped the carriage, my son looking up from his journal that he had returned to after our conversation had come to an end.

At the edge of an unassuming part of the forest, not even one of the named ones, I smiled. "Dalton, go wake everyone. We travel the rest by foot."

After some jostling and yawns, our group set out. I held Natakia's hand, making sure not to travel at a pace too fast for my desert flower, and watched as Daka scurried around the group, looking at all the new trees and rocks around.

As she stared inside the hollow trunk of a tree, I was almost envious of her sight. A familiar question of how beautiful the Vitae of the forests must look to her crossed my mind, followed by a smile, but it faltered as I remembered our last conversation regarding such things.

She had not dwelled on it, from what I could tell, but perhaps the singing of the fish could cleanse our lingering worries and doubts.

"Uncle Rakta." Macy's rare, quiet voice broke the silence. "Are we going to be fishing at the lake?"

A lesser man would have choked at the idea, but I shook my head after a slight pause. "No, no, Macy. This is a . . . sacred site. No one should disturb the sanctity of it."

I heard Dalton mutter something about the value of singing fish as pets for nobility, but I decided to ignore such a sacrilegious thought.

Singing, a beautiful weaving of stories, was not a cornerstone of Ruskan traditions as our own spoken stories were, but we cherished it still. For fish to have taken up the practice, well, I had been very excited when Lydia had found this place for me.

Coming up to a larger bush, almost like a wall, I looked back to everyone. "We're here."

"That's a bush." Doh stroked her chin, not looking entirely awake yet.

I nodded at the astute observation. "It's behind the bush."

Grabbing at a part of the bush that Lydia had found for us on our first visit, I pulled back on the vegetation to reveal a pathway forward toward the beautiful, enclosed pond ahead.

"Welcome to the beautiful singing pond of the Certillian Empire." I smiled at my children and my friends, echoing my wife's past words, said moments before the world was filled with beautiful music.

And yet, my own words were simply met with silence.

14

The pond was exactly as I remembered it as I stepped through the bushes with an uncertainty in my gait. Every bush, every flower. It was a place that I had considered safe from even time's cruel hand.

And yet, it was silent. The pond's crystal-blue water was completely still, with no ripples at all. Perhaps the fish were asleep? They could not sing every second of the day, of course.

"You okay, Rakta?" Dresden was beside me as we crept into the concerningly still clearing.

I looked around, glancing back to Doh and the children, who were all slowly making their way into the clearing behind us. "It's quiet."

Daka was looking around, her brows furrowed. Natakia was looking at me, a silent question in her eyes.

"The fish must still be asleep," I offered. "Doh, did you fetch the fish feed?"

With a faint look of nausea on her face, she brought out the dried grasshoppers. "Uh, yeah. Here, kids, go see if the fishies are hungry."

Watching her pass out the grasshoppers, my heart whispered quiet words of hope and optimism as my children took small little bundles of insects, Daka getting two big handfuls, while her siblings took one or two each.

"Eat up, fish!" Daka threw her feed into the pond, the insects plopping onto the rippleless crystal surface and making for the first movement in the water since we'd entered.

As her siblings and Macy followed suit, feeding their bundles of food to the bottomless crystal lake's carnivorous surface, I waited for anything.

I waited for the insects, floating across the surface of the water, to be nibbled at and eaten. I waited for the first harmonic tunes of an old song that never came.

Doh came up to my side, her voice low. "How long has it been?"

"Too long." I had no other answer. Had I really deluded myself into thinking that this pond would never change? I'd thought this place sacred and indelible, untouchable by the gods themselves.

Obviously, I had been mistaken.

"Dad." Daka came running back up to me. "Where are the fish? Did, um, something happen to them?"

Dalton was by her side, but he didn't look curious as his sister did. More like there was an answer in his eyes, and he saw fit to see if I matched it with my own.

I patted her on the head. "Well, it seems, that . . . that the fish perhaps left. Predators or changes in the surroundings could have . . ."

My attempt at an answer failed as I suddenly choked up. There was emotion welling up in the back of my throat, pushed out of my chest by the silence of the pond.

Had someone taken them? Killed them? A dark whisper in the back of my head offered the questions, my deep sadness threatening to burn with anger.

"Are you okay?" Daka was looking up at me with her blue eyes, Lydia's blue eyes.

Feeling weak, I sat down on the ground, sighing. Natakia and Macy had come to surround me as well, Dresden and Doh looking on with concern.

"I'm sorry." My apology was offered in a dry whisper, my throat barely able to get the words out. "Your mother and I . . . When we came here this place was beautiful."

Even beyond the silence, the sharpness of this place's beauty had dulled over the years to me. Now, the only thing that was sharp was the memories plunging into my heart and twisting.

I rested my head in my hands, trying to collect myself. This trip was supposed to be filled with the fun and joy of an adventure.

It wasn't fair to them that I had brought them to this place only for me to become a victim of my own grief.

"I think it's fine."

Quietly, I looked up to Dalton, confused. "What?"

Dalton shrugged, his cold gaze looking across the pond. "It's quiet, peaceful, and the air is fresh. It's fine. Tell us about the fish."

Tell them about the fish? I looked at Daka and Natakia, both of them nodding along with their brother.

"Yeah, yeah, I wanna hear about the fish! And, uh, did you really propose to Mom here?" Daka was suddenly wrapped around my arm, smiling at me.

Natakia sniffed, looking at her hand. "I'm just glad I don't have to feed them."

Were they trying to cheer me up?

Chuckling at the thought of my own children trying to comfort me, of Dalton trying to do so, I got to my knees and brought them into a hug.

"Yes, yes." I squeezed them gently. "Your mother brought me to this place after I found myself longing for home. She said the fish would quell my wanderlust with their singing."

Letting them go, I looked at all of them, feeling a heat in my chest. To have children as special as mine, with their oddities and their quirks and their infinite potential for spectacular things, I considered myself a lucky man.

"I got down on one knee, just like this." I pulled up one leg from my kneel, bring my foot to the ground and my knee up. "Your mother was an amazing dancer."

"She was?" Daka smiled.

I nodded, noticing the gaze of both Natakia and Dalton following my tale. "We danced together for hours, from the ballroom waltz to the celebratory rekan of my people."

One of the greatest dances I had ever experienced.

"And then, when the fish departed"—I motioned out to the pond's surface—"I knew I never wanted to let our dance truly end."

Natakia's eyes were shining. "And that's when you proposed?"

"That's when I proposed." The look of surprise in Lydia's eyes had been enchanting, the one time I had ever caught her off guard.

Dresden spoke up, holding Doh and Macy close. "I can see why this place is special."

For a moment, a part of me wished to contest that, that the pond had lost its glow, but a thought stopped me, an epiphany. Did not every great warrior perish long before his stories would?

Did a man's life become less special, less beautiful, when it ended?

"Yes," I agreed, holding my children close again. "This place is special indeed."

Perhaps I simply needed to enjoy this place for what it was, not purely what it is right now. Through my stories of this place, my children could appreciate what I had brought them here to see.

Even if it wasn't entirely as I remembered.

My most rambunctious daughter was comfortable in my arms for a few more moments before she broke out of it and cheered, "Now we get to swim!"

What?

Before I could react, Daka swiftly leaped through the air and straight into the water of the pond, something Lydia and I had never so much as considered when we found this place.

"Daka!" I was conflicted with worry and a bit of shock, maybe even a little anger. Beyond the possibility of there being remnants of magic here, this was a sacred area!

Soaking wet, Daka came bursting up from the surface, her grin blinding as she took in a big breath. "It's so cold! Come on, Dad, swim with me!"

Natakia frowned. "I didn't bring a swimsuit."

I shook my head. "No, no, we are not . . ."

Daka's smile stopped me. Half-submerged in the water, looking happy to be here, how could I truly be angry at my daughter for enjoying this pond in her own way?

Would Lydia have swum in the pond? Would she have called her daughter back to the shore and reprimanded her?

I noticed that the others were slowly getting ready to join Daka, Macy bringing over a spare swimsuit for Natakia.

Feeling something tight within my chest unravel slightly, I rubbed my forehead, giving a jerky nod. "Alright, let's swim."

"Have fun with that." Dalton sat himself at the base of a tree, pulling out a book to read as everyone gave a little cheer and headed to the water with passion.

After hours of swimming and enjoying the crystal-clear pond, we returned to our carriage and set up camp for the night.

Doh was tending to Macy's sunburns from our day in the sun, simultaneously ignoring her own. Thankfully, my own children's skin was far darker, used to the unforgiving Ruskan heat that my ancestors had adapted to.

The others were making idle chatter, Daka staring into the raging fire of the center pit as our food cooked. Natakia and Dalton were whispering to each other.

Dresden, polishing his blade, sat next to me. "So, what did the fish sing?"

That got the others to look over at us, but I took a moment to make sure the chicken would not burn before I glanced at him. "Hmm?"

"The fish. Do you remember what they sang?" Dresden smirked. "I'm sure you remember some of the songs, right?"

I thought about that for a moment. "It's been quite a while."

My children, Daka most of all, stared at me expectantly. I had told them so many stories that they could only assume that this was easy for me, but remembering the delicate words of a song after so long . . .

"Actually." A thought struck me. "I do remember one quite clearly."

Doh pulled back from rubbing more oil on Macy's nose. "Let's hear it then."

Meeting every gaze around the campfire, I let the beginning words of the song roll out of my chest in a rumble. "In the mountains, high as clouds, with no worries and no doubts . . ."

A nameless song, one of a bright future that the bard had shared with the fish so long ago. Of leaving your regrets behind to enjoy tomorrow's sunrise.

To enjoy the love of today and tomorrow, rather than the tragedy of yesterday.

The song that had joined Lydia and me as I proposed to her.

". . . Tomorrow comes with a joyful hour, prosper, laugh, and never sour."

Opening my eyes, I found the camp entranced with my words as they came to an end, but as my song faded, I heard the sounds of sniffling and noticed tears streaming down Daka's cheeks.

"That was, uh." Daka wiped her eyes, smiling through tears. "That was a really good song, Dad."

I was instantly by her side, hugging her, before I noticed an absence in the circle around the campfire.

"Where's Dalton?" I looked to Doh, who was wiping her own eyes.

She pointed off back toward the carriage. "He, uh, got up and left during the song. Didn't want to stop him."

Wiping my daughter's cheeks clean of tears, I gave her a kiss on the forehead before going to find her brother.

NOON INTERLUDE: DALTON VELBRUN

Congratulations on the view, Abe." Dr. Warrick sniffed his wine subtly, habitually testing the scent for any tampering, before taking a slow, gentle sip.

I didn't even bother to smile back. "It is a view, yes."

The Neo York City Arcology was a sprawling cesspool of filth and depravity with the dregs of society littering its stained floor. From my new office on the top floor of ZehrTech Industries, of course, you could barely make those features out behind the blinding neon lights and incessant advertising.

Dr. Warrick gave a chuckle, a horrid sound that echoed in his mouth, from his fat, old cheeks to his toothless gums. "After your little stunt with Cromby, you've got the board's confidence, but we can't let up now."

Cromby had been a bad product, a defective clone of the original. Letting him degrade over the last few months after making the switch made it easy to outplay and outbid him for his position as CEO.

"No." I nodded. "I can't."

Dr. Warrick paused for a moment, his smile dipping into a frown. "Now, don't go forgetting we're a team, Abidemi. We do things together."

"We haven't been a team since you murdered my mother." I glanced at him, letting the cold anger I'd felt for the man in front of me for years show itself in my eyes.

Any response the old man had was stopped as he grabbed at his throat, his wide eyes filled with fear and panic as he fell to his knees, his arms and legs jerking around sporadically.

I watched him fall, sipping my own wine. "You trust your implants far too much. Cutting-edge is only so sharp for so long."

Vulnerability was a fact of life in this strange fantasy world of monsters and gods. True technological innovations were a thing of the distant future, and the equivalent magical breakthroughs were bizarre.

And yet, nothing had sent tremors through my stolen body like Father Rakta's song. I left the campfire, ignoring the glances, and returned to the carriage.

I didn't give a shit about what they thought of me. I didn't give a shit about them at all. Emilia, or rather Natakia, had kept trying to speak to me like we were getting closer during the trip.

"Parasites have to stick together, don't they?" I questioned myself, feeling a tightness in the young body I had inherited after a few words with some cosmic intelligence.

At least she had some distinction about who she was now and before. Daka was obviously from Earth, as well, but she seemed dedicated to her little isekai farce.

Shaking my head, I took out my journals. Most of the journals were for detailing out local laws and business practices that such an under-developed culture would be vulnerable to. Others, of course, were dedicated to the expenditure of my resources and how to best use them.

Thinking about it, I took the moment to check the contents of my account, some sort of metaphysical fund that kept track of one thing in particular.

The 1,341 sil that I currently had, accumulated over a long life of frugal living and selling all that I was confident was unnecessary or worth more to me in its value than its benefit to me.

I'd been able to profit off of a few flowers I'd picked in the clearing while everyone else had been swimming. Selling them, I'd earned a couple of credits, but nothing big.

Better than nothing, but I'd need thousands of flowers to have enough capital to afford anything exotic or impressive in the shop.

Holding one of my business journals in hand, I let my gaze wander to the last journal, one that I rarely added to and read only in complete privacy.

The one meant for myself, the life of Abidemi Nel.

* * *

I scanned my bio-tag implant against the door and waited patiently as all the security locks disengaged. Opening the door, I stepped inside my home.

"Nine-one-three-two-one-alpha-oscar-seven." The swiftly spoken command code disengaged the secondary-security automated turrets.

Putting my briefcase down against the wall in its specific spot, I disengaged the tertiary-security localized explosives.

Everything taken care of, I was finally back in the safety of my own home, but my mind hadn't ceased spinning. I'd finally done it, CEO of ZehrTech.

My penthouse was windowless, or rather, it appeared to have windows, but they were merely digital displays embedded into the reinforced concrete of the walls and wired to exterior cameras.

"I guess it's time to celebrate." The silence of the room greeted me, which I appreciated. Other people would have simply snuffed out the joy I'd managed to wrangle from this life.

Retrieving one of my sterilized wine bottles, I brought out one of my finest glasses of wine and poured myself a few ounces of Corton-Charlemagne.

I took a sip, before calling out, "Messages."

The soft, feminine voice of my home assistant, Georgia, responded efficiently, "You have three messages, sir. Would you like to hear them?"

"Play them in ten minutes. I'd like to enjoy the silence."

Nothing could be better than the life I had now. It was worth the sacrifices I made. It was worth the atrocities I'd committed. Everything was worth the life I had now.

I poured myself another glass of wine.

"Dalton?" My hand stilled mid-page turn.

Rakta opened the door to the carriage gently. "The others said you left during the song. Are you okay?"

Keeping my gaze free of the tumultuous thoughts and feelings that were roiling inside of me, I coldly looked at my body's father. "I'm fine, Father. I'm just not a fan of music."

Silence was always preferred. Music was often just noise that desperate people applied meaning to in order to feel better and placate themselves toward the unfairness and injustice in their lives.

Obviously not feeling the dismissal I'd been hoping to send with such words, he stepped farther into the carriage and sat opposite me. I hated the look on his face.

The love in his eyes, for me, the dead man who had festered away within the body of his glowing newborn just to selfishly live again.

"You don't like music?" Father seemed honestly perplexed at the idea, but I didn't blame him. As I already knew, music was for those desperate for meaning, and I couldn't imagine anyone was more desperate than Rakta and the rest of his people in Rusk.

I put away my journal, careful not to draw too much of Rakta's attention to it, and nodded. "It's just noise."

"I see." He seemed to think about this for a moment, before smiling softly. "Is that why you were fine with the . . . the fish being gone?"

That was a misconception. I wasn't fine with them being gone at all. The value of such exotic beasts would have been off the charts, even if my shop didn't take living creatures.

Still, I shrugged. At the time, I'd had little motivation to comfort the man about the lack of fish beyond the fact that he was my biggest supporter in this strange land and I was already betraying him with my existence.

For a time, there was silence between us, and a strange tension grabbed at my chest. He looked at me in a way that felt too knowing, too invasive.

"Son, is there . . . Are you okay?"

"Hey Abe, uh, it's DeDe, was just . . . calling to let you know that Clark's in the hospital. They say he, uh, he . . . There was some old shrapnel in his system that tore up a . . . a lot." The message went silent for a moment. "So, I know it's . . . I know it's been a while. I know we haven't talked much, but the bills . . ."

And on and on the message went. My sister had never acknowledged the danger of her husband's outings as a courier. The money was good, yes, but the life expectancy was horrible.

At this point, even if Clark recovered, he'd never carry another mission, much less be able to keep having his implants repaired. He was a dead man who would push his moving corpse around just to put one more little notch on his belt.

"Georgia, send DeDe the credits she needs for the medical bills, no more, no less."

She never came and talked to me anymore. Why would she? She knew who I was, and I knew who she was; we both lived in different worlds now. DeDe had decided that the speck of filth we'd grown up in, that our father had left us in, was our home, and I'd realized that it was a fucking cage.

One I rattled hard enough until someone heard and let me out.

"Abidemi." A new message began in a deeper, darker voice. "ZehrTech Industries is yours. Now, you pay back the debts you owe us."

And then it ended. Excalibur, the group of couriers I'd paid to make the switch between Cromby and his clone, were professionals. Ones that made sure they got paid once their services were complete and extra if certain requirements, like my appointment as CEO, were met.

"Georgia, send the package to Neon and his crew. It's time to clean the board." You didn't owe debts if the man on the other side of the table was dead.

Instead of Georgia's response, however, my body froze as the dark voice from before spoke again.

"Yes, yes, it is time to clean the board. Death to oath breakers."

And everything went white.

I closed my eyes at the question. Was I okay? Ha, was I okay? He provoked me into thinking back to the past, and he has the gall to ask if I'm okay?

I hated his concern and his love. I'd woken to this life and watched another mother pass away right before my eyes. And yet, he didn't know, did he?

How could he know that his children were all fakers? All his love and little tokens of paternal affection being dropped down the bottomless pit of us horrid parasites.

"Dalton—"

I flinched away from his warm, concerned grasp, away from the fucking lies that I'd thought I was okay with. That I had to be okay with to survive this fucking world.

Never show your weakness. Never hesitate to betray. Never show all your cards.

This fucking world of horrific beasts and unimaginable dangers, of magic and sorcery, of an existentially omniscient cosmic thing that had put me in this fucking place—it was all too much.

Truth rattled around in my chest as I looked up at Father, fuck, Rakta, and it flew from my lips soaked with venom before I recognized the benefits I'd be throwing away.

The store, the keep, everything this father had given to his son and I'd received in his place.

"I'm not your fucking son! I'm not your fucking child! None of us are! We never fucking were!"

I gasped at my own words, grabbing my head to regain my center. It was too noisy in this carriage; there was too much noise. I needed quiet.

15

I'm not your fucking son! I'm not your fucking child! None of us are! We never fucking were!"

The words struck me harder than any blow ever had in my life. Even the death of Lydia had left less of a wound upon my person than the venom in my child's words.

Dalton was half-bundled-up, inching away from me as he grabbed at his head like he had a headache. I moved closer, instinctively stilling as he flinched away from me, his father.

"Dalton?" I tried to make my question simply curious, but it was a fragile facade held up by the underlying desperation in my mind. "What do you mean? You are my son. You always have been."

He didn't answer my almost pleading statements, simply glared at me with a wounded heat in his fearful gaze.

My mind was turning over, trying to understand what could have possibly brought on this horrible fracture between us. Had it been the song? Had I broken some sort of promise?

I expected these tantrums from Natakia when she did not get what she wanted, but Dalton? To blow up with such emotion, this couldn't be something so simple; it had to be . . .

An understanding blossomed in my chest. Shawn had spoken of my children's past lives, their lives on Earth. Had his memories of said lives made Dalton doubt the love I felt for him?

I backed up, giving Dalton some space, my hands lowered. "Dalton—"

"That isn't my name." His young voice squeaked with anger, a touch of hysteria.

Of course it was his name. It had been his name for years. The name of my meticulous, intelligent son.

Frowning, I tried to figure out how to explain what I knew. How did I explain the prophecy without burdening my children with the weight of destiny? Was I right to reveal Shawn's own displacement to Derra? It felt like such a deep secret to offer without explicit permission.

Waiting in silence for a moment, not making any more attempts to speak, I watched as my son calmed down ever so slightly, enough that I felt comfortable enough to speak.

Not that I felt comfortable. The sheer pain in my heart from my son's words was debilitating.

"Then," I began softly, barely above a whisper, "what did they call you on Earth?"

Dalton froze. I could see the questions flickering in his gaze, but eventually he croaked out, "Abidemi."

"Abidemi." I tested the name and nodded. "I . . . prefer Dalton, but if you are more comfortable—"

"You knew? All this time, you knew?"

My son had relaxed enough that I took the moment to approach, bending down to take his cold hands in mine. "What is there to know? That my children are special in ways I can barely understand?"

Dalton frowned and his words were sullen. "Your children died when we stole their lives. You're raising parasites."

Parasites. My son, no, possibly all my children, thought they were parasites? The children that I had cleaned when they were young, fed when they were hungry?

My eyes burned, and I watched my son's face tremble as tears began to flow down my cheeks.

"Dalton, Abidemi," I began, my voice unsteady. "You are no parasite; you are my child. One with memories, a soul, from another world, but never . . . never a parasite. You think yourself a thief? That you stole from me? Stole from another?"

Overwhelmed by my emotions, I grabbed him into a hug, pulling him to my chest even as he made a token resistance.

"Dalton, you have given me everything. You and your sisters are my everything. How can I mourn the love I never felt for another when it pales to the love I feel here and now for you and you alone?"

"You're . . . delusional." His arms wrapped around me, and he choked into my chest, "We aren't . . . I'm not . . ."

I sat with him against my chest and gently swayed with him, rocking back and forth in the carriage seat, remembering when the young boy in my arms was just a baby. "No matter who you are, no matter what you are, you will always be my son."

He quieted against me, his hold on my tunic tight. I was sure he'd have questions; he wouldn't just let me get away with knowing about their nature, their origins. And yet, for now, we embraced in peace.

"You . . . need to shave," Dalton's sleepy, petulant words were the last I heard from him before he fell into a gentle, exhausted slumber. "Hey," Doh sat beside me as I watched the smoldering campfire. The children had been put to sleep, Dalton thankfully a heavy sleeper.

I nodded back to her. "Doh. Is Dresden out on patrol?"

"Yeah, he's making sure nothing's poking around. How'd it go with Dalton?" She absently threw a leaf into the smoldering flames, watching the cinders quickly take it.

Truly the question of the night. How had it gone? It had been the most emotional I'd ever seen my son, but one of the few times I truly felt like I connected with him.

"It was very heavy." That was all I could say about it. The prophecy, Earth, my son's idea that he was some kind of parasite—it was all so heavy.

Doh nodded. "Yeah, yeah, I get that. Wanna talk about it?"

I stared into the flames for a time and watched the ashy cinders crackle and pop, sending glowing chunks of charred wood jumping through the air, their heat quickly dying against the cool breeze.

"My son"—for that was what he was, no matter his thoughts on the matter—"he thinks he has hurt me, that he is undeserving of my love. That he is some aberrant creature."

Doh hummed at that, tapping her chin. "Is this, uh, about the prophecy?"

"Is it that obvious?" It was almost surprising that she'd even ask. After helping me remember it, Doh had fastidiously avoided the topic of what she had helped me discover.

She made a weird gesture in the air that had no meaning as she shrugged. "Eh, I mean, ugh, I guess so? Like, I can't imagine why he thinks that, and . . . with how important that whole thing seemed to you, I always suspected it involved the kids. I mean, they're special."

"They are." In ways that I barely comprehended and yet admired all the same. "They don't know of the prophecy, but it . . . I think they understand that they are different. And that difference . . ."

How did I even put it?

". . . makes them feel a disconnect from the world around them?" Doh offered, a knowing glint mingling with the flame reflected into her gaze.

I nodded, slowly. "I think that is the case."

The conversation lingered on the silence between us for a moment, before Doh broke it once more.

"When I told Macy about what we were . . ." Doh paused, hesitating for a moment. "Not just what we could do, but what we . . . we go through. The memories, the fear, it all scared her."

I nodded, remembering the days of long conversation I'd shared with Doh and Dresden on the matter. I couldn't imagine how much they'd spoken together in private about revealing the full truth to Macy.

She scratched the back of her head. "She doesn't really spend time with the other kids much anymore, you know? Natakia is basically her only friend, well, close friend."

Our problems were so different and yet so alike. It felt good to bond over such a thing with an old friend, even if the doppelgänger-blooded magician would tease me for calling her old.

"I'm sure she'll find her confidence again, as will Dalton. We just need to listen to them and love them." For what more could we do? How else did we defeat their inner demons?

Maybe that was the true question to focus on.

Doh nodded. "Yep. Macy's blood hasn't awakened yet, but when she does . . . I'm sure that'll open up, like, a whole new set of questions and weirdness, right? Like, your identity gets weird when you can be anyone, you know?"

"I'm sure it does," I agreed. "It's good that Macy has such an amazing mother and father guiding her through it all."

Doh tucked a stray tangle of hair behind her ear, smiling. "Oh my, I can see why Harriet fell for such a sweetheart like you."

"Doh," I groaned. "Harriet is just—"

"—A friend. I gotcha, I gotcha." Doh winked at me. "Welp, it's getting late, and I'm already horrible in the mornings. Time to go to bed, yeah?"

I shook my head but got up, helping her up as well. "Time to go to bed. I'll go relieve Dresden so you can both rest."

With that, I wandered into the forest to find Doh's patrolling husband. With Dresden relieved of his duty with little ceremony, I walked through the forests of the empire around our campsite, my eyes sharp for any movement.

This wasn't a well-traveled trail, but wolves and bandits could turn up anywhere. Letting your guard down was the quickest way to be proven wrong.

And yet, while I kept my senses sharp, I didn't expect to run into any danger.

"Rakta."

I stilled, my axe in hand, ready to fill the entire clearing. The gentle breeze of the wind through the forest continued, the sway of the trees did not pause, and nothing disturbed my patrol.

Had it been a simple mishearing of the wind? I'd barely been able to make out the voice, make out what it sounded like, but it had sounded . . . familiar.

Perhaps I was simply stressed from my conversation with Dalton.

Even so, my patrol became even more stringent, making sure to root through all the trees and bushes to make sure nothing got close to my family.

16

The world was a blur around us, our carriage speeding toward our next destination. While my thoughts lingered on my conversation with Dalton and the strange, perhaps imagined, whisper in the woods, I was beset by a more pressing concern.

"Natakia, my desert flower, there is no reason to starve yourself." We had only been traveling for a short time when Natakia's stomach grumbled.

Natakia huffed, looking away. "I don't want to gain weight before the gala."

Breakfast had been a delicious serving of stew that Dresden had cooked with the travel rations and spices we'd brought along. Puzzled over the night's events, I'd missed Natakia barely touching her food.

I gently grabbed her chin and turned her back to me. "Natakia, you won't gain weight; you will stay healthy."

"Healthy?" Natakia turned her nose up at that. "That's just a kind word for fat."

I blinked and suddenly felt like I was crossing a narrow bridge over a deep ravine. Was this an issue born from Natakia's past life? Did I bring it up to her now?

Speaking to Dalton about his own life, or rather, merely revealing my knowledge of it had led to a heartbreaking conversation. Was the moment right for such a thing with Natakia?

And when did I bring it up with Daka? It was hard to believe that my little warrior had a past life filled with horrors, but the fugues she would fall into, the night terrors she had . . .

"Perhaps you could train with Daka and me, then? Exercise is great for keeping one's figure." It was the only card I could confidently play in this conversation.

"Horrible, overdefined muscles are only slightly better than being fat, Dad." Natakia frowned. "I'm not going to ruin my figure by becoming some meathead like Daka."

Daka's figure was ruined? What? Lydia would have been able to handle this so much better than I. She was quite good at eating and staying trim.

"You shouldn't call your sister such things," I began, lightly chiding her. "And a little exercise won't . . . give you too many muscles. It'll simply let you eat properly and burn off the excess."

Not that I really knew all the exact specifics regarding the process involved. Food gave your body the energy to move, but I knew that other more scholarly magicians had found proper terms for the more mundane science of the body and all that it consisted of.

"I know what burning calories is."

Ah, yes, that. I suppose with all the talk of my daughter giving tips to the women of Gelvurt on keeping their . . . figures, she would have a better grasp on such words.

I nodded. "Well, then, are you against exercising?"

"No?" Natakia was frowning slightly, playing with her hair. Her magical mirror was tucked away in the carriage for safety, but I could see her gaze automatically shifting to where it'd be in the air beside her.

Taking a moment to make sure the horses stayed on the trail, I gave her more of my attention. "Then why not exercise with us? We can keep it light, and you can eat with more . . . confidence."

She looked at me, and for a moment it felt like her gaze knew every worry and doubt I held before she lightly blushed and looked away. "I, well, I don't like being sweaty. It isn't right for a lady to be sweaty."

Suddenly I was reckoning with a more familiar concept. I was not dealing with some holdover of her past life in this small moment, but something passed along by one of the nobles in Velbrun.

"Don't let the ladies of House Velbrun color your life, Natakia. There's nothing wrong with sweat." Sweating actually helped one cool down quite a bit, especially useful in the Ruskan desert.

She made a small, irritated noise in the back of her throat, so I backed off from the conversation, instead retreating back to my thoughts on my children and their prophesied lives.

Besides, Natakia's empty stomach may have been a blessing in disguise today. She'd have plenty of room for our next destination.

Her mother's favorite eatery, the Hallowed Hollow. "I'm not going in there."

Natakia's voice was clipped and firm. She had turned her head the moment we had pulled up to the eatery on the outskirts of Kagg, a small village on the edge of House Kire's influence.

I didn't entirely blame her. The Hallowed Hollow was as I remembered it. It was larger than an eatery of this renown truly had any right to be, and I knew that a large portion of that size went to the fighting rings in the back.

"Yeah, uh." Doh looked around, holding Macy to her side. "Rakta, this place is really bad news. You know that, right?"

Making sure Daka's helmet was affixed and her hair wasn't unduly tangled underneath it, my little warrior fearless in the face of the intimidating restaurant, I nodded. "Yes, yes, this place is a hive of scum and villainy."

"And you're okay with bringing our kids here?" Dresden looked ready to draw his blade, glancing around suspiciously everywhere.

I pointed over to a part of the wall of the establishment, the dark wood of the building looking slightly newer compared to the wall behind it. "Back when Lydia and I traveled alone on our way to the capital, we stayed here for a night. Lydia grew . . . fond of the food, but the service required me to step in."

Over the years of adventuring, Lydia would often drag me and the others in the group to this place, cleaning out the nastier sort between our meals. Eventually, only small-time crooks and thieves remained, hiding between the cracks of our attention.

Still, it had been a while. Thinking about how much had changed at the pond, the lack of fish after so long, there was no telling what kind of criminals had regathered at this place.

"Hmm," I sighed. "You may be right. It is perhaps too dangerous for the children to go into. If Shawn and Penelope were also here, maybe, but there is no telling . . ."

Daka frowned. "But Mom liked the food?"

"She did; the chef here seemed to have a remarkable hand with spices. Still, I can't expect the food to stay the same after so lo—"

"I want some!" Daka smiled. "If Mom liked it, then I'll like it too!"

Natakia sniffed. "Mom liked bathing."

"Natakia." I gave her a familiar look before turning to Daka. "I'm sure you would, but . . . Hmm, Dresden could keep everyone safe in the carriage? I could go inside alone and come back with food."

The swordsman looked around a bit. "Yeah, of course. Doesn't look like any of these guys linger outside the place anyway."

Good, good. Then I could go inside for some food and bring it out to the others without endangering the younglings. It was a much better plan that everyone, well, mostly everyone seemed happy about.

"Aw, I wanted to go inside!" Daka hugged my leg. "Can I come with you? Please, Dad? Please!"

With her Vitae and her helmet, Daka was probably the safest of my children physically. Still, I was somewhat reluctant to bring her inside.

And yet, nothing defeated me with greater ease than the wide blue eyes of my daughter.

"Alright, you can come," I relented with a great sigh.

She cheered, bouncing around me and her siblings. "Yay!"

I grabbed her arm, hoisting her up into the air. "You need to keep close to me, Daka. I won't be happy if I lose track of you in there, understand?"

Daka loosely swung around in my grip, smiling. "I hear ya, Dad. Let's get some nosh."

Smiling, I nodded before carrying her inside. I hoped the quality of the food would surprise Natakia like it had her mother. Stepping inside, Daka holding my hand firmly, I definitely noticed the scattered gazes focused in my direction. There was Vitae and Mana in the air, enough that gave away that more than just simple crooks plagued this restaurant alone.

No spells or techniques were primed, and Daka would grip my hand tightly if she saw anything strange. Thankfully, our traveling attire did little to give our nobility away, and few in Kire would believe someone with my heritage could ever attain such a title.

Walking silently to the bar, I gave a few knocks on the wood. "Good day."

The man behind the bar, a rotund but thickly muscled man with a large beard that mostly stretched across the underside of his chin gave me a look. "Long time since a Ruskan came knockin' here."

He gave my daughter a look as well.

"Even longer since anyone's brought a kid with 'em."

"We won't be here long. Does Quark still run the kitchen?" He'd been Lydia's favorite chef and truly the genius behind some of their specialties.

"Yeah, yeah." The man nodded. "Quark runs the kitchen. Who's askin'?"

I threw down a few golden sils. "A paying customer in need of food to go and peace while he waits."

"Hmm." The bartender, who was certainly new since my last visit, looked down at the coins. "Peace is expensive these days."

I threw down a few more, the sounds of scattering sil cutting through the air between us. I didn't need a fight when I was with my daughter. And yet, I did push some of my own Vitae into the air, Daka following suit.

Soon, none of the Vitae and Mana that had lingered in the air remained as the atmosphere grew heavy with our life energy, the other criminals tensing as they felt the change in the room.

"I know what peace costs," I said. "We'll take seven of Quark's special and some hard cider. Don't overcharge me. I know the price."

Giving a shaky nod and a quick tilt of his head to a few pair of eyes around the room, the bartender passed along our order, and I paid for the meals. The price, it turned out, had actually gone up since I'd last been here, but I trusted it was an honest increase in cost. I was sure it would have been less honest had I not been so confident.

Daka looked up at me with stars in her eyes. "Dad, you're so cool."

While I would rather not encourage threats as an admirable way of diplomacy, it worked far better with this ilk than any other. Still, not what one often wants to be praised for by their daughter.

"You're cool, too, Daka," I patted the top of her helmeted head. She grinned before her eyes widened and she suddenly struck like a snake and grabbed something, no, someone.

With her hand around the pale wrist of a long arm, which I followed up to the spindly, lanky form of a tall man that I hadn't noticed in the room at all.

A deeply unsettling fact rooted itself in my chest as I noticed the serrated knife in the man's hand, a single foot away from where my back would have been moments ago.

"You . . ." Daka's voice was shocked for a moment before it quickly transformed into something dark and vengeful. "Were you trying to hurt my dad, you disgusting piece of shit!?"

The man was grinning, his smile wide and unnerving and filled with too many teeth. He barely reacted as my daughter held his wrist tighter and tighter, the sounds of bone beginning to break.

No, not bone. I knew what breaking bone sounded like. This sounded . . . chitinous.

And then the unnaturally pale man's body began to deform and mutate.

17

Time slowed as the full gravity of the situation settled into my bones. The immense threat I was met with making my Vitae boil in my veins without consciously doing so.

Daka was rearing back, her fist glowing with raw Vitae, the pale assassin was transforming, and the patrons of the Hallowed Hollow were reaching for their weapons, their magics, preparing for a brawl.

One thing was certain however. Among all this insanity, I decided that this was no place for my daughter.

My Vitae thrummed, and I circulated it through my body as my **Skip Dash Technique** activated. One moment, I was standing in the center of the chaos, and the next, I was outside, redirecting my daughter's punch into the empty air.

"Ha!" A distant tree exploded as Daka shot the air around her fist out as a crude weapon, but her anger quickly drained as her new setting registered. "Wha?"

I knelt, knowing the storm was only a few paces behind us. "Go back to the carriage; make sure the others are okay."

Daka looked worried. "But . . ."

Wait, could I send her alone? What if there were other untraceable assassins? I had not expected one at all, much less an entire group of them.

I looked around, Vitae blossoming in my eyes as the world was stained in the revealing cerulean of the **Deep Blue Technique**, the Hallowed Hollow becoming awash in blue, but not its denizens.

The assassin stepped out, his form chitinous and his robes torn by the multitude of monstrous needlelike protrusions that had emerged from his body.

"Your girl has a nice grip, Lord Velbrun." The assassin giggled.

A quick look around; there were no traces of any other assassins in the area. I couldn't be sure how he'd escaped my notice before, but I trusted my vision. "Get back to the carriage."

"I'm not gonna leave you!" Daka got into her own fighting stance, ready to do battle with this horrific nightmare.

The assassin grinned, his face elongated and breaking into a larger, jagged insectile maw. "Then I'll eat you first."

He blurred forward, straight toward my little warrior. His protrusions pointed outward to skewer her a thousand times over. Daka began to move, but she was far too slow to even begin to react to the speed of a more capable fighter.

I wasn't. Crow was in my hands before he'd taken his second step.

The Vitae-elongated blade, powered by my **Horizon Throw Technique**, sheared the man's protrusions to little, flat nubs, his form suddenly crumpling to the ground.

"Ah— Agh!" The assassin had no time to appreciate his loss of limbs as I dashed over to his form and stomped him into the ground, something breaking underneath my foot. "How . . . ?"

"Try to kill me all you like, assassin." I glared, dropping my **Deep Blue Technique** for the moment. "Even look at my children again and I will make this very long and very painful."

Daka fell to the ground, her eyes wide as she crawled back in shock from the assassin's waylaid attack. "He was . . . He was so fast . . ."

"Daka, get back to the carriage." I noticed the door of the Hallowed Hollow was opening again.

"Bu—"

"Now!"

The Vitae in my voice kicked up the dirt around the downed, bleeding form of the assassin, my daughter gulping as she nodded and turned to run back to where the carriage had been stopped.

Looking over to it, a knot unfurled in my chest as Dresden opened up the door, welcoming Daka inside and making eye contact with me. He'd keep them safe.

It was at that moment that I felt a stabbing pain in my leg, as I looked down to empty air below my feet, even as my foot still rested upon the back of the assassin.

Feeling punctures going up and down my leg, I ripped my leg away, Vitae returning to my eyes for my **Deep Blue Technique**, to once again see the strange assailant as he picked himself up, his sharp protrusions having once again emerged, healed.

"Perfect invisibility," I said, pumping my leg with Vitae to heal the tiny, pinprick wounds. Something about this situation felt too familiar; it was bothering me.

A voice called from behind me, "That's not fair at all!"

As the assassin righted himself, I passed a glance backward to see another figure bathed in the red of my visual technique, their form somewhat difficult to make out with the current coloration.

Their voice was just on the edge of masculinity, sounding youthful but not young, and they were short. Most importantly, however, they didn't seem hostile.

"You shouldn't . . ." The assassin seemed off-kilter, his form swaying and his voice less confident. "You shouldn't be able to see me. Nobody can see me. I'm the best."

He certainly didn't seem very competent beyond his aptitude for hiding his form.

I fell into my **Grace Stance**, not wanting to lose too much blood to this man. "I'll give you a chance to tell me everything you know. Are you one of Zactrik's?"

"Can't fail." The pale man's form began to shake and twist again, this time beginning to lose all trace of his fading humanity as his arms extended into vicious-looking scythes of mutant bone. "Won't . . . fa—"

The transforming man's form fell backwards onto the ground, with a fading duplicate of Crow lodged deep into his head. I'd wanted to ask him more questions, but they weren't worth letting him finish whatever terrifying transformation he was going through.

"Man, I'm gonna have to clean that up."

I blinked, letting my vision return to normal, before looking over at this strange commentator that seemed, uh, very casual regarding this bout he had walked up on.

Golden-blond hair and short, as I'd noticed before, he looked early into his young adulthood and wore a dirtied apron. His eyes were crystal blue, a lighter shade than Daka's, but bright all the same.

I looked at the beast and him. "Ah, my apologies for the fight. He attacked my daughter, who I should really be making sure is okay."

"Oh, yeah, it's fine." He shrugged it off. "You paid for peace, and I'm kind of the person who has to keep it here, or Quark'll get on my ass."

Then he must be quite capable. I hadn't heard any inkling of a brawl inside, so it must have been handled quickly if one actually broke out.

I motioned to myself. "Rakta. Thank you for taking care of the corpse."

"Pup. And no problem. Your food'll be out soon." With that Pup began to weave magic through the air, but I did not stick around to see the cleaning process. I opened the door to the carriage. "Is everyone okay?"

Five pairs of healthy gazes looked back at me, but one rocketing missile of a small girl rammed into my chest before any words could be said.

Daka looked up at me. "You . . . You won, right? You're okay?"

"Yes, I'm fine." My leg was somewhat sore, even after healing it, but I didn't want her to worry about such a minor injury. "However, I'm afraid this marks a change in our trip."

"So it really was an assassin?" Dresden spoke up.

Hugging Daka, I nodded. "This man wasn't here to kidnap anyone, like we were warned, but this still feels like Zactrik's doing. He was certainly here to kill me."

I remembered where I'd seen such horrendous traits before, back when I and the others were besieged by calkers. And yet, I couldn't understand why or how I was targeted here specifically, or why the assassin was so ill-equipped beyond his innate invisibility.

Doh held Macy tight. "Then we need to get to the capital quickly."

"I agree. We'll leave as soon as possible." Honestly, at this point, the food here was not worth the wait—

"Hey," Pup called out. "I got your food!"

Looking back to see that the polite peacekeeper did in fact have platters of food balanced in his arms, no signs of the previous corpse anywhere I could see, I nodded and looked to the others in the carriage. "Get ready to leave."

Putting Daka back into her seat, gently untangling her from my chest and whispering gentle comforts to calm her worries, I went over to Pup. "Thank you for the food."

"Just doing my job and, uh." Pup smirked. "Quark said it'd been a while since he'd seen ya. Sure you don't want to come and say a few words with the old man?"

I looked back over my shoulder at the carriage. "I would, but I must get going. It'll be safer for my children in the capital, and I don't want to waste any more time."

The young man nodded before pulling out a dirty-looking note and handing it out to me. "The guy's corpse had this on it. Probably good for you to have it."

"Thank you." Grabbing the food and the note out of his hands, I gave him a nod before returning to the carriage and getting ready to head to the capital.

18

Hallowed Hollow. Noon. Eighteenth of—

The rest of the dirty note was incomprehensible, stained by blood and grime. I rode alone up front as the sun set in the distance, all my children sleeping in the carriage proper. There was so much to think about, my concerns for the now mingling with my worries of the future.

I was familiar with assassins, with some in the past having attacked me on my travels, but not since my children had been born had I dealt with such nuisances. And this had been no normal assassin.

While I could question his skills, they only came up short in comparison to the innate calker-blood invisibility he possessed, an impossibility realized before my very eyes. He had been capable. In fact, if Daka had not seen him with her special sight . . . I could very well be dead.

It was a sobering thought.

"And someone knew I would be there." I rubbed my eyes, tired. "Someone has been following us. That whisper from last night . . . Was that a sign I ignored? A threat? A warning?"

It was all so confusing, but I knew I had put my children in harm's way unnecessarily. I'd wanted to show them places their mother had loved, but I had deluded myself to think it safe.

The only silver lining was that Natakia had truly enjoyed the food, something I'd have to thank Quark for if I was ever in the area again.

Regardless, once I was in the capital, I could speak with Shawn and make sure my children were safe from whoever was behind this, Zactrik or not.

* * *

It was in the middle of the night, hours later, that the horses slowly pulled the carriage up to the gates of the capital, the midnight guards watching closely as I came up. I had waited patiently behind a number of travelers and merchants seeking entrance, as well, time I spent observing the guards.

There was a tension in the air among the platoon of guards, and unless my eyes deceived me, there were certainly more of them on duty than the usual.

"Greetings." One of the guards spoke to me as my turn approached. "Name?"

"Lord Rakta Velbrun of Gelvurt."

The guards looked at one another before the one that had spoken looked back at me and nodded. "We've been told to expect you, Lord Velbrun of Gelvurt."

Unsurprised by the news, I pushed my horses onward as the guards allowed me through, completely entering the capital and heading toward the palace that lay at the heart of the city.

I heard muttering and movement in the carriage behind me, the occupants having stirred as we passed by the various lights of the street. Even so late at night, the world was bright within the walls of Cerula ever since Penelope had been tasked with installing new magical lights throughout the main streets.

It was, well, it was quite beautiful. Brilliant white lights that marked the main cobblestone paths for all those who entered. I'd heard that there was talk of future installations throughout the entirety of the capital streets and homes.

I hoped my children enjoyed the lights.

Eventually, I approached the gates of the palace and was relieved of my carriage and horses by some of the men there, my family and friends retrieving their things.

As Doh and Dresden made sure that Macy had her bags, I gathered my own children around me and knelt to them, meeting their eyes.

Daka was bright and happy, her attention eagerly given to me, as Natakia blinked slowly, her eyelids looking heavy with exhaustion from the day's travel.

Dalton watched me carefully, his expression guarded. We still hadn't spoken, truly spoken, since our last conversation, and I knew I needed to speak to him soon. All of them, really.

"Welcome to Cerula." I smiled. "I know it's been a somewhat difficult trip, and I'd . . . hoped to show you all many things before we arrived here, but things have, well, changed."

They all shifted in their spots, Natakia looking more awake.

I swallowed hard. "The world is a dangerous place, and I hope to always be by your side to protect you, but when I am not, I need you three to stay together, understood? Trust your siblings; protect them."

Daka frowned. "Are you going somewhere, Dad?"

"No, no." I shook my head. There was nothing that could tear me away from my children at this point, not without a fight.

"You want us to stay close?" Natakia once again had that look in her eye, like my life was laid out in front of her. "Are we in danger?"

There was a fear in her eyes, a glint of concern for her own safety that burned at me, but also something else. Something that felt different than fear, but I could not quite place.

"Yes, stay close." I pulled them all together, even Dalton, and hugged them. "We're safer here within the walls, but danger is always where we least expect it. Stay close to one another, to me."

I felt the three nod their heads, and I released them, taking Daka and Natakia's hands in mine as I began to lead them into the palace, Dalton keeping close to my side.

"Wow, so this is the king's place?" Daka looked around. "Does Uncle Shawn work for the king?"

Her siblings glanced at each other before Natakia leaned over to her sister. "Daka, Uncle Shawn is the king."

Daka looked around the large platoons of guards, the monolithic towers emblazoned with the royal family's colors and crest, and blinked, her eyes wide. "Oh." Our things were quickly taken from us by the royal attendants to our guest rooms at the palace. I trod along the carpeted floors to the throne room.

It was a walk that I was familiar with, even before Shawn had taken on the power of the throne, but the others buzzed with excitement around me. Often, I had to pull Daka back from touching something valuable or assuage worries that we were not dressed correctly.

"It's fine, Doh." I motioned to our traveling clothes. "This isn't an official meeting or anything ceremonial, just simply meeting with Shawn and Tracy like we did weeks ago."

Doh squinted. "Well, it feels different, okay! They don't exactly roll out the red carpet when they come by for a drink. I'm feeling underdressed, lock me up!"

The guards nearby looked at one another at Doh's words.

Natakia, were she not slumbering in my arms, would have most likely agreed with her. Thankfully, my little flower had quickly exhausted whatever energy the excitement from entering the capital had unearthed.

"So wait, does that mean Winfred's a prince?" Daka was stuck between the excitement of walking through the palace hall and the confusion surrounding her newest revelation.

I nodded. "Winfred is a prince."

"He never told me!" Daka's cheeks puffed up. "And he's my best friend. They're supposed to tell you everything!"

Dalton spoke up. "Oh, have you told him everything about yourself, Daka? Everything?"

Daka flinched, and I spoke up, deflecting my son's very targeted words. "Regardless, Winfred meant no harm, I'm sure."

"Is Shawn really okay about seeing us this late at night?" Dresden was carrying Macy in his arms. "I'd thought he'd be asleep at this hour."

Readjusting Natakia in my arms to make sure she didn't slip, I said, "I thought the same, that perhaps we could simply sleep and wait until the morning, but the guards were told explicitly to waste no time."

Shawn really wanted to see us as soon as possible, and if I were to be completely honest with myself, the haste was making me somewhat worried. A few more minutes of walking and we finally made it to the large, ornate doors of the throne room. The throne room was an impressive example of making a man feel small regardless of his height or power. Decorated with stone depictions of past kings, when one walked before the king's throne, they walked before the gaze of every monarch that came before them, staring them down.

The king's throne, adjacent to a somewhat smaller throne for the queen, was a large chair adorned in the finest marble and silk and comfortable linen. While I had never sat in it myself, Shawn had often said that the comfortable seat was one of the greatest perks of the job.

Although he may have been joking.

"Hey, buddy."

Shawn did not look like he was joking now.

With bandages wrapped around his chest, the telltale signs of blood seeping through the fabric of his dressed wounds, the king of the Certillian Empire and my friend looked pale and weak upon the throne.

"Shawn." I almost choked over my words. "What happened?"

The others around me were in similar states of shock, Doh and Dresden looking worried as the children all sat stunned, unsure of what to do or say.

Even Dalton looked somewhat disturbed at seeing how frail his uncle, always strong and bright, looked at this moment.

"Assassination." Shawn nodded, like he was agreeing with himself. "Tracy and Winfred are fine; the assassin only went for me, but he got me good before I killed him."

"I've had my own similar experience." I glanced at the additional protection around the room. "Is this why all the guards have been on such high alert?"

"If another assassin comes to finish the job, I'm not in a great state to defend myself. Can't let the people know though. That'll just cause panic, and, uh, the nobles might get antsy." He wheezed a bit, catching his breath.

I got closer. "Will you get better?"

There were certain toxins that could slow or resist the usual methods of encouraging the body to heal through Vitae and other nefarious concoctions that could do even worse.

"Yeah, yeah." He waved a hand in the air. "The poison is, uh, annoying. Nothing I can't work out of my system eventually, but we have other things to talk about."

Frankly, I couldn't imagine what would be a more important conversation than the life and health of one of my closest friends, but I nodded, letting him change the subject.

His gaze narrowed in on me, weak but intense. "It's about the plan I was talking about. We need a shake-up of power to get one over Zactrik."

"A shake-up of power?" I stroked my chin.

"Yeah, a shake-up." He wobbled before pointing at me. "It's time for a new house to have influence in this empire."

An uneasy feeling welled up in my chest.

"Rakta, will you be the first high lord of House Tribus?"

19

Wine?" Shawn offered me a glass, but I declined with a simple wave of my hand. After Shawn had revealed his plan, I knew it was going to be a long conversation.

One that my children did not need to be a part of. With a nod of confirmation, Doh and Dresden had taken the sleeping Natakia and her siblings to their rooms, guided by some of Shawn's servants.

"I'd like to keep my head clear tonight." There had been so much to consider, but truly, what was there to consider now? Shawn had made it clear that this plan was already in motion.

And I was sure he had noticed how displeased I was at that.

Shawn frowned, shifting slightly in his chair and wincing from his wounds. "I wanted to wait until you got here to, well, make the final decision, but after the assassination attempt . . ."

I frowned, looking around the small, private room we were in. Magically enchanted to keep any prying eyes and ears away, the room was perfect for these sensitive conversations.

"Explain to me," I began, softly. "Explain to me the reasoning. A target on my back is one thing, but if this makes my children even more of an interest to those that would hurt them, I will be . . . upset."

I did not want to be upset at Shawn. I knew that there was not a single malicious bone in his body, and perhaps, I owed him for his years of support. I would listen to his words carefully.

"There are a few reasons." Shawn took a sip of his wine, groaning a bit in discomfort. "One is the situation with Zactrik."

I nodded. Most things these days had something to do with Zactrik.

"Zactrik has a good idea of the game, of the politics. I need to shake up the board in a way he, or rather, his agents won't expect. House Tribus will effectively change the game." Shawn spoke slowly, his voice tinged with the months of thought that had gone into this.

I sighed. "So House Tribus is intended to act as a mouthpiece for future changes? I can't imagine a new house will have the same influence as older ones, so how much change would I truly represent?"

"Enough." Shawn nodded. "Zactrik has seeded his plans, for years and we need to do the same. House Tribus is a blank slate, free of corruption and small enough that any attempts at intrigue will be noticed."

There was a logic to his plan, but I was still concerned. Did the reward outweigh the risk in this situation?

"And why does it have to be me?" I had my suspicions, but it was important to hear Shawn's reasoning.

He smiled. "Because I trust you, buddy. And, uh, I wanted you to think of it as . . . as a way to finally get away from the Velbruns."

I raised an eyebrow.

"You're strong, no doubt about that." Shawn emphasized his words with a cutting motion with his hands. "But influentially, you pale in comparison to other Lords Velbrun. With this, you're finally able to make big decisions. Even a fresh, new high lord is going to be more influential than a simple lord."

That was an enticing thought. As a high lord of my own house, I would no longer have to seek out permission for major improvements, no longer make concessions to the other Lords Velbrun for aid. And yet, they would also no longer have reason to aid me in my matters.

In fact, if House Tribus took land from House Velbrun, that would be the spark of a generational dislike that I was already not in a good position for.

As if hearing my inner concerns, Shawn continued, "House Tribus will inherit the land that you own as Lord Velbrun of Gelvurt, as well as the land of the two other lords I have in mind."

So we would be taking land from House Velbrun. I wondered when they would be alerted to this fact.

"I assume you mean Jorge and Caitlyn?" They were the only two I personally trusted after working together for so long.

Nodding, Shawn took a sip of his wine. "They'll be offered the title of Lord and Lordess Tribus and the benefits of independence from House Velbrun. The Velbruns will be notified at the upcoming council meeting, but they can't go against me on this. Creating a new house is one of my vested powers as King Certimov."

"They may not go against you," I said, "but I doubt they will stay their hand against me and other lords of the new house."

"I'm not doing this carelessly," Shawn said, a weary look in his gaze. "I know how they'll react; I know what I need to do. I'm not going to lie, it's going to be a bother for you, but . . . I need your help with this, Ratka. I hope it benefits you, I really do, but at the end of the day, the empire needs a new house."

It wasn't a satisfying answer, but I could tell that Shawn was burdened by a great many things. To do so much for this empire, caring for it even with the knowledge that it wasn't his true home.

And the way he spoke, that tinge of desperation. As if he was racing against time.

My eyes lingered on his bandages. "How are your wounds, Shawn?"

He was quiet for a moment, his hand lightly touching his gauze. The slight flinch at his own touch, the way his skin paled around the edges of the bandage. My mouth felt dry.

"It's not good, buddy." He smiled, as if his words hadn't made my heart drop into my stomach. "The healers are, uh, good at what they do, but they can only buy me more time."

"How is the poison untreatable?" Such legendary toxins and venoms could not be so easily procured. My mind went to the attack on my own person. Had my assassin's blade been poisoned as well?

I hadn't even checked.

Shawn sighed. "It isn't poison or venom."

He stood up and slowly began to unravel the bandages around his abdomen, slowly revealing more and more of his wound. My heart pounded in my chest as I saw what my daughter had saved me from.

While I had seen the skin pale around the bandages, I now saw the full wound. A deep gash into his side, a truly minor injury for a skilled cultivator of Vitae, but I gasped at the sight of this one.

A deep-black sludge seemed to have stained the wound, lightly pulsing within the gushing hole of the injury. Dark veins spiderwebbed out from the entry point and protruded through Shawn's pale skin, visible in a sickening, almost taunting fashion.

"It's an infection," Shawn said. "One that sucks up any Vitae or Mana we try to cure it with."

The words brought forth a disturbing memory of a woman who had drunk deeply of our energies in the past. The woman that had taken Lydia's face as her own.

"How long?" The words fell from my lips before I had decided if I wanted to know the answer.

He shook his head. "Three months with treatment. I think my healers are being optimistic though."

Three months? Three months to live? That was . . . I could barely comprehend the state of my friend. How did it come to this?

"Who did this? Is Zactrik behind this?" No one would tell his story after I was done with him.

Shawn shrugged. "Who else? An assassin went after me, you, and Penelope. I've sent a messenger out to make sure Ulric is okay, but I doubt he got snuck up on. He's kept sharp."

Wrapping up his wounds once more, Shawn settled back down into his seat across from me and reached out for my hand to grip with a strength that paled in comparison to the strength I was familiar with.

"I don't have long, Rakta." His smile was sad but determined. "That's why we need to work together. Zactrik may think he beat me, but people like him never expect others to have the strength to keep going. Will you help me?"

I thought back to the lovely dinner I'd shared with all my friends and family back at the Velbrun estate in Gelvurt. It felt like such a distant memory now.

"Of course, my friend." I would not abandon him in this dark time.

* * *

It was early the next morning that I gathered up my children after breakfast. Shawn was not present, undergoing treatments, but Tracy and Winfred were in attendance.

Daka had done an admirable job cheering up her friend, but the state of his father had truly dampened the prince's mood. Even so, I could tell he did not understand the full extent of his father's injuries.

Tracy had a look in her eyes, one of pain and impending loss, that gave away that she, unfortunately, was not so ignorant as her son.

"What're we doing, Dad?" Daka was walking backward in front of me, her back turned toward the crowds.

Natakia spoke up. "Are we going to look at dresses? I want Macy to come if we're looking at dresses."

"Macy is getting a tour around the palace with her parents, but she'll be joining us at the dress shop later." I would not risk the ire of Doh's child.

"Later?" Natakia frowned. "We should do it now."

Natakia had been in a mood since she'd woken up, irritable after having her sleep disturbed so many times, but thankfully the incredible softness of her bed had eased her complaints.

I held up a hand. "Dresses later, Natakia. We are going somewhere else first."

My gaze went to Dalton, who eventually looked up to meet my attention, a glint of uncertainty in his eyes.

"Let's go take a look at your shop." I rested a hand on his shoulder.

I felt something small lift from my heavy shoulders when he did not resist.

20

Was the capital safe? That was the biggest question in the back of my mind as I walked with my children down to the market district of Cerula.

If Zactrik had invisible assassins, perfectly invisible, then what stopped them from infiltrating the streets? Could I truly rely on Daka being able to see them with her own unique sight?

Relying on my child was out of the question. Protecting us from harm was not her burden to bear at her age and experience.

And so, as I walked with my children, I regularly pulsed out my Vitae, my eyes burning with intermittent uses of my **Deep Blue Technique**.

Draining? Perhaps. And yet, Shawn had mentioned that Penelope and her fellow artificers were figuring out an answer to this new threat. Until she did, I was not letting down my guard.

"Are you okay, Dad?" Daka gripped my hand tightly, looking around as I pulsed out my Vitae. It must have been quite obvious to her what I was doing, the technique I was using.

Natakia was not paying attention, her eyes looking around at the various passersby on the streets, but I could feel Dalton's attention on our conversation.

"Ah." I had never wanted to lie to my children more so than right now. "I'm fine, but very concerned. And, Daka, please don't use the technique you see right now. It's dangerous."

Daka's face scrunched up, as if she wasn't satisfied, but I could see her eyes flicker as her mind went to a different question. "Is Uncle Shawn going to be okay?"

There was a tremor in her voice, one that was worried, but I could feel something much more knowing beneath it. I hadn't even considered that Daka's sight might have given her insight into his true condition.

What had such a horrific state looked like to her?

"Let's speak of that later, Daka." I made a small gesture to the streets. My daughter looked around, noticing the crowds around us. After a moment, my point registered with her.

These people did not need to know the state of their king; it would only cause panic among them. Exactly, I expected, what Zactrik and his agents wanted from their attempt on his life.

She gave me a small, firm nod. Dalton's silent gaze promised that he would not allow such a conversation to happen without him. It seemed I would not be able to shield my children from the larger truth of the empire for much longer.

"Rakta?" A sudden voice interrupted my train of thought, making me tense as I wasn't entirely familiar with whoever was speaking to me.

Turning to the voice, I saw a strangely familiar-looking man. Long, dark hair that fell down below his shoulders and olive complexion that seemed to have been tanned naturally out in the hot summer sun. He wore a loose collection of traveling gear that hung from his clothing and bags.

My children all watched the man with some confusion as he approached, but I blinked as I realized who this was. "Tenon?"

"Hey!" Tenon smiled. "Wow, it's been so long, and you still remember me. I guess you don't save many people from goblins, huh?"

"Dad's saved a whole bunch of people from goblins." Daka stood defiantly against this man. "I don't know who you are though!"

"Children," I gently broke in, "this is Tenon. He's an author, a writer of a grand encyclopedia of monsters, isn't that right, Tenon?"

He smiled. "Yes, sir. Just got back from Prayers, so I've been trying to relax for a while. I'll be meeting with a couple of my patrons to get my funds back in order, but . . . I have gotten the first volume of my book published!"

I blinked, thinking that ten years was certainly more than enough time to do that, but smiled all the same. "I'm happy to hear that."

"Actually." Tenon rifled through one of his satchels before producing a heavy tome. "Here, for your help and, well, saving my life."

I looked down at the book. "*Tenon's Worldwide Monstrous Encyclopedia Volume One*," and gave him an appreciative nod. "This will be a fine read indeed."

"It comes presigned." Tenon grinned before he blushed at saying that out loud, turning toward a different direction with a hurried vigor in his step. "Welp, it was nice seeing you again and good luck growing older, kids!"

With that, he was off, and I found myself watching him leave alongside my children. He bumped into a few people, apologizing on his way out, before finally disappearing from view.

We were silent for a moment.

"That guy was kinda weird, huh?"

Daka could only be quiet for so long.

Turning away from the direction that Tenon had gone and gently pulling Natakia closer, making sure she did not get lost in the growing crowds of the morning streets, I coughed. "We're almost there."

The property for Dalton's store had cost a few shiny sils, but it was in a good spot. A single-story building with a large front room and two spacious supply rooms and a personal office, Dalton's store was set in the middle of a bakery and a larger building often used for meetings by the local guilds. I imagined he'd appreciate the connections this might afford him by simple proximity.

"Wow!" Daka crept over to the front windows, smooshing her face up against the glass. "Your store is amazing, Dalton!"

Natakia pulled her away from the glass. "Stop smudging up the glass. It'll have to be cleaned."

Dalton paid little attention to his sisters, looking around with a sharpness in his gaze. His eyes wandered from the front door to his neighboring buildings, to the alchemy store across the street.

I knelt beside him, my attention slipping from my surroundings for a moment to focus on my son. "What do you think?"

"It's fine." Dalton closed his eyes, turning slightly away from me. "I'll have to see inside first to be sure."

Smiling, I dug through my pockets. "Then do the honors."

I held out my hand to my son, Dalton's eyes opening to see the glistening metal key in my palm, made for the new locks I'd had installed to the building. They were strong and resistant to being picked, with some minor enchantments layered into the metal.

Reaching out to take the key from me, Dalton's hand shook slightly as he gently pinched the key from my hand, taking it over to the door. He barely looked at me during all of this, but I could see the edge of his lips trying to curl into a smile.

Of course, I gave a quick pulse of my Vitae as he approached the door, searching for any assassins. If Zactrik was targeting my children and me, then I wouldn't put it beyond him to place hidden assailants within my child's new property.

Thankfully finding nothing amiss, I smiled as Daka and Natakia crowded around Dalton, both intently watching as their brother unlocked the door and took his first steps into his new building.

"At least some things on this trip won't be ruined," I muttered to myself, following my children inside. "Ugh, dust." Natakia was the first to speak as we walked in, noticing the thin layer of dust and cobwebs scattered about the place. This place had sat unused for quite a while, held up in various ownership issues that I had leaned on with the help of a few favors I was still owed from my adventuring days.

Daka ran around, her eyes wide before she whipped her head toward Dalton. "It's so big! What are you going to do with all this space, Dalton?"

That was an exceedingly good question. One that my son ignored as he continued to walk around, eyeing up the surroundings like he was preparing an ambush.

Perhaps he was. I had yet to truly speak with him about my deeper concerns with his planned business practices. I did not want to ruin this by interrogating him, however.

As the children walked around the front, I did a quick survey of the many different rooms, my vision blue as I tried to root out any attempts to hide from my earlier pulse of Vitae. Thankfully, I found nothing.

Confident that, at least for now, the building was free of threats, I came back out to the front, seeing that Daka and Natakia were over near the walls looking at the peeling wallpaper. "Girls, I believe there are some cleaning supplies in the supply room. Why don't you go get them and we can start tidying up?"

Natakia's face soured, but she had barely any time to protest before Daka had whisked her off down the hallway, some cheery mantra about cleaning echoing through the building.

Leaving me some time alone with my son.

"Dalton." My son looked at me, a resigned glint in his gaze. "Or perhaps, you would like me to call you by your past name?"

"No point. I don't need to start having to explain to people why I prefer a wholly different name." Dalton was dismissive of the idea, but if the true identity of the Warlock King were to ever come out, I was sure few would fault him for distancing himself from his namesake.

"If that's what you're comfortable with." I walked over to him. "I want to talk about this business, my son, this business and . . . your past life."

It was hard to gauge his reaction, my son merely tensing at the mention of his origins. I doubted that it would ever be a topic we spoke of freely, but it was an important one.

"This really isn't the place to talk about past lives, is it?" Dalton's voice was crisp, logical. A practical reason that made sense, exactly what I expected from him.

I looked around the room, hearing the clamoring of Daka and Natakia as they began their cleaning in the back rooms. "Perhaps we can wait until tonight, when we have our privacy, but your business . . . What are your intentions, Dalton?"

For a moment, I thought he might not answer me. We'd talked at length about the practices and strategies he would employ, but the actual business itself was still a mystery.

"I need to study the area first to be certain what the local market is like," he eventually started. "However, I think a furniture store would suit my needs."

I raised an eyebrow. "A furniture store?"

"The local carpentry guilds are the easiest to work with," Dalton explained, a new glint in his eye. "And furniture is like art: it'll attract noble customers easily enough. I already have a few designs, but I'll need a carpenter to work on them."

Art? I thought back to the grand pieces hanging on the walls of my keep. Daka had ruined one during some of her indoor training. I had gotten a letter explaining just how expensive it had been to purchase.

The amount the Velbruns had paid was almost embarrassing. To put a price on a painting felt like trying to put a price on a story. Why go so far as to own something that flourished among the public? It wasn't even a family painting.

"And then," my son continued, my gaze refocusing on him. "I'll broker my way into antiques and other businesses before settling on a few monopolies."

That sounded as strong as a business plan as I could think of myself. I had never seen my son show interest in furniture, but I doubted the beauty of chairs was what drew him to the market.

I looked around the storefront, smiling. "You'll do well, Dalton."

And yet, I knew I needed to be there, to guide Dalton away from the edge that he neared every time he spoke of his business. He didn't need to be like the other merchants that squeezed money out of those around him. My son was smart enough to be so much better than that.

And much, much worse.

"Rakta." I felt a pang in my heart as I looked over at Dalton, uncomfortable at how he addressed me. He wavered, like he was unsure himself, before he relented, "Dad, how did you . . . know about me?"

I took a knee, getting eye level with my son. "There is—"

"Dad, Daka splashed dirty water all over me!" Natakia's shrill scream echoed throughout the entirety of the dusty, empty store.

Daka's call came soon after. "You got in the way of cleaning! And it's just on your shoes!"

I blinked, sharing a glance with my son, before standing up. There would be time tonight to speak with my son about the prophecy, about what it meant to him and his sisters.

First and foremost, however, I needed to make sure Natakia did not kill her sister. After calming down Natakia, whose cheeks were still stained by tears she shed at her shoes getting dirty, I made Daka apologize and helped both of them get to cleaning while Dalton examined his personal office.

Natakia had, well, not been keen on cleaning, but I was firm with her. Sweeping up dust, I'd convinced her, was the least she could do to help with her brother's store.

Daka, on the other hand, was covered in the dust and filth of a building left mostly unattended for months by the end of it. She happily swung her feet as she sat on a ladder I'd fetched to dust the cobwebs from the corners of the room. "So, where are we going next?"

Dalton, by this point, looked satisfied by how clean his store was and the space it provided. Natakia, hearing her sister, looked at me imploringly.

"Natakia," I said, enjoying the way her eyes widened moments before I said the words. "We're going to the dress shop."

My darling desert flower cheered.

21

Tatiana Pellorana was one of the most renowned dressmakers of the Certillian Empire, with few within the higher circles of nobility unaware of her craft and skill with threads, both mundane and esoteric. For while other clothiers could weave their art skillfully, only a few of them possessed anything close to Tatiana's talent with magic.

The Queen's Gown, a name bestowed upon the abode by the current queen's late mother, was a truly beautiful storefront. Taking up the entirety of the city block, it was as charming in design as it was massive in size.

"Can I stay here forever?" Natakia looked close to tears as she peered in at the magical dresses lightly dancing past the windows of the capital, the animated finery doing twirls and spins.

It was slightly bizarre to me, seeing clothing move on its own, but my children seemed fascinated by the display, even Dalton inches from the glass of the boutique's window.

Macy looked up at her mother with the same question, Doh making a little snort as she watched the display herself.

"Sorry, kids." The maid ruffled her daughter's hair. "Can't imagine the good Miss Pellorana will want your grubby little hands all over her place for that long."

My desert flower pulled back from the window to look at Doh, a slight frown. "My hands aren't grubby."

"No, they are not." I stepped in, pulling Natakia away from the beginnings of a tantrum as I motioned her and Macy to the doorway of the dress shop.

Getting a fitting from Tatiana was not a simple request. There was a waiting list for even the most influential of merchants and nobility, but thankfully, I'd had my own strings to pull for this one.

Making sure all the children were following, I opened the door and walked inside, smelling the sweet, perfumed scent of apples in the air. For some, the smell might have been surprising.

I didn't blame them; those people could never have known beforehand that Tatiana loved apples.

"Dad, help!" Daka's strangled cry suddenly broke through my idle thoughts, and I turned around with intent to kill, only lessened by the laughter of Doh and the others.

I watched, somewhat stunned by the sight, as one of the dresses hanging on the various stands throughout the room was trying to force itself onto Daka, my daughter looking panicked as she wrestled with pink lace and finery.

I moved to help her, my fingers barely managing to get underneath the tight lace before a sharp whistle pierced the air and the threads of the dress suddenly melted away, sliding off of my daughter and slinking back to the stand it had been hanging on.

Daka took a deep breath as I held her, my little warrior clinging to me as she gave the dress a dirty look. My own gaze drifted toward the banister of the stairs.

Natakia's giggling fit at the sight of her sister's struggles melted into awe as she followed my gaze. "She's beautiful."

Covered in resplendent golden weaves that seemed to flow around her like water, a red-and-blue shawl wrapped around her shoulders, a cream-skinned woman with long red hair leaned over the railings of the upper platform of the store.

Her chin gently nestled between the knuckles of her open palm, Tatiana smiled down at the five of us. "Now, I do believe I have signs around. You touch the dresses at your own peril."

In the years since she was a traveling seamstress, Tatiana had gone from eccentric merchant to a figure that filled the room with her presence even without the use of Vitae or Mana.

"I apologize for my daughter," I said, standing up with Daka and allowing her to step forward, her cheeks aflame as she muttered her own apologies.

Tatiana waved them away. "No harm done, not that there is really any risk. My dresses only cling to those who wish to wear them."

Natakia's trance broke as she looked over at her sister, a teasing edge to her smile. "Daka? You wanted to wear that pretty dress?"

"Humph." My little warrior clung even tighter to me. "I just wanted to see if I could fight in the stupid thing."

"Of course you just want to get it dirty." My desert flower rolled her eyes at her sister, her nose scrunching up in disgust.

I stepped in. "Natakia, Daka, please. Miss Pellorana's time is very valuable. Let's not be rude and waste it by arguing."

"Yeah, it feels like I'm going to have to go into debt just to breathe the air in here." Doh walked up alongside me with Macy at her side.

I gave her a look. Wasting her time was far from the only way to be rude to Tatiana, but we hardly needed to figure out how many different ways that could be accomplished.

Melodic giggles shattered my concern, Tatiana beginning to walk down the long, winding stairway she had been looking at us from. "Please, take your time. Any friend of Rakta's certainly doesn't need to pay to breathe my air."

"I can't believe I'm going to get a dress from the real Tatiana Pellorana." Natakia was sounding entranced again, her hands reaching out for Macy and pulling her close, as if to help her stand.

Macy smiled, before looking up at the beautiful woman approaching us.

As if answering a question in her gaze, Tatiana began to pull cloths and fabrics from stands as she neared us, her flowing golden weaves coasting across the floor around her feet. "Oh yes, both of you, my dear."

Doh's daughter wrapped her arms around my desert flower as if she suddenly needed the same support. "She wears everything quite well," Tatiana said as she pulled me aside from the rest of the group. The last hour consisted of nothing other than measurements, fittings, and keeping Daka from touching everything in the store.

Of course, Natakia had loved it all, excluding the latter, with my desert flower and her best friend adorning themselves in the most extravagant of colors and giggling to themselves.

I nodded, looking over to where Natakia was fluffing her current attire, a pink dress that turned blue when she twirled, while gazing into her personal mirror as it floated around her.

"Natakia is her mother's daughter. I'm not surprised." Lydia had never seemingly put much effort into looking beautiful but had never looked unappealing. "Thank you for doing this, Tatiana."

Dress aside, seeing my daughter look so openly thrilled was worth any price.

The seamstress smiled, following my gaze toward my desert flower. "Think nothing of it. I was surprised when you got in touch after so long, but I'd never forget the Dancer that saved my life."

"Life?" I thought back, never having done much more than any other adventurer would have. "I seem to remember that I only fetched materials for you on occasion. Shawn was the one who introduced you to the royal family."

Certainly, it had never occurred to me to bring together those two parts of my life. My friend was always better at connecting people.

"And yet, you were the one who introduced me to Shawn and the rest of your friends. A humble seamstress on the side of the road, no business the entire day except for a Ruskan needing a new shirt," she giggled.

Thinking back, I could vaguely remember the old, limping cart that she had been working out of back then. None of what she sold was purchased from another; it had all been handcrafted with her own thread and needle.

"I could tell your clothes flowed better," I said, thinking back to those old threads. Certillian attire was much more confining, didn't breathe.

"Yes." She smirked, looking proud of her old work. "When you're the best, why should you shirk comfort to look good when you don't have to?"

Lydia hadn't been the keenest about Tatiana's clothing, but even she couldn't argue about the results once Tatiana began to feel the benefits of having wealthy patrons that depended on her.

"Have you an idea about what my daughter would enjoy?" Unfortunately, the complexities of fashion were lost on me. And while Dalton had seemingly paid silent attention to the conversation, Daka had definitely inherited ignorance from me.

My little warrior was currently doing a handstand in the corner, silently counting how long she could keep her balance steady.

Tatiana raised an eyebrow. "I'll be honest. I'm almost tempted to offer her a job."

"I'm sorry?" I wasn't sure if I'd heard that quite right, somewhat distracted by Daka for a moment.

"Your daughter, Rakta." She motioned over to her. "Natakia just got done telling me about some truly divine ideas she had for a clothing line."

She shook her head, as if still struggling to believe it. I was a tad surprised by Natakia's interest going beyond simply wearing dresses, but not truly. In retrospect, her love for fashion was much too great for that.

"And the way she led the conversation, Rakta!" Tatiana dramatically fell upon me, her forehead against my shoulder. "No girl should have such a grasp on subtly and charm! How many tutors has she had!?"

I wasn't sure what to tell her. Natakia's etiquette teacher had effectively put her in charge of helping the class alongside her after a few weeks of teaching her all he knew.

Gently straightening her up, I considered her words. "All my children are talented, Tatiana. I'm glad Natakia has found another who appreciates her interests so openly."

The way Natakia could read another was unmatched, something that was impressive even with the knowledge that she was far more than the average youngling. "How do I look, Dad?" Natakia spun around for me, her purple dress seeming to hum as the golden embroidery began to glow at the movement.

"My desert flower," I said, taking her arm as she stopped and looked at me expectantly, "you look beautiful. I'm sure you and Macy will be the talk of the entire gala."

She smiled, looking away with a touch of bashfulness as she returned to gazing at her own reflection. "It's nice being beautiful."

"Hmm?" I raised an eyebrow.

"Oh, well." My daughter seemed to start for a moment before calming down. "I've just always heard how beautiful Mom was from you."

Ah, yes, Lydia had certainly passed down her beauty to our daughter. The idea of my daughter comparing herself to her late mother, of course, was slightly concerning.

"Natakia, you make your mother proud every day." I had no doubt that, if Lydia were truly watching over us from her Great Beyond, she only had reason to be disappointed in me.

She smiled, her gaze drifting back to her own reflection. "Miss Pellorana is very nice. Even though she's making us our own dresses, she's let us try on so many."

Tatiana certainly was kind. That she felt like she owed so much of her success to me I was somewhat dubious about, but I would not argue with the results. My daughter had never looked so pleased.

Before I could continue the conversation, the door opened, and a pair of men walked in, both adorned in finery and armor dipped in the colors of House Iriend.

Between them, walking with the familiar air of a noble, was a young girl, perhaps only a few years older than my children, wearing a beautiful walking gown that she lifted up with her fingertips as she strode inside.

"Miss Pellorana." The young girl's polite voice echoed throughout the store in a small display of talent with Vitae. "This young mistress of Iriend would be pleased to have your attention shortly."

I looked up the stairs where I'd seen Tatiana depart while she gave my children and Doh some time to enjoy the clothing of her dress shop. When I turned back, the young Iriend had stridden further into the store, approaching myself and my daughter.

Natakia pulled away from herself as the older girl approached, seemed to easily slip into the etiquette she had been taught. "Greetings, Lady Iriend."

The Lady Iriend focused on my daughter, glancing at me before narrowing her gaze. I stepped forward to introduce us, as expected for members of the Velbrun family, but her next words stopped me.

"I see Miss Pellorana allows the help to frequent her wears." She smiled. "I do so hope they are cleaned before they are put back on display for the proper young ladies such as myself."

I blinked, unused to such a flagrant insult from such a young child, before I glanced at my daughter to make sure her words had not struck her too deeply.

Natakia's eyes had widened at her words before her smile twitched a single time and became just a smidgeon bigger as she stepped up.

I realized, in that moment, that Natakia might have inherited far more than beauty from Lydia.

<h1 style="text-align:center">22</h1>

A proper young lady?" Natakia asked, far too politely for the chill in my stomach.

The young Lady Iriend raised an eyebrow at the question. "Yes, a proper young lady. Did staring at the desert sun make you go blind?"

I looked to the two guards accompanying the young noble, noticing that they were keeping their gazes firmly on me, far more than they were gauging my daughter. The comment burned at me, but striking a child was certainly not my intention.

"Natakia . . ." Her name left my lips on instinct, but I went ignored. Words between these two young ladies had started this, and I believed that words between them would be the only end.

"A proper young lady would be more educated in knowing who they speak to, Lady Annabella Iriend." Natakia tilted her head, almost curious in her barbs. "Of course, this Lady Velbrun would be happy to lend aid if a scion of Iriend was in so desperate need of it."

I watched on as, while her feet remained firmly rooted, Annabella's gaze took a metaphorical step back from my daughter in shock. And yet, that anger once again lashed out as my daughter's last few words registered.

"I do not need help from anyone." Annabella almost hissed, her hands tightly clutching at her dress as her own polite smile fractured just enough.

Natakia took a curtsy in her beautiful dress. "Of course, Lady Iriend, perhaps, with the boundless respect you command from your parents, you've proven such a thing tenfold?"

Annabella froze, and the belated realization struck me that I had no idea how Natakia had known this young lady's name or, as the young lady wordlessly mouthed to herself, these words to say.

"Perhaps"—Natakia gave the lady no reprieve—"if your sister is around, then she might be able to take care of this."

The guards glanced at each other, but seemingly had no interest in the blades being thrust into their young charge. Of course, I hadn't a clue about what was going on, either, only that the young lady's mouth had closed, and she was beginning to shake.

"Y-you," Annabella stuttered, her countenance broken. "What is your n-name?"

My daughter had begun to turn away at this point, almost as if speaking with the Lady Iriend had started to bore her.

The look on her face—the lack of interest in someone's mere presence in a conversation—it reminded me sharply of Lydia when she was angry.

And yet, she turned around, her eyes wide in mock surprise and little mercy. "Ah, did your ears not catch my father's call for me? Has your hearing been impaired by all the lessons you ignored?"

Natakia primly stepped into Lady Annabella Iriend's personal space, the guards paying more attention now to her but making no moves to stop her. I certainly wouldn't allow them to put a hand on my child.

"My name is Lady Natakia Velbrun," my daughter said to her, in what might have been a hushed tone if it were not purposefully loud enough for all to hear it. "And if you ever lay such disrespectful words at my feet again, I will not be so kind in our next encounter. I hope to see you at the Rose Gala."

And with that, she disengaged, taking steps away from the noble and turning away and heading back to where Macy was watching from afar. I was sure that if my daughter had not handled herself so well, her friend would have been ready for support.

And yet, while my daughter's interest had waned, my gaze went back to the young noble as she stared at where my daughter had stood, a haunted look in her eyes. She swallowed hard and began to leave the store, her guards accompanying her and her dress forgotten.

No matter the rudeness that the young noble had shared, I doubted

I knew the true depths of the words my daughter had said to her. Had Natakia gone too far?

It warmed my heart that she had defended herself, and yet I felt an itch at the back of my head at the memory of the venom that had dripped from her tongue.

"Did something happen, Dad?" Daka came over, obviously drawn by the minor commotion. She looked over her shoulder as the door swung closed behind the young Lady Iriend.

I shook my head, rubbing her head affectionately. "Nothing to concern yourself with. Natakia handled it."

Scarily well, I noted to myself. My children were certainly full of surprises. After some more discussion with Tatiana, my children and I wrapped up our visit and pulled Doh away from the dresses, which was far more difficult than pulling Macy away.

"Just one more dress!" Doh struggled in my grip. "And I think I saw a suit that would fit me really well if I just make a few changes and—"

Getting out of the boutique and Tatiana's hair, Macy was silently hugging her dour mother, and I simply shook my head at the sight. Natakia and Macy were showing much more maturity in leaving the place.

Daka and Dalton were walking beside me, Natakia off to the side by a few paces as she looked inside the various windows of the jewelry and beauty stores common in this part of the city.

"Rakta?" A new voice caught me off guard, calling out to me from behind. I stopped, turning around with mild amounts of apprehension, but the voice registered in the back of mind as I saw who approached.

With her arms rigid at her sides with a hint of nervousness, a large leather satchel at her hip, and a large pair of bulbous glasses that seemed to glint in the afternoon sun for a moment, Harriet Pillops shifted nervously as she came closer, a briskness in her step.

I smiled, the tension in my body relaxing. "Ah, Harriet, good afternoon."

"Good, um, afternoon to you as well," she said, a halting nervousness in her voice. "I see you've been in to see Tatiana. I'm, uh, glad you're getting ready for, well, the Rose Gala."

Nodding, I was moments away from voicing my gratitude for all the help she'd provided when a soft cough stopped me. I turned around, seeing that all of the children and Doh were looking at the new woman with wide, curious eyes.

"Dad." Natakia smiled sweetly after clearing her throat. "Care to introduce us?"

Ah, yes, introductions were important. As much as Shawn and Penelope had discussed Harriet around my children, it had escaped me that they had never truly met the woman before.

"Children, Doh, this is Harriet Pillops. Harriet, these are my younglings, Dalton, Daka, and Natakia." I motioned to my children before motioning to Doh and Macy. "This is Doh Booker and her daughter, Macy."

My children, Natakia specifically, seemed to watch the new woman intently as she shyly smiled at all of them, waving her hand in greeting. "Um, well, hello. Yes, uh, my name is Harriet. I hope to, uh, I hope I'm not intruding."

"Not at all!" Doh quickly sidled up next to the woman, grabbing her hand up into a fierce shake. "I've heard so much about you! I couldn't wait to meet you!"

Harriet looked flustered by Doh's advance. "Rakta, uh, Rakta spoke about me? A lot?"

"Nope," Natakia said. "It was mostly Uncle Shawn and Aunt Penny who talked about you. Hey, Daka, what did they call her again?"

Daka looked confused for a moment, her focus on the merchant broken for a moment before recognition lit up in her eyes. "Oh, a—"

"Anyway," I cut in, feeling a tad defensive of the poor woman. Natakia certainly seemed to still be in a combative mood for some reason. "Harriet here is the reason you and Macy have invitations to the Rose Gala, Natakia. What should you say?"

Natakia looked up at me, a strangeness in her gaze, before she let out a soft whisper of a sigh and stepped forward toward Harriet, who looked somewhat overwhelmed, before curtsying.

"Thank you for the invitation," she said, Macy quickly walking up alongside her and curtsying in a perfect imitation of Natakia's poise.

Doh gave the frazzled woman a squeeze, smiling. "I'm pretty grateful too. My darling little daughter gets to make a name for herself at the Rose Gala!"

"Um, well, yes, it's a very big deal for young ladies." Harriet started, rubbing her arms. "You're welcome, of course. I, well, when Rakta came to me, uh, told me about all of you . . . Well, what else could I do, but help?"

She shrugged, uneasy. It seemed like there was something weighing on her mind, but I wasn't sure what it could be. Harriet had mentioned, when we reconnected, that ever since her father died a couple years ago, she'd inherited most of his business dealings and the stress of it all.

"We're truly thankful," I said. "Natakia and Macy would not have this opportunity without you, so please, let me know if you're ever in need of help."

Daka flexed beside me, smiling. "Yeah! We'll help you move boxes or beat up any thieves!"

"And maybe," Dalton added quietly, "if you ever had a moment to spare, we could discuss business in the area."

Harriet swallowed, straightening her glasses, before she nodded. "Um, yes, that would all, well, be very nice and . . . Thank you, you truly have wonderful children, Rakta."

"Yes." I laid my hand on Dalton's and Daka's shoulders. "I grow prouder of them every day. I'm sure Lydia would feel the same."

There was a warmth in my chest that I let sit for a moment, only dulled by the absence of Lydia on this street. I wondered, truly, what advice she would have had for Natakia and the upcoming gala.

Harriet, on the other hand, had stiffened. "Ah, yes, I'm sure she would be. I, um, need to get going, but . . . Rakta, would you be free tomorrow night? I thought we might discuss som—"

I was already trying to arrange the words as politely as I could to decline. Harriet was a wonderful friend, but with Shawn hurt and the state of the empire, any distance from my children filled me with worry.

Unfortunately, Doh interrupted both of us.

"Yes," she yelled, looking like she'd just gotten proposed to by Dresden again. "He's super free, schedule is completely empty!"

"Doh," I said reproachfully before I sighed looking at Harriet's hopeful face. "I suppose I do have the time, but you've already done enough for me, Harriet. This will be my treat."

The way she smiled at that was reward enough, but my concern endured. Perhaps the children could spend some time with Penelope tomorrow night?

Natakia, for her part, was sending an annoyed look toward Doh, Macy instinctively matching it, but as Doh dramatically staggered under their dual looks, Harriet said her farewells, and we continued our trek through the market before heading back to the palace with the setting sun behind us. Later that night, I was pacing in my sleepwear, the sounds of my children getting ready for bed in the adjoining bathroom that connected our rooms filling my ears.

Thoughts of House Tribus, Zactrik, Harriet, Shawn, and many other things filled my head, but nothing more so than the discussion of the prophecy that I planned on telling my children tonight.

"Daka and Natakia deserve to know as much as Dalton does," I said to myself, trying to persuade the part of me that was fiercely against revealing such a heavy burden at such a young age.

And yet, no story that began with lies and omissions of truth ever ended in anything better than bittersweetness. They should know; they deserved to know.

And perhaps, well, perhaps this was a chance to finally discuss Earth with them, the land they came from. With Shawn here, as weakened as he was, he could speak with them about their origins in a way I could not.

And yet, as they began to file out of the bathroom, all of them ready for their bedtime stories, I felt a shake under the soles of my feet as the whole of the palace was suddenly rocked by a great and powerful noise.

Natakia looked alarmed. "What was that!?"

"An explosive?" Dalton had instinctively gotten low to the ground, his eyes glancing to the side.

Daka had frozen up, a haunted look in her gaze as another episode shook the whole of the palace around us, my form quickly stepping forward to grab her and the rest of my children up.

"The palace is under attack." I could hardly believe the words that fell from my lips, but they stank of a deep fear that rose from my chest as their certainty gripped me.

The palace was under attack, and my children were in the midst of it.

23

Very few times in the past decade had I truly needed to protect my children after I'd made it clear to the Velbruns what would happen if assassins found their way to my doorstep.

Neither bandits nor monsters had neared the keep, and until Zactrik's latest schemes were revealed to me, I'd thought that the value I had as a target had waned. My duplinium axe at my side, I cursed my own importance.

"W-where are we going!?" Natakia sounded scared, no longer the confident child that had meticulously tried on dresses to find the one that fit her perfectly.

Speeding down the hallway, all my children in my arms as I wasted no time with my **Great Wind Sprint Technique**, I barreled through the doors of the room, racing toward the other rooms across the hall. "Doh! Dresden!"

Dresden's blade was unsheathed at my entry, his ready stance relaxing as he recognized that I was no enemy. "Rakta, what's the situation?"

Behind him, Doh was carrying Macy, the young girl looking sleepy and not yet aware of the danger around her.

"I do not know," I said, readjusting the frozen Daka in my grip. Dalton was currently on my back, hanging on to my neck, while Natakia latched on to my side. "We need to get the children to safety."

The palace shook once more, and yet, I could feel it was from a different direction. A pincered attack? Why had Zactrik suddenly made such a direct attack?

Regardless, with my friends gathered, we ventured down the hallway together. I looked around, trying to remember the layout of the palace from the many years I'd had to study it.

There were warded rooms on each floor that would offer protection. And yet, I was not sure I even knew where to start.

"Lord Velbrun!" A guard called to us as we rounded the corner, just one of a small patrol rushing down the hallway to greet us. "Come with us. We'll get you to safety."

They were wearing the royal colors, five of them all wielding large halberds that they kept at the ready for any sign of trouble. It was relieving to have them nearby.

"What's going on?" I made to follow them, Doh and Dresden following suit, but before the lead guard, a nondescript-looking man with black hair, could answer, my daughter interrupted.

Natakia screamed in my arms, pointing at the guards. "Dad, they want to kill us!"

The guards tensed, even as another explosion rattled the palace, making for the third, and I felt my entire body tense as my Vitae blossomed throughout my arms and legs.

"What . . . Hey! We're here to get you out! Don't you hear the attack going on?" The lead guard was more tense now, holding his halberd just a tad too aggressively for my liking.

The other guards were the same, all of them thrown off by my daughter's words. Honestly, so was I, but I would be long dead and forgotten before I ever disregarded the words of my children when they spoke with such certainty and terror.

"Dresden." I untangled my children from me, dropping them behind me as I took a step forward. He nodded, his hands on the hilt of his blade as he readied himself.

Feeling confident in my children's safety, a small pulse of Vitae revealing no living creatures around me beyond those I could see, I narrowed my eyes at the guard. "I would have you tell me your intentions."

The guard, frustrated but not scared, steeled himself, and I felt the shift in Vitae among the group before he ever spoke a word. When he did finally speak, it was not to me. "I guess we'll do it here, then."

And as another explosion shook the palace, the guards, no, the intruders leveled their blades at me. I frowned, feeling a deep anger welling up inside of me, sprouting from the fertile soil of my fear.

"I have little patience for men who point weapons in the direction of my children." I could feel the world begin to slow down as the attackers took their first step toward me, halberds shimmering with Vitae.

And then their forms froze before toppling forward unconscious, revealing a new form walking in our direction down the hall. A drawn blade by his side, Tanner raised his hand in greeting.

"Lord Velbrun and company, come with me," he said, stepping over the impostor guards as if he had barely noticed their presence. I could feel the instinctive uneasiness welling up inside of me at the sight of the man, but Natakia seemed to calm at his presence.

Daka, however, had gripped onto me even more fiercely.

I nodded, taking the man at his word. "What's the nature of this attack? Where are you taking us?"

While I would have words with Shawn, I did not need to leave my children out in the open during this attack. And the sooner they were sequestered somewhere away from the ire of assassins and disguised intruders . . .

"There is no attack," Tanner interrupted my thoughts, beginning to walk back down the hallway. He never even missed a step as the palace rumbled once again from a massive explosion.

"An illusion? Truly?" Even after I had flexed my Vitae and forcefully dispelled the Mana-born delusions, managing to guide Daka into doing the same, I was still flummoxed at the notion.

Doh and Dresden were taking care of Macy, guarded by trusted men, but I had not even humored the idea of my children being away from me after such an incident, even if it was only a phantasm.

We sat, Daka and Natakia sitting in my lap as Dalton stood beside me, all of us focused on Shawn as he took a sip of some silvery water, most likely some rare medicine.

We were currently sitting in one of his private, secure chambers, a small, crackling fire at the center of the room keeping it aflame. Tracy and Winfred, Shawn had mentioned, were elsewhere for the moment.

He nodded, putting the glass down. "An illusion, truly. Penelope was called for, so she'll be able to make better sense of it than either of us, but my own great minds have never seen an illusion so complex and subtle in their studies."

I ran my hands through Natakia's hair as I tightened my grip around Daka's waist. Natakia was frightened, yes, but Daka had still not said a word since the illusion had gone off.

That, more than anything, had me truly worried. My only solace was that I was not the only one worried, Natakia's hand drifting over to hold her sister's.

"And these stones." I looked over to the table, seeing the weathered, squarish rocks covered in the runic markings of ritual work. "Your men never noticed them being set up?"

"The only physical part of the illusion was the intruders," Shawn said. "Another example of some master illusion work done on their armor to pierce the palace's defenses and alarms and set up the ritual moments before it went off. And once they'd completed that part . . ."

I frowned. "They came after me and mine."

There was no telling what would have awaited my children and the others if I had followed those guards. It had only been Natakia's own quick instincts that saved us from perhaps running straight into a trap.

"One of Zactrik's people," he said. "First, those half-calkers, and now we have an illusionist plaguing us? There's no telling what kind of monster is behind all of this, but we'll get them, I promise."

And yet, as his promise left his lips, his shoulders dropped like it was just one more burden for him to carry, buckling under the weight of his responsibility and, by the look in his eyes, regret.

"I'm sorry, Rakta, kids," Shawn said, lowering his head. "I told you it was safe. I really thought it wouldn't get quite so . . . busy during your vacation here."

He winced, not from his words, but from physical pain as he let out a small breath of air. The only indication that his affliction was just as serious as when last we'd spoken.

Dalton spoke up, sounding calm for one having been through such a ruckus. "It's fine, uncle. You don't get to decide when the enemy makes their moves."

It was strange hearing my youngling speak to the king with such wisdom, but I agreed with his words. In fact, perhaps there was potential wisdom to be shared by all in this room right now.

"Shawn," I started, gaining my friend's attention. "I know you are busy right now, but I'd like your presence after I tend to my children. I wish to have a talk with all of us present and focused."

I'd speak it now, of course, but I looked down to the still statue of my little warrior clinging to my chest and taking shallow breaths.

My friend's eyes sparkled with some confusion for a moment before recognition sparked and he gave a slow, hesitating nod. He knew what I wished to speak of.

And I thought having him there might be enlightening. Resting back in our rooms, my eyes wandered over my younglings as they truly began to collect themselves after such a loud and visceral scare.

Natakia, trying to hold herself together and not let her own emotions show as she indulged in her own reflection; Dalton, who seemed calm and yet could not hold back the shake of his hands; and finally, Daka . . .

She was quiet, besides the whispered words of an old, strange-sounding song spilling from her lips about the shade of an old apple tree.

For a moment, I felt helpless. I rarely had peace of mind myself, so how did I intend to invent some for my younglings as they wrestled with this new fear? This danger that had knocked at our door?

"Children, gather around." I might fail to bring them solace, but I would have failed on a far more fundamental level if I lacked the courage to even try.

They collected around me, Daka being the slowest of the three to move, but she had not been far from me since the first explosion went off. I sat them down on the bed in front of me as I stood, wanting their full attention.

Three pairs of eyes, each filled with its own unique struggle with the fear of trickery, of death. I cursed Zactrik's games and the way they had sewn uncertainty into their hearts over the last few weeks.

"Tonight, we were targeted by someone who meant us harm," I said, knowing little to say other than the truth. "If not for quick thinking, sudden insight, we may have gotten hurt. And while we are right to be afraid of those behind this, do not let that fear taint tomorrow."

There were nights spent afraid like this, when the Warlock King's forces marched against us. Overwhelming armies, monsters sworn to his service—it eventually became that some feared the rising sun for what new horrors it brought.

"Tomorrow," I said, "we will still be here. I will still be here. All three of you will still be here. We have only lost something tonight if we allow them to take away our certainty of such things."

For a moment, my children were quiet. Dalton glanced at Daka, who seemed to be listening but still seemed so very far away, before Natakia spoke up. No matter how long she had spent tidying herself up, smoothing out the wrinkles in her nightdress, she was still obviously shaken.

"They were . . . they were targeting us, Dad," she said. "You. They wanted to kill you. Kill us. This . . . this isn't fun anymore. It isn't supposed to be like this."

No, it wasn't. Unfortunately, the world seemed reticent to easily provide the nice and peaceful life I'd longed for my children to have. Lydia would have foreseen these struggles far better than I had.

"And yet, it is. There are dangers in this world, too many to count." I motioned to the window, to the city beyond the palace. "Even in a place like this, we have to be careful, but I will protect you three. There will still be dances, there will still be time to train, and there will always be demand for good prices."

The last thing I wanted was for my children to lose this opportunity to enjoy themselves. They were far too young to get wrapped up in the struggles of the empire and the machinations of a madman.

I took Daka's hand, bending down to meet her distant gaze at eye level. "My little warrior, come back to us. You do not need to be scared. There is nothing in this room but love."

Slowly, far too slowly, she blinked, and I could see the familiar light in her eyes flicker back into being. She gave a weak smile, like those she gave after her nightmares, but it was a welcome recovery.

A light knock at the door came, and I was relieved to notice my children did not flinch at the noise.

"Rakta." Shawn spoke through the slight crack. "I'm ready if they are."

No one was ever truly ready for prophecy, but I would not allow the fear stirred by my enemies to sway my actions. Tonight, I would tell the children of the strings of fate bound around them.

And I would reveal what I knew of Earth.

24

The stories my people had regarding prophecy were not pleasant ones. Most were tales of Ruskans like Shunta the Caller, who had heard of his death due to a mistake of the wind and had fled his responsibilities in leading his people.

He later fell prey to the gray sands that swallowed him whole.

Would my children flee from their prophecy? Would they fear that which bound them? My thoughts lingered on Dalton and his insecurities that I'd become privy to in his moment of weakness.

"Children," I began, my younglings before me and Shawn at my side. "I promised Dalton answers to some very important questions, answers I would be remiss to exclude any of you from hearing."

Daka had focused on Shawn's pale form as he shuffled in. "Are you okay, Uncle Shawn?"

"Oh, well, I'm still recovering." Shawn weakly smiled, shifting as best he could in his seat. I kept my face from showing my discomfort at his words. Recovery for my friend would take a miracle.

None of my children seemed to relax as their uncle's words, but Dalton barely glanced at the conversation, his gaze firmly set on me.

"So you're really going to tell us? How you know we're—" I cut him off with a firm but gentle grabbing of his hands, cradling them as I held his gaze with mine.

"I'm going to tell you everything I know about the three amazing souls that entered my life," I corrected the unuttered words I dared not even consider in my thoughts. "And the burden that I believe will rest on your shoulders for years to come."

Natakia swallowed. "A burden?"

"One that I've thought a great deal about," I said, but I knew I needed to get to the meat of the subject before my audience grew impatient.

And so, I told them and left nothing out. From the fate that Lydia, their mother, had divined from the gods of Derra to my knowledge of Earth, the origin of their souls. Each word that left my lips lessened the burden on my shoulders, but the guilt that replaced it was equally heavy.

Children should not be cursed with the knowledge that their fates have been tangled by the divine. My younglings should have led their lives free of such worries, but there was no telling what the future held. With the attempt on my life in the back of my mind, I knew that I couldn't have answers dying with me.

Shawn's turn of fate had already proven that the new dangers were burgeoning, obscure, and esoteric ones that had no grounding in the reality we knew. I could not have the same faith that my strength would see me through the next few months untouched.

As I finished, I was left in a room of silence. I watched the expressions of my children shift as I explained what I knew, watching fear enter Natakia's gaze and understanding filter through Dalton's. Daka had become distant, almost barely listening it seemed, as I spoke of Earth.

Shawn was the first to speak. "I'm from Earth, as well, but I didn't get sent here as a baby. If you have . . . questions, then I can hopefully answer them."

"I knew it," Dalton said, glancing at his sisters. "Natakia already told me, but to think you've known the whole time . . . That's . . ."

Natakia was entirely focused on me, her nervous eyes almost examining me as if I were a new person. "Dad, this whole time . . . you knew? And you still . . ."

She looked terrified, like the world had become glass around her. Perhaps I should have picked a better time, a better place, but when would the world allow me such mercies? Had it not already taught me to spend the moments I was blessed to have wisely?

All I could do was comfort her and the rest of my younglings, show them that nothing had changed with how I loved them.

I knelt, swallowing hard. "I know this—"

"Wow, you guys are from another world?" Daka's question interrupted me. I slowly turned to her and found that her eyes were still distant but with something harder at the center. "That's bloody amazing."

The room was quiet for a moment as my little warrior's words settled upon us like a fine layer of soot. I glanced at Shawn, and I saw my own concern reflected in his eyes. Was Daka denying her origins? Or perhaps she did not come from Earth?

Dalton had closed his eyes, looking annoyed, but Natakia rounded on her sister, an almost desperate energy as she fiddled with the hem of her dress.

"Daka," Natakia said, in an almost panicked whisper, "stop it! It's time to stop playing pretend, okay? This isn't fun anymore. We could have actually gotten hurt!"

"I'm not playing pretend." Daka smiled, one that almost stung to look at. A bright, joking thing that her eyes turned into a cold mockery.

Natakia grabbed her sister by the shoulders, all grace lost in the moment. "Yes, you are! I've heard you speak English! I've heard you talk about British food! Slang! You're from Earth! Stop lying!"

I moved forward to pull Natakia off of Daka, breaking my daughters off from each other. "Natakia, calm down—"

"No!" My desert flower writhed in my arms, and I didn't have the strength of heart to hold her tight enough to keep her in my grip. "She's lying! All she wants to do is lie and pretend she's different! She's not different!"

Daka's breath hitched at her sister's words, and I felt the tension in the air, laden down already by the threats and illusions of the night, begin to break, and I felt a terrible knot in my stomach suddenly twist into being.

Natakia pointed a finger at Daka. "My name is Emilia, and your name is Geor—"

The sound of wood breaking cracked through the room as my senses suddenly heightened out of instinct, my body tensing, but nothing could have prepared me in time as I watched, almost in crystal clarity, Daka step forward and attack her sister.

A single fist, charged with Vitae that I could almost smell in the air, impacting into the center of my desert flower's nose and knocking the latter half of the name upon her lip away.

Natakia flew backward, hitting the ground hard as blood began to gush from her face, her eyes wide and full of pain as she tried to remember where she was, what had just happened.

And as her first scream of agony broke the silence in the room, I heard the window shatter as Daka erupted out of it, Shawn moving to my daughter's side as I instinctively did the same.

"Daka! No!" My words left my mouth like an afterthought, no good to anyone as I began to try and heal Natakia and stem her bleeding.

A hand grabbed my wrist before I could begin, my eyes turning to Shawn with a vicious protectiveness that had uncoiled from my chest like a viper.

"I'll heal Natakia," he said. "Go make sure Daka is safe."

The rationality of the suggestion struck me dumb for a moment, but thankfully my body was not quite so uncertain. It knew that the blow had been powerful but not deadly.

One nod of the head and a quick whispered word of love to my injured daughter later and I pumped Vitae through my legs, jumping through the window of the palace.

The search for my wayward daughter had begun. As the brisk night air simmered against my hot skin, I knew that this was my fault. I had opened up too much, had been too irresponsible with the truth. How could I have let it get this far?

And yet, I still wasn't sure how I could have done it better. Should I have waited longer before telling them? When they were older and more equipped to deal with the revelation?

Or should I have started younger? Showed them that it was natural to have peculiar origins, to have given them a chance to express how they felt about Earth so as not to bottle them up for ten years?

"Daka! Please, slow down!" The small blur that was my daughter in the distance was barely visible, but I could feel the path she left in the air with her own **Great Wind Sprint Technique**.

Could she even hear me over the wind of her own technique? Did she want to? We had long left the confines of the capital, startling guards and raising alarms throughout as we dashed over the walls and into the countryside.

Daka had attacked Natakia, her own sister. I hated it, I hated what I had pushed my own daughter to do, I hated that I had been unable to protect Natakia from her sister's fear, her desperation. Violence between siblings left a stain, something that could never be washed away.

And it struck a chord too familiar for my liking.

The heaviness of Daka's potent Vitae in the air was like a cold blade against my ribs. Like a young scorpion unable to control its venom, Daka was scared and unstable. While both of us used the same techniques, I had a stronger foundation, and catching her was only a matter of time, but . . .

It would mean nothing if my reward was the corpse of my daughter, drained of life by her own recklessness.

"No." That would not happen, I would not allow that to happen. I landed heavily on the branch of an old and sturdy oak, feeling it's wood cracking under my weight and power.

In swift movements that I could feel my body complain about, I let my Vitae soak into the air around me, and I began to move with the tension in the night wind, the static bouncing between the clouds, all under the watchful eye of the moon.

For that was the way of the **First Dance Stance**.

"**First Dance Technique**." I could feel the energy around me vibrate, wind flowing through my fingers, as I watched my daughter run away to her death. "**Twister Through the Valley**."

The oak I stood upon was rewarded for its aid by being horribly sundered as the wrath of the air around me gathered in a cyclone that soaked into my body, lending me its power, but more importantly, its speed.

I ripped through the air, riding the path left in the wind by Daka, and through the darkness of the night I could see her form now more solidly, her nightwear stained by the leaves and dirt thrown up by the chase and her helmet left back at the palace, leaving her hair a wild mess.

"Daka!" The cyclone around me echoed my words, a monstrous roar that could not be ignored. Her head flew back at me, and I could see the shine in her eyes, the shine of burning Vitae.

In her surprise, her fear, I watched as her foot slipped on a branch and surged forward as my daughter began to shoot toward the ground, unprepared for a landing. Catching her in my arms, tightly hugging her to my chest, I wounded the earth with my landing, breaking the dirt around me as I dug my foot in to stop my momentum.

The cyclone dissipating around me, I breathed heavily with Daka in my arms, a stark relief filling my bones even as fatigue hit me. It had been quite some time since I'd been required to push myself with the **First Dance Stance**, but it was nothing I couldn't handle.

Being tired was worth my daughter being safe and sound any day, keeping her from being alone in this trying moment. She writhed in my grip, fearful, but I just held her in my arms.

"I love you," I said, the strongest words I could find to say. "No matter who you are, who you want to be, you will always be my child, and I will always love you."

I could feel my daughter melt in my arms, her struggling ceasing as she wrapped herself around me. The silence of the clearing after my words was quickly broken as she cried out.

"Dad," Daka sobbed into my chest, gripping at my chest with a desperate strength that quickly faded as she pulled her Vitae back. "I'm Daka. My name is Daka!"

There were times I wished I were a smarter man, perhaps one with the magic words to heal whatever wounds my child had that were beyond my comprehension. I hugged Daka as strongly as I could without hurting her. "And it always will be, to me."

She continued to sob, holding me tightly, and I kept a still vigil in the middle of the shredded clearing as my daughter let loose with all her emotions.

25

Returning to the palace was a simple task marred with uncertainty and questions that I had no answers to, with Daka deep in a torrid sleep within my arms as I carried her back to bed.

It was hard to truly know how long I had given my daughter to spill her heart out as she had done, but by the time I returned to the palace, guards stepping out of my way, I found Shawn standing outside of my children's room.

Our gazes met, and I wondered if Shawn would have done better with these brilliant children of mine. A soul from Earth, as well, perhaps he would have a greater insight into their plights? Unknowing of my thoughts, Shawn looked troubled himself.

"How is Natakia?" I broke the silence between us, the last I'd seen of my desert flower having been her bloodied face on the ground, wailing in pain.

Shawn glanced away, breaking the gaze he'd held with me. "I healed her, but she's upset. And worse, it's obvious that . . . she's scared."

"Scared," I said, a mutter under my breath that did not encapsulate the failure I felt at those words. I gently ran my fingers through the hair of my little warrior. "Scared of Daka?"

Shawn closed his eyes, unable to answer beyond a nod. I considered that for a moment, feeling my chest tighten at the mere thought of two siblings turning against each other due to a mistake in the heat of passion.

"She's with Doh and Macy," Shawn continued before he looked toward the door of the bedroom. "Dalton, he's . . . he's fine. He went to bed after I told him that you'd be handling Daka."

I was relieved that at least one of my children was faring well in the face of tonight's revelations, but Shawn's troubled expression tightened at his own mention of my son.

I stepped closer, making sure that Daka was still sound asleep. "Shawn, is there something wrong?"

"Your son, Rakta." Shawn licked his lips nervously, taking longer than usual to gather his thoughts, but I listened tensely. "Dalton said . . . something that we need to talk about. Come see me after you make sure Natakia is okay, alright?"

Although I pressed him on the matter, Shawn had other responsibilities to attend to after the attack, and so I agreed to find him later.

I couldn't blame him. There was still much to do to evaluate the situation within the palace. I could only be grateful that he'd stayed with my children until I returned despite his royal responsibility.

After putting Daka to bed, tucking her in and making sure she was comfortable, and making sure that Dalton truly had gone to sleep himself, it was time to approach my last concern for the night.

Through the heavy door of Doh's room, I could hear the faint sounds of comforting inside. Was it truly the right time to intrude? Perhaps Natakia needed the more subtle comfort that Doh provided?

"No," I whispered. I could not leave my child unattended after what had happened, not after I had left her side when she'd just been struck. Doh and Shawn had done well, but that did not absolve me of responsibility to my child.

Knocking on the door, the voices inside went quiet, and I spoke through the solid wood. "It's me."

"Rakta?" Doh asked through the door. "Hmm, what monster did Dresden dream up fighting that one time a few years back?"

I heard Dresden give a start through the door at his wife's question, but I answered clearly, "I believe he dreamed of fighting a feathered troll."

Less of a true breed of troll and more like a somewhat common mutation among the foul beasts, there were stories that it was due to remnants of ancient breeding with harpies that showed up every now and then.

With that said, a small click of the lock later and the door opened a crack, Doh glancing around through the slit. "Rakta, hey, sorry. Just a little on edge with this whole illusion magic going around. You can't trust a thing!"

Perhaps another time, another place, I'd say a few teasing words to a shape changer worried about trusting what they can see, but the severity of the night had left me little spirit for amusement.

"We'll have to handle this illusionist, yes," I said, none too happy about their role in all of this, but I quickly focused on my true goal. "Natakia, is she here?"

Nodding, Doh opened the door for me and let me inside. The room was nice and, much like my own and my children's, had a door that opened into a conjoined hallway leading to an adjoining room for Macy.

And there, upon the floor and with her back against the wall, Macy quietly beside her and trying to comfort her in ways only a friend could, was my desert flower, Natakia, looking down into the reflection of her silver mirror.

I was struck dumb by the stains of tears upon her cheeks, the remnants of blood on her upper lip where she'd been punched. The bruise that would never form on her face still viscerally flashed before my eyes.

Another time, another place, I had seen this before. A darker skin, tanned by the Ruskan sun, but there was a tightness in my chest that arrested me for but a moment, a memory that lined up tragically with this one.

"Natakia." Her name tumbled from my lips in both a call to her as it was to me, a call for me to return to the present. "Natakia, my desert flower . . ."

I knelt down to her, her eyes still low to the floor. She had stiffened at my voice, but I pressed onward, gently taking her hand in my own. I was relieved that she did not pull back from me.

I was unsure what to say. Ask her if she was alright? Ask her if she hated Daka now? And yet, something kept thumping against my chest, something that had struck me in the moment as I left for Daka.

"I'm sorry," I said, holding her hand now in both of my own, hoping to warm her cold fingers in my warm grip. "I'm sorry I left you when you were hurt to go after your sister. I'm sorry I did not protect you when you most needed it, when your sister lashed out in anger and fear."

For a time, the room was quiet. I distantly noticed Macy being pulled away gently by her mother, privacy being allotted to my child and me. A courtesy I had not expected but appreciated.

Eventually, after what felt like hours but could only have been minutes, Natakia finally spoke in a shuddering voice filled with unshed tears.

"Dad, do you . . ." Natakia's head bowed lower as her voice shook. "Do you love . . . Daka more than me?"

I sat down next to her as the weight of the question fell upon me, my mind filled with how utterly I had failed, and yet with this failure I was filled with no grand insight into how I could have done any better.

"No, Natakia." I wrapped an arm around her shoulder and brought her to me, her head falling into the crook of my armpit as her face smooshed into the side of my chest, a fresh wetness from her cheeks staining my tunic. "I . . . I love all of you. Daka, Dalton, and you . . . No matter what, that, I . . . I could never love one of you more than another . . ."

My tongue felt heavy, unsure of what to say to a daughter that doubted my love for her. How did I even begin to confront that? Assuage those feelings?

"You left me," Natakia said, and I could hear the tone of loss in her words. "I was hurt, and . . . and . . . you left to go after Daka . . . who punched me. I . . . why didn't Uncle Shawn go after her? Why weren't you healing me, Dad?"

Try as I might, any words I had failed to realize themselves before Natakia continued, her hands pulling from my grip as she pushed herself away from me, her eyes coming up to finally meet my own.

And in them, I saw sadness quickly curdling into anger.

"I'm smarter this time. I'm prettier this time," Natakia almost growled, gritting her teeth. "So how come I'm not the favorite, huh? Why am I not the one you stick by? Why am I the afterthought? Why am I always the afterthought!?"

She was yelling now, trembling in fear and anger, but had turned her emotions into a bladed edge with which to stab me. My mind was filled with doubt.

Had I favored Daka over the others? Had I truly shared more love and attention with her? There was certainly more I had in common with Daka, but . . . but Natakia . . .

It was a familiar ache in my heart as I remembered that there was someone who could have done this better, who could have made sure that Natakia never had reason to feel this way.

I felt a wetness begin to spill down my cheeks.

Natakia paused, her eyes wide as she stared at me. "Dad? Are you . . . ?"

Pulling my stunned daughter into my lap and against my chest, I cried as I hugged her. "Your mother would have loved you so much, my desert flower."

The words spilled from my lips before I knew if they were the right ones, but I knew they would be true. Every hour I spent training with Daka, every game we played in the forest, would have been an hour spent by Lydia shopping with Natakia, perhaps teaching her the ways of divination.

"I do not know dresses," I admitted, my voice shaking. "I do not know how to spend time with you as Lydia would have. I can only be there for you, support you, and yet, I have failed even in that."

She was quiet against me, but she held me tightly. Tighter than I had ever remembered her hugging me, her face pressed up against my shirt.

"I could not tell if I loved any of you more than the others, Natakia," I said, combing my fingers through her hair, fondly remembering the Lydia I could see in her. "In the same way I would not be able to tell how bright a star was compared to another. My love blinds me to such differences, but in my haste . . . I've hurt you, and I'll never forgive myself."

Natakia looked up at me from the hug, her eyes wetting once more as her anger began faltering. "You're . . . not lying, Dad."

And even as she said this more to herself, I was comforted. I took it desperately, like a drowning man would gulp down air in between the waves of the sea.

As Natakia fell asleep in my arms, I knew in my heart of hearts that this truly only felt like the beginning of more tribulation between my younglings.

The prophecy echoed in my ears. Hours had passed after my children had all been put to bed. I was fearful of what the morning would bring, but hopeful that Daka and Natakia could forgive each other.

Was I sure of why Natakia's had provoked Daka in such a way? No, but I had spent these waking moments where sleep eluded me thinking about the origins of my children.

Not just the knowledge or maturity they possessed, but the scars they must carry upon their otherworldly souls. I knew my children, but I did not know who my children had once been.

And they, those strangers that I loved, I could only imagine that they may hold the answers to the words shared tonight, but in my ignorance, I found no truly satisfying answers.

"Thanks for coming to see me, Rakta." Shawn sighed against his throne, documents in his lap that he'd let fall as I walked into the grand chamber room.

I nodded. "I would have come sooner, but . . . I had much to think about."

There was a silent understanding between us. The night had been little kind to either of us. And yet, Shawn still held on to my son's words with an uncertain energy. I could tell they still weighed on him.

"I won't keep you from your children for long," Shawn continued, "but your son spoke to me when you went after Daka, after Natakia left for Doh's room."

Had my son shared some insight into Earth that Shawn did not know himself? Or perhaps he had noticed a stranger in the halls of the palace, a suspect of the true identity of the illusionist?

"Rakta." Shawn rubbed his cursed wound. "Dalton said that he may know of a way to cure me."

That was not what I had expected.

26

If asked, it would be one of my deepest desires to honestly answer that the palace recovered after the attack, but it would be with a heavy heart that I would have to say otherwise.

The damage done to the structural foundation of the palace had been mostly illusionary, besides a few minor explosives, but the peace that had been broken by the falsified assault could not be put back together so easily.

Common folk and nobles around the empire were now buzzing with a strange energy, the whispers of war on the horizon with the second coming of the Warlock King. For who else, other than a reincarnation of such a vile man, could be behind such a bold attack?

My disagreement with the sentiment set aside, it was an idea that was now bringing new faces to the capital, some I was not looking forward to seeing.

"Dad?" Daka interrupted my thoughts, finishing with her morning exercises. It was the only thing that took her mind off of the events of a few days ago.

I shook my head, smiling as best I could for the sake of my daughter. "It is nothing, Daka. A passing thought merely made me pause."

Finishing up my own routine, I glanced at the surrounding guards that kept themselves a distance from Daka and me as we pushed ourselves in the training field of the palace. Shawn had set some of the most trusted of his rank and file to protect his family and friends.

Still, it did little to calm my worries. Natakia was out with Macy, followed by Doh and Dresden, and accompanied by Tanner, who had promised me he could see through any invisibility if attacked. They were preparing for the Rose Gala at some local perfume shops.

Natakia had been distant and had barely spoken to Daka since the troubling incident between the two of them. Daka had tried to apologize, but it seemed my little warrior had been deserted of all her confidence recently . . .

"Ha." Daka side kicked the training dummy that she was intent on making the victim of her latest technique, something she'd picked up from a local brawler that had been training here earlier. **"Lock Kick Technique!"**

As the dummy creaked under the force of the blow, I watched as I finished my final push up, pulling off the weights from my back as I stood up. Daka's nightmares had woken her every night since the palace was attacked, but now she seemed to throw herself into training instead of talking about it.

It was all I could do to keep teaching her and making sure she wouldn't hurt herself until she was ready to speak about it to somebody.

"Alright, what next?" Daka was voracious, consuming lesson after lesson, her own axe dangling off of her side as she'd brought it out for training.

I nodded. "We're going to be doing some throwing exercises to warm you up to the methods behind properly throwing one, and then we'll be doing some training regarding a few of my own stances."

"Easy peasy!" Daka got straight into it, not wasting a second as she began to follow my examples and lessons.

And so it went, exercise after exercise, teaching my daughter all that I could without feeling like I was giving her too much to digest at once, nor did I wish to give her anything that she could possibly hurt herself with.

As she worked to polish her own techniques, those that she wished to master, I began my own exercising up until my daughter came by, impatience on her face.

"Done with exercises, Dad?" Daka came over, an eager smile on her face. "I wanna spar!"

Mopping up some of my sweat with a small towel, I threw it aside and nodded. "Let's start with general enhancement first, Daka. Then we can spar with techniques."

As I began to spar with Daka, my thoughts once again turned to other things. Dalton was with Penelope, speaking with her about local merchants while he began to set up his business here. His initiative had impressed his aunt, but she'd declined to help him too much.

She was always about building things up with her own two hands, something I was sure had not been a part of the curriculum as an Iriend. It was, like all houses within the empire, ruled by nepotism.

"Ha!" I dodged as Daka flew by me with a straight kick, grabbing her by her extended arm and swinging her back to her starting point.

She huffed, straightening her leather helmet. "Dad! You're just standing in one spot again!"

"I am a mountain, Daka," I said, mirthfully. "I will not simply move from a breeze."

Her face squished up into an annoyed squint before she smiled impishly. "This breeze is gonna trip you up!"

For a moment, I could forget about how distant my children were with one another right now. I could smile and laugh with my little warrior, and it gave me hope that I could do the same with my other younglings soon.

"The academics aren't sure about how to implement Dalton's idea," Shawn said, leaning back in his chair as we spoke privately in his royal office.

I scratched the back of my head. "I can sympathize. I have no doubt about my son's aptitude, but for a method that can be simplified down to 'cut it out,' well, I'm not sure how to either."

When Shawn had first spoken to me about the plan, I was optimistic. Any chance of curing my friend of his deadly ailment was, well, a balm on my soul. I wouldn't wish this affliction on anyone, certainly not one of my most trusted friends.

"It's more complicated than that," Shawn said. "Honestly, it isn't a bad idea. Back on Earth, we do something similar for cancer. It's a, well, it's nasty. I hadn't considered the method myself, but if we treat this thing as something . . . living, then if we find what can kill it, we might be able to do so and cut it out."

I gave him an uncomfortable glance. The problem with this plan, we both knew, was that currently we weren't sure how to kill the thing inside of Shawn without killing him as well.

"We'd need a natural poison, strong enough to kill it, but not empowered by Mana or Vitae," I said. "Then, we'd also need a way to localize the poison or some other way of keeping you alive. Furthermore, we have no way of knowing how this thing inside you will react."

There was a particular cactus flower in Rusk that could be used in a paralytic tea, but that was the extent of my knowledge of deadly admixtures except for a few rare species of scorpions.

"Yeah," Shawn said, "my scholars are trying to subtly put out words for some alchemists in the area, but I'm having difficulties trusting anyone or anything right now. The illusionist could be anywhere."

I looked away, feeling some emotion of my own welling up at the thought of the perpetrator of the palace attack. Could I blame them for Daka and Natakia's fight? Perhaps not easily, but it certainly made me feel better to try.

"Have your guards found anything yet?" I asked, not expecting much with such a sly character behind all of this.

He shook his head. "Nothing. Interrogating the captured invaders involved currently has us on a wild-goose chase. Penelope is trying to develop an anti-illusion device, but . . ."

He trailed off, unsure of how to finish his sentence. Penelope had been busy, very busy, and constantly pressuring her to create new answers to the myriad of problems Zactrik employed only furthered that pressure.

I wondered if he had ever considered how much easier this would be if Lydia was here. The illusionist would have never even gotten close to the palace without her knowing about them.

"In other news," Shawn said, breaking up the silence that had grown between us, "I heard that you have a guest coming."

I sighed, not wishing to think about that. It had taken me off guard, actually, to hear from him after so long. Even with the visits the children and I made, we had rarely seen him or heard about him. The other Velbruns were very hush-hush about his whereabouts, but I could only guess as to why.

"Yes," I said. "Markus Velbrun is coming to the capital and has asked for a meeting."

And no matter the genial words in his letter, I doubted that he simply wanted to meet his nieces and nephew. He'd never been a familial individual beyond his sister and brother.

"Do you think it is about House Tribus?" Shawn tilted his head, speaking of his plan to install me as the high lord of a new house. "The council meeting for that is soon, a week or so after the Rose Gala."

The implication was clear. I had little time to fully accept the raiments of the new position that Shawn had thrust upon me. It was not a comfortable feeling, being rushed.

"Perhaps, perhaps not," I said, my head ticking with any other sort of news that would be important enough for such a change. "After so long, I fear that Markus only brings ill omens with him."

With that said, a knock came at the door, with the queen calling out for Shawn. He'd barely had time for his family recently, especially with the extra protections layered throughout the palace, so I bid him farewell and let them speak alone.

Gathering my children was not a difficult task, per se, but it was truly a challenge not to broach the tension among them as we walked to the nearby Velbrun estate beyond the palace walls.

Tanner was with us, his sharp eyes keeping watch alongside my own and Daka's, although my daughter's suspicious gaze certainly did not exclude our dragon-blooded Protector. The group of guards surrounding us kept the surrounding crowd of peasantry at bay, but I still doubted their worth in the face of an assassin meant for me.

Natakia and Daka stood on either side of me, away from each other and barely acknowledging the other's presence, with Dalton deep within his own writings even as we walked.

"Dalton, how are your plans for the shop coming along?" It was an easy question, having not heard yet about what aid Penelope ended up providing him.

Dalton barely looked up from his journal. "A man by the name of Frant John has been hired to work the shop while I'm away, and Aunt Penelope has given me a few leads on deals to follow up with."

He paused, mid-stroke of his pen, before he shook his head.

"She wouldn't give me the discounts I wanted," he said, obviously annoyed. "Still, nothing I can't deal with by going through with my rental plans. For every noble, there's an upper-middle-class peasant that wants their abode to look more noble for a fee every month."

He muttered something about differing cultures and needing to integrate subscription as a payment model within the area, but I wasn't entirely sure what he meant by it. Perhaps something from Earth?

Nodding, I smiled. "I'm glad you're so invested in the shop. I think you'll go very far, Dalton."

My son glanced up at me from his journal, a strange look in his eyes, before he looked away without betraying anything else on his face.

"And what about you, Natakia?" I turned to my desert flower. "How did the perfume shopping go?"

She lightly sniffed, looking away from me without letting go of my hand as we walked. "You would know if you came along, Dad."

I felt a sting in my heart at the unfairness of the remark. I had offered to go, but Natakia had recently been reluctant to have me along, even as I made an effort to do more things with her. Doh said she was just in a mood, but it felt like my efforts to reconnect with my daughter seemed to push her away more than they helped.

Perhaps she did not think my attempts were genuine? The words she had spoken to me that night—I wish I had had a better response to them.

"You will look grand at the Rose Gala, Natakia," I said, gently rubbing the back of her palm with my thumb. "I hope you will still allow me to walk you in."

Natakia didn't spare me a glance as Dalton had, but she nodded and spoke with a softness that belied its fragility. "Of course I want you to walk me in, Dad."

I glanced at Daka, but she seemed to be dutifully watching out for dangers, a glint of fear in her eyes as she watched every peasant and noble that shuffled around us. It hurt to see my young daughter looking at the world around her in such a way.

Before I could calm her worries, we reached the Velbrun's capital estate. Ten years had added more gray to Markus's hair than it had to my own. That was the first thing I thought as he opened the doors to House Velbrun's capital estate.

Draped in the colors of his house, albeit with more finery than I had last seen him in, Markus' attire marked him as one with higher favor within House Velbrun, but I supposed it was inevitable that Markus would rise throughout the ranks of his house.

"Rakta, it's been a while." Markus smiled.

As my children observed the man that, by blood, was their uncle, I stepped forward to greet him, albeit with an uncertain energy making my hands twitch at the sight of that smile. "Hello, Markus, it's been quite some time, yes."

He squinted at me, looking me up and down, before his gaze went to my children. I tensed, remembering his frequent attempts to steal away my younglings for the high lords of Velbrun.

"And you three are Lydia's children." Markus's words were warm and made me even warier. Perhaps he truly had grown some sort of familial love for them in his time away?

Instinctively, I doubted that. Daka and Dalton didn't seem too keen on the man, although Dalton certainly had a glint of interest in his gaze. Natakia, however, she held my hand even tighter as she eyed her uncle.

Watching us for a moment longer than I found comfortable, Markus motioned us inside. "Come, we have much to discuss."

Led inside, I wasted little time in getting to the root of the matter, distinctly unconvinced by the welcoming demeanor of the man before me.

"Why have you asked us to come here, Markus?" I looked around the halls for any assassins or nefarious traps. "Or has ten years truly changed you so much that this is indeed a simple family visit and nothing more?"

Markus stopped leading us outside of what looked like a dining room, making me tense once more and begin fluctuating my Vitae in response to any attack. And yet, he simply gave a great sigh.

"Ten years? No, I don't suppose time would have ever enlightened me," he said, looking over his shoulder back at me with an unexpected softness to his gaze. "I changed for the same reason you did, Rakta."

Before I could even begin to decipher his meaning, Markus glanced inside the room he led us to and smiled. "And yet, perhaps it's best to show you."

As if taking his words as a cue, I could hear the soft footfalls clicking against the estate's floors as a child walked out of the dining room and joined Markus's side.

Wearing a beautiful silver dress that ruffled gently against her alabaster skin was a young girl, perhaps the same age as my own children, with eyes like polished sapphires and a face that felt distinctly familiar and dangerous.

Daka's and Natakia's grips on my hands tightened immeasurably as even Dalton seemed to sense something strange about the girl before us.

"My name is Esmeralda Velbrun," the young girl smiled as she curtsied to us all. "It is a pleasure to meet all of you."

27

The name cracked through me like lightning. For a brief moment, I could hear the cackles of an inhuman monster in the back of my mind, the echoes of a perversion of my late wife's voice.

The familiarity that had tugged at me at the very sight of this child now sharply trod upon my heart with soles of iron as I realized that this was no simple child. I could see the traces of Lydia in her face, each scrap of my late wife almost amplified to an almost outlandish degree.

I pulled my children back behind me, feeling my heart beat against my chest as I kept my eyes on her. "Markus, what have you done? What is this supposed to be?"

Markus narrowed his gaze, walking up alongside Esmeralda as he placed a hand on her shoulder, the monster in the shape of a young child looking dour at my response.

"Rakta, there is no need to be so troubled by a child." Markus gestured to the young girl at his side. "I promise that any danger you fear from my daughter comes from a place of misunderstanding."

Misunderstanding? Ten years may have dulled my memory, but there was an absolute clarity within my mind that there had been no misunderstanding in regard to this thing. She had attacked us like a wild animal, had killed the entirety of that village . . .

Every passing second spent near Esmeralda made me more and more aware of how close my children were and how very fast she had been the last time we'd fought. And yet, she didn't move, almost didn't even breathe from what I could see. She simply watched me as Markus gauged my movements.

"Then tell me," I said, ready to grab all my children and run, the Vitae churning in my limbs threatening to burst at a moment's notice. "What is this? You must know who this is."

Or perhaps he didn't. Perhaps he was ensorcelled or had gone mad. Or, if Esmeralda was truly an agent of Zactrik, perhaps this was all an elaborate assassination attempt? I could not doubt a Velbrun would join the madman in his warpath against common decency and humanity.

Markus moved in front of his daughter, as if she were the one in need of protection here. "I understand that this is an unsettling introduction, but I promise there is no ill will here."

Natakia barely relaxed in my arms, but both Dalton and Daka stayed as tense as they were since the young creature's introduction. Daka in particular, I could feel, was ready to burst from my arms and . . .

No, the very idea of Daka fighting Esmeralda was a frightening one. We had barely managed to defeat her last time, with even our greatest efforts proving fruitless if the one standing here truly was the same monster. Daka wouldn't have a chance.

"Then have her leave," I said, brooking no argument with my voice. "I will not ignore this threat for what it is on the pretense of good faith. I will hear you out, but not while I believe my children are in danger."

"They are not in danger, you . . ." Markus shook his head, sighing as if he were the one being slighted here. The sheer self-centeredness, to impose upon me with such a troubling revelation as this.

He turned to the child behind him and knelt down to her, brushing a stray curl of hair back behind her ear. "Esmeralda, dear, I need to speak with your uncle alone for a moment and clear up some details, alright?"

The tenderness with which he spoke to the girl would have been oddly nice to see coming from a man as cold as I remembered Markus Velbrun. And yet, as his supposed daughter gave a sad little smile and nodded before she turned around and walked off, I was filled with little else but uncertainty.

As she left, I was at least relieved to feel my children begin to calm down, with Daka relaxing her muscles and Dalton now lightly pulling at my arm around him, trying to get free.

Natakia herself surprised me with her boldness as she spoke up. "That girl isn't human."

Markus's gaze snapped to her, filled with a familiar coldness that I was much more accepting of in this current situation. "I'm sure that there are plenty who would say the same about you regarding your heritage."

She flinched back, and even I found myself surprised at the intensity of the barb, but that did nothing to sway me as I pulled her closer to me and met Markus's stare with my own.

"Speak carefully, Markus," I said, less than pleased about every aspect of this. "I'd save your words for the explanation that I'll be taking back to the king after this is all said and done."

After a moment, my brother-in-law relaxed and gestured to a different room. "I'd hoped to discuss this over some food, but follow me to the tea room. There, I'll tell you everything you want to know about Esmeralda, who and what she is, and how we've come to help with Zactrik."

Truly, I wished Lydia were here right now. If only to save me from the headache and heartache her family so often caused me. With my children sitting comfortably in the tea room's chairs, with Dalton appraising them with a glint in his eye, I myself sat across from Markus, having declined any refreshment until the tale had been woven.

"I found Esmeralda half-dead, or rather, her trace memories of Lydia led her to me," he said, swishing some wine in a glass that he had poured himself. "I, well, I can't say if it was compassion or something else that motivated me in that moment, but I took her in."

I was going to need a little more detail, but as he met my gaze I could at least recognize that he'd realized that himself. All my children were listening intently at this point as well. Although I had never spoken to them about the fight with Esmeralda in detail, I'd mentioned a horrible shape-shifting monster before.

"I quickly found that she fed on Vitae and Mana," Markus continued, "but not only that, she also was haphazardly stitching herself together with the memories and thoughts that she derived from them."

That would, at the very least, explain her abject insanity. I was still unclear about where the fascination she had with me had come from, but I supposed that was not the main point here.

Markus looked out a nearby window, taking a sip from his drink. "She was unstable, both physically and mentally. Some days, she thought she was Lydia. Those were the . . . easier days. And so, I began to care for her and slowly feed her a steady supply of Mana and Vitae from *ethical* sources."

He stressed the word *ethical*, and yet I still had my doubts. However, I wasn't keen to interrupt him just yet.

"She spoke of a ritual, called herself a mistake, but as the months went on, she began to . . . stabilize," he said. "I taught Esmeralda how to compartmentalize, how to structure her mind, to meditate on the strange energy that makes her up, and eventually, she started to become more than simple scraps of memories."

For the first time, I spoke up. "And she spoke of us? Zactrik? The path of carnage she wove through the empire's countryside?"

"Yes," Markus said, as if he were agreeing with the sentiment that the sky was blue. "That and more. He attacked her, you know, after she managed to escape your attack on her. Zactrik is what left her in such a horrid state, not so much you."

"You do not care about her crimes?" I frowned, filing away that little tidbit for another time and promising myself to ask more about Zactrik later.

Markus gave a little chuckle. "Not really, no. By the time she was sane enough to even begin telling me about all that she'd done, I knew it didn't matter. She'd long since ceased being a mere replacement for my sister."

I watched him for a time, the affection in his eyes. Unless he had been truly enchanted or ensorcelled, there was little explanation for the change in the man before beyond a true parental love for Esmeralda.

"And so, you've come to help with Zactrik," I said, unsure of how to feel about Markus's apparent change of heart. "How and why?"

Markus put down his glass, frowning as I said the name of the madman. "Raising Esmeralda in secret these past ten years has made me an expert on the fundamentals of what she is, of what Zactrik is."

From his robes, he pulled out a collection of files, tucked neatly together, before placing them on the table and pushing them over to me.

"Take these. I'm sure a brighter mind will be able to make more sense of them than you," he said, seemingly unchanged on his personal opinion of me.

That said, Penelope would be happy to have more information.

"And why?" Markus smiled. "Is that even a question? Zactrik represents a great threat to the empire, of which I am sworn as a royal denizen to defend with honor and bravery."

"That's not it."

I blinked, glancing at Natakia who was staring at Markus with eyes like daggers. He turned to her, not letting his surprise at the interruption take root in his expression, but I could read a man fairly well these days.

"You want to take revenge on Zactrik for hurting Esmeralda. You want to prove you're better than Dad to Esmeralda by taking Zactrik down yourself," Natakia said with cold confidence. "You want to be the hero that takes him down or maybe even use his findings to make you strong like Esmeralda. You don't give a shit about the empire, my lord."

Markus and my daughter stared at each other for a moment before she reached over to me. I took the cue, holding her cold hand in my grip, as I turned to him with a frown.

"I trust my daughter's insights," I said, fully committed to my child's words. "Thank you for your information, but if that is all, I believe this visit is over."

Ignoring Markus's choked response, I stood up, followed by Natakia. Dalton and Daka were quickly by my side, as well, although Dalton couldn't keep his eyes off of his uncle, with Daka the same, albeit with more anger in her gaze.

Hugging Natakia to my side, I began to walk out of the tea room before Markus called to me. "Rakta, believe me or not, but do not take that information lightly."

I turned to him, my gaze flickering around in case of an attack. "Brighter minds will judge it fairly."

"Just"—Markus swallowed hard, for the first time looking frazzled—"please, understand that Esmeralda is different now. I am . . . better, and so is she. I know what I want . . . But her safety comes first."

Watching him for a moment, I glanced down at Natakia, who met my gaze with a single nod. That was more than enough proof to me that his words, in this regard, were true.

With that, my family and I left the estate and didn't look back.

"Dad," Daka said, as we left the vicinity of the Velbrun grounds, her voice fearful and slightly mystified. "That girl didn't have any Vitae at all . . ."

I simply kept my children closer, counting down the steps until we once again reached the safety of the palace, away from the monster that had taken my wife's form and the noble that sought to protect her.

"So, was Markus's information worth the scare to my children?" I asked, still a little sour about how my brother-in-law had decided to introduce his daughter to us.

It had been three days since my visit to the Velbrun's capital estate, and I had managed to finally speak to Penelope after she'd had time to look over the findings that Markus had provided.

No one had taken the news of Esmeralda's survival well, albeit Shawn had decided that attacking and imprisoning her and Markus would only create a new enemy. Instead, he had spoken to them himself.

I was still unaware of how that conversation had gone, but Markus walked free with Esmeralda, who was currently a volunteer in a series of experiments that Penelope would be overseeing in the next few weeks.

Penelope cracked an eye open, turning on her office lamp as her hourly mininap came to a close. "Yes, yes, I . . . I, honestly, I don't believe we'd have ever come to some of these conclusions on our own."

That was a relief, but my heart wouldn't rest until I'd heard more. A part of me was uncomfortable with interrupting Penelope's complex and, in my opinion, overly complicated sleep pattern, but the topic was of too great a concern.

"And what conclusions have you made?" I asked. "What kind of horror is Zactrik?"

Slipping out of her resting chair and slinking back over to behind her desk, Penelope, I could tell, was gathering her thoughts as she began to flip through the documents, both her own and those provided by Markus.

Eventually, she laid the documents down and met my gaze with a seriousness that I respected by turning all my attention upon her.

"He's undead; that's the simple answer," she said.

Undead? Necromancy was considered taboo in some corners of the world, but it was still an art that was founded upon Mana, enchanting cadavers to move at the whims of the mage.

Seeing my confusion, Penelope continued. "Like I said, that's the simple answer. What we know of as undead is simple puppetry, but this . . . Whatever Zactrik did is something beyond that, beyond living."

That matched more appropriately with the horror that seemed to follow Zactrik in his trails.

"Mana and Vitae," she said, taking on a lecturing tone. "These, along with Primus, are living energies. The living produce them, use them. Some scholars believe that everything in life is made up of these energies on a foundational level."

Penelope's tone grew more severe as she picked up one of the documents, and I could read the exhaustion and trepidation on her face as she spoke.

"Whatever Zactrik did to himself, what Esmeralda did to herself, they generated something new," she said. "It's something the dead produce, something that feeds on the energy of the living and corrupts it and grows. The few scholars I've shared this with have taken to calling it death energy."

I felt coldness blossom in my heart at the very idea of it, something so monstrous being introduced into the world that my children lived in.

"Markus called it Mortum in his notes," she finished, worn out from revisiting it herself.

With so much to think about, I thanked Penelope for her time and apologized for interrupting her sleep before taking my leave. It was a heavy weight to carry, but perhaps this was the price of knowledge.

It was one more step toward finally taking Zactrik down.

However, for now, I could not think of such things. I must tuck away such dark thoughts as tomorrow brought something else upon the horizon.

The dawn of the Rose Gala.

NOON INTERLUDE: NATAKIA VELBRUN

My love, for too long we have been kept separate by the scheming of my parents," Prince Kerns said, his voice breaking from the sheer emotion weighing upon the words.

Princess Arete, excitement blazing in her gaze, smiled. "I have ever thought the same, my prince. For too long the world has gotten between us."

"From now on"—the prince took his beloved's chin within his fingers—"you are my world."

And they kissed, the visual novel sprites fading into one of the twenty different CGI endings that A Fallen Kingdom *had, with Princess Arete failing to build her kingdom back, but having a high enough relationship level with Prince Kerns to enter into a relationship.*

"If a pretty girl looked at me like Prince Kerns did, I'd be okay with being a failure too," I said, finally rolling out of bed, feeling heavy and disgusting, but that was fine. I was fine.

My room was darkened, the beads of light from outside barely squeezing inside through the cracks of my shades. I felt sweaty, but I wasn't interested in taking a shower right now.

Mom was having a little gathering later today. Allassandra was already on her way. She'd just gotten back from some big shoot in Hawaii, so she was expected to brighten things up with some fun stories.

I, in comparison, was expected to stay in my room and keep the noise to a minimum. Not that I made much noise anyway, but sometimes I liked to watch Mom's parties from the stairs, listen to them make small talk like royalty.

"Maybe if Allie doesn't make it back from Hawaii, Mom will ask me to come down and talk about all the cool stuff I do," I said, glumly looking back at my game.

Forgetting why I had even bothered getting out of bed, I fell back under the covers and got comfortable with my game. I could eat later, maybe when Allie brought me something from the party.

Distantly, I heard the echoing music of my mother's phone going off.

A few moments later, the relative quiet of the house was broken by her screaming.

I looked so cute in this dress. It's beautiful trail falling behind me as I walked, each step followed by my adorable floating mirror that seemed to know each of my best sides. A great distraction from the nugget of worry in my stomach.

As the grand doors opened to the main chamber of the Iriend estate, I tightened my grip around the large, warm hand of my father, feeling the world realign itself after so many days of assassinations, of danger, of things that should exist in the background.

The smell of fresh flowers, picked this morning, of the soft, warm scent of pastries and confections, all for me and the other ladies of the gala. Not that I would be tasting them beyond a few princess bites.

The Rose Gala. I was finally here. My very own debut, the first step I would take in this beautiful fantasy paradise as a recognized lady of my royal standings. Of course, I was of strange origins. Dad wasn't exactly a typical noble, but that just made my story more interesting.

Interesting in a good way, of course. A nice, peaceful interesting filled with intrigue and gossip rather than weapons and bloodshed. A kind of interesting that suited a princess.

"You look beautiful, my desert flower." Dad's warm words calmed the anxiety in my heart as I glanced up at him, forcing myself not to stare too long at any of the nearby corners.

'Rakta Velbrun. Your father. Loves you, wants the best for you. Hoping today makes up for his failure to make you feel loved. Trying not to embarrass you in front of the other young ladies.'

The whispers that the wind carried to me warmed me up even more.

I knew he loved me; he loved all of us. He just didn't love us equally all the time.

And yet, today was my day.

"Thank you, Dad." I smiled up at him. "I'm glad you're walking me in."

I could feel his relief and see it with the help of the whispers. I was glad that he felt guilty. That was ultimately what proved he still cared about me, that he wouldn't abandon me.

As we entered the chamber, nearly two dozen other young ladies of similar ages to me turned to look at us, each of them dressed in pretty little ensembles that their parents had gotten for them. Blonde, brunette, some wilder colors that certainly couldn't have been natural on Earth . . .

A small glance at my mirror for a quick comparison and I was reassured that no one here was prettier than me. And certainly, none of them had prepared for this day as much as I had.

All eyes were on me, and I was going to pick each and every one of them apart.

Sometimes with how pale I was, I forgot I had the same Hispanic heritage as my sister. Her skin was like cream; mine was like a cracked yellow sidewalk that had been bleached by the sun.

That, of course, was what my mind decided to focus on as I stared down at her dead body, her face a serene smile that somehow managed to look smug and superior even at her own wake. Like she was basking in the glow of having so many people here mourning her.

Drunk at the wheel, the police had said. Apparently Allie had gotten a little sauced on the flight over and had driven straight off a cliff. Only fifteen minutes away from the house.

"Why? What did I do, oh lord!? Why have you taken my baby from me!?" Mom wasn't taking it very well, down on her knees and hugging the casket.

"You still have me, Mom," I wanted to say, down on my knees right beside her. Tears would be in my eyes, and I would magically become pretty and outgoing and everything else Mom loved about Allie.

Or, more realistically, she'd start crying harder. Hell, I wasn't even sure I could cry right now. The only thing I felt was this numbness in my head that had been growing since I'd heard the news.

Scientists always talk about how the moon's glow was just a reflection of the sun's light. I guess when the sun dies, the moon just becomes a dark, cold rock that everyone gives even less of a shit about.

My stomach rumbled, breaking up my thoughts. I hadn't eaten much since the news broke.

"Oh, Martina." One of Mom's friends comforted her on the floor, more tears in her voice than in my entire body. "No one should have to lose their only child like this. Oh, you poor thing."

Only child? I blinked, walking away from the casket and back over to the corner in the room. It felt weird, so many people in one room, one of them my own mother, and no one batted an eye as I retreated.

No, it wasn't weird. Allie was here, and no one ever paid me attention when she was around except, well, her. She was dead, though, dead and soon six feet in the ground.

I saw myself for a moment, like I was someone else. I was short, where Allie was tall. I was sickly, while Allie was healthy. I was awkward, but Allie was confident.

I was alive. She wasn't.

How hard could it be to replace a dead girl?

Watching Macy walk in with Doh was only slightly less breathtaking than my own entrance. In her beautiful dress and her cute deep-black eyes, my best friend looked happy as her mom walked her in.

If I hadn't had Dad walk me in, Doh was my second choice too. Although, I would've hated stealing her away from Macy. Speaking of Dad, he had stepped away to join the other parents on a nearby balcony overlooking the gala, mentioning that Aunt Penny was up there and they had business to discuss.

'Wants to stop the kingdom being destroyed. Trying to keep you and the others safe. Learned something recently that has terrified him, but doesn't want to ruin your day by letting his fear show.'

Things that didn't concern me, no matter what a prophecy said. Dad and the others were the heroes of the story. They'd keep me safe and sound.

And I didn't need any distractions as Macy walked over to me, her head held high just like I showed her, her walk barely making any noise. She was just naturally quiet, which I rather thought suited her.

'Macy Dresden. Your best friend. Very happy that you brought her.

Trying to walk like you showed her. Wondering why that girl walking up to you looks so angry.'

Hmm?

I turned to the side, making sure I looked properly dismissive as I smiled at the approaching Lady Annabella Iriend, holding up the ends of her dress as she made a path through the other gathered ladies, a duo of unfamiliar girls following behind her.

'Lady Annabella Iriend. Remembers you. Going to show you your proper place. Going to ruin the Rose Gala for you. Almost didn't come out of embarrassment. Older sister talked her into coming.'

"Oh, Lady Iriend." I smiled as gently as I could, going for a curtsy. "I was hopi—"

As expected, Annabella interrupted me, her hands shaking as she ground her teeth behind a demure smile. "I'm surprised to see you here, Lady Velbrun."

I blinked, wondering where she was going with that kind of introduction. The whispers reached out, and I heard a torrent of words as I glanced at her retinue.

One was a piggish-nosed girl with a figure that would better be described using circles and squares than any more sophisticated descriptions. Mannish shoulders, far too much of a slouch in her gait.

'Lady Uriel Kire. Hates you due to your heritage. She thinks you're going to take out a knife and attack someone at any second. Is scared you'll hurt her. Is glad that Annabella is taking the lead.'

The other girl was smaller, glasses dangling from chains that wrapped around her ears, with plenty of seashell adornments upon her sea-colored dress. As beautiful as it was childishly themed.

'Lady Hope Taine. Heard that Annabella humiliated you last time and made you cry. Wants to stick close to whoever is the most politically powerful. Recently lost her pet fish.'

Ah, so that was her game? A move worthy of a C-tier beginner court rival, but that was all it was. I'd seen better attempts from the academy children at boastful lying and bullying.

"Oh, why so?" I smiled, tilting my head, looking over to the two other young girls in welcome. "Lady Uriel Kire, Lady Hope Taine, I'm glad to finally meet my peers."

At this point, Macy had made it to my side, easing a part of me that I hadn't realized was getting a little worried about being ganged up on. My best friend was a balm on the little bits of useless anxiety I could feel bubbling up in my fingertips.

Both of her retinue blinking as they were so readily recognized, Annabella frowned, which was more like a polite scowl. "After our discussion at the dress shop, I was rather expecting you to skip the gala altogether."

"I seem to remember being quite excited to see you again, actually," I said, giving her my full attention. "You must have misunderstood through all those tears in your eyes after we spoke about your sister."

The poor young Lady Iriend flinched, looking caught off guard by the blatant mention of her own weakness, of how fucking useless she was without her sister to guide her.

'Wants to impress her friends. Wants to impress her sister. Thought last time was a fluke. Thought she was better than you. Thought she could humiliate you easily.'

"I wonder," I said, pouncing onto the silence, "is she up there on the balcony? Watching you come over here and play at being a proper member of noble society? Or did she even bother coming?"

Annabelle froze, her eyes glancing up to where I knew with self-assured confidence that my father was standing, always proud of me.

'Knows that her sister isn't here.'

I leaned in closer, almost stage-whispering, "I thought not. Next time, apologize, or I won't even acknowledge you by name."

With that, I daintily weaved my fingers through Macy's hand and smiled at the other ladies as we made our way to some of the empty seats of the various tables, plenty of noble ladies just waiting to be befriended.

Life was so easy when you were pretty.

No matter how little I ate, no matter how much I got outside, nothing I did would ever be enough. That was what I realized as I sat alone once more at the dinner table, a single candle lit just for me by one of the servants.

Mom was gone, having left on a retreat yesterday. She'd refused to take me with her, no matter how much I wanted to go. She said a lot of things to me, a lot of things she didn't need to say.

I think she just wanted to.

"Thank you for the meal." I finally remembered to thank the chef, but I was pretty sure she couldn't hear me at this point. It was a nice meal, smelled and looked good. Something with chicken? It was hard to focus on the specifics, but it was a pleasant-looking meal.

It made me sick. Just thinking of eating, of wasting all the work I put into being there for Mom, of being loved. I'd spent months trying to lose weight, but I was never skinny enough. Fasting, purging, protein shakes, exercising until I wanted to die—nothing was enough.

If I started eating, I might not be able to stop.

My online friends said I needed help when I'd told them what I was trying to do, who I was trying to be. I opened up to them, the only ones I had, and they thought I was crazy for trying to be someone I wasn't.

I didn't talk to my friends anymore. Best part about removing online friends? They can't bother you if you block them. They can't tell you that you aren't meant to be anything other than a freak.

Popular, loved, the girl in the spotlight. Not for Emilia. Those spots could never be filled by an ugly girl like Emilia. I'd give anything to be beautiful, to be at the top of the world like Allie.

Mom had yelled at me when I'd tried one of Allie's old dresses on. I didn't blame her. I'd looked at myself in the mirror just before she caught me and barely kept myself from throwing up.

I was so hungry. I could probably take a few bites, maybe even eat the whole dinner if I tried. If I felt bloated later, I could just deal with it then.

And then . . . I didn't know what came after that. I felt so cold. Just like the moon would when the sun went out. There would be no more light, no more warmth. Just a craggy surface that the people of Earth decided to visit a total of six times and then decided to never set foot on it again.

My eyes caught on the lit candle. In a daze, I watched the flame, the only warmth in the room. It danced, free of care or concern. Just like the sun, people loved it and feared it.

I wanted that so much. So, so much.

But the sun was gone now, and the moon was just overstaying her welcome.

I decided to eat after all. I'd take it slow and cherish each bite.

* * *

Waking up as a baby in a strange new land, I'd always wondered if this was what heaven actually was. Did everyone get a second chance? Did everyone get to live their dreams out like I was?

Had Allassandra gone on to have her own adventure? Her own prophesied descent into a world of wonder and charm? When I first woken up and watched my new mother die right before my eyes, I thought I was having a nightmare.

Instead, it was a dream. A dream I was still in and never wanted to wake up from.

The last half hour had been filled with everything that I ever wanted out of a gala. Sure, it was for all of us young ladies, but it was easy to wrap each and every one of them around my finger, one small compliment at a time, besides the few that shied away from me and stuck close to Annabella.

I had a table full of gossiping young ladies all around me, each of them glancing at me from time to time, as if making sure I was still paying a modicum of attention to their words.

"Are you okay?" Macy whispered, having allowed me to do the speaking for the both of us, as per usual. "I know you and Daka haven't really—"

"Don't ruin a good time, Macy," I said, a gentle note of warning as I caught my smile in the mirror that floated around me. "Daka is just a brute. Can we really blame her for doing the only thing she knows how to do?"

And I knew how much she hated what she'd done. I could literally hear it through the whispers about her. I could also hear what she thought about Doh, who didn't deserve having such horrid things being thought about her.

Macy didn't answer, but I was feeling a little uncharitable about her bringing up the nonsense with my stupid sister. That said, I still eventually glanced over at her, not able to ignore her silence for long.

'Wants to know what happened with Daka. Enjoying herself. Hoping that she isn't replaced by one of these other girls. Wants to keep you safe. Thinking about Annabella.'

Why was she thinking about that sad girl? I glanced at the young lady in question, her moping figure surrounded by a few of her friends that I hadn't pulled away from her with a few quick words.

"Don't worry, Macy," I said, putting a light hand on her shoulder. "None of these girls could ever mean more to me than you do."

I didn't say it loud enough for said girls to hear me, but she smiled nonetheless, distracted from her errant thoughts. It was wholly the truth too. I couldn't imagine not having Macy by my side, always wanting the best for me. A comforting loyalty that I returned.

"Ah, Lady Natakia Velbrun, what a pleasant surprise." The familiar, smooth voice was like a cup of ice-cold water being splashed across the warmth in my chest.

I turned, and two blazing sapphire eyes, far too close for comfort, stared at me with wide-eyed enthusiasm and delight, the alabaster skin of Esmeralda shimmering underneath her beautiful green-and-gold dress.

"Oh, greetings," I said, feeling my entire body chill as I kept myself from shying back from the horribly insane thing that had tried to kill my father years ago. "I wasn't . . . expecting you here, Lady Velbrun."

The eyes around the table were all on Esmeralda, with Macy taking my hand. She didn't need a cheat ability to notice how nervous I was at the sight of this new girl.

But it really, really wasn't the way that Esmeralda looked that freaked me out.

'Barely holding herself back. Wants so much. Wants to live. Wants to kill Zactrik. Wants to be loved. Wants Rakta.'

The whispers around her were rough and insane. Everything about her was an alarm that kept blaring that I should stay as far away from her as possible, but what could I do here without making a scene?

"Oh, well, getting an invitation was quite fortuitous." She smiled. "Unfortunately, there was some delay in getting here. I hope I haven't missed anything important."

As if to save me from having to answer, a horn sounded throughout the room, signaling that the time for idle socializing was over and it was time for official introductions.

And then I noticed a pair of eyes watching me from the balcony that I did not recognize and screams erupted all around me.

28

In Rusk, the celebrations, my memories of them distant as they were, were often very musical events, with the honored guest of the occasion often the focus of loud recollections and stories shared from person to person about them. For some, it was quite overwhelming to have your life story shared so freely.

And yet, as was often the case, the parties of the Certillian Empire were devoid of such liveliness, with the air filled with only the light, ambient music of distant violins that were nowhere to be seen, and the grumblings and soft whispers of nobility.

"Ah, Lord Velbrun of Gelvurt, I'm glad that you could make it," High Lord Gren Iriend said. "I've heard much about you from Penelope's stories, when she deigns to share them with her family."

I smiled, raising a glass to the host of the gala. "It is a pleasure to be here, High Lord Iriend. I thank you for the invitation; it's truly a gift Natakia will cherish for the rest of her life."

Of course, I doubted that High Lord Iriend had much to do with an invitation being offered to my family, but that did not mean I could get away from withholding any sort of expected gratitude for the man. He had far too much political power for me to treat irreverently, no matter how little I truly respected him.

"Oh, I'm so happy to hear that. It always warms my heart to offer a chance to rub shoulders with capital royalty. Let me know if she ever needs any kind of break from the pressure among so many of her peers." He chuckled good-naturedly, with a touch of condescension.

I doubted Natakia would be the one who needed any sort of break from the gathering down below, but I simply smiled as politely as I had been trained to before taking my leave. The light snub aside, paying respects to High Lord Iriend for hosting the Rose Gala hadn't taken long, and now I simply observed those around me.

"That one seems to have quite the lay of the land already." An older gentleman knocked his glass in the air toward where some of the young ladies down below us were gathered.

A wizened noblewoman raised an eyebrow in the same direction. "I do so hope they aren't gathering around Caryla trying to tell one of her atrocious jokes."

Taking a careful sip of the offered wine, I followed their gazes toward that specific group and felt a welling up of pride as I watched Natakia smile and giggle among her peers. It was nice to see her still manage to smile after the recent difficulties.

It was obvious that she was made for the courts, her young beauty only uplifted by the crafty and cunning mind behind it. On some level, I was worried for her, but I would put that aside for now and merely be grateful for the world's gift to my desert flower.

Perhaps I should go find Doh. She had walked Macy in quite gracefully, and it certainly wouldn't do well to have her be alone if she got a penchant for mischief among all these nobles.

"Rakta?" A familiar voice broke my reverie, and I turned to look as Harriet Pillops approached, adorned in a conservative blue gown that stood in contrast to her usual merchant attire.

For a moment, I was stunned. Not by the dress or the way Harriet looked in makeup, but rather the realization that we had not spoken since the attack on the palace. I'd entirely forgotten that she wanted to speak about something, the memory flashing back with a touch of guilt lacing it.

"Harriet," I said, taking more effort to smile at the woman that had made this moment for my daughter and her friend happen. "I'm sorry I didn't reach out before today. Things I have been . . ."

Harriet giggled, seeming a little nervous. "Busy? I, uh, well, it's been busy for me too."

Busy was a very good word for it while in polite company. I was grateful that she didn't seem to hold my silence against me. Even after so many years of practice, it was still hard sometimes to keep in touch when it mattered most.

Approaching the railing of the overlooking balcony and settling in beside me, Harriet fumbled with a small note in her hand, her eyes glancing around the room, as if checking for something.

"Keeping busy?" I asked, following her gaze to numerous decorations around the room. "You've done a wonderful job preparing the estate for the gala."

"Oh, uh, well Lord Iriend expected a lot from me. You wouldn't, ha, believe how difficult it was to convince him that a, uh, a common merchant could handle the job," Harriet tucked a strand of hair behind her ear, smiling. "He's certainly kept me on my toes. Work, work, work. I don't know if Lord Iriend being an old friend of my father's, uh, helped or hurt, ha ha."

And yet, even as she stumbled over her words and looked at the edge of an accident, I could tell she was in control. Losing her father, having to run each and every one of his businesses—it wasn't something just anyone could do.

"He would be proud, I think." I moved to make sure she didn't trip as one of the roaming nobles bumped into her.

Harriet tilted her head, still glancing at her note from time to time. "Who?"

"Your father," I said, smiling.

She paused for a moment before folding the note and nodding as she gave me her full attention. "I always hoped he would be, one day. Maybe when we meet again, he'll be able to look past how I did things and recognize their worth."

There was a lot of meaning in those words, but it was hard to decipher the complex emotions within them. Merchantry was hard and, if Dalton's own plans were anything to go by, diverse in methodology.

Any words I had to share in response died upon my lip as I noticed a familiar figure moving through the roaming bands of nobles, making idle introductions and chatter as he approached.

"Ah, Lord Rakta Velbrun and the organizer for this gala, Harriet Pillops, I believe." Markus came up, a glass of wine already in his hand. "I'm sorry for being late. Troubles with the carriage, unfortunately."

Harriet blinked, looking surprised to see Markus. "Oh, uh, carriage trouble, Lord Velbrun? I'm, well, I'm glad to see that you made it."

"I'm glad as well." Markus nodded at her before passing a side glance at me. "My daughter is very interested in making friends this evening. I'm hoping her efforts are not in vain."

Ice filled my veins as I turned to focus my attention at the sight below, quickly narrowing my gaze as the familiar form of Markus's daughter approached my own. I gripped the wooden banister of the balcony and had to stop myself from vaulting down to be between the two of them.

"Nothing is going to happen down there, Rakta." Markus was at my side, as if his voice or words would ever be a source of comfort for me.

Esmeralda was far too close to my daughter, but before I could flex my Vitae and channel it to my ears, to hear the words she shared with my desert flower, a horn rang out throughout the room.

And as the horn sounded for the young ladies to approach for their formal introductions, I watched my daughter turn away from Esmeralda and look up toward me, or rather, the balcony, searching for me.

I did not know what caught her gaze, but I could see the moment that she went from self-assurance to mortal terror and fell from her chair in fear and began to scream as she startled toward one of the many doors in the manor.

I was following before I recognized it myself, the sounds of jeering children and haughty nobility a forgettable buzz in my ear. "Natakia!" I rushed down the hallway, calling out for my daughter. She did not know this estate, and neither did I, and yet, at every intersection, I could not find her, and she did not call for me. "Natakia! Call out to me!"

The royal colors of House Iriend flew past me as I kept a steady pace, pushing Vitae through my limbs more and more as I checked each room and doorway with growing desperation.

What was happening? What had she seen? Something had obviously terrified my daughter, to the extent that she had dropped all decorum and hastily fled, and yet I had noticed nothing?

And now, for the life of me, I couldn't catch up to my own daughter!? Daka, I could understand to a certain extent, but Natakia was truly her mother's daughter, and Lydia had been more of a jogger than a sprinter.

I should have been able to catch up with her. I should have been able to notice what Natakia noticed.

"No," I said, feeling something shift in the air now that I was more alert. "She saw what someone wanted her to see."

Fear and worry coalesced into anger as pieces began to fall into place, my Vitae bubbling out now as I shattered the hallway around me, revealing an entirely different part of the estate as thin Mana powering the illusion surrounding me, drowned in the energy that I released.

"The illusionist is here," I said, feeling a certainty grip me. "The illusionist is targeting my daughter."

It had been some time since I had so viscerally wanted to murder someone with my bare hands, and yet the idea that my daughter was alone with the illusionist around gave me ample reason.

"Calm down, friend."

Slowly, missing the weight of my axe, I turned to the voice and found myself finally standing face-to-face with the illusionist that had caused my family so much grief.

A tall man with orange hair that seemed to struggle out from under a wide-brimmed hat and blossomed down the sides of his face and into a light ginger beard. His eyes were wide, unnaturally so, and full of a blackness like the night sky.

Looking into them I felt something shift around me, something that did not feel like Mana. Seconds later, I was slicing through the air with wind gathered into the **Wind Axe Technique**, a facsimile of an axe made of the air itself, cutting off his head and hearing it topple to the ground.

And then the world shifted.

"Oops." The wide-eyed illusionist chuckled from the same distance away from me, as if time had reversed between us. "I think I won this little tussle of ours a tad too quickly. I really expected more."

I frowned, my eyes burning as my **Deep Blue Technique** activated, and the world was bathed in reds and blues. The illusionist was red; the hallway was blue. Everything that I expected to see and yet illusions were involved. This couldn't be right.

"Petur Benoit," the illusionist said. "That's my name, friend. I tend not to give that out."

I pushed out my Vitae, attempting to shatter the Mana in the air, but there was nothing to break, no illusion to destroy. At least, not one I could feel, not one laced with the familiar glass-like impression even some of the most exceptional illusions had from the way the Mana within them was shaped.

Petur smiled, holding his hands in mock confusion. "Simply strange, isn't it?"

Something flared in the back of my head, and I instinctively jumped to the left, but no attack came. Nothing that I could see, even with my **Deep Blue Technique**.

"Oh, that was impressive," Petur chuckled.

An illusionist with strange eyes that I couldn't pierce the illusion of. Something about this felt familiar, and yet I knew there was no time to figure out his trick at this point. Obviously, Zactrik was involved somehow, but I was constantly distracted from the here and now by the absence of my daughter.

And so, I decided my priority in this matter.

"Hey!" Petur's voice raised as I tensed my body, and I could hear him shouting down the hallway as I raced down the hall, continuing my search for my daughter. "Don't ruin a good showing!"

I ignored him, trying to figure out the extent to which an illusion such as this would have to work. Was there a focus somewhere? An object the magic was tied to? Perhaps I'd been infected with some kind of enchantment myself? I let my **Deep Blue Technique** fade, its worth nil in this situation.

All that mattered was figuring out where Natakia was and getting her to safety. I was sure Penelope was here. I doubted that she'd not notice that something was going amiss. And yet, I hadn't seen her on the balcony with the rest of the guests. Her absence, once innocent, sent a chill down my spine at the implications.

"Dad?" The soft voice stopped me as I dashed down the hallway, leaving dents in the polished wood of the estate as the force of my momentum slammed down into the floor.

I whipped toward the sound of her voice. "Natakia?"

And there she was, tears down her cheeks, sitting in the corner of what looked to be an emptied guest dining room, the chairs and tables missing, presumably taken out to seat the numerous guests for the Rose Gala.

"My desert flower, I know today has only just begun, but it is not safe here," I said, kneeling down to her. "We must leave."

"It . . . It was terrible . . . They were all laughing at me, screaming that I was ugly, Dad," Natakia sobbed, none of her usual decorum present. "And I ran away! I'm so embarrassed!"

There was no time for this, but my heart went out to my daughter. The illusions had not been real, but her reaction certainly had. I could only imagine the mercilessness of the other young ladies ready to attack her for the show of weakness, but there was no time to discuss that now.

There were much greater things to be worried about.

"Ah, finally caught up," Petur chuckled.

Much greater things indeed.

I put myself between him and Natakia, readying myself. "You have made a grave mistake, Petur. If you harm even a single hair on my daughter's head, you will find no solace in death."

"You really don't know the rules to the game yet, do you?" Petur confidently gave a crooked smile. "You looked into my eyes, Dancer. I'm afraid it's all over for you."

I frowned before I flashed to the other side of the room, Natakia in my grip before I pushed her behind me. I'd felt it again, another attempt on my life. Something that I couldn't see through an illusion I could not break. Something that no human could do . . .

"This is another one of Zactrik's tricks," I growled. "You've been changed, a man cut up and fused with the essence of a monster. There is no Mana here, only Primus."

It was why my Vitae had no effect on this illusion; even the most powerful of Vitae could do little to influence or diminish the impact of primal energy and the monstrous capabilities it powered.

"Ah." Petur shook his hands in mock surprise. "That's one cat out of the bag, I suppose. Really don't think that should have been much of a leap of logic to make, but I guess old age is a hell of a drug."

"A pooka," I said, suddenly understanding the situation.

For the first time, Petur had no response, merely lowering his hands and giving me an amused look with his large, wide eyes, but my thoughts were elsewhere. A pooka was a harmless creature, but not one to be recklessly provoked.

To look into a pooka's eyes was to surrender your world to lies, giving dominion over your five senses to the trickster creature, allowing the beast to escape without much difficulty. Harmless, usually, but given the right mood, it could gut you without you even realizing it had struck.

If he truly had the eyes of a pooka, then even my **Scourger Bloodhound Technique** would be all but useless, and any of my **First Dance Techniques** would likely hurt Natakia if I didn't know where she truly was. And yet, I could tell there was something I was forgetting . . .

I lowered my body into my **Grace Stance**. "Your trick is impressive, Petur."

The fact that it would not be enough to win went unsaid, but despite the illusion, I could feel the air change around me as Natakia huddled behind me as much as she could.

The true fight was about to begin.

29

A mirage was a dangerous but rare hazard in the lands of Rusk. An intangible force of Primus that the intelligence of was widely questioned by foreign scholars. Caught up inside a mirage yourself, it was easy to start asking similar questions as your greatest wants were used to bewitch you.

Inexperienced travelers through the sands of Rusk fell prey to the creatures hidden beneath the dunes while lost in their own personal hallucinations. Not to mention the risk of heatstroke and adding days to your travel as your supplies dwindled.

There was certainly an intelligence to this illusion that I had been caught in the web of, the almost affable countenance of Petur barely changing as he seemed to wait for me to do something, anything as the air tensed.

My Vitae rumbled beneath my skin as it became laced with the speed-enhancing edge of the **Grace Stance**, feeling the beginnings of the **Guard Periculum Technique**'s danger-sensing aura roll off from my body alongside the tightening of my ligaments as my **Instinctive Reflex Technique** took hold.

There would be no room for error here. No information could be trusted, and any attack, if it hit, could be a fatal wound with little chance for recovery.

I even began to pump Vitae through my body to close any injuries I wasn't aware of, just in case I was being played for a fool by this crafty illusionist. The many-layered techniques took a toll on my body, but I held fast, and I easily kept the strain from showing on my face.

"Let's see if you are nearby," I said, gripping onto air with my **Wind Axe Technique** and surging forward with the incredible speed packed deep within the muscles of my body.

Natakia held against me as tightly as I could safely hold her, I flashed across the room, ignoring Petur's apparent location in the room, and made testing swipes, putting barely any strength in my blows as I tried to narrow down any kind of specifics for the room I was in.

Petur tilted his head. "If I knew you were going to swing that thing around so recklessly, I would have gone through with tricking you to kill your own daughter."

The sheer possibility of that sent a chill down my spine as I continued to slash around, hoping to learn something and gain a better bearing on my environment.

And then, I felt my **Guard Periculum Technique** fluctuate for just a moment, my own senses outpaced, as I twisted my body and flashed away from something that felt particularly dangerous.

And yet, I still felt a flash of pain across my body, a wetness suddenly soaking my side.

"Heh, looks like that one didn't quite miss," Petur smiled.

My royal clothing was now soaked with blood, feeling warm and wet with my own life essence slowly but surely leaving my body. Or rather, it would, if I didn't examine my Vitae with a quick **Personal Health Technique** and feel it's unaltered flow, having not changed from before.

"I doubt those blades you're attempting to hit me with," I said, "are simply normal weapons, am I correct? I doubt Zactrik would give his assassin normal blades."

In fact, I knew what kind of blades Zactrik gave his assassins. The same kind of blades loaded with the special parasitic poison that had infected Shawn and slowly but surely started draining him dry of Vitae.

"You don't seem worried." Petur crossed his arms. "I'm sure you won't be so confident when I poke your child full of holes."

Natakia was still held against me, barely saying a word, but I made a promise to myself that I would rather die a thousand times than let her get hit by even a single one of these blades. Perhaps, a pragmatic voice in my head wondered, that sentiment was already a part of their plan.

"You'll have to go through me to get to my daughter," I said, standing by my promise.

Petur snorted. "Yeah, sort of the point, friend."

And then Natakia was no longer in my grip, the world flexing around me as Petur changed what I perceived, what I saw, before I stood once again in the same room, albeit larger than I remembered.

And before me was not only a single Natakia, but five of them, each of them looking terrified about this sudden shift and the presence of duplicates of herself.

"Go on, Dancer." Petur seemed to barely suppress a chuckle. "I want to see you protect your daughter." Time was relative, and in a world beholden to the imagination of a cruel assassin, I found myself unable to keep track of the minutes and hours passing as I was run ragged throughout the room, trying my best to continue dodging while simultaneously defusing Petur's attempts to kill my daughter.

And yet, beyond my control, I had seen my daughter die more times than I could take in the last few moments. Torn apart by unseen weapons, claw marks ripping her to shreds, and falling to the ground, writhing as a parasite like Shawn's destroyed her from the inside out.

"You do nothing but make your inevitable end that much more painful," I said, trying to ignore how distracted I was by the many deaths of my daughter's image.

The very idea that one of them had been the real one, that I had saved an illusion at the expense of my real daughter, made my heart thump dangerously quickly in my chest.

Petur looked annoyed at this point, motioning to the world around him. "Oh, Lord Velbrun, I'm only just now getting started! Don't you think I'm taking it easy on you?"

Was he? It was a possibility, but I rather thought this was an attempt by a barely experienced combatant with exceptional illusionary talent that was trying to do their best on their own. I kept quiet, continuing to dodge the strange pressure of danger as it came, which I had had very little time to think about.

And yet, in the time that I had, one thing had become apparent. If all my senses were truly Petur's to bend, then such a sharp feeling of danger shouldn't have been present. I prided myself on my ability to perceive danger, of course, but all my perceptions were not mine to use at the moment.

I was sensing something else, something that felt inherently dangerous and yet was so alien to the senses that the only thing that could be sensing it would be my Vitae alone.

"The Mortum in the blades," I said, quickly moving to pull another crying Natakia away from a small pulse of danger. "I can feel the Mortum through your technique."

Petur, for the first time, seemed somewhat shocked by my sudden revelation. "What? You can, no, but . . . no!"

And yet, I could. Mortum was such a vile feeling energy that it seemed like my Vitae had a physical reaction to its direct threat upon me that I felt as danger. I gave thanks to my ancestors and the stories they weaved, for they were surely looking out for me.

"And now"—I looked around the visages of my daughter—"the next step is figuring out which Natakia is the true one, getting her to safety, and then killing you."

And my constant rescue of my daughter's many different versions running around had clued me in on slight details that I was confident Petur had not realized.

First, Petur had done his research. He had gotten down a lot of behavioral patterns of my daughter, meticulously controlling each figment of my daughter to perfectly act as her. Second, Petur must be in the room somewhere, and where would be the safest place other than the disguise of the one thing I would never hit in this room?

Clues that may not have helped a layman, but putting them together as I dodged for my life, sweat covering my form, I realized one very key detail that Petur had missed.

Scared or upset, Natakia always looked toward her mirror rather than away from it, something that each and every one of the copies in the room had failed to do.

Petur must have felt my intent change, frowning now. I could only imagine what he really looked like compared to that of what he allowed his figment to emote. Was he truly this calm and collected?

I would soon find out.

"I'll give you one chance, Petur," I said. "Zactrik did a horrible thing to you, made you a freak of nature, but you don't have to be a monster because of it."

He laughed, "Oh, what a valiant hero you ar— Ughk!"

Mercy wasn't ever on the table, of course. Perhaps, if Shawn were here, but I had no intentions of leaving him alive with the threats he'd laid at my feet. I just needed him distracted for the second it took me to flare my Vitae and dash through each and every one of the Natakia fakes in the room until he reacted exactly like this.

There was no feeling of flesh underneath my grip, no sense of touch or weight to give away the hold I had on his neck, but I knew I'd grabbed him with my left hand. Instantly, I felt the pain of a thousand imagined dagger cuts upon my arm, each one going to the bone, but I never wavered in my grip.

And then, the world changed around me in an underwhelming blink of an eye, my senses returning to my control as I finally felt the weight of Petur in my hands.

Less changed than I had expected, with the empty room we were in shrinking to its original size and the immense pain in my left arm fleeing beyond the ghost of feeling that I felt would last a long time. The most alarming change that I noticed as I glanced around was a very important one.

There was no Natakia in this room.

"Hagh? Hagh!?" Petur tried to choke out a question as I looked him up and down, noticing that his face was somewhat vulpine in appearance, but more akin to that of a coyote upon closer look.

"A pooka can hold their illusion for quite some time, but the more changes they do, the more alterations they make, the more exertion it takes," I said, slowly tightening my grip on his neck, watching his face pale. "I knew if I grabbed you, you'd panic and use up all your energy. Where is my daughter?"

I could feel the idle illusions in the air, Petur seemingly genuinely skilled in silently layering them around the area even while choking, break as my Vitae soaked the air and destroyed them. I lightened my grip, just enough for Petur to answer my question.

"Dead! Killed by my brother!" he choked out at me. "Just like you will be!"

Petur went for a blade at his side, a dark iron-looking shortsword, but stilled as a crack broke the tension in the room. Or rather, he stilled as I broke his neck. His permanently wide eyes began to finally close as I threw him to the side, a deep anger and worry welling up inside of me.

Another illusionist? One that had targeted Natakia!? My entire body was cold, my Vitae bubbling, as I began to sprint toward the damaged door of the room, one of my attacks having torn it asunder.

"Rakta!"

And almost smashed straight into Penelope as she came into the room, looking hurried and cut up, but otherwise fine. At her side, one of her magical cannons hung from a strap around her shoulders.

"Penelope," I said with a dry throat. "Where is my daughter? Have you seen her? The other illusionist—there were two and . . . and . . . the one that went after my daughter—"

What would I even do without my desert flower? How would I have the strength to continue as a parent knowing I had failed one of my own children, one of Lydia's children, in such a terrible way?

"She's fine!" Penelope caught me as I slumped against her, the words an instant and powerful spell that had wiped me of all strength. "She's fine, Rakta. She's safe and sound. No harm, not even a mark on her."

"Thank you, Penelope," I said from the bottom of my heart. "Thank you for saving my daughter. Please, I need to go see her. I need to hold her in my arms."

She nodded, but her face scrunched up with discomfort as she began to walk me out of the room, a legion of guards coming into the room to collect the pooka hybrid's body.

It was hard not to notice as my techniques began to fade, the hyper-awareness I had to maintain for the entire fight slowly dwindling. "What is it, Penelope?"

As my friend continued to hoist me, help me back through the estate, the little hints of where I'd traveled through the Iriend property became apparent, from the dented floors to the cuts along the walls, all being a portrait of what my battle with Petur had truly looked like.

"Rakta," she said, taking a deep breath. "I wasn't the one who saved Natakia."

I blinked, slowly digesting that. "What?" Walking into the heavily guarded room, I felt an immense relief and sadness as I found Natakia sitting in a chair, staring straight down into her mirror laid out in her lap. Her dress was slightly torn from the light scuffle and running she'd done, no doubt.

It was my greatest hope that we would have a moment alone, to speak about what had happened, or at least to comfort her with the knowledge that she was safe, but I glanced at the other individual in the room.

Esmeralda, prim and proper as she'd been since our introductions at House Velbrun's capital estate, her eyes on me as I entered. Watching her, I could still feel the way she had fed from Vitae so many years ago, some of which I had never fully recovered even now.

And yet, she was no longer just a monster, was she? A daughter, a young lady, and the savior of Natakia, having followed after Natakia when I had been led astray and ultimately slaying the other Benoit that had been set to kill my desert flower.

"Natakia," I said softly, sitting down next to her, reaching out to my ancestors to give me strength. "I'm so happy you are alright."

There was silence for a moment before Natakia looked up at me, tear tracks down her cheeks and an edge to her gaze that outlined the sadness and fear within it.

"Alright?" she whispered. "I'm not alright. The gala was ruined, and I almost died."

As if remembering it all for the first time, Natakia's eyes began to well with tears again, and I swiftly took her into my arms, feeling her wrap herself around me tightly as I did my best to comfort her.

And once again, I wished Lydia were here to have seen this coming, to have been a mother when I failed to be a father and protect our daughter.

<h1 style="text-align:center">30</h1>

The Rose Gala was unceremoniously canceled after word spread about the attack on nobility. As distant as I was from the conversations, Doh had said that there were a lot of split sentiments.

Most seemed to blame the perpetrators, some naming Zatrick and spreading his name, others simply pointing fingers at the main interlopers, the illusionists, as the problem. Others, unfortunately, seemed to take issue with House Iriend and Shawn for their inability to provide a safe place for their children to socialize.

I had retrieved Doh and Macy, taking them alongside Natakia back to the safety of the palace to recover from the attack and put distance between Natakia and her savior. Even now, a few days after the events of the gala, I was still conflicted about the involvement of my brother-in-law and his daughter.

"I'm glad Natakia is safe, Rakta," Shawn said as a servant laid drinks down between the both of us before leaving to give us privacy.

I glanced down at my reflection in the wineglass, my displeased expression pronounced after weeks of my children's celebrations getting ruined. "Is she, Shawn?"

Natakia had not left her room since, the only silver lining being that she had returned to sleeping near me, her issues with Daka entirely forgotten or, at least, put to the wayside for the time being.

"We're still investigating that." Shawn sounded frustrated, mostly with himself. "There's a traitor somewhere, I'm sure of it, but getting High Lord Gren Iriend to work with us to find them . . ."

"Could High Lord Iriend not be who is behind all of this?" I asked, finally picking up my glass of wine to sip at it, if only to quell a familiar old anger rising. One that wouldn't hesitate to kill anyone behind this.

Shawn nodded, but he didn't say anything more on the topic. "How are the others? I hope Natakia was able to sleep with the extra posted guard."

My daughter had given each of them a hard look before she felt relaxed around them and asked questions that only their closest friends or a natural divination expert could have known.

"She slept . . . better." It was the best I could say on the matter. "But Daka has still been quieter than usual, and Dalton has seemingly retreated into his business plans. With the pressure of their origins, Shawn, and Zactrik's constant interruptions, I fear for them."

"Because of the prophecy?" Shawn asked.

I glared at him, feeling my anger rise. "I have never once cared for prophecies, especially one that has done more harm than good every step of the way."

The intentions of the gods were beyond me, but I was confident that they had done nothing but make my children suffer far more than they should with the burden of fate upon them. And I, like a fool, had made them aware of it, thinking that it would do anything resembling aid.

"Whoa, Rakta, buddy." Shawn weakly reached out and grabbed my arm. "I get it, I really do. You want your children to be safe, I know that. I'm sorry I've been such a, well, a horrible friend in that regard. I've really failed you every step of the way, it feels."

That, no, that wasn't true. Shawn had always done his best. All of us were trying. I could see Penelope running herself to exhaustion most days trying to keep up with new issues, Shawn was slowly dying, and I had this sense of doom every moment my thoughts lingered upon the prophecy.

"We're all doing our best," I said. "And yet, I know of plenty of stories where that has not been enough."

Shawn smiled. "I think we'll be one of the stories where it is."

It was all that could be said, but coming from Shawn, it did more to comfort me than had I heard it from anyone else. I knew that he was going through my same struggle, keeping his family safe.

"Honestly," he continued, "I take solace in knowing both of the illusionists are dead. Taking Zactrik's pieces off the board is the best way to slowly whittle his resources and plans down."

"Was the illusionist's sword recovered?" I asked, feeling comfortable enough to move on from the earlier topic for now. "Was it as I thought?"

Answering my question, Shawn brought out the aforementioned blade from a sheath beside him that I had not noticed. "It's been scraped clean of the Mortum-powered poison. Penelope took samples back to her workshop to start getting a better read."

"Will it help with your surgery?" I was hopeful, knowing that any advantage during the upcoming procedure could be vital to saving the life of my friend.

He shrugged, not looking too hopeful, but that might have just been his exhaustion showing. "I think that's the hope."

I nodded before we continued to discuss the attack on the gala, although making sure to steer clear from any discussion about Esmeralda and Markus. Gratitude blended with suspicion about the two, from their sudden presence at the gala to their aid.

Eventually, it was time for me to return to my children and give Doh a chance to spend time with her family without having to keep an eye on mine. Macy's mood had fallen as much as Natakia's in the wake of the gala's cancellation, but each other's company had done little to improve their moods.

And yet, as I stood to leave, Shawn spoke up once more.

"Three days from now, Rakta," he said, looking away from me, "the high lords will be gathered, and I will officially decree you as a high lord of House Tribus. Have you prepared the letters for your associates?"

My brow furrowed. "Yes, I have. I'm sure they will be ecstatic."

Just another reminder that things would never be as simple as they once were again, a thought I put aside for now as I left to see my children. I could only hope they were doing well.

Approaching the slightly opened door of my children's shared room, I was caught off guard by the words that greeted me as I stopped, stunned by the door.

"What are you going to do?" Natakia's flat voice said with an acerbic edge to her words. "Punch me again to prove your point? Prove once and for all that you're just a monster—"

Daka crashed through the door, leaving the bedroom, and stopped as she made eye contact with me, her helmet slightly off-kilter on her head. Her wide blue eyes were wet as she held my gaze, surprised, before she gave a big smile.

"I'm gonna go get some practice in!" And with that, Daka ran off, leaving me almost instinctively reaching out to the air for her before I pulled back and turned toward the door.

Walking in, I saw that Dalton was in his own corner of the room, writing in one of his journals, while Natakia was in her bed, resting against the headboard, a pillow propping her up as she watched me come in.

"I guess she decided to run away," Natakia lightly scoffed, almost sounding bored.

I frowned, approaching her. "Natakia, there is never a reason to call your sister a monster."

"Instantly defending Daka, Dad?" Natakia smiled, tilting her head. "How typical. I can't even get a word in, and I'm already the bad guy, aren't I? I certainly feel like I'm being punished."

I felt like I had whiplash for a moment, mentally retreading my steps to figure out where exactly I had already gone wrong in this conversation. Natakia was not in a good mood, that was clear and very concerning.

"Natakia." I sat down beside her. "I know you're upset that the Rose Gala was ruined."

"What invaluable insight." Natakia looked away from me, toward her floating reflection in the surface of her mirror. "I'll be feeling better in no time."

"Natakia." I understood that she was frustrated, but I expected her to be mature enough to at least speak with me about it, to properly discuss the issues at hand.

For a moment, there was a silence between us that I let settle, watching as my daughter began to lightly fidget with her blanket, glancing at me from time to time, before she finally spoke. "I'm sorry, Dad."

"Don't apologize to me, Natakia," I said. "I expect both you and your sister to apologize to each other when you next speak, do you understand?"

She didn't quite acknowledge my request, but I knew she'd heard me. I sat by her side and laid back alongside her, holding her hand in mine. I was grateful she did not pull away from me.

"I know that the Rose Gala felt like a once-in-a-lifetime event, but you are more than your first day in the limelight, Natakia." I began to brush her hair slightly with the back of my hand.

She frowned, a slight dip of the edge of her lips. "How would you know? Some of Mom's stories?"

Lydia had never made a habit of speaking much of her time in the courts of House Velbrun. I wasn't particularly curious as to why.

"No." I gently tightened my grip around her hand. "Because Natakia Velbrun is too charming and spectacular of a young lady to allow such a thing to keep her from where she belongs."

She looked down at our hands before looking back up at me, a smile growing on her lips, the first hint of such a thing since the Rose Gala. "You really think that."

I could tell it wasn't a question, but I nodded regardless. "I understand that times are turbulent right now, but you have your brother, your sister, and you have me, Natakia."

"And Macy," Natakia said, rubbing her arms. "Doh and Dresden . . . Everyone back home."

"That's right," I said. "I'm going to go speak to your sister now. I think Macy would enjoy you visiting her if you're in the mood to leave the room."

I could still see it, the fear she had for the world outside after such a terrible event, but I knew that there was courage when around loved ones.

After a moment, she nodded. "You're right, Macy's day was ruined too. I guess I was just . . . too upset about it myself to really talk with her about it before."

With that, I helped her out of her bed and watched as she left the room, glancing over to see Dalton raising an eyebrow in my direction, having paid attention, somewhat, to the conversation.

"Something on your mind, Dalton?" It had been a while since my son and I had a moment to ourselves for any kind of discussion. Quiet, determined, but perhaps also feeling left out?

Dalton seemed to think about that for a moment, glancing at his journal, before he nodded. "I'd like to talk about what I'll need to help Uncle Shawn and how I'll be doing it. As well as . . . the compensation."

For a moment, I was troubled by his desire for compensation, but I wouldn't fault him too soon. I was glad he had come to me, however, for I was eager to speak on such matters myself.

"Let me go find Daka and speak with her first. I don't want her overdoing her training," I said. "Afterward, I'll come find you, and we can sit down and talk."

He nodded before going back to his journal, letting me depart the room without further question.

In the wake of the attack on the palace and the Rose Gala, the training yard had been much busier, many of Shawn's personal squadron of Protectors and some hired CADs littering the area, polishing their skills and weapons in the event of a true assault on the capital.

I nodded to a few, having properly gotten to know some of the men and women who were putting hours into keeping the palace safe for my children, but before I could find Daka, I was approached by a familiar man bearing the regalia of Shawn's personal guards.

"Good morning, Rakta." Tanner walked up, the general feeling of unease that naturally surrounded him easily ignored for the moment. "What brings you to the field?"

Smiling, I continued looking around for a moment, searching for a familiar blur, before giving him my full attention. "My daughter Daka came down to train a moment ago. I wanted to speak with her."

Tanner nodded, looking around. "I think I saw her earlier, but I'm not sure where she went off to. I know we were busy at the time. I think she might've gotten told to wait until some space opened up for her."

I frowned at the idea. My little warrior had been quite upset. I wouldn't doubt she ran off to go work out her emotions elsewhere if the training ground had been full.

"If you see her," I said, "let me know. Have the guards keep an eye out."

I wouldn't raise the alarm yet, but if I couldn't figure out where Daka had gotten off to, then I would be left with no choice. The experience of almost losing Natakia was far too fresh to come anywhere near that possibility again.

"Of course, Rakta." Tanner made a sign with his hands for some of the nearby Protectors, and they seemed to stand at attention, ready to keep an eye out.

As I stepped away, I heard a familiar sound out in the horizon, outside of the palace, and perhaps even outside of the capital walls entirely. The sound of something shattering, the roaring of pressure that stretched across the lands in an introduction befitting only one man that I was aware of.

Ulric the World Breaker had arrived at the capital.

31

When I used my **Scourger Bloodhound Technique** to heighten my sense of smell and start tracking, it was with a growing feeling of trepidation that Daka's path had completely left the palace, which I would be talking to her about, and had, in fact, left the capital completely.

I sped up as each of these new details unfolded, a deep concern gripping me at the idea of someone having coerced Daka into following them outside the capital.

And yet, a new feeling began to blossom in my chest as I realized her trail, which was quite fresh, seemingly turned on a swivel from its original path and straight toward the direction Ulric's roar of shatter magic had erupted from.

"Damn it, Daka," I said, momentarily cursing my little warrior's curiosity. Of course she would recognize the sound of Ulric's magic after so many stories.

At the very least, I doubted Daka was in any true danger approaching Ulric; he was not the type to hurt defenseless children. I knew that intellectually at least. My heart still remembered old words Ulric had told me, threatening my children just so I would fight him.

Shaking my head of such thoughts, I bent back down and continued my tracking, eventually coming upon a clearing amid a loose gathering of trees. Loosening my technique, the sounds that had escaped me before now rang clearly.

"And what did you do next, Uncle Ulric?" Daka's voice was clear and present, full of joy and life, as if the last few weeks had just been a dream.

And the deep, jovial voice of Ulric boomed back, "I did what every self-respecting Fjordic man would do when his honor was questioned! I punched him straight in the face and knocked his teeth out!"

It was a testament to Ulric's dedication to that exact method of dealing with disrespect that I had no idea which story he was sharing with my daughter.

"Now," I said as I walked out into the clearing, "was this the time when the man was a simple merchant trying to sell you rotten fruit or that one lord whom we had to compensate for one of our members assaulting him?"

"Dad!" Daka cheered as she dashed away from Ulric and jumped over to hug me as I made myself known, her eyes bright and shiny. "Uncle Ulric's here!"

I laid a hand on her helmeted head, sighing. "Yes, I heard."

Ulric had stiffened as I made myself known, looking somewhat caught off guard, but the suddenness of our first meeting in years didn't pause him for long as he stood up and grinned. "Ah! Rakta!"

"Ulric, it's good to see you again," I said, honestly feeling a bit safer with Ulric's might to aid in whatever came next, before looking down at Daka. "I thought you'd be at the training yard, Daka."

Blinking, Daka seemed to belatedly realize where exactly she was and the full extent of how far outside of the palace she had wandered. "Oh, uh, sorry, Dad."

"You worried me, Daka." I bent down to give a kiss to her forehead. "But this is a fine place to train with the proper chaperone."

"Uncle Ulric was chaperoning me, yeah?" Daka seemed eager to jump onto that idea, glancing back to her uncle as if he would jump on board.

Upon which he did, seemingly with no hesitation.

Ulric nodded. "I did that, I did! Yeah, I found her, and I was like, your Rakta's girl! And we started talking, and, well, I was telling her stories . . ."

He trailed off as I continued to stare at him, Daka eventually pulling my hand to get my attention and looking up at me with her big blue eyes.

"Well," I said, powerless, "this time, I suppose Ulric was here to make sure you were safe, but . . . we will talk about this later."

I made sure they understood with some pointed looks that would be with both of them, separately, and for entirely different reasons. Daka was a child, strange origins or not, but I felt a little defensive in regard to how friendly Ulric was being. I doubted he had forgotten that night when we'd almost killed each other.

It was discomforting to hear Daka label the man that had once threatened her and her siblings as her uncle so readily.

"Okay, Dad." Daka wilted somewhat. "I'm sorry."

I hugged her to my side, giving Ulric a look. "I'll take it from here, Ulric. I'm sure Shawn will want to see you now that you've arrived."

He gave a nod before lumbering off past me, waving goodbye to my daughter before catching my eye and having the decency to look somewhat sheepish about how this had all gone down.

Waiting until he was out of sight, I patted Daka on the head. "Alright, now it's time for me and you to talk, my little warrior."

"Oh." Daka looked a little taken aback before she sighed and forced an upbeat tone. "Can we train a bit before we talk, Dad?"

I could allow that small mercy. Eventually we both settled down into our cool-off positions, spreading our bodies out wide to give them ample space and breathing room to cool off from the intense but short training session.

Daka certainly seemed to have worked out some stress that I hadn't been entirely aware that she had been holding on to, some of her kicks and punches feeling a tad too real for sparring if I were a normal cultivator of Vitae. It was too bad she'd forgotten her axe back in her room.

"How are you feeling?" I asked, taking in slow and steady breaths, slowly stretching my body to make sure it stayed moving and flexible as I came down from such exertion. My years of refining Vitae kept my body from the worst that aging had to offer, but plenty of old wounds were quick to show themselves.

Daka was doing the same, although she didn't seem as worried about pulling anything. "I'm fine."

It was painfully obvious by the way she tensed and seemed to look away from me as she said so that she was anything but fine.

"I heard what Natakia said." I decided the direct route would be the most effective with her. "I didn't hear much, but I . . . heard her call you a monster."

There was a silence as we eventually finished cooling off, settling down into the grass as Daka sat on my leg, looking deep in thought, her eyes distant in a way that I disliked.

"She . . ." Daka started, grabbing a hold of my shirt. "I was trying to apologize for . . . hitting her, that daft cow, but I . . . She was in such a bad mood, but I thought . . . an apology would help. I couldn't do it though. I was scared it would just make things worse."

I hugged her close, hoping that she never called Natakia a cow to her face. "That was when she called you a monster?"

"Natakia always knows what'll hurt the most."

"Do you," I asked carefully, "fear being a monster?"

I thought back to Daka's reaction when the half-calker assassin had made an attempt on my life back at the Hallowed Hollow, the murderous darkness in her voice as she screamed at the man.

"Monsters are killers." My little warrior said it with such deep-seated belief, as if she were saying the sky was blue. "I can't kill people or I'll be . . . a monster."

Each word seemed to take a lot out of my daughter, each one another nugget of truth about her life on Earth. The soft implication of *again* went unsaid.

"Your sister was upset, Daka. Her words were said from a place of her own hurt, not from any truly held belief," I said, relatively confident in my words. "I hope that when she apologizes, you take the opportunity to apologize to her as well."

"What if she doesn't apologize?" Daka pulled away from me, her face twitching with fear as she glanced around, trying to find something to focus on that wasn't me. "What if I don't want to apologize to her? What if I really am just a monster? One that'll hurt people . . . only hurt people."

She laid the question at my feet, her concern laid as simply as it could be for me to judge and answer. It was times such as these I wondered if other parents were faced with tasks as impossible as my own. Guiding such unique souls as they truly found themselves for a second time.

And yet, as impossible as my little warrior's concerns were to answer, they struck a chord within an old and familiar part of me. One that had grown up asking similar questions amid the sandy dunes of Rusk.

"Daka, I understand the questions you ask." I met her gaze, connecting with the older glint that seemed to stare out behind my daughter's innocence. "Once you have killed, once you have taken a life, are you anything more, or perhaps, can you ever be anything more than a killer?"

It isn't an answer, not quite yet, but it was what I had once thought about long ago when I was younger. My daughter watched me, entranced, as I considered my next words carefully before I realized nothing I could say would have the proper meaning without . . .

"Let me tell you a story, Daka." I stood up, lifting her up to her feet.

Daka blinked, tilting her head. "A new story, Dad?"

Taken aback by the sudden turn, I could tell she was, but the growing excitement on her face outshined any confusion as I nodded, holding her hand in mine.

"One of a young boy who grew up wondering if he would ever be more than the killer that he had been trained to be by his tribe, his family, and his sister," I said.

It was on one of the less-beaten paths back to the capital, one rarely used by merchants or travelers, that I began to share the story, Daka riding on my shoulders as we passed by a small crack in the earth, one of the Certillian Empire's many ravines.

There had been silence after I'd offered my tale, but not one that I had spent staying idle. My own stories, this one in particular, were not ones I had much experience in telling. Certainly not for the ears of my own daughter, who had the most to learn from my own life.

"On the Ruskan sands, life is different than what I've become accustomed within this empire. Instead of courts, we have tribes, and in place of politics between the houses, words are traded between chieftains, Storytellers, and the Grand Cipher of Kakrel," I said, feeling the world around us begin to blur as I felt the heat of the Ruskan sun upon us. "I was as young as you are now, Daka, when I killed for the first time . . ."

She was silent and tense, but I could feel her interest as I continued to weave my own personal tale.

"It had been a hot summer day, the worst of the season at the time, and the roaming tribes throughout Rusk had been feeling the heat in their bones for weeks at that point." I frowned at the memory of that summer, that horrible summer. "Heat that could drive even the sanest of men wild with rage and mindlessness if not given a chance to breathe."

"My tribe had not escaped the wrath of the sun but had found momentary salvation in the sweet relief of a wandering oasis, a solution that would not last long." It had barely lasted a week, from what I remembered.

"Your tribe?" I could hear the budding smile in Daka's voice. "The Kroterruk Tribe, right?"

I nodded, keeping an eye on our surroundings as my daughter lost herself to the spirits of the story. "Yes, the Kroterruk Tribe, although in Certillian, we'd be called the Last Dancing Bird Tribe."

For a moment, I was about to continue, but I stayed my words. I felt a question growing among my audience, and any Storyteller worthy of their craft respected such interest.

"You don't talk a lot about your tribe, Dad." Daka sounded curious, yet worried. "Is it because of what your about to tell me?"

My pace across the grasslands of the empire toward the capital slowed for a moment, but I did not let my gait waver long. "I love the stories of those around me more than those I left in Rusk, my little warrior."

I gave her a moment to respond, but when no question came, I resumed my story. "While my tribe had found momentary reprieve," I reiterated, "other tribes had not been so lucky."

The sounds of sand being overturned, blood being spilled across the dunes in every direction, and the words of Storytellers coming to life and slaughtering the living.

"I had only become a warrior of our tribe when the Buruk Tribe, those of the Iron Lions, attacked us for the water we desperately guarded," I said, feeling my side begin to burn, where my first scar had been engraved upon my skin. "It was a battle waged with reckless abandon, the warriors of the Buruk Tribe having lost their minds after losing their tribe's younglings to the heat."

At the time, young and immature, I had scoffed at their weakness of will and lack of stalwart spirit. Today, I feared for my own sanity if I were to ever have to deal with such a tragedy.

"Among my peers, I was considered exceptional," I continued, feeling the weight of my first weapon, a spear. "My father pushed me hard, Daka, prepared me to fight and kill for the tribe, to protect our people from that which encroached upon our way of life as we traveled our lands."

I made a habit of keeping thoughts of my own father, and the way he had raised me, at a distance. I never wanted to learn anything from him beyond foresight into the mistakes a father could make in regard to their children.

"And when the time came, when the Buruk Tribe attacked"—I sighed, feeling the old screams rear their head—"I fought back with merciless-ness, each man and woman that came at me cut down as I carved a path through rabid animals that seemingly welcomed death as a reprieve to their pain."

It was a side I never wanted to show my children, but it seemed to become harder and harder to manage in the wake of Lydia's death and Zactrik's constant attempts on our lives. Traveling with Shawn and the others had taught me countless lessons as we fought back against the Warlock King.

The art of knowing when and whom to kill, yes, but also of mercy and of kindness. Things that my tribe had taught me, but only in regard to those of our way, of our tribe.

"That battle, my first battle, there was a moment when I could not tell where I ended—" I said before Daka interrupted me.

"And the weapon began."

Her words were old and somber, and I felt a connection with my daughter that a father never wanted to feel. One that should have been only felt by veterans of long wars, of yearslong campaigns across pillaged lands.

"Yes," I said, holding Daka steady on my shoulders. "It was a sensa-tion that startled me, that made me lose my center. My certainty faltered, and my lapse of focus almost ended in my death, a lone warrior bursting from the sands as he leaped upon me with his blade drawn and blood trailing from his mouth."

It was still vivid in my head. The heat, the feeling of my mind entrap-ping me, the way my body began to move so slowly as the Buruk warrior aimed for my throat, easily beheading me had it landed.

"What happened?" Daka's voice was tense, a strange blend between that of a child listening to an exciting tale and that of an older curiosity.

I smiled, a bittersweet chuckle dryly falling from my lips as the moment played out in my head as I spoke. "Natakia, my sister, saved my life."

32

W hat!? Natakia!?" Daka bent down to look at me in the eye from her spot on my shoulders. "Whaddya mean Natakia!? Dad! Natakia is my sister! Not yours!"

I laughed, lifting Daka off my shoulders and holding her in my arms as we continued to walk, carrying her at my side. "Your mother named her for the past, Daka. Her reasons are still somewhat beyond me, I admit."

"So wait," Daka said. "Who am I named after?"

"Unfortunately for you, I was given the honor of naming you," I said, "which means my lead tongue simply gave you the first thing I could think of when I held you."

I truly was powerless to those shining blue eyes, my youngling so tiny and yet so mighty to bring me to my proverbial knees. Lydia would have done better, but I was glad to have been a part of the moment.

"Aw, I love my name, Dad." Daka hugged me, easily lightening my spirits, before she pulled back and pouted. "So I'm really not named after anyone?"

Seeing her obvious interest in the subject, I thought back to any notable ancestors that shared her name before I shook my head, not able to bring to mind any such individuals.

"I'm afraid you have the task of being the first to bring your name to glory, Daka." I smiled at her. "I think there will be many children proud to be named after you in the years to come."

Daka looked stunned for a moment before she smiled and laughed. "I'll give them something to shoot for, yeah?"

"Indeed you will," I said, having no doubt that each of my children would be immortalized in history for one reason or another, prophecy or not.

They were simply too special for history to merely forget them as I'm sure it would me.

"So is Dalton named after someone?" Daka asked guilelessly, and yet the question made me falter for a moment, but I quickly followed through with my next step, gliding over a stray stick in the path.

I glanced off toward a cloud in the sky. "Yes, he is, but that is a story for another time. I believe I was telling you about my own sister."

"Oh yeah." Daka giggled. "Sorry, Dad!"

In my heart of hearts, getting off track from the story was completely fine if it meant my child had a moment to smile and laugh again. I would never rebuke her and sully these moments together, especially as I knew my tale was far from over.

I began to once more weave the story, reiterating some of the details to build upon the scene as it happened, the sand bursting upward from the eruption of the hidden warrior and the moment my sister saved my life.

"Pushed to the side by my sister," I continued, "the blade merely pierced my side. Deeply, yes, but nothing that I could not live from by circulating my Vitae."

Natakia had been not much older than me, barely a year into her training as a warrior. Never as pushed, as focused on, as I was by our father, but she was already showing an expertise with bladed chains.

"She saved my life," I said, admitting that freely, "but that moment stuck with me for years. I grew angry with my tribe's way, especially as we began to cross into neighboring countries. Compared to the ruthlessness my tribe showed to those not even of our lands, that battle I witnessed was tame."

It was why I understood the pain of those who lost loved ones to those of my kin, even if I would never accept their channeling of that pain into ostracizing those of Rusk that meant no harm. Many Ruskans had died simply wishing to leave their bloody tribes.

"You were a bandit, Dad?" Daka frowned at me, her smile having dwindled as I continued my story. I knew she may never see me in the same way again, but I accepted the burden of my mistakes.

I nodded, but I felt like more was needed to answer such a question. "I was what my tribe wanted me to be. I've killed people who never wanted anything more than to protect their families."

It was, in part, why I never personally sought out any glory for the monsters that I slayed or the lives I saved. It would have been disrespectful to every death I had not been held accountable for.

"When I was eighteen," I said, continuing on, "I left my tribe, having finally found the courage to leave their ways behind me. It was years later, after I'd been traveling with your mother and the others for a while, that I finally spoke with my sister again and it was . . . not pleasant."

We'd been on the hunt for some ancient texts that a merchant from Prayers had hired us to find after a group of bandits had ransacked a traveling caravan when it was discovered that said bandits were my old tribe, led by Natakia after the death of my father.

It had, in the kindest interpretation of my memories, not been a happy reunion between the two of us, and I wasn't sure if I was ready to share that story with my young daughter.

"So when you question yourself, Daka," I said, looking up to stare into the blueness of my child's gaze, "when you wonder if you are a monster for killing another, know that you never have to remain a monster. The blood on my hands, perhaps on yours, will never wash away, but it will dry."

I stopped walking and grabbed her hand in mine, grimly looking at it resting in my palm. "We can never change what we have done, but it is always within our power to change what we do."

Daka looked down at her hand in mine alongside me and I wished, for just a moment, for the kind of insight Lydia and my own desert flower seemed to be blessed with. That simple knowing of how one was thinking, of how they felt.

"Dad," she said, after a long moment of silence between us, "do you think that Natakia and I will end up like you and your sister?"

When I left the tribe, I had reached out to my sister and tried to convince her to go with me. Against my tribe's ruthlessness as I was, even now I could not deny that I was still led by my anger then. When she refused to come with me, called me a coward and a traitor . . .

With as much certainty as I could harness from the world around me, I gripped onto her hand resting in mine. "As long as I live, Daka, I will do everything in my power to keep this family together."

Daka smiled, before it dwindled slightly. "And you're going to live for a long time, right?"

"For as long as I need to." I kissed her on the forehead as we continued on towards the capital. On our way back, there was a quiet between my daughter and me, but not an unwelcome one. I had given my daughter a lot to think about, had unearthed many memories for me to think about, but I felt a weight had been lessened between the two of us.

There was still so much, I felt, that needed to be discussed between us, but there was no need to rush it. Pulling teeth from the mouth of a bull often leads to getting the horns, as they say.

Instead, when we did speak, it was about the good food of the palace and Daka's excitement at finally having been taught some new techniques. Introductory, they were, but they would help shape Daka's development as she grew up.

One couldn't simply start to dance overnight, a lesson learned from personal experience.

Eventually, making it back to the palace, I encouraged Daka to go speak with her sister once again and finally put the ill feelings between them to rest. The world would only get more dangerous, that I knew from experience, and there would be no room for dissension between siblings.

She seemed unsure, but willing to try. That was all any of us could do.

That left me, after I'd seen her off, alone to find my cunning son, but before I could trace his whereabouts, I found myself on the trail of a different quarry.

"And with a mere push of my magic, the mighty dragon was shattered clean out of the sky!" Ulric's voice echoed throughout the mess hall of the palace, the raucous cheers of off-duty guards celebrating the climax of the story.

It seemed that time had not quelled Ulric's enjoyment of spreading tales of his great feats and heroic deeds, although even I could admit the spectacle of watching a dragon slam down in the earth was not easily forgotten.

Before the World Breaker could enter into another grand story of his own making, in the literal sense, I stepped out from behind the pillar I had waited behind and caught his gaze.

"Oh." Ulric blinked before he smiled. "Friends! The time for stories is over, but I will be in the capital for quite some time. Perhaps we will get a chance to make legends together before I leave!"

With the backdrop of another surge of cheering, Ulric stepped off of the table he was standing on and lumbered over to where I waited, following as I turned and led him out to somewhere more private to speak.

"I'm sorry," Ulric said as I closed the door to a nearby private chamber, my slight surprise showing on my face as he waved it off with a hand. "I know how you feel, I should not have . . . Well, I was surprised when she called me uncle, and . . ."

"Ulric." I clasped a hand on his shoulder, feeling him tense. "It's good to see that you're alright."

With Zactrik out on the prowl, the lives of everyone I knew were at risk, especially those I had once traveled with. Our differences aside, I held no desire for Ulric to be assassinated or worse.

For a moment, the Fjordic warrior was stunned before he grinned. "It is good to see you, as well, Rakta. I was pleased to hear that the whole illusionist situation worked itself out before I got here."

"Yes, well, once Zactrik's forces have the time to truly become experienced with their strange abilities, I fear they won't be so easily dispatched," I said, thinking about Petur's capabilities.

Exceptional talent, yes, but there was no mistaking the illusionist as an experienced fighter. He couldn't adapt once his illusions and unique ability failed to instantly bring me down.

My growing concerns aside, I refocused my attention on Ulric, who seemed to agree with my statement, his own thoughtful expression fading as I turned back to him.

"That said, I want to thank you for keeping Daka company and making sure she was safe," I said, frowning at the still-pressing issue of my daughter having simply left the capital by herself. "I still haven't forgotten that night, but . . . I know you care for them. I know you aren't a monster."

It had been ten years since that night, and even now my feelings had barely faded, but I knew that there was no time for grievances between friends. Perhaps my grudge could have prospered in a time of peace, but I could feel the winds changing.

"That . . . Thank you, Rakta." Ulric looked down at his hands. "Since that night, I have been doing what I can to make up for the destruction that I caused. It keeps me up at night, the birthdays I only hear about."

A pang of regret coursed through me at the melancholy in his eyes. My feelings were valid—this man had attacked me—but had I allowed my anger to keep my children from having even more family? Was I truly so blind to Ulric's sorrow that I'd withheld forgiveness for years?

"There will be plenty more birthdays," I said, smiling. "Perhaps, next year, you could celebrate with us? I'm sure Daka would love to hear more of your stories."

Ulric closed his eyes before looking up at me with the slightest hint of wetness in his gaze. "I would like that very much."

Perhaps we would never be friends in the same way as we once were, Ulric and I, but he could surely be a part of my children's lives if he was so determined to be.

"I have so many presents to make up for!"

Ha, more competition. I was sure my children would be ecstatic. Searching for my son after catching up with Ulric properly—apparently he'd been busy sinking ships in the northern parts of the empire—I found him in the palace library, guards posted around to keep him safe.

I approached smiling, seeing that Dalton was at a larger desk by himself, but with a large stack of books with peculiar titles like *Hosmon's Lex Theory*, *Lineage and Power*, and *The Dangers of Flora Volume Two*.

I recognized *Lineage and Power*, an older text that outlined the powers of nobility and the passage of inheritance, something that I had personally read to familiarize myself with the royal culture of the empire. Inheritance was a hefty and complex subject, one fraught with complicated rulings.

My son's interest in the title was not, by itself, worrying, but a part of me did balk at the idea of having my children fighting over any of the titles I would leave behind. Especially now, as I believed that Dalton had been there when Shawn had first spoke of his idea to ascend me as a high lord of a new house.

"Dalton?" I settled into the chair beside him.

Dalton looked up. "You took a long time."

My son, for all his ambition, was a very quiet child and seemed to outwardly not have much interest in causing problems. In reward, it seemed like I was paying him less and less attention these days.

"I'm sorry, son," I said, leaning over and resting a hand on his shoulder as I looked over the passage he'd looked up from. "The passing of estates?"

Dalton fidgeted under my gaze before he regathered himself and stoically nodded. The passing of estates was less about inheritance and more about the fierce political process in deciding if and when land was transferred between two different houses, usually due to a marriage.

"It's good to understand how this backwater empire wastes everyone's time," Dalton said quietly to himself. I was sure he'd rather not have the guards hearing his words.

It was strange to hear the empire be besmirched in such a way, but I myself had questioned the complicated nature of this nation's politics. I certainly would not be defending it.

"Well," I said, looking to veer to a different topic, "I believe we have a lot to speak about."

Nodding, Dalton pushed his books aside for a young scribe to come and reorganize them as we stood up together and left the library in search of a place to speak.

33

One of the biggest differences between my son and his sisters, I felt, was that he always seemed to be working toward something. There was never a moment where he stopped and played or relaxed.

Daka had been training for years now, but she still enjoyed having fun with others her age, especially Winfred, and Natakia was entranced by the social life of royalty, but she still seemed to have a life beyond that, speaking with Macy about dresses and makeup.

Ambition—that was what I often felt from my son. From when he began helping me organize some of the paperwork for Gelvurt to when he slowly but surely began to get his furniture business up and running, each action he took felt like a stepping stone to something greater.

Perhaps I should have been concerned, but what father did not appreciate his child reaching out toward a goal with such determination? It was not my place to stop, but rather guide him, yes?

"I know you have spoken a lot to your uncle about this plan of yours, Dalton," I said as we sat down together in one of the private chambers of the palace, "but I would like you to talk to me about your plan, what your intentions are, and what compensation you expect."

With the illusionists gone, Shawn had been able to more confidently get the word out about the materials he would need for his procedure, but Dalton certainly seemed to desire payment for his idea.

Dalton took out a single golden sil from somewhere and placed it on the table. "That's what I want, Father."

"I see." I picked up the sil, looking it over. "Shawn may be thankful for your idea, son, but I don't know how much he'd be willing to give you for simply that."

Dalton's brow furrowed. "I don't expect him to give me that simply because of having the plan. I expect him to compensate me after I provide all necessary materials and aid with the procedure."

Alchemists across the world were currently being subtly tapped for information on the reagents and expertise needed for such a task, and yet here my son sat with the confidence of a man who knew everything.

"And," Dalton continued, looking back at his book, "I'll be needing Natakia and Daka to help me as well. Their talents will be put to use."

"Hold on, Dalton," I said, placing a hand in front of him to get his attention. "I've never doubted your capabilities, but this is beyond the works of you and your siblings. What gives you such confidence in finding these things, much less performing the procedure yourself?"

He paused, glancing at the sil in my hand, before reaching out and gently taking it from me. My son gazed down at it in his palm before he sighed. "Father, you understand Daka's expertise with Vitae? Her unique sight?"

I nodded, staying quiet and allowing my son the time he needed to think and speak. My son had thrown himself into his business, retreating from his family, so I would not squander a chance to connect with him and learn more about him.

"There is a value to everything in life," Dalton said. "Knowledge, tools, even the most mystical ingredients all have a specific, quantifiable value."

He placed the golden sil against his open book, slowly dragging the coin across the heavily decorated passages of noble processes.

"This book has a value: fifty golden sils," he said. "The hours it takes to make, from treating the paper to the copying of the scribes, each book has a value decided by its inherent worth and its subjective worth, with its true worth being somewhere in the middle."

And then, with no burst of Mana or flexing of Vitae, I watched the book Dalton had been reading suddenly leave existence. One moment it was there, and the next moment it was gone. I had not even blinked, and yet I could not tell where it had gone or that it had ever been there.

"Dalton," I said, mystified by what I had just seen, "what did you just do?"

My son looked down at where the book no longer was before focusing his gaze on me once more. "I sold it. I've been selling things of minor to medium worth for ten years now, from the moment I was born."

All those toys, those gifts, that is where they had gone? They had been sold by my son for their worth in coins?

"And I buy things, anything really," Dalton said. "That's how I know spells; that's why I have Mana. It's even why I've been saving up money to start investing into Vitae and into techniques. It all has a value to it that I have to purchase, a price tag to obtain something I want."

This went beyond Daka's talent for Vitae and into a world beyond that of normal understanding. A technique based on the pure concept of value? Buying materials and knowledge from the world?

"If Uncle Shawn gives me the money I need, I can buy everything we need for the procedure as well as obtain the needed surgical skills and medical knowledge to do it myself," he said, looking at me, no, watching me. Carefully observing me for any hint that I was taking this badly.

"Dalton," I said, "why would you hide this from me?"

Dalton shifted in his seat, looking slightly uncomfortable at that question. "There was no reason to tell you. I needed no training; I needed no guidance. It was a trump card, an advantage I wanted to keep safe."

"Dalton . . ." It was a heavy day for a parent to learn that their child had thought it important to keep such a secret from them. And yet, he was telling it to me now, explaining it to me openly. "Why tell me now?"

"Ah." He seemed more comfortable with that question. "Well, Father, there is more advantage to telling you than there is to keeping it from you. I can't help if you and Uncle Shawn don't believe I can help."

That made sense. I had doubted my own son's capability to help, so it was not difficult to imagine my friend's dubious reaction to such a claim as well.

"So, what kind of compensation are you intending on asking for?" That was the next big concern, although I was still trying to slowly wrap my mind around Dalton's unique ability. Did Natakia have an ability of her own as well? Was that why she often seemed so observant of others?

"Sil, obviously," Dalton said. "I want to be paid back for the resources I lose buying the needed ingredients and knowledge. Beyond that, perhaps easier quotas for the next decade for Gelvurt."

A decade of easier quotas? That was . . . not exactly what I had been expecting.

"You would use your compensation to better the lives of those in Gelvurt?" I asked, wondering where this compassion for the people of the village had come from.

"Gelvurt isn't going to grow on its own, Father." Dalton shook his head, almost smirking. "With less going to quotas, our farmers will be able to make more money, which will open up possibilities for expanding the town even more through proper, guided investment."

It seemed my son had very high hopes for Gelvurt. I had done my best over the last decade to improve upon every aspect of the town I could, but it seemed Dalton had even higher goals for it to reach. Regardless if it was for the benefit of the people or simply himself, I could not fathom how this would not help both.

"I will speak to Shawn about this, Dalton," I said. "I will explain to him your ability, your offer, and . . . Well, why will you need the help of your sisters?"

The final question to pique my interest, realizing Dalton had said they'd be important to succeed in saving their uncle's life.

"I'll provide the ingredients and the knowledge," Dalton said, "but Daka's sight can aid in finding the source of the infection, and Natakia, well, she'll be able to tell me exactly how it's reacting to the procedure in real time."

She would? Was my desert flower truly aware of such a thing?

At my silence, Dalton smiled, a slight and practiced expression. "We're very useful parasites, aren't we?"

"Dalton." I reached out and ruffled his silver hair, smiling down at him. "I'm so proud to be your father."

Perhaps it was simply a trick of the light, but I thought his smile became just a bit more genuine before he frowned and started to comb his hair back into place.

Leaving the library and giving my son time to study, and repurchase the book that he had sold, I found myself walking back toward my bedroom to make sure that Daka was still there and check to see if Natakia had returned.

And yet, there in front of my door, I noticed Doh waiting with a worried expression, her foot tapping as she looked down at her hands knitted together across her stomach.

"Doh? What's wrong?" I asked, having rarely seen my maid and friend so openly worried about anything. "Are the children safe?"

Doh looked up, a bit surprised, but pleasantly so. She came up to me, glancing back at the bedroom door, before whispering, "Daka and Natakia are talking, but we gotta chat, okay?"

"Of course, Doh," I said, quickly following her as she turned to head toward her shared room with Dresden and, after the palace attack, Macy. "Is Macy okay?"

She stopped, sighing, before pausing at the door and glancing at me. "That's the issue. Macy, she . . . The stress of the whole thing with the gala . . . I thought it'd pass, but . . ."

I had a sinking suspicion bubbling in my stomach as she opened the door and I looked into the room, noticing Dresden currently attending to Macy as she lay in bed and what was clearly vomit on the bedroom floor.

It was gray and disgusting, looking like no ordinary vomit. Certainly nothing a child would produce if they were healthy or, of course, if they were a normal child.

"It's happening," Doh said, her voice tight and low, whispering into my ears as she moved into the room. "I just know it's coming. This is . . . This has to be how it starts. I don't know everything, but it's a feeling I have. Macy's heritage is awakening."

I closed the door behind us, making sure with a few quick applications of Vitae that there were no spies encroaching upon our location. I trusted Penelope's magical wards, but not recklessly so.

"What can I do to help?" I asked, everything else falling to the wayside for a moment in my friends' time of need. Doh and Dresden had been steadfast companions for years now. I would do everything in my power to aid them with their daughter in such a state.

Dresden looked up from the dazed and confused-looking Macy. "I think Doh wants to go home."

"Truly?" I turned to look at Doh. "Is it safe to move her during this change?"

Doh seemed nervous, glancing around. "I don't know, but with everything going on, the palace being attacked and the gala . . . I don't feel safe here anymore, Rakta. I feel like there's way too much going on here in the capital right now."

I could not fault her for believing that with my own confidence in the safety of my children having been damaged these last few weeks. And yet, with Zactrik's interest in the palace, I was worried about how truly safe such a move would be.

"And you believe Gelvurt will be safer?" I asked, not outright disagreeing, but trying to get at the root of the issue. Honestly, with my children and me as targets, I certainly didn't feel safe leaving the expensive protections and wards afforded to us by the palace and capital guards.

And it seemed like Doh understood my own feelings quite well as she shifted uncomfortably. "Look, I love you and your kids, but we're not . . . Dresden and I and Macy, we aren't the ones being targeted, okay? This was a really fun trip, but I feel like we're getting way too deep in this stuff!"

And oh, how I envied them for the lack of interest given to their lives. The idea of being able to live with my children with half of the complexity and danger was near paradisiacal.

However, I did not blame Doh for her thoughts. How could I blame a mother and father for their concern over their child's life? Especially as she began to go through such a traumatic event?

"Buh, Mom." Macy suddenly spoke up, her words heavy and clumsy. "I wanna . . . I wanna stay . . . with Natty. I'm, uh, I'm fine."

"Hey kiddo," Dresden rubbed her back, "it's gonna be okay. Natakia's not gonna be away from you for too long, just a . . . few weeks probably, just while all this gets sorted out."

I appreciated the optimism, but I honestly did not have much hope that this would get handled quickly. My only hope would be to wait until I was given the status of high lord in a day or so and lean on that for increased protection and military force in Gelvurt.

"Doh, Dresden, if you want to return to Gelvurt, I understand," I said, sighing. "I don't think it's the safest option, but I find myself . . . lacking in safe options these days."

"Rakta," Doh began, "we don't want to abandon you and the kids . . ."

I raised up a hand as I shook my head. "I understand. This is no place for Macy to go through her changes, not with Zactrik so interested in those with your unique heritage."

"Oh, Rakta." The black-eyed maid came up to give me a hug. "Just be safe, okay? It's gonna really suck if you get hurt and we hear about it in a letter, okay?"

"I will be fine," I assured her, hugging her back and giving Dresden a nod of confidence over her shoulder. "I'll speak with Shawn and get the both of you outfitted with a guarded caravan, something that will get you home swiftly and safely."

Pulling back from the hug, I looked at Doh. It was strange to imagine that she had once stolen from me so many years ago, now one of my closest companions.

"Is there anything else I can do for Macy?" I looked at both of them.

At that, Macy suddenly held a hand to her mouth before throwing up over the side of the bed again, just barely missing a chamber pot placed out on the floor for her.

"Uh, a maid?" Dresden looked down at the gray sludge.

"Nah, nah, nah." Doh spoke up. "I got this. If you could fetch some extra towels and some cleaner, then we'll be good. Don't need to be tipping off any spies. Thanks, Rakta."

With that, I left the couple to their business, not seeking to intrude upon them any longer. Stepping over into my children's bedroom, I found both Daka and Natakia resting on their respective beds, with none of the negative feelings in the air that had become pungent over the last few days.

On the side of Daka's bedside table, I saw Tenon's book, *Tenon's Worldwide Monstrous Encyclopedia Volume One*, had been opened and flipped through, most likely by Daka. Perhaps I should refresh my memory on the local monstrous wildlife, especially if Zactrik was involved in the area.

That said, both of them glanced at me and looked away, embarrassed, as I smiled in pride at seeing them once again feeling like siblings. I wished Doh the best with Macy but was happy to see my own family was no longer falling apart around me.

It gave me more room to worry about other things.

34

Doh's departure from the capital with her family in tow was a swift and secretive measure, with no one wanting her to be seen as some target to hold hostage in an attempt to get at me and the children.

I had spoken to Shawn about Dalton's abilities and his willingness to help with proper compensation, with my friend not being as surprised by the existence of the ability as I was. Apparently, he'd told me, he had once had a gift of his own that had aided him during our adventuring days.

Unfortunately, he mentioned that said ability was out of his control and had seemingly disappeared since he'd taken the throne, although I felt he wasn't being entirely honest.

"High lords of the Certillian Empire, we can all agree that special precautions need to be taken in regard to the increasingly bold and disruptive actions of Zactrik," Shawn said, his Vitae filling the room as loudly as his words. "However, Zactrik does not operate with an army or known aims like the Warlock King. We cannot confront this foe as we have done with others."

The court had gone well, from what I had observed from the sidelines. Only a mere lord of House Velbrun, I was not allowed to join the conversation unless specifically called upon by a high lord with the permission of King Certimov or the king himself.

Each of the houses of the empire was present, represented by two to four high lords. House Velbrun was in attendance, albeit with only a single representative, alongside House Lyle, House Taine, House Iriend, House Kire, House Oron, House Saren, House Zel, and House Montae.

"Where did this Zactrik come from?" A random high lord from Saren asked, looking a little greener than the others around him. "I cannot imagine such a fiend would simply come from nowhere."

I fought my urge to look over at the representative for House Velbrun. Revealing that Zactrik had originated from Velbrun's nobility would certainly hurt their trustworthiness, but I doubted Shawn wanted to alienate them during such a difficult situation.

"We know that he originates from the empire," Shawn said, "but where he came from matters less than dealing with him now."

High Lord Heron Zel nodded, "I agree, my king. I put forth the motion that we invest in foreign agents from the Continental Adventurers of Derra to act on the interests of the empire in this matter."

"I second the motion," High Lord Yatalia Montae said, smiling as she looked over the budgetary records that had been passed out to the other representatives.

A raucous chorus of whispers erupted through the court, with each representative looking to their adjacent noble. With the motion made and seconded, the floor was open for the matter to be discussed before the king pushed for a vote to be made, unless he made a decision on the matter himself.

"And why," High Lord Garen Kire asked, looking moderately upset, "are our own forces not adequate to root out this cretin? I am offended on behalf of the men and women of my lands, my king."

Another high lord, High Lord Teal Saren, giggled. "High Lord Kire of Frankwin, bold as he is, does have a point, my king. Do we not seek outside aid too quickly? Do we wish to seem weak?"

King Shawn Certimov-Hanchett shook his head, his weakened, poisoned state hidden by his clothing and flexing of Vitae. "This is not a matter in which we are concerned about appearances, but rather one that requires us to be strong enough to reach out to allied organizations and nations to deal with this threat."

"And why are we not investing these resources into the protection of Cerula, my king?" High Lord Leon Velbrun said. "With the attacks upon it, we should be more concerned with defense than an issue that seemingly intends to move on from our lands in time."

The situation with Zactrik, as it had been explained to the high lords, was that he was an immensely powerful mage with strange abilities and unique expertise that allowed him to empower his followers with exceptional abilities. In properly identifying him and his actions, Shawn had proclaimed him an enemy of the nation at the beginning of the court, marking him as a threat akin to that of the Warlock King.

However, some high lords seemed to think, since Zactrik was not presently in the nation, that all there was to be done was to clear the empire of his followers and allow another nation to deal with him.

"Zactrik is an escalating threat whose goals are mysterious and unknown," Shawn said. "Even though he does not currently tread upon our lands, he will return. We must either kill him before he becomes even stronger or seek allies to aid in our defense when that moment comes."

"House Kire will not stand for any attempt to seek aid from the Grand Cipher of Kakrel," High Lord Stefan Kire said, his arms crossed and his glare barely contained.

Talk of whom to ally with was also of hot debate, but soon Shawn called for a vote to the original matter, that of the investment of funds into CAD for talent foreign agents.

In a 16–12 vote, the motion carried, and the discussion of a payment plan from each of the houses to support this investment was held. The frustration from some of the houses, mainly that of House Taine and House Kire, was palpable to the rest of the court.

As the discussion of the matter died down, Shawn held up his hand in the sign of an additional matter to be introduced to the court, and I felt my body stiffen.

"High Lord Leon Velbrun," Shawn said, "I ask you to call upon Lord Rakta Velbrun to stand before me and be presented to the court."

The high lord in question raised an eyebrow, the other nobility in the room breaking out into whispers, but eventually he raised his hand into the air. "Lord Velbrun of Gelvurt, present yourself to the king."

Stepping out from behind one of the closer loose tapestries of the court, I could feel the eyes upon me as I made my way to the small, raised platform in the center of the chamber. Shawn's eyes, no, King Certimov's eyes were strong and unfailing, the gaze of a ruler, as he stared down at me.

It was not my first time to walk down into the focus of so many nobles, but it was certainly never something I enjoyed. The subject of today's spectacle, and the implications and headaches that would be sure to follow, made it even worse.

"Lord Rakta Velbrun of Gelvurt, the Dancer, Slayer of the Warlock King," Shawn said, my full titles resounding throughout the room. "You stand here today as a hero of the Certillian Empire, not only in your service in killing an enemy of the nation, but your humble work as a mere lord of House Velbrun."

Some of the other representative high lords in the audience found amusement in the wording, some glancing at High Lord Leon Velbrun, but most were enraptured in curiosity by the king's words.

"Your work with Tribus Academy, in offering education and facilitating the improved lives of the common folk, alongside Lord Velbrun of Niers and Lordess Velbrun of Alwur, has impressed me," he continued. "And so, due to your character and efforts, I find the need in my heart to reward you, both in honor of your service and in preparation for the conflicts to come."

Now every single one of the representatives was paying attention, the House Velbrun representative frowning as all eyes either lay upon myself or the king of the Certillian Empire.

"In accordance with my power of the throne," Shawn continued, "I decree that the land of Gelvurt, Alwur, and Niers will now henceforth belong to House Tribus, which will be placed within the authority of the newly titled High Lord Rakta Tribus and his associates, High Lord Jorge Tribus and High Lordess Caitlyn Tribus."

The eruption of the room was likely heard in all but the farthest and most isolated corners of the palace, with each and every representative loudly reacting to the news.

I gazed up into the eyes of my friend. "I accept this honor, my king, and will act with the countenance and wisdom expected of a high lord of the empire."

As noise entirely consumed the court at my response, I glanced to see the still-frowning expression of the High Lord Leon Velbrun, his eyes flickering to my own, before he stood and made his way to one of the many exits. With all the power I now held, I knew that my tribulations would only grow to match it.

Looking down at the newly embroidered house symbol—a triangle of rope with knots tied at each point—that had been grafted to my clothing, a formality as I would need to establish royal colors not of Velbrun's influence, I felt tired.

"That went well," Shawn said, drinking a glass of wine as Tracy gave him a look, doing her best to look over what seemed like some work that Winfred had done in class.

Shawn, no longer acting as king, had eagerly relaxed his demeanor after dismissing the court and retreating from the chamber. I could only imagine what kind of strain using his Vitae to appear healthy caused to his system, but perhaps he would soon be able to recover.

I sighed, still having a bit of ringing in my ears from the reactions. "I'm not quite as convinced, Shawn."

"Yeah, uh, it certainly got loud," he admitted, "but I was really expecting the whole of House Kire to blow a gasket about the whole mess. They were really the one I was most worried about when I made the announcement."

I wasn't entirely aware of what a gasket was, but House Kire certainly could have reacted worse, all said. I'd feared that they would entirely walk away from the court or that my rising as a high lord would incite some kind of civil war.

Seeming to notice my feelings on the matter, Shawn patted me on the knee. "Don't worry, buddy. With this, we can start to pull some strings that Zactrik won't expect."

"And I will be able to get some more safety for my children," I said, trying to find the silver lining of the situation. "Although I'm not convinced that this won't simply increase the need to protect my children."

I did not want to have to deal with assassins from the other houses, but that was certainly a possibility now. Not that I would allow such things to go unanswered.

Shawn flinched a little, nodding. "Yeah, again, I'm sorry. Even with the procedure coming up, I can't even begin to imagine not following through with this. Everything I said out there was true. You deserve to be more than just a lord of a small town."

"I appreciate the reward, but not the dangers that come with it." I took a sip of my wine. I'd have to explain to the children that their names were Tribus now.

It was somewhat melancholic, honestly, to be leaving House Velbrun. Those of the house could rot for all I cared, but the name itself, well, it was one of my few connections remaining to Lydia. It was her name that I had happily taken, not that of her family.

And yet, my children were more than enough, and there was simply nothing to be done in regard to sanctity and tradition of names within the empire.

"Speaking of the procedure." I changed the topic. "You plan to move forward with the aid of my son?"

Tracy shifted, looking over from her son's classwork. I knew she had been very busy these last few weeks, her husband's weakened state leaving much work for her to do for him. I wasn't surprised to see a few new gray hairs peeking out from her blonde locks. I'd seen some fresh ones in the mirror myself.

Shawn nodded, glancing at his wife. "Honestly, yeah. Having him actually perform the procedure is a no go, but providing the reagents and having Daka and Natakia help, well, with your permission, would be great."

I still needed to speak with my daughters about lending their aid to their uncle. I was sure they would agree, but I did not want to pressure them. Having the life of a loved one in your hands was never easy, much less if the worst were to happen and you felt responsible.

And yet, keeping them from doing so, even if I wanted dearly to keep them from all threat and danger, would be an even more heinous of a crime that I felt I would surely regret.

"What exactly is he purchasing for you?" I was still somewhat unsure of how Dalton's ability worked, but I no longer doubted its potency.

Although, I was glad he was not the surgeon in the matter. Knowledge and expertise were important, but I doubted Dalton could purchase firsthand experience with such capabilities.

"A golden-speckled rose from the Prell Islands," Shawn said. "Hard to grow anywhere else, but the poison in its petals is very lethal, strong enough to kill an ox in a few minutes, but very treatable. A pretty good combination for what we want."

"And what of Dalton's compensation?"

Shawn had been willing to pay Dalton for whatever material he was requested to supply but had been antsy about the reduction in quotas. He'd shared his concern with me, privately, that House Tribus being given such a reward carelessly could look like a particularly shameless breed of favoritism.

"Well," he said, "we'll be buying plenty of the flowers. The alchemist I managed to find will need to synthesize a lot of poison, more than we'll really need, but I'm only able to give him eight years of quota reductions and not nearly as much as he wanted."

Dalton would not be pleased, but he was a haggler at heart. I would not doubt that he had simply asked for more than he truly wanted to receive exactly what he would be given.

"When will you have the surgery?" That was the biggest question. Every day doom lingered over us, and the longer we waited, I assumed the lower his chance of successful recovery would be.

Shawn took another sip of his wine. "I'll be talking with the alchemist today to set things up, but Penelope is getting a room in the palace prepared for the procedure."

He paused for a moment, resting a hand on Tracy's as he smiled at her encouragingly. She smiled back at him, taking his hand and resting it on her stomach.

"It'll be a week from now," he continued. "A week from today, I'll have my best chance to live."

35

After the craziness of the court, I had not expected many allies to be forthcoming from the houses. Frankly, I didn't care to have allies among nobility, besides a few exceptions, but I knew they would be important as I began to build upon the foundations of Shawn's decree.

House Tribus would be a small domain for years, I was sure, only having a few minor lands to its name, and yet, it still allowed me a few powers that were exceptional. As a high lord, I was able to pull from the House Tribus treasury, which was protected from taxation.

It was effectively my own bank, albeit shared with Caitlyn and Jorge back home, and it wasn't just a culmination of our lands' funds, but also a hefty starting monetary gift that all newly appointed houses were promised by the royal family.

Deciphering the new advantages and disadvantages of my life, however, I had not expected to receive a letter from House Velbrun as quickly as I did.

And certainly not one inviting me to the Velbrun capital estate once more.

"You'll forgive me if I am hesitant to relax, Markus," I said as he once again welcomed us at the door. Natakia, at my side, was dressed in a new outfit that Macy had gifted to her before she'd left the capital.

Markus smirked. "I understand, High Lord Tribus, but I promise you that the business I called you here about today is nothing that'll cause you or Natakia any harm."

I'd have certainly preferred to have left Natakia back at the palace with her siblings, who were both excited at their new surname, albeit Daka being disappointed that she was named after a school. Dalton had spent hours after I told him about our new station reading books on high lords.

"Well, I certainly hope so," I said, glancing at my daughter. "She is quite interested in properly giving her thanks to her savior."

While considerably less depressed since finally talking with Daka, it wasn't hard to notice that Natakia had started eating less and finding fewer reasons to leave her room.

"Ah, of course. Esmeralda is just inside freshening up and getting ready for dinner." Markus led us inside, the Velbrun estate looking no different now that I no longer belonged to the house.

There was talk of a capital estate being built for House Tribus within the year, but I did not hold my breath for it to be as big or magnificent as any of the others, nor would I want it to be. I imagined it being of similar size or quality would simply be another smack in the face to those like House Kire.

"Thank you for inviting us, Uncle Markus," Natakia said, seemingly much more open to the man after the Rose Gala.

He nodded back to her, smiling more genuinely. I was not keen on Natakia establishing a familial relationship with Markus, not with his coldness in the past, but there was very little I could do. She seemed better aware of the man's aims than I often was.

Soon, we were sitting around one of the dining tables in the many chambers of the estate. I kept an eye on the man as the servants began to bring out the food, with the dishes soon set as Esmeralda finally walked into the room.

She was dressed as she was for the Rose Gala, an exceptionally beautiful dress that she wore on her petite figure, her smile a pristine and practiced thing that barely twitched as she looked at me before she zoned in on Natakia.

"Natakia," Markus said, "Esme here was looking forward to seeing you again."

Natakia blinked, looking at Esmeralda, a small tremor in her hands that she seemed to put out of sight in her lap. "I was looking forward to seeing her as well. I never got a proper chance to thank her for saving my life.

Markus's daughter came over, a grace to her steps that hinted at how little was likely human about her, and tilted her head, her eyes glistening with excitement as she neared my daughter.

"Natakia, I really hope we become great friends." Esmeralda giggled. "I really think we could do great things together, you know?"

My daughter, for once in her life, didn't seem to know how to respond to such a statement. Esmeralda tiptoed away from her before she could respond, returning to her father's side and sitting down as the meal, roasted chicken, was fully served.

"Please, dig in," Markus said. "I hope you don't mind discussing some business over a meal?"

I shook my head, beginning to eat after subtly circulating Vitae through my nose to smell for any obvious poisons. "Feel free, although I was expecting High Lord Leon Velbrun to be in attendance."

"Unfortunately, Leon was quick to return to Velbrun after the court a few days ago," Markus said. "By the way, congratulations on attaining your own house, taking some of Velbrun's scraps with you."

"Father," Esmeralda pouted, "I told you to be nice."

Markus seemed genuinely scolded by his daughter, looking slightly embarrassed as he gave me an apologetic nod. "Excuse my tongue. Tonight truly isn't intended to be a casting of judgment on recent politics."

I appreciated that, if only because politics often ruined my appetite. Still, if not politics, I was concerned about Markus's exact motivations for bringing us here. Perhaps to share more information about Zactrik? Surely it wasn't just a chance for our daughters to become friends, was it?

"So, Natakia," Esmeralda said as she nibbled on some chicken, as if that was what she truly needed to satiate her hunger. "That is a beautiful dress you're wearing."

I merely glanced at my daughter and knew that she had appreciated the complement, her lips twisting up into a slight smile, one that'd been rare after Macy left.

"Oh, well." Natakia took a small sip of her water. "It was a gift. A friend of mine got it for me before she had to head back home to Gelvurt."

I met Markus's gaze and felt the slightest of understandings reflected back in his eyes as our daughters began to talk about dresses, makeup, and other things that were beyond us.

"I hope you're comfortable with Esmeralda showing Natakia her room?" Markus came over, offering me a foul-smelling cigar, which I declined.

Comfortable wasn't really the word for it. I was more resigned to Esmeralda's interest in my daughter and over the course of the meal had not noticed an iota of malicious intent regarding my desert flower.

An intense interest, there was no doubt, but nothing that I could perceive as duplicitous or aligned with the intention to cause her harm. That coupled with Natakia's own interest in seeing Esmeralda's collection of dresses and masquerade masks meant there was little power I had over the process.

"I plan to check on them soon. Have no doubt about that," I said, no interest in staying tactful with my brother-in-law. "However, I thought I should owe her savior at least some benefit of the doubt as thanks for being there for her when I could not."

It was a sour point that I still could not think about without feeling like a failure, but I would not downplay the truth of the matter.

Markus nodded. "Yes, she was very concerned about your daughter when she ran off. I don't want to even imagine what would have happened if we had not been there."

"Yes," I said tightly. "I would also hate to imagine that."

Thankfully, he seemed to get the implications and moved on. "I wonder, have they found the perpetrator, the one who organized everything from the inside?"

"No." I kept my eye on him. "Although I wasn't aware that such information had become public."

There was, of course, the very real possibility that Markus himself was the man on the inside. A notion that nothing could dissuade me from.

"Public? No, merely an incontestable fact that such an attempt on your life couldn't have been done without some sort of preestablished plan," he said. "The magic involved in the illusions throughout the estate couldn't have been done quickly nor quietly."

I looked away, the thought irritating me. Someone on the inside had also been involved in the attempt to trick my family into walking into a trap at the palace, of which I was still wary.

"I understand your displeasure at the skullduggery, Rakta," Markus said. "I myself was the target of such an attack right before the Rose Gala began."

I paused, slowly turning back to him. "I'm sorry?"

Markus had not yet lit his cigar, which I was grateful for, and instead looked down at it with a thoughtful gaze, rolling it around in his fingers.

"I'm an enemy of Zactrik, Rakta," he said, a seriousness to his words. "Our carriage was attacked by a band of mercenaries disguised as House Velbrun guards. Of course, they seemed ignorant of Esme's true talents and were swiftly dispatched."

That was . . . No reports of such an attack had been made. Had I simply not been made aware of it, or had Markus not even gone to the trouble of reporting it?

Markus glanced up at me, raising an eyebrow. "Yes, yes, I'm sure it's a surprise to hear. I didn't see any reason to report it, certainly didn't want my daughter getting questioned. She's very shy."

His last words were ironic, but he certainly seemed ready to stand by them. I wasn't sure I'd ever recognize shyness in the way his daughter had eagerly whisked off with Natakia.

"Well, I'm glad you survived." I wasn't sure how else to put it. Esmeralda making it to the Rose Gala was quite a benefit, even if I had no evidence that this attack had happened. "Do you know who sent them?"

He thought about that for a moment, putting his cigar away. "I know it wasn't Zactrik. At least, it wasn't him personally."

"Oh? How would you know that?" Any insight into the man was valuable.

"Because." Markus stroked his chin. "Zactrik would have known exactly what kind of threat Esmeralda is. He wouldn't have sent normal mercenaries. No, this was most likely prepared by the traitor in question."

Which was a clue, perhaps, and certainly something I'd pass along to Penelope and Shawn, but nothing that I personally could do anything about. I already had my hands full with high lord responsibilities.

"So," I asked, "is that it? Is this what you wanted to speak with me about? An attack on you and your daughter and believing that the traitor acted independently in doing so?"

If I were to consider it for longer, the traitor acting independently meant that Zactrik's original preparations for them hadn't exactly worked in their favor, which I assume was due to Shawn's machinations and Markus arriving with Esmeralda in tow.

"No, no." Markus waved me off. "That isn't why at all. You see, I was hoping to warn you about House Velbrun."

"You," I said, pointing at him, "wish to warn me about House Velbrun."

Truly these were strange times we were living in, with Markus Velbrun of all people coming to me in regard to what House Velbrun had planned. This was so blatantly going against the tides of our relationship that it was almost difficult to see it as anything other than the absurd truth.

Markus looked down at my finger, before he shook his head. "Against all odds, we're allies now, Rakta, against Zactrik and whatever he does next. So I want you to hold on to your children tightly."

This man had threatened the sanctity of my family many times, had been the herald of the high lords years ago, but now he was telling me to hold on tightly to my children?

"What do you mean?" He spoke as if something disastrous were waiting in the wings.

"What I mean," he said, "is that you made a deal with House Velbrun, to give your children an opportunity to properly join them once they were of the age to make a decision. They'll fight tooth and nail to keep that bargain, even with your new status."

That was, no, that couldn't be . . . I thought back to the deal, the one I had forced House Velbrun into to leave my children alone until they could make their own decisions, when they became of age at 16 years old.

"It'll be years until your kids reach adulthood," Markus said, "but that doesn't mean they won't do what they can to put them in a position to relinquish their Tribus name for Velbrun."

The very thought made me bristle, but I held in my emotions, calmed down the anger I felt every time someone sought to manipulate me or my children.

"Thank you for the warning," I said, my voice tight, "but I believe it is time to collect Natakia and go."

With that, I stood up and began to walk toward the nearest stairs to go find my daughter and leave as soon as possible.

"Farewell, Rakta," Markus said, finally lighting up his cigar.

36

The days leading up to the procedure were difficult, with getting House Tribus situated, sending and receiving letters from Caitlyn and Jorge as they, too, were accosted by the difficulties of change, as well as finding time to spend with my children.

While I trained with Daka in the mornings, I now invited Natakia and Dalton to join, getting to finally see my children exercising and playing alongside one another for the first time in a while. Additionally, I had procured a magical tutor for my daughter and son, with the mage already heading their way to Gelvurt.

Dalton was excited, although it would be hard to tell if you didn't know him. He'd mentioned, after I surprised him with the news, that learning such things would be a good investment of his time, something he was always interested in.

Daka was eager to sit in on the lessons, too, even if it was mostly to cheer on her siblings and, as Dalton had once put it, to ask the questions Dalton and Natakia didn't want to. I was glad he wanted her involved, at the very least.

It was while I was folding some clothes that one of the maids had forgotten to put away that Natakia finally approached me about it herself.

"Dad." Natakia, her hands behind her back demurely. "I wanted to talk about the magic lessons, if you had a moment."

I put the clothing aside and turned to her. "Of course, my desert flower. What is it that you wish to know?"

I sat down on my bed, smoothing out the blankets beside me to offer her a seat, which she took with a small hop onto the bed. I noticed her hands were slightly smudged by ink, a remnant of her latest hobby of writing letters to her newest friend, Esmeralda.

That was . . . a conversation for another time. It seemed they'd grown attached after meeting once again, and it was the only thing that Natakia seemed to spend her time doing beyond practicing her makeup and doing some light exercises with Daka and me.

"I wanted to know." She shifted in her seat, leaning against me. "I want to know if this teacher can show me how to use divination magic."

I blinked, feeling my pulse quicken. "You wish to learn divination magic, Natakia?"

She looked up, her eyes bristling with nerves as she met my gaze, but she quickly calmed as she held it, a shy smile breaking out on her face.

"I know Dalton already, well, mentioned that I have a special talent," she said, "but I think I can do a whole lot more with it if I could . . . use magic like Mom did. Is that okay?"

For all the stress that had been building up in my heart over the last few weeks, for every trial or tribulation I had to deal with from within and without, I found myself smiling brilliantly.

"Natakia," I said, resting a hand on her shoulder, "there is no young lady more deserving or more capable of learning your mother's magic than you, do you understand? I do not wish to pressure you, but I would be honored—your mother would be honored—if you pursued those studies."

Her eyes glistening halfway through my sentence, she threw her arms around me as far they could go, and I reciprocated, uncaring of how I ruffled up her hair or had to calm the light tremors as she began crying against my chest.

"Shh, my desert princess." I smiled. "Don't cry. Your mother would be so proud of the fine young lady you've grown up to be."

I felt wetness run down my cheek, just imagining a world where Lydia had been able to teach Natakia her magic with her own hands. And yet, through my stories of her, she'd managed to live on and inspire Natakia, the truest measure of how powerful a story was.

* * *

The next day, still riding the emotional high of Natakia's interest in divination magic, I smiled as I walked into the room with Shawn and Penelope, the both of them far more ragged than I was currently feeling.

Ulric was also there, standing in the corner of the private chamber with his arms crossed and an expression that blended focus and confusion.

"Good morning," I said, taking a sip of my coffee as I sat down. "Is there any news?"

Shawn yawned, looking to Penelope, who shook her head and made a gesture back to him, the king of the empire bowing to his similarly tired friend's request.

"Well," Shawn said before he started to cough, each cough sounding rough like his throat was sandpaper. He held up a finger, asking us to give him a moment.

Penelope rolled her eyes sleepily, but I could tell she was worried underneath her exhaustion. "I got the room for the procedure set up. Emergency teleportation device, strong wards, a couple of trusted CADs, some trusted royal guards, the whole works . . ."

That was relieving. If something were to happen and we needed to step in, it would be beneficial to have so many experienced fighters on hand.

"That's good to hear," I said. "With Zactrik's informant still likely among us in some way, there is a chance they know of our attempt to keep Shawn from dying."

There had still been no breakthrough in identifying who was responsible for the leakage of information, but at this point, Penelope was confident they were using some kind of subtle spell work to mask their intentions or aid in the subterfuge.

"Yeah, Penelope, you did a great job getting it all figured out." Shawn's pained compliment got a nod back from the artificer. "So, on my end, I found an expert who can do the procedure with the help of a very special friend of Rakta's."

Wise to my friends' humor now, I shook my head. "I'm glad that Harriet was able to help, Shawn. I assume you've checked to make sure he is legitimate?"

"Oh yeah." Shawn nodded, groaning a bit as he shifted in his seat. "I had a couple of my men make sure he was on the up and up. It's been said he's from House Saren's land, but he's capable and something of a savant when it comes to surgery, apparently."

That was good, very good. Shawn had been forgoing the treatments that his aids had recommended to him for the last few days to prepare for the procedure, but that combined with his general exhaustion had made him increasingly ill.

I could only hope that my friend would get better soon.

"My children are willing to help," I added, somewhat hesitantly, "although Dalton does wish he'd been given the responsibility of handling the operation himself."

Penelope giggled. "Dalton wishes for a lot, doesn't he?"

"Dalton has powerful wants that he considers needs," I admitted. I still gave her a bit of a look, not wanting my son to be spoken of in ill words after the aid he'd provided.

"Calm down, Rakta," she sighed. "By the way, I have some emergency teleportation amulets prepared for them if anything does go down. Should send them to a secure bunker in the Iriend capital estate."

"The same estates where the illusionists were able to penetrate?" I asked, feeling a little dubious of the true safety of such a place.

"You got a better place, Rakta?" Penelope raised an eyebrow, her gaze becoming colder and colder. "Perhaps High Lord Tribus would like us to send them to House Velbrun's estate?"

I frowned, disliking the very idea. "I understand that there are not many spectacular options, but these are my chil—"

"Oh, yeah, I know! I've been trying to keep them sa—"

"Guys!" Shawn suddenly interrupted the both of us, a surge of strength to his voice. "Calm down, okay? I get it. We're all tired. We're stressed. Let's all remember that we're doing the best we can do. Nothing will ever be completely safe with Zactrik around, so we have to take the steps we can take and not fall apa—"

And as soon as his strength came, it went with another round of coughs that seemed to physically shake Shawn. I frowned as he caught his breath, his coughing eventually evening out into a steady respiration.

"You're right, Shawn," I said, before turning to Penelope. "I'm sorry, Penelope. I know you've been working tirelessly to make your home safe once more."

She shifted in her spot before tying her hair back into a frizzy ponytail. "I forgive you. I'm sorry I brought up House Velbrun. I know you've still got a lot of politics in your future with them."

I had not been shy about informing my friends about Markus's warning, with Shawn confirming that they would indeed be within their rights to reach out to my children eventually.

"I know. All is forgiven," I said, not capable of holding my friend accountable for much she said when she was literally doing everything in her power to prepare us. I had been busy myself, but I was not so pressed by my new high lord responsibilities as to need to stay up late for days at a time.

If Zactrik were not such a great threat, I would press her to rest, but there was simply no reason I could think of that would have enough weight in her mind. Shawn had mentioned that she did plan to rest tonight before the procedure, but the body was not an instrument that could be retuned over a single night.

"So, tomorrow is the day of the procedure," Shawn said, nodding in confirmation to everyone in the room. "We're as . . . prepared as we're ever going to be. I really appreciate everyone's hard work, and if I don't make it out of tomorrow's operation—"

"Tracy and Winfred will be taken care of," Ulric said, breaking his silence as the air around him vibrated from his Mana. "No force on Derra could get through me to hurt them, I promise."

There was no doubt that Shawn could see the same resolve on my face and Penelope's, letting him relax back into his chair, smiling in relief. "Have I ever mentioned I love you guys?"

"Yeah," Penelope mumbled, "once or twice."

I smiled, turning my head to lock eyes with Ulric. He met mine with a familiar grin that he seemed happy to share with me again. Perhaps things would never be the same, but I was glad that, for a moment, it felt like it was.

On the day of the procedure, I received a letter from Doh that they had made it back to Gelvurt with little to no issue. It was her handwriting, her scent on the paper, and she'd even included an anecdote of our past together, all of which comforted me that this wasn't a trick.

Macy had also sent a letter, which I'd passed along to Natakia, who was pleased to receive it. Doh had mentioned in her letter to me that her daughter was, well, doing as well as expected.

Thankfully, it seemed like she wouldn't be going through what her mother did to the delight of my friend. Memory magic wasn't a common magic, so it was fortunate Doh had become so adept at it.

"He is arriving soon, yes?" I looked toward Tanner. "I thought this doctor would be punctual with all of the high praise I've heard."

"Perhaps he had a bit of trouble on the road?" The dragon-blooded guard shrugged. "We sent out some of our fastest riders to go collect him, so I imagine we won't be waiting much longer."

Being a part of the greeting party for the doctor wasn't exactly what I had in mind for how to prepare for the procedure, but it was really all I could do to help except channel some of my Vitae into Shawn to strengthen him for the day's events, which I'd already done.

The others were getting ready as well, with my children having been given their emergency teleport necklaces, while I waited in the cool evening air at one of the main gates of the capital alongside Tanner. I regularly checked to make sure Crow had not been disturbed in its holster. I was not keen on being in a fight without my weapon of choice again.

And yet, before any conversation could be had, the sounds of an approaching carriage broke the silence, both Tanner and I tensing as we saw it riding up the road, the coachman pulling on the reins of the two black stallions that were harnessed to the vehicle.

"Good evening, traveler," Tanner said. "Do you come bearing gifts?"

The coachman nodded, his face grim and stoic. "That of broken toys and forests lacking trees."

"Terrible gifts," I responded easily. "Show us."

With that, the coachman leaned back and gave a single solid knock on the wood of the carriage, followed by an additional two weaker knocks. For a moment, I'd wondered if this coded play-by-play would really work out before a single knock was heard from the inside and the door to the carriage opened.

Stepping out of the carriage was a brown-haired, masked individual wearing a large coat that came down to his knees and holding a cane in his hand. A little shorter than me, the man stepped carefully out of the vehicle, a waver to his steps that he tended to by placing his cane firmly down onto the ground.

His mask was made of stiff leather with a long beak like that of a bird and two large holes for eyes that were fitted with a dark-tinted glass that I supposed he could see through just fine.

"Richard Roe?" I asked, already taking stock of the man that would be at the forefront of the effort to save my friend's life.

According to Harriet, he was a very intelligent man that had no talent with either Mana or Vitae and still proved himself capable when compared to physicians that did. An exceptional understanding of medicine and capable of keeping a low profile, despite his attire.

He took a moment to steady himself before his mask turned to me and nodded. "I fly to the king. Please lead on, merry men."

That was the end of the coded phrases I'd been given to receive. I glanced at Tanner, and he nodded, no issues currently seen. We'd have him checked by Daka to make sure that there was nothing strange about his Vitae, and Natakia could read his intentions, but for now, I rested easily.

"Allow us to escort you, sir," Tanner said, motioning for the doctor to follow as the coachman pulled on the reins to lead the carriage elsewhere.

"Please," the physician said as he unsteadily followed, "call me Dr. Roe."

He seemed like a strange man, his mask certainly not being something I expected, but I trusted Harriet's recommendation. That is, if this man was who he made himself out to be.

We'd find out in due time.

37

Vitae was not a delicate energy, not like that of Mana. It was bold and harsh, powerful and difficult to tame for some. Powerful techniques could be derived from it, yes, but they were rarely subtle or complex like that of those fashioned from spiritual energy.

Information gathering, for instance, was one such avenue that Vitae had the capability of facilitating, but not in the complex way that Mana could be utilized for. And yet, I was not lax in using everything in my power to observe Dr. Roe as we walked through the streets of the capital up to the palace.

There was nothing strange about his scent, nothing that any of my techniques to pierce illusions could find out about the man beyond the obvious and what I expected to find. Even as I vibrated my Vitae in the air to subtly test any reaction from the man's possessions, none of Richard Roe's equipment responded as they would if they'd been enchanted with Mana.

"Tell me about yourself, Dr. Roe," I said as we began to leave the beaten trail of the cobblestone path that headed toward the palace and instead went toward an ancillary building.

"Nothing much to tell." His voice was clear, genial, like someone who often spoke with politeness, even informally. "I have no family, few friends. I make my skills available to those who need them, even if they aren't the finest sorts."

Tanner looked back at the doctor. "Are you referring to criminals, Dr. Roe?"

The dragon-like aura around the guard had spiked somewhat, nothing that I couldn't brush aside, but Dr. Roe seemed to pause as he felt in full.

"Yes, I am." Dr. Roe continued walking, small stumbles in his slow gait as he followed us. "I've found that everyone deserves medical care, even if they aren't appreciative. I took an oath, you see, to provide aid to all who need it."

That was very honorable of him, although I could think of many who certainly did not deserve such oath-bound kindness. I hoped that he was not actively aiding murderers and kidnappers.

"An oath?" I asked, curious as to what it fully entailed and wishing to not judge too quickly.

"Yes, an oath, High Lord Tribus," Dr. Roe said. "You see, I am bound to do no harm, or rather, I am bound to either help or do no harm if help is impossible. It is a nuanced binding, one that I've not always adhered to perfectly."

I could only imagine what examples of breaking his oath he held. Derra was dangerous, both human and monstrous threats alike, and I could only say that I would find it difficult to adhere to such an oath indefinitely with the tribulations the gods seemed apt to place in my path.

I was comforted, however. I heard no deceit in his voice, nothing that I could sense that would cause me worry or concern. Perhaps this truly was the perfect man for Shawn's procedure?

"Why do you hide your face?" I asked. "The mask is disconcerting when trying to prove your identity is sound and there are no tricks being played."

Dr. Roe stopped, with both Tanner and me coming to a halt, as well, as we turned to him. He, without a moment's hesitation, pulled the mask up from his face to show a very real, very normal visage. Blue eyes, a slight smile, and younger than I had imagined.

"A certain amount of mystique," he said, "is beneficial when dealing with the more criminally inclined. Also, I place nice-smelling flowers in the beak of my mask, to keep my stomach from turning during a surgery."

I had never seen any other physicians or alchemists wearing such a thing, but I could understand the benefit. With all my experience with the **Scourger Bloodhound Technique**, I had become quite numb to even the most powerful odors of viscera.

"How did you meet Harriet Pillops?" Tanner asked, heading up to the wall of the side building to the palace, placing a hand on the stone pattern of the solid structure.

"Oh, Harriet." Dr. Roe seemed to consider that for a moment. "I can't say much. It's truly more her business than mine to share, but I can tell you that she needed help. Help that I, well, was uniquely capable of aiding her with."

Harriet had a medical issue? Or perhaps she had sought out Dr. Roe for his wisdom? Nonetheless, it truly didn't seem like my business, but I would ask Harriet when we next spoke.

"Well," I said, "I believe that you are true in who you say you are and your intentions. Tanner, if you would?"

Nodding, the guard began to draw with his finger on the wall, sliding it against the surface of the stone in the depiction of a spiral with an eye at the center, the national symbol of the Mana Wastes.

As he finished, the stone suddenly shifted and began to fall in on itself, the individual cobblestones of the wall animating and retreating to reveal the passageway of the secure area where everyone was waiting.

"After you, Dr. Roe," Tanner motioned.

Even though I was reasonably sure that Dr. Roe was not an agent of Zactrik, I found myself tense as he led the way down in the depths of the secure area. Each ward that we passed, each member of CAD that I nodded to as we went deeper, I felt less and less comfortable.

The spell work within each layer of protection should have detected any ill intentions, with a dedicated mage reading our surface-level thoughts as we descended downward.

Something was off. I felt like something was very off. And yet, what could I say? What could I do? The doctor had passed every test. He seemed completely fine. He wasn't as nervous as one might be when asked to tend to the king, but perhaps he simply hid his nerves or was made of stronger will?

And yet, he had faltered slightly when Tanner's aura spiked. Had the aura simply surprised the doctor? Admittedly, there was a difference between dealing with common nerves and the Primus-powered majesty of a dragon.

It all felt very natural with little trickery involved, but my eyes continued to watch the doctor and my surroundings as the uneasy feeling persistently grew. Could I really ask for the procedure to stop simply because I was paranoid?

Eventually, we walked up to the final layer of wards placed by Penelope and the other mages of CAD, a powerful occlusion magic that would keep out any attempts to perceive within the area. And right outside of it, an unexpected welcomer.

"Dad! You finally got here!" Daka came up and hugged me, passing by the doctor. "I thought we were going to be waiting for hours!"

"Daka," I said, hugging her back, patting her on her protective helmet, "you are not supposed to be outside the warded area. It's dangerous!"

Or at least, it certainly felt like that to me for some reason. Which was more than enough for me to be worried about my child willfully leaving even one facet of the protections laid upon her.

"Sorry, Dad." Daka smiled, her eyes crinkling. "I just . . . You were taking so bloody long and, you know . . ."

Ha, patience—my little warrior had little of it. Perhaps she got that from me? I certainly had not been enjoying the long wait at the gate for the doctor.

Speaking of whom, he had stopped, not going any farther, as my daughter came up to greet me, his glass gaze focused on my daughter as she pulled away from me and looked at him herself.

There was tension for a moment as they both watched each other, my daughter looking him up and down, before Daka gave a thumbs-up to Tanner and me. Not the coded gesture that we had decided upon, for better or worse, but I gave Tanner a look to make it clear that the doctor seemed fine.

No strange Vitae, nothing out of the ordinary. I would have been able to tell from how Daka reacted, her sensitivity to "disgusting" Vitae being still very high and untamed. A matter for later.

It was almost a relief, really, that the doctor had passed that part of the checkup, but what if he hadn't? I'd have had to protect Daka as I defended myself from whatever Zactrik had created or purchased or whatever was the case for this instance of his madness.

"Alright, Dr. Roe, we'll be going through the last ward now," Tanner said. "It's a powerful concealing magic, but it will also block unauthorized forms of teleportation, both in and out."

Dr. Roe nodded. "I understand. I don't have any intentions of shirking my responsibilities here. All I want to do is help cure the king."

Still no signs of deceit. No uptick in pulse, no slight catch of the breath. And nothing that was drenched in the corrupt, rotting feeling of Mortum, but we knew so little about that there was no telling what was really possible in the hiding of it.

"We have one more test," I said suddenly.

Tanner glanced at me. "Another test?"

"Yes." I nodded, meeting his gaze as the doctor simply bowed his head at my words. "My associate here is going to flare his aura at you."

If he were to crumble and fall to the aura, knocked unconscious, then he would be confirmed as just a normal individual. Only experienced adventurers could withstand the full force of a dragon's aura.

Tanner blinked. "I could really hurt him, Rakta. If he's really just a normal doctor . . ."

Dr. Roe didn't look like he was going to disagree, not even a hint of resistance from him at the idea of such a test being done, but Daka looked a little worried herself. I doubted she was looking forward to Tanner doing this test any more than he was.

"But if he isn't," I said, "then we'd be allo—"

Suddenly Penelope appeared out of nowhere, stepping through the occlusion ward. "Shawn's just started convulsing. Get the physician in here now!"

Dr. Roe, for all my suspicion, acted quickly as he followed Penelope swiftly, moving through the last ward and into the room, followed closely behind by me and Tanner.

Was the sudden shift in Shawn's condition suspicious? Yes, it certainly was. Did I even have a moment to consider attacking the doctor out of that suspicion? No, not when there was still a likelihood that he'd be the only one capable of saving him.

The procedure room was a large underground chamber, the space excavated and built through the use of techniques and spells throughout the last week under the cover of night. It was a shielded stone room, large enough to be segmented out into multiple rooms if needed.

And yet, right now it was entirely open, with few individuals awaiting us inside, all of them focused on the king of the empire, Shawn Certimov-Hanchett, as he convulsed on a metallic-stone raised slab in the center of the room, numerous tools and supplies surrounding him.

Ulric was looking helpless, an expression I rarely saw on the Fjordic warrior's face, as he stared down at the pained, writhing form of his friend. Dalton and Natakia were away from the slab, my son looking ready to step in at any second while his sister seemed entranced by the horrid sight.

"Clear the way," Penelope yelled as Dr. Roe came through. "Everyone get out of the fucking way!"

The only two others in the room, Garrick and Zerota, members of CAD whom Penelope trusted implicitly, kept their distance from what was happening. Zerota currently had a number of smaller beads of pinkish light at the ends of her fingertips while Garrick's large war axe fluctuated with Vitae.

They both looked ready for a fight, especially as Dr. Roe began to examine Shawn's form.

"Begin circulating the poison," Dr. Roe said. "Who here is capable of reading the patient's vital signs?"

We'd informed Dr. Roe, through coded messages, exactly what he should expect in very loose terminology. The supplies and personnel, like my children, that we had on hand. Nothing in detail, but we wanted him to understand what he would have during the surgery.

Daka stepped up, putting on a brave face as I watched her hands tremble in fear at the state of her uncle. "I can see his Vitae being eaten! And, uh, and where it's going!"

"Come here. Wash your hands in the hot water and place them in on the patient's body where the infection is. Move as needed." The physician seemed to take to this task like a fish to water, no hesitation in his calm but expedient tone.

My daughter instantly went over, wanting to help as much as she could. I followed her, placing a hand on Penelope's shoulders as she activated the small magical device that began to circulate the diluted poison of the golden-speckled rose into Shawn's body, near the initial entry wound.

Dr. Roe nodded as Daka placed a hand on Shawn's side, looking ill as she touched the pale, veiny wound, keeping her fingers away from the black, sludge-like pus that spilled from it.

As the doctor began his work, getting out his scalpel and cleaning it, I realized that Natakia was still only watching, that she'd yet to approach the slab to give her own insights into the reactions of the unliving, parasite-like poison.

"Nataki—" I called over, looking toward my children, but then stopped. Natakia was pale and frozen in place, looking squarely at Dr. Roe.

Her gaze whipped to mine at the sound of my voice, her body suddenly untensing as she yelled out, filling the entire room with words that changed everything. "Dad! That's Zactrik!"

The entire room froze, Dr. Roe's scalpel barely an inch from piercing Shawn's skin to begin the surgery to try to save his life.

"Oh," Dr. Roe, no, Zactrik said, not seeming too bothered. "Well, isn't that a neat trick."

And then a lot of things happened at once.

38

There is a trust that exists within the bonds of comrades. One must trust those that they fight alongside to understand their intentions when a battle starts.

In a few brief moments, just as what Natakia said registered, we were all flying in different directions, each of us with a different parallel goal in mind. In a flash, Daka was in my arms and I carried her close to my chest as I retreated back with the rest of my children.

Penelope had instantly activated one of the emergency teleportation devices, sending Shawn's writhing body, and Tanner, to the secure secondary location at the Iriend capital estate. Ulric, moving as soon as Shawn was gone, shattered the air in front of Zactrik, sending air pressure barreling straight into where he stood.

Or rather, where he once stood.

"Well," Zactrik said, standing on the opposite side of the room. He looked barely fazed by the sudden attack, even as the air pressure decimated the stone wall that had once been behind him.

The room was silent for a moment, everyone still as Zactrik seemed to simply look at where the destroyed wall slowly crumbled and cracked. Not a single one of us moved, glancing at one another to figure out what the next step would be.

One look at my children, all of them still in shock at the sudden turn of events, and I knew what I needed to do.

"I love you all very much." I swiftly activated each and every one of

my children's own emergency teleportation devices, each of them looking up at me in shock as they realized what I'd done.

"Wait, Dad, no!" Daka yelled out, terrified.

Natakia screamed, trying to hug me. "Don't!"

Dalton's mouth seemed to move as if he wanted to say something.

And then they were gone, having been sent to the same place that
Shawn had been. Hopefully the additional forces and protection there
would keep them safe. Keep them away from Zactrik.

"Very good idea," Zactrik said. "I'd hate for the children to be hurt
unnecessarily. Although, I suppose it was a part of the plan to kill them
at some point."

That sent a chill down my spine, but I ignored my fear in favor of my
anger as I pulled out Crow, holding the weapon with a fierce grip, even
as I tried to figure out exactly what I could do against a monster like
Zactrik. He was like Esmeralda, wasn't he?

"Did you plan on killing the king, Zactrik?" I got down in my **Grace
Stance** for now, activating my **Instinctive Reflex Technique**. Dodging
his initial attack, reacting quickly, would be the difference between life
and death.

Zactrik stroked his chin, no longer standing with his cane as if he
needed it. Penelope took the moment to slap her hands together, activating a protective field around herself and inflating a pair of gloves around
her hands into larger-looking gauntlets.

"All-Gear Gauntlets," a feminine voice, akin to a younger Penelope,
echoed from the gauntlets as they powered up with a soft blue light.

Ulric held out his hands, palms out, and I could feel the tension in the
air around his body, the Fjordic man was most likely the least rusty when
it came to direct combat compared to Penelope and me.

"Oh," the madman said eventually, as if finally finding an answer. "I
had no intention of killing the king. Really no reason to. Now, recovering the parasite, absolutely. I can only imagine that the body of such
a renowned warrior would make for a remarkable environment for
growth."

He said the words without a hint of malice, although there was an
edge of coldness to his tone. No, not cold, professional. As if he were one

of Penelope's assistants, dutiful but somewhat eager to see the result of an experiment. Penelope tensed, obviously hearing the same similarity.

"Where is the real Richard Roe?" Penelope asked, her gauntlets charging up. "What did you do to him?"

Zactrik looked confused before a glint of understanding passed through his gaze. "Oh, I see the issue here. No, Dr. Roe never existed. He's a simple fabrication."

I frowned. That couldn't be true. We'd heard a lot about him from . . .

Before the thought could be finished, I reacted on instinct as it seemed we'd decided to attack Zactrik during my momentary distraction.

Zerota, her long, spindly fingers whipping through the air as she completed her delayed spell work, shot off the pink balls of light that had been resting at her fingertips. And running at Zactrik, Garrick began to go in for a slash of his empowered blade.

Penelope held out her palm and shot out a tightly bound ball of blue light that sped toward the stationary-looking Zactrik, Ulric beginning to shatter the air around the man. All the while, I began to throw out as many Crows as I could, filling the air with duplicates that began to rush at the humanoid monster.

The air was filled with destruction, Mana and Vitae saturating the air, and for a moment it was hard to tell what exactly had happened until the air cleared and Zactrik remained standing where he was. Cuts and scrapes from attacks that had pierced him slowly faded away, as if nothing had happened, leaving only holes in his clothing.

"Ha," Zactrik said, shaking his head. "Was that it? Is that really what the heroes of this nation have to offer? Truly makes you think the Warlock King was a bit of a pushover, don't you think?"

Pulling off his mask and tossing it aside, Zactrik revealed his maskless visage, his expression looking slightly disinterested in all of us.

"You two"—he pointed at Zerota and Garrick with his cane—"don't even really have enough prestige to be here."

And then the air changed, and Penelope's eyes widened, and I tried to move fast enough, but in a moment Zactrik was no longer where he'd once been, and a large hole the size of a crystal ball was blown into the broad chest of Garrick, his magical axe being split into two halves as he crumbled.

"No!" Penelope rushed toward Zerota to try and save her, the Waste-lander looking toward her friend in fear as Zactrik was suddenly behind her.

"Oh." Zerota's unnaturally wide eyes suddenly rolled up into the back of her head as her chest exploded outward into a similarly sized hole to the one that had killed Garrick. Her garment seemed to shimmer, as if trying to stitch her back together with contingent magics, but the magic ceased after a moment.

I darted forward, grabbing Penelope as I dove to the left, feeling whatever had killed Zerota continue on and pass by me, barely missing us both as it left an impression on a nearby pillar.

As Garrick's and Zerota's bodies fell to the ground, I gritted my teeth, Penelope standing up from being dove at, and Ulric regrouped closer to us. We wouldn't even have a chance of winning without working together.

"Mourn them later, Penelope," Ulric said, the air around him still vibrating and ready to crack. "I won't be able to get a clean shot without you and Rakta holding him down."

"His speed outmatches us," I said, watching as Zactrik simply observed the corpse on the ground before him, his attention barely on us. "I doubt I'll be able to get a hold of him easily."

Left unsaid was that I was also less confident about the chances of our old plan of attack against Esmeralda working this time around. She'd been nowhere near the speed and power of Zactrik, and we'd barely gotten a hold of her. Not to mention that she'd been insane, lusting for blood and, well, myself.

"We need to regroup, buy some time," Penelope said.

I nodded. "It's time to retreat."

Leaving was far too easy, with Zactrik's clinical gaze trailing us as we retreated from the room and exited through the first ward, with Penelope instantly making a motion in the air, the ward suddenly vibrating fiercely.

"I've turned the ward inward," Penelope said, a tightness to her voice. "I'll do the same for every ward we pass. It should keep him busy for a little bit of time."

I nodded but did not hold out much hope for that being the case. If Zactrik were anything like Esmeralda . . . I could see that Penelope had the same thought as me. The wards may very well just be a nice snack for him.

"Hurry up," Ulric said as he began to race upward, motioning us forward as we began to follow suit. Each and every ward we passed, Penelope turned it inward, collecting members of CAD as we traversed to the surface.

Throwing them at Zactrik would just be pushing lambs to the slaughter, and a few seconds of additional time to plan and think wasn't worth their callous sacrifice. With every face that Penelope knew by name as she called them to her, I knew that such a thought was doubly so for her.

"Where's Garrick?" Another Fjordic man asked as he began to follow, his expression souring as he was shot a pained look by my friend.

Penelope choked slightly. "We . . . we don't have long! Just keep running!"

These were her friends. And I, in my failure and weakness, could not promise that any of them would live until the morning sun broke the horizon.

As we made it to the surface, with twelve CADs in tow, the sound of something shattering back down in the depths of the passageway shook us all to the core, the first and strongest of the dozen wards having been broken. There was little hope that he would humor the remaining eleven.

And yet, that was not the only thing we noticed.

Stumbling out into the courtyard of the palace of Cerula, the capital city of the Certillian Empire, we stopped as we were greeted, not by palace guard, but by a band of cloaked individuals, each lacking any kind of markings or bearings of allegiance.

I counted thirty of them, each of them wearing enchanted-looking armor and fine weapons underneath their nondescript cloaks.

Around them lay the dead guards of the palace that had been posted to keep such a thing from happening. Each and every one of them gutted ruthlessly, with the last breath of one of the guards wheezing out as we exited through the secret passageway.

"This is your chance to surren— Ughk!" one of the cloaked individuals, an older male voice, tried to say before one of my Crow's many duplicates lodged itself inches into his skull.

As the cloaked individual fell down, I cracked my neck. "At least some of you die normally."

With that, the CADs around me roared and surged forward toward the cloaked mercenaries, with Ulric leading the charge as he kept the back line safe from Zactrik's men and free to cast their spells.

"Rakta!" Penelope had stayed back with me as the CADs began to fight the enemy, shooting balls of light out of her gauntlets that detonated and killed cloaked figures one after another. "Zactrik has to be on his way. We have to figure out something to do!"

I took a moment to think, entering into my **Dancing Star Stance** to mentally direct the many Crows flying through the air to hinder numerous foes at a time. We needed something that could hurt Zactrik, actually, honestly, hurt him, but that would need to be something he didn't expect and dodge . . .

"The golden-speckled rose," I said, whipping toward Penelope in my epiphany. "That is what we know, or believe, hurts even a creature such as him? A powerful, mundane poison?"

Penelope's eyes widened. "I think that'll work, but . . . damn, we left the poison behind! Down there, with the guy whom we need to kill with it!"

"Shawn had a lot of poison synthesized," I reminded her. "I can go and get more of the poison from the palace lab while you and Ulric handle him."

"*Handle* is a funny word, but we'll give him the runaround and buy as much time as we can. We'll try and pull him into the palace." She let out an exhausted breath that I could practically feel reflected in my soul before she stomped her feet and her magical boots began to raise her off the ground.

She was getting ready for the chase, so I dared not waste any time.

Killing one last cloaked figure for the road, I nodded and was off without another word. I hoped I would see Penelope again because such a departure did not do our friendship justice.

Rushing through the palace with my **Great Wind Sprint Technique**, I saw that it was not only the palace guards on the outside that had been hit by the cloaked figures of Zactrik's forces. However, compared to the outside ambush, which seemed to have been a clear victory, I was dashing through active battles as I made my way through the palace.

For every guard slain, I saw two or three cloaked figures fall, showing the worth of Shawn's investment in the overall training of his men. I helped where I could, a Crow bisecting an enemy here and there, but I kept my gaze ahead, focusing on each twist and turn toward the lab.

"Ah!" One of the cloaked figures noticed my approach. "Seems like it's time to slay the great Danc— Ughk!"

The figure fell to the ground, drowning in her own blood as I continued past the downed foe, not even passing them a single glance as I finally arrived at the door to the lab, which had been left open, a smear of blood upon it in the vague shape of a handprint.

Kicking the door open, I marched through it with purpose, walking into the expansive, two-level palace lab, the general equipment on the lower floor that I had walked in on and a set of stairs spiraling up toward the second floor, which overlooked the lower part of the lab from a balcony.

It was also where the storage was, where the synthesized poison would be.

After slaying a few more cloaked figures that had made a mess of the lower area, I swiftly proceeded up the steps to the second level of the palace lab.

And found myself walking into what looked like the disturbing aftermath of an alchemical experiment gone wrong, with brilliantly colored chemicals staining the last few steps to the second level and overturned tables and chairs that seemed half-dissolved by strange admixtures.

"Ah," a familiar voice from across the room said as she came through one of the opposing doors. "This is a dreadful surprise. I really am not ready for our first date."

Harriet Pillops, walking into the room with confidence I would never have ascribed to her before seeing it myself, looked nothing like I remembered seeing her just the other day. Long flowing hair that trailed off into a colorful display, her eyes a twisting rainbow of color.

"Has Zactrik already finished up, then?" she asked with a tilt of her head.

39

With Zactrik's words fresh in mind, the casual mention that Dr. Richard Roe had always been a falsehood in all aspects, I knew that this simply confirmed my most recent suspicions. It was with a heavy heart that I regarded the woman I had once thought of as a friend.

"Harriet," I said, sorrow tempering my anger, "I see that it is as I feared. You were the informant all along, the traitor that has been working for Zactrik."

Harriet smiled. "I know. It's not exactly the way I wanted all of this to happen, but when you reached out to me about the surgery, I knew Zactrik would be interested, and . . . well . . . you can figure out the rest."

There were so many questions I wanted to ask, so many words that I knew would tumble uselessly from my lips if I were to open them, so I kept them sealed. My heart would not sway me from treating this woman like all others who betrayed me.

"Rakta?" Her eyes widened.

I dashed toward her, a downward **Heavy Strike Technique** hurtling toward her clavicle before it made impact, and her physical form suddenly erupted into, to my surprise, a deluge of colorful chemicals that almost splashed all over me in my shock before I instinctively blurred away with my **Skip Dash Technique**.

The chemical mound of liquid that once was Harriet trickled quickly toward one of the corners, building in on itself back into the vaguely humanoid shape of the woman I had just attempted to kill.

"Rakta." Her voice was very watery. "I understand you're angry, but I think we can communicate like normal people if you just give me a chance."

I could see the wooden floor under her liquid-like form sizzle and decay from the acidity of her gelatinous form, relieved that I hadn't been entirely soaked by the solution, but feeling the slight burning as droplets of her acid ate into my clothing and skin.

There was no seconds to spare to deal with yet another difficult and frustrating opponent, not when my friends were fighting for their lives merely to buy me time. The poison I was looking for would be in a lead box in the back of the storage room, one that I knew the combination to.

I needed to end this now.

"Thank you," I said, unable to stop myself from speaking, "for the good you have done."

Perhaps it was the growing anger within me that allowed me to flush the air around me with my Vitae so quickly, the same ferocious anger that Brota had drawn upon during his dancing, his passion inflamed.

"Rakta." Harriet could feel the change in the air, I could hear it in her voice. "I really do think we could talk. I mean, think about the—"

For I moved with not only the wind around me, but the rumbling with it, the potential for destruction. For I was the storm, and the storm bubbled within my veins. I provoked the anger of the world into one solid stroke, a stroke I wrote in the air before me.

For that was the way of the **First Dance Stance**.

"Oh shit!"

"First Dance Technique," I said, aiming my open palm toward the fleeing form of Harriet, her body jumping toward one of the nearby windows to the courtyard below. **"Flash of Summer Lightning."**

A solid bolt of lightning flashed out from my hand, my Vitae screaming as I used such an advanced technique, and I watched it scorch through the liquid body of Harriet, sending her screaming in pain as she burst through the window and fell to the ground below.

I dropped my stance, already beginning my Vitae-recuperation exercises, and rushed over to the lead safe where all the chemicals were kept.

There was no telling how much had already gone wrong, how many of my friends were already dead. I couldn't waste even a single second.

* * *

Rushing back through the palace, my first destination to try to find my friends was the largest room that I thought possible for Penelope and Ulric to lead Zactrik to.

The throne room.

Kicking open the heavy doors of the throne room's back entrance, I rushed inside to see Penelope and Ulric entering from the front, the large doors closing on their own as they made their way inside, both of them covered in new wounds.

The worst of what I could see, Ulric's long hair had been shorn, more of an emotional injury, and one of his arms dangled uselessly at his side, while Penelope's left eye looked like it had been glued shut by the blood covering it.

"Rakta!" Penelope dropped onto the ground, her boots deactivating as she stumbled toward me. "Tell me you have the poison!"

I pulled out from the folds of my clothing the vials I could find of the poison synthesized from the golden-speckled rose before noticing that my friends had arrived alone. "Where are the others?"

"We had them scatter, help the fight for the palace," Ulric said, grunting in pain at his loose arm. "They weren't necessary for the chase. Zactrik is only interested in us for the moment."

That was good, much better than the dark thoughts that had filtered through my head when I saw that my friends had not been followed by others from CAD.

I came over, channeling my **Healing Flesh Technique** into Ulric's arm, keeping an eye out as my Fjordic friend slowly regained the use of his appendage. He gave me an appreciative nod, but Penelope stopped me as I turned to do the same for her injury.

"Save your energy," she said, taking out a small-looking disk and placing it over her ruined eye. "I have a thing for this."

I watched as the small disk seemed to glow for a moment before grafting itself to Penelope's damaged eye, the side of the disk facing outward flashing with a teal light before it shifted to become something akin to a metallic-looking eye patch.

Penelope's tricks always surprised me, or rather, the time she had to constantly come up with new tricks would always surprise me. Her ingenuity was never to be underestimated nor her work ethic.

"Alright, Rakta," she said, taking most of the vials except for one. "Pour the poison on your axe. It should take effect if it enters the body through a wound."

"And if it doesn't?" I was no poison expert and certainly not with this one in particular. That said, I instantly began to pour it all over the edge of my blade.

"Let me handle that," Penelope said. "I'm gonna need a little bit of time to rig something up quickly, but we should have a moment or two befo—"

The throne room doors slammed open, cutting her off as we all assumed our fighting positions. Stepping inside, moving far too gracefully to ever need a cane, the monster of the hour entered the chamber.

"Ah, there you are, Rakta," Zactrik said, nodding to me. "I was thinking that you had gone off somewhere, perhaps where your children were sent off to."

Even the mention of my children coming from his mouth made me tense in disgust and fear. What would a horrid man like this do to them if he ever had the chance?

"Rakta." Penelope took a few steps back, giving me a meaningful look. I needed to buy her some time, especially if the poison covering my axe did little against Zactrik.

Ulric stepped up alongside me. "I stand with you, Rakta. Let us remind this doctor who took down the last 'unstoppable' threat."

Bold words, even I thought, but the confident grin he gave me relaxed my tension. He was right; this was no time for doubt or hesitance.

I readied Crow as I settled back into the **First Dance Stance**, feeling my Vitae flow through the air around me, as I readied myself for the toughest fight of my life.

It was time to dance with Zactrik.

"First Dance Technique," I yelled, retaining my focus, **"Twister Through the Valley!"**

Despite every advantage I had, it was difficult to even come close to wounding Zactrik.

His speed, while inhumanly impressive, wasn't unmatchable in short bursts using my **Skip Dash Technique** and **Instinctive Reflex**

Technique alongside the speed of the tempest that pushed me forward toward him. Intensive, yes, but doable.

And as we flitted throughout the room, every attempt I made to cut him with Crow missing or failing by just an inch or two or being blocked by his cane, Zactrik asked me questions.

"How is Gelvurt?"

No matter how much I struggled to slice at him, he was always a second ahead of me, with no hint of exertion on his face as I tried to match his speed.

"Where was the king sent?"

He asked the questions as if we were not in a pitched battle for our lives, which—perhaps I was the only one in such a battle. It could have been disheartening, but I did not allow my heart to sway. Nor did I waste moments thinking about if Shawn had even survived the transit.

"How much longer do you think you have before you tire?"

Questions that I ignored for the sake of my sanity and lack of breath as I put my all into laying a mark on the invincible creature before me. To give Penelope as much time as she needed to get whatever device would win the battle ready and to prove that even this dark thing could bleed.

And yet, the moment finally came. The moment that Ulric shattered the air and sent a plume of air pressure barreling toward Zactrik in one of his blind spots, barely inconveniencing him, but pushing him forward.

Toward me and toward my waiting blade as I surged against him, the power of the tempest fully behind my axe's strike as I aimed for the throat.

His eyes widened, the first reaction I'd ever seen break the man's professional placidness, before Crow carved into his face, his howl of pain echoing as he was sent sprawling toward the floor. I was honestly surprised at how animalistic the noise sounded, such a primal cry of agony that seemed to echo throughout the throne room more than it should.

"Agh, you . . . You hurt me!" Zactrik slowly struggled to stand up, his cane falling to the floor as he grasped at his face. "You—"

I dashed toward him, readying my blade to finish the job now that something had finally seemed to hurt the monster, the light at the end of this horrible night on the horizon.

Slashing down at the man, I found my blade suddenly embedded into the ground, having not even realized that my quarry had moved.

"Rakta, behind you!" Ulric called out.

I tried to move to the side, but found myself stopped as the strongest grip I'd ever felt suddenly had me by the back of my throat, an inhumanly long pair of fingers wrapping themselves around my neck. I lashed out, slashing at the appendage with my axe, but it was quickly caught and tossed aside.

"You." Zactrik's voice now had the tinge of insanity in it that I always knew the man had. "I expected the king to give me trouble, had my little friend not taken care of him, but you . . . You have the gall to harm me? To attempt to ruin everything?"

I kept calm, circulating my Vitae to aid in breathing as his grip got tighter around my neck, but it was more and more difficult as I felt the horrid sludge-like essence of Mortum begin to enter my body.

"Rakta!" Ulric's voice called out, and I could make out the sound of Penelope's boots getting closer as I heard her beginning to yell as well.

"Don't move a muscle," Zactrik said, "or I kill him quickly."

The throne room was quiet, and I was slowly turned around, unnaturally so, while still stuck within his grip, the tempest empowering my limbs fading as I stared down at the torn visage of Zactrik. His face ripped to shreds, his eyes gleaming with hate, and his nose nearly cut off.

If these were my final moments, I rested easily knowing that I had shown that this was a monster that could be stopped, that there was a possibility of a world without him in it.

"I've given up so much to be the perfect life-form, and you think that this is enough to kill me?" Zactrik tilted his head. "The only reason I even humored you and let you live this long was because Harriet's always saying just how much of a wonderful, upstanding guy you are."

The grip around my throat tightened, but I kept my cool and made to look toward my friends.

"Look at me." The hold around my neck tightened even more, Zactrik's hand twisting into something larger and darker and more mutated as his hold became firmer and firmer. His gaze was suddenly looking through me, as if he were speaking to someone behind me. "Do I not interest you?"

"There are thousands of monsters in this world," I gasped out. "There is nothing of note in you being one that we have yet to kill."

"You." Zactrik's focus was on me once more before he smiled. "I've never enjoyed killing. I think you'll be an exception."

I closed my eyes, thinking about my children and the lessons I would never get to teach them. I would never be able to sit down and work out Daka's issues with those of monstrous heritage, Natakia's insecurity in her own life, or Dalton's tendency to put aside his morals for profit.

Would someone else teach them for me? Would the others survive and live on and pass along the lessons that I so desperately wished to? I was jealous, envious of those that had yet to live.

And yet, as I felt the hold on my neck begin to jerk, beginning to bend the bones in my neck even as I enhanced them with Vitae, I smiled at the thought of existing within the stories of others.

The ones that I could walk alongside Lydia in.

And as I felt Zactrik begin to tense and push my bones to their limit, the throne room doors slammed open once more in a sudden burst of spectacular golden light.

"Put him down." King Shawn Certimov-Hanchett walked into the room with a golden aura of Vitae spilling out around him, his **Valiant Hero Stance** glowing with the full might of a king's majesty as his crimson armor rippled around him, ready to defend its newly restored wearer.

40

The relief I felt at Zactrik's sudden release of my neck, throwing me to the side, was only matched by the relief I felt at seeing my friend walking into the room, looking vibrant and healthy.

"Shawn." Penelope's words were thick with the relief I felt, her eyes wet. "Is that really you? But how?"

Drawing his blade, Road Less Traveled, Shawn nodded, giving an encouraging smile to the three of us. "I had a little help."

"The infection," Zactrik said, sounding mystified. "Someone removed it."

"Well." Shawn glanced at me, before turning back to Zactrik with a smirk. "You aren't the only doctor around. The stitching was kind of rough, but I think I'll pull through."

He couldn't mean . . . Dalton? Had my son, with the aid of his sisters, actually continued on with the procedure? That was, I could not even begin to express the pride I felt in that moment.

"No, this is very interesting," Zactrik said, slowly trying to mold his marred face back together as he spoke. "I think it'll be very interesting to see what kind of impact the infection had on your body, so I really can't let you recover too much."

And as he blurred out of existence, heading toward Shawn with a speed that didn't even allow me to get into the correct stance, Zactrik's speed allowed my glowing friend just enough time to smirk.

And suddenly Zactrik was thrown back, impacting the wall of the throne room and leaving a spiderweb of cracks across the stone surface.

"Oh, sorry." A new figure landed between Shawn and where Zactrik once stood. "I didn't see you there, mister."

Esmeralda tossed her hair back, looking pristine and ready for a gala with the dress she wore, albeit covered in blood and viscera as her lips pulled back into an unladylike snarl that belied her polite tone.

"I brought a friend," Shawn explained, looking at us.

The young lady took a moment to stop snarling at Zactrik to haughtily sniff. "I brought myself."

I was too startled by the sudden entrance of what I once thought to be one of the greatest foes in my life and found that it was very pleasant to have such a monster, nominally, on our side for the time being.

"I've got a lot of questions," Penelope said as she moved closer to Shawn and Esmeralda, "but for right now, I've got this, which should take down Zactrik."

She pulled out what looked to be a large syringe-like attachment that had been fashioned onto one of her magical blasters, with a prominent capsule of poison embedded at the center of it all.

"Awesome," Shawn said, readying his weapon. "Esmeralda, run interference. You're our only consistent match in speed with Zactrik. We'll keep him from hurting you."

The young girl, looking around my children's age, nodded and seemed eager to get into the fray. I glanced at my Fjordic friend, our feelings on the strangeness of this new alliance resonating with each other.

Ulric frowned, turning toward Esmeralda. "I am conflicted about this, but today we fight as comrades!"

He and I moved back with the others, as well, and I picked up Crow on the way, it's edge still soaked in the poison that could actually hurt Zactrik.

"Comrades?" Zactrik suddenly spoke up, having picked himself up off the ground. "I can't believe anyone would want to spend time around that failed experiment. You really were so close to perfection."

Esmeralda narrowed her eyes, and her grin became inhumanly wide. "I'll show you how perfect I've become."

With that, both sides settled in for the fight. I fell back into my **First Dance Stance**, feeling the strain of the day beginning to wear on me and knowing that I truly wasn't prepared for a long fight. I could at least support my friends and give them a chance to end this.

"I hope you don't mind if I shake your throne room up, Shawn," Ulric grinned, the air vibrating all throughout the room.

Shawn's blade glowed as he took a step forward. "I don't think I'll be bothered one way or another, buddy."

Penelope's syringe device was absorbed by her gauntlets as her boots began to carry her off the ground once again. "I'll pay for the damages."

"That's a first." I chuckled, enjoying the brief moment of levity.

"**Black Art**," Esmeralda screamed, "**Rose Garden!**"

Piercing our conversation with the yell of her technique, Esmeralda's cry had the rest of us reacting instinctively as Mortum soaked into the world around the young girl and began to surge toward Zactrik in the form of delicately shaped flowers tipped in razor-sharp thorns.

Esmeralda quickly followed her garden of deadly energy, rushing toward Zactrik with clawed hands stretched outward.

Using the **Swift Throw Technique**, I flung duplicates of Crow into the air, surging forward with the original as the tempest of the **First Dance Technique: Twister Through the Valley** began once more.

Shawn surged forward even faster than I, his **Valiant Body Technique** seemingly bringing his physical capabilities up to a level I had never seen before from him. His sword glowed with the telltale signs of the **Valiant Strike Technique**, Road Less Traveled readied over his head as he dashed toward Zactrik.

Ulric and Penelope were of like minds, staying back as they began to unload properly onto the area around, filling the air on either side of Zactrik with shattered plumes of dangerous air pressure and detonations of explosive force.

And yet, as we all approached, each of us with the intention to kill Zactrik, he simply watched us surround him, or rather, he was staring at Esmeralda.

"Art? No," he shook his head. "When we use Mortum, we don't call it an art."

He stretched his hand forward, and I felt a pulse of evil spread out toward us from where he stood, something that went against the very nature of existence and creation.

"**Sacrilege Against Time**." Zactrik grinned. "**Broken Clock**."

And with a harsh, grinding scream, as if the world itself fought against the very idea of what Zactrick was doing, the throne room was overcast in a deluge of gray as everyone and everything stopped moving.

All except for Zactrik.

While my body was frozen in midair, my mind was free to consider exactly what was going on. This couldn't be a technique, or rather, a sacrilege that he could keep up for too long.

Such an immense effect, to freeze the world around him as if the concept of time were his to defy, couldn't be one that he could do without exertion, right? Or was I simply a fool to believe there was any kind of limitation to this sickening energy?

The one limitation I noticed, as Zactrik began to weave his way through us, was that he couldn't seem to interact with us. He observed us, even mumbled to himself, but never attacked us in our paralyzation.

And yet, as I noticed the world begin to brighten, as if his hold on the local time was beginning to fade, I saw Zactrik stride up to Esmeralda of all people and place his hand up against her chest.

"Sacrilege Against Space," he said, **"Black Hole."**

And there, right in front of her body, a small, black, spherical orb now floated barely ahead of where she'd naturally continue to move when time resumed itself. Even for one that I thought of as a monster, I sympathized with the fear she must be feeling, the pain she was about to experience.

And then time resumed, and the sound of tearing dress and flesh could be heard as Esmeralda flew into the orb, her horrid scream of pain filling the air. I reacted as quickly as I could, everyone scattering from the dangerous spherical object, but I reached out and pulled her away from the ball of disaster.

Darting away from it, I could feel Zactrik's gaze on me as I peeked down at the young girl in my arms, frowning as she whimpered in my grip, her touch greedy as she began to instantly latch on to my Vitae.

"Be careful, Rakta," Zactrik said, his voice polite and helpful once more. "She'll drain you dry. A flaw in the process, I'm afraid. Needing any kind of sustenance to survive is just so . . . human."

I let Esmeralda feast upon my Vitae for a moment longer, letting her repair herself as much as she could, before I settled her down to the ground and stood over her. "I don't see any issue with being human."

"Of course you wouldn't." Zactrik looked at me like I was stupid. "You've never had the chance to be anything else, anything more."

The crazed man was still standing near the spherical orb of blackness, looking undisturbed by the destructive force that he stood so close to. Would it simply not affect him? Was it worth a try?

Shawn called out from a distance away, on the opposite side of the spherical orb from me. "Rakta! Is she okay?"

"She'll live," I said, for whatever the definition of the word would be for her. "I tried to help her recovery as much as possible."

"Alright, interference is down." Shawn nodded, still gleaming with energy. It was hard to even imagine that he had been bedridden just a few hours ago. "I guess we'll have to do this without Esmeralda for now. Just keep him on his toes. Ulric!"

"Say no more." Ulric grabbed the air around him and smirked at Zactrik. "I will bring the whole world down on you, puny monster."

Zactrik was fast, but as the tempest around me flared to an extreme, I knew exactly where he was going to be as I whipped my axe toward him just as he tried to close in on Ulric, the doctor rearing back at the sight of my axe before a bright light flashed behind him.

"Valiant Strike Technique!" Shawn sliced into the back of Zactrik as he reared back from my attack, flat-footed and surprised by the unending onslaught.

"Agh!" Zactrik's voice distorted as he screamed. "That hurt me!"

Before he could turn to face Shawn, the world around him shattered, and in his moment of pain and distraction, he seemed incapable of dodging quickly enough as air pressure shot down into him from overhead, cannoning him down into the ground, cracking it as he screamed.

We regrouped again, backing up as we took in the situation. I, specifically, wasn't inclined to try and take advantage of his apparent pain, having already almost died.

"Shawn?" I glanced over at him.

Shawn smiled, wiggling his blade a little. "I thought soaking my blade in the poison would do some real damage to him. Seems like I wasn't the first to have the idea."

"Cutting him up will only make him angry," Penelope whispered, looking at Zactrik who, while enraged, hadn't seemed to be slowing down or tiring in any noticeable way. "We need a larger concentration of the poison in his system."

"Easier said than done," Ulric said, looking pleased that he'd finally managed to give a little hurt back to the good doctor.

As we spoke, trying to figure out a plan, Zactrik stood up from the ground and shook his head. "I see that now is no time for experiments or peace. I should have simply killed all of you from the start and just autopsied your corpses."

As he spoke, Esmeralda slowly started to stand up, but she still looked like she was feeling the effects of the sacrilege. She was a little wobbly but seemed to try and focus on Zactrik.

"You can learn a lot more about a person when they're alive, Zactrik," Shawn said, his blade ready. "About their hopes, their dreams, their loves, all the things that make them better than a corpse."

"What are you going on about?" Zactrik simply staggered around for a moment, looking around, before he shook his head. "None of that matters to my pursuits."

The king of the empire smiled. "And that's why you'll lose."

For a moment, there was silence, before Zactrik suddenly blurred toward us and the fight was on once more.

41

If Zactrik had told us that he had been playing with us before, I would have believed him. Suddenly, he was faster, stronger. Every second his attention was on me, I was in pain in one way or another.

Esmeralda, getting back into the fray, tried to run interference, pulling us away from attacks or knocking Zactrik's blows aside, but even her speed was dwarfed by that of the doctor.

Having learned his lesson, Zactrik stayed away from the blades of Shawn and me, the fear in his gaze palpable every time we neared him with a swing of our weapons or caught him off guard, although such things were happening less and less frequently.

Was he simply learning how we fought, or was he slowly revealing just how outmatched we were? I was covered in bloody cuts and sweat at this point, my Vitae near exhaustion. And yet, he never killed us, hadn't attempted to do so yet, despite his earlier words.

Why? What was he waiting for? What was our worth in keeping alive if he could kill us easily? Did he simply think he could exhaust us and make us surrender?

I was already tired from feeding Shawn some of my Vitae earlier today to keep him stable, not to mention the intensive Vitae usage I was putting myself through beyond that. Ulric and Shawn, however, they could go on for a while, and Penelope, I was sure, had something to make up for any failing of stamina.

"Corner him!" Shawn began to try to carve his way toward Zactrik, trying to push the madman back, but the throne room was too big, even as I stepped in to help, albeit slower than I would have liked to be.

Getting Penelope a chance to inject him with the full dosage of the poison was our best chance at this point, the one thing that we were sure could balance this fight.

And yet, while he didn't seem to be avoiding Penelope like he was Shawn and me, he certainly didn't seem keen on letting anyone get too close to pull out any tricks. We'd have to distract him, truly, but I was beginning to doubt if that would be possible during simple combat.

In a brief moment of respite, as Zactrik seemed to give us from time to time, I said as much to my friends and Esmeralda. "I believe we need to figure something else out."

"What's your idea?" Shawn nodded, open to anything as usual.

Zactrik was willing to converse before, but he was very calm and placid. Now, he was more unhinged, anger and pain getting to him. If I could get his attention, if we could irritate him . . .

"Throw him off. Antagonize him," I said. "Right now, he's still careful, trying not to overextend because he's afraid of our blades. Give Penelope a chance to blindside him."

He'd lost calm once before. If Penelope could capitalize on it properly, we'd only need him to lose it once more.

Ulric laughed. "I see! I see! Time to make fun of the doctor. I can tell I am going to have a good time!"

And that, unfortunately, seemed to be the end of our mild break, as Zactrik was once again on us, each blow he laid was enough to knock us aside and bruise us, but nothing that would be fatal.

Even Esmeralda had not been eviscerated again, although she was giving her all to returning the favor between trying to keep us from getting hit. It was hard to see Markus's daughter within the insanity of black sludge that kept slashing out at Zactrik as quickly as she could.

"What happened to do no harm? Your oath?" I asked as I dashed out of the way an attempt to grab me, barely saving myself from a nasty blow on the shoulder. "I thought that doctors were meant to help, not hurt."

"What?" Zactrik stopped, seeming almost dazed by the question. "I'm not hurting anyone."

Ulric continued on from where I'd left off as he filled the air with loose shatterings. "I'm not surprised a monster such as you cannot recognize harm! You have no idea what you're doing. You're insane!"

"I'm perfectly sane," he insisted, dashing away from the attempt to blast him.

"I'm glad I had someone else do the surgery," Shawn swiped at Zactrik as he moved away, trying to slice into him with his blade before the doctor could dodge, but failed as Zactrik managed to dash away. "I don't think you could have even saved me while trying!"

Each comment came with more force than the last, Shawn, Ulric, and I berating the false doctor with comments regarding his ethics, his talents, his failures, sometimes simply falling back to immature name-calling more appropriate for a child.

Zactrik gritted his teeth. "Stop this right now!"

And so it went, with the majority of us throwing out insult after insult, trying to rile the madman up, including Esmeralda when she wasn't busy screaming bloody murder, and leaving Penelope to slowly become a part of the background, the quiet participant that could do little more than fire ineffective blasts.

I could see it whittle away at him, each comment tearing at him a little more, before the air around him changed as I went for a swipe of my blade, a comment about his stature ready to fall from my tongue.

"You want to see me do harm?" Zactrik wondered with a deceptively calm voice. "I can do harm."

And then I felt pain, hearing the sounds of all my friends and allies, as I realized that Zactrik had struck us all in a moment too fast for us to perceive, Ulric being blasted back into a nearby pillar while Esmeralda had become a smear against the ground, slowly picking herself back up out of it.

Shawn stood in shock, his gaze flitting toward our downed friend, as Penelope looked like she'd only barely registered what had happened.

Nearing the extent of my Vitae after such a long and drawn-out battle, I was unable to do much of anything as he suddenly stepped toward me, his hand flying up to be right above the center of my chest.

"I can do without you," he said, not sounding particularly happy about it, a heavy resignation to his words. **"Sacrilege Against Creation: Disintegration."**

The world screaming out against his action, I could feel Zactrik's hand seemingly catch against something solid and forbidden, sparks of glinting dark spraying out from the contact until the Mortum seemed to catch flame, his hand erupting into a strange whisper of black, white, and gray fire that writhed around and through his fingers.

And as his hand blared into a monochromatic torch, the world slowed as it was pressed toward my chest, and I felt the strangest sensation. Not thoughts of my final moments with my children, their futures, nothing of the sort. Sadness did not wet my cheeks, nor did anger make me ball my fists.

Rather, I felt a rock of cold horror drop into the pit of my stomach as I felt the glow of the morning sun upon me and the feeling of someone pushing me out of the way of the sacrilege, turning in midair to watch as the hand was placed firmly against Shawn's shoulder, easily melting through his armor and lighting his bare flesh on fire.

"Ah," Zactrik said, "what a shame. It seems the king will die after all."

It spread quickly; that was the worst part. As Shawn looked down at me and down at the spreading flame beginning to eat his flesh, a small pain gasp erupted from his throat.

"Shawn," I asked, dropping Crow to the side in shock, "why?"

He simply watched the flame begin to spill out from his armor to the rest of his body before he focused on me, giving a little shrug and a smile. "I guess it was just instinct, you know?"

Ulric made a groan of pain from where he'd barely gotten up, standing up to stare in horror at what had happened as Penelope stood locked in place, looking like she'd forgotten the importance of moving.

Shawn convulsed for a moment as the flame began to eat through his armor, digging in deeper as he suddenly took a knee before falling to the ground as he grunted in pain. Through the flame, I could see the sacrilege eating away at his very bone.

"Hey, Rakta," Shawn said as the sacrilege began to eat away at his shoulder and spread across his body. "I'm sorry I never got to help with the kids. I, well, I guess I just couldn't accept that I wouldn't be around for much longer."

"No, Shawn, no." I carefully placed a hand on his head. "I have never had a friend more helpful and kind than you. You are the epitome of a hero. I'm sorry I . . ."

I could hear Penelope crying somewhere, somewhere that wasn't important right now. All that mattered was staying here by my friend, a friend that I had gotten killed by my stupid idea.

"Hey, I know what you're thinking." Shawn shook his head. "It was a good plan. Honestly, I didn't expect to leave this fight alive, but you, Rakta, you've got people to look out for, your children to raise."

My children's terrified gazes as their teleportation amulets sent them elsewhere flashed before my eyes. They were out there, waiting for me to return to them. And yet . . .

"But what about Winfred?" I asked, feeling my heart break for the soon-to-be-fatherless child. "Does he not deserve a father? Does he not deserve to grow up without this weighing upon him!?"

"He's a strong kid, and he's got his mom. Agh, I've already said my, ugh, my goodbyes." Shawn smiled, tears beginning to flow from his eyes as he continued to writhe in pain, obviously repressing how much torture he was truly feeling. "And I know you'll look out for them. You just gotta make it through this, alright? You, Ulric, and Penelope all gotta be strong, okay?"

The flame had burned away half of Shawn's body at this point, my friend holding on to the mortal coil with the sheer might of his Vitae alone. It was a testament to the power my friend held that he could still breathe, much less talk.

"We'll be fine, Shawn," I promised him, feeling a heavy sense of melancholy begin to fall around my mind. "I will make sure stories are told about you in every corner of the empire and beyond."

"Ha, that sounds pretty sweet." Shawn closed his eyes, his dimpled smile flashing one last time as the flame began licking at the bottom of his face now. "It was nice feeling like a hero one last time."

And then he stilled, and I felt the life leave my friend's body, going off to be remembered in the stories of all those he had saved, of all who had benefited from the light of Shawn Certimov-Hanchett.

Zactrik watched on, his expression neutral as Shawn burned away into nothingness in my grip, looking somewhat curious before he looked down at my hand where I had grabbed a hold of Shawn's shoulder.

And that was when I, myself, noticed that the sacrilege that had just taken away one of my closest friends had not stopped at Shawn's body, but had seemingly jumped to my right hand as he was entirely consumed.

"Pity." Zactrik smiled, although it looked dead. "You'll be gone, too, and I won't even have a corpse to study."

As Ulric recovered, desperately trying to regain his focus for his magic, I could see Penelope slowly beginning to act, as if the plan was slowly returning to her, but all that faded as I remembered the man that Shawn was.

"Rakta," Ulric yelled, sounding hurt and rushed, "what do I do?"

He wanted to save me, somehow rescue me from the fate that had enveloped our friend right in front of our eyes, with none of us able to do anything. I was so weak, I couldn't even attempt to save him.

Looking down at my slowly consumed hand, I breathed in and out. "Give me a moment."

I could already feel it, the way it ate away my skin and began to devour my muscles and bone. For a moment, I allowed it to continue, to feel, even for a moment, the agony that my friend had felt in the last moments of his life and committed it to memory.

Because, if it was ever within my power, I would make sure Zactrik suffered this and more. That was a promise I tucked away in my heart before I began to channel my last remnants of Vitae into my right arm and picked up Crow with my left.

"You are a sick and lonely man, Zactrik," I said before driving Crow straight into my elbow, cutting my burning forearm off. "That is what you said, correct?"

The last bits of remaining Vitae I could spare went into restricting the flow of blood, keeping me alive and conscious as I watched my appendage hit the ground, the flames spreading all over it.

Shawn had been a man rich with family and friends. He had charm and wit, but compassion that kept him from lording all that he knew over those around him. He only ever sought to help, never sought to harm.

Zactrik seemed stunned, either by me cutting off my arm or my question. "What?"

"No family, few friends," I repeated, approaching the monster with my axe, ignoring the loss of my dominant arm. The haze around my mind was strong, memories flashing of a dimpled smile I would no longer see again. "I found no deceit in those words, and I don't think you're a master of deception, Zactrik, I just think you're insane. That you believe what spews from your lips like it is from the gods themselves."

Even in my darkest moments, when I had abandoned them and there had been no debt between us, Shawn had forgiven me, had given me support and had aided me in reconnecting with a world I had retreated from.

Zactrik backed up, away from me, from fear of my axe or my words, I cared not as I continued to approach him. There was no additional strength in my limbs, no great swelling of Vitae as I approached in the wake of the death of my friend.

All I had were my words, spewing from my lips with vitriol only blunted by exhaustion and the shock coursing through me at the sudden death that, for all intents and purposes, should have been mine.

"No stories will ever be shared about you," I said, shaking my head. "And the stories you live on in will be caricatures of your madness, your loneliness. You will be a boogeyman that scares children, nothing more. No one will ever tell the story of Zactrik Velbrun or care how smart or clever he was, only that he was a monster."

It was not simply the truth I spoke, but rather, an omen. An omen that would follow and chase him down until the day he died and was forgotten by those around him.

Zactrik said nothing for a moment before he looked up at me with a dark gaze, something having changed as his marred face stretched out in a truly mad grin. "Nothing, you say? I'll be nothing?"

As he stepped forward, I swung at him with Crow, but it was a weak strike and lacked even a hint of the strength my anger wished to bear against this man. Zactrick caught the swing by my wrist, tightening his hold on my sole remaining hand as I barely struggled, nothing left to fight against him with.

"Stay away from him!" Ulric suddenly came crashing through, having recovered his strength, but it was all for naught as Zactrik simply grabbed a hold of Ulric by his neck and threw him across the throne room, barely glancing in his direction.

Esmeralda was a blur herself, screaming something resembling my name, but she too was thrown to the wayside with barely any acknowledgment given. All that Zactrik cared about was me.

"If you think being remembered is so important"—the madman smiled, a dread filling my heart—"I think it's only suitable that we make it difficult for you to remember anyone."

The fog of anger and mourning that had clouded my mind began to clear as Zactrik's words pierced the veil around my mind. I took a step back, but I knew that he was too fast and his abilities were too strong to resist, especially in my weakened state.

Stepping into my face, he gave me a hard shove, sending me sprawling to the ground. The thought of forgetting my children, my friends . . . I tried to stand up, but my body was barely listening to me.

And yet, as my body failed, I could hear the sound of someone else running in my direction.

"**Sacrilege Against Mind**." Zactrik stared down at me like a god of death, unknowing or uncaring of teary-eyed, pissed Penelope running up behind him. "**Shattered Glass**."

I could feel something horrible slither inside my mind as the world around me went monochrome, as if I were slowly drowning under a black sea that began to encroach upon my vision.

The world shook and screamed within me, what should have been the sanctity of my own mind. It felt nothing like the delicate, compassionate spell work of Doh. No, this felt monstrous, it knew it was monstrous, and yet it continued to destroy me all the same.

The last thing I saw as the dark world of black sludge and insanity consumed me entirely was the sight of Penelope injecting Zactrik with her device.

I fell asleep with a smile on my face.

FROM NOON TO DUSK
INTERLUDE:
PENELOPE IRIEND

The clock in the estate was two minutes fast.

That meant that it was faster than the other clocks around it. And yet, as I watched the horologist from the street shops of Mulwin begin to peel back the layers of the clock, I wondered why it was so wrong for the clock to be faster.

Why couldn't a clock just be faster than other clocks? Was it wrong? I would love to know how that clock worked, why it was two minutes fast.

Sometimes I felt two minutes fast. It never felt wrong to be two minutes faster than other children. I got done with my tutoring faster than most other kids my age, and I was impeccably punctual.

Was any of that wrong?

"Penelope, dear," Mother called from the kitchen, "I need you to come here and sit still for a moment, alright? It's dangerous to go around getting in the way of the help when they're working."

The horologist continued his work, as if he'd barely heard Mother, and I really envied him for that. Sometimes I wished I never heard her, no matter how loud she yelled or spoke. I was never sure how she did it, but I was pretty sure her yells were magical.

"Coming, Mother," I said back, with the regal enthusiasm, or rather the lack thereof, I'd been taught to show for most things, from the most amusing to the dreadfully boring.

It was unfortunate because I really did want to show the horologist just how much I loved what he did, but it wasn't my place to be excited. It wasn't my place to show that kind of love for just a clock.

And yet, it wasn't just a clock, was it? It was a clock that ran two minutes faster than all the other clocks in the estate. Perhaps there would be a good time to tell Mother just how much I loved clocks.

Zactrik stumbled back as the full syringe of poison was injected into him from behind, his gaze whipping toward me in anger as his face almost seemed to deform. "It seems I will just have to kill each and every o— Agh!"

He suddenly crumbled, looking like he was convulsing as he began to writhe, his humanoid form splintering and breaking at the joints as he tried to shake off the effects of the poison.

"Ulric!" I said, bringing out my own weaponry, knowing we had to finish the job now, ourselves. I blasted him as much as I could, my perfected blasters merely denting his form and barely leaving any kind of mark, certainly no wound.

Ulric began to shatter the air, and Esmeralda flew in toward the downed madman, but with one final groan of pain, he suddenly shot up to his feet and looked at me square in the eye. "I will rain hellfire upon this empire, do you hear me?"

And then, enduring glancing blows, stray columns of air pressure, and the dogged pursuit of Esmeralda, Zactrik was able to do the unthinkable and escaped, smashing through one of the ornate glass windows on the far side of the throne room, letting the moon's light bleed in on the failure that I was.

I stood there in shock for a moment, wondering what had just happened. Zactrik had been hurt, in pain from the corrosive poison of the golden-speckled rose, and . . . and he just got to leave?

No, I was not going to allow that. It was time to get a search party ready, one made up of the finest members of CAD. I'd get Zerota to . . .

Oh yes, she and Garrick were gone.

There were others, though, other members of CAD and the royal guard who would join me in hunting Zactrik down to the far corners of Derra. Zactrik had to be of utmost importance; not a second could be wasted on anything else but finding hi—

"Penelope!" Ulric's call stopped me as I began to head toward the exit. "I have a pulse!"

I looked over and felt my heart stop as I saw Ulric standing over Rakta's limp body, feeling a great sense of relief rush through me. I'd thought that he'd died, that Zactrik had killed him with that last sacrilege!

Esmeralda giggled, not able to hide the malicious anger in the sound. "Well, it is a shame that Zactrik got away, but I must be going now. I have a curfew that I'm currently breaking."

And she was off, the strange monster of a young girl fleeing from the throne room, back to wherever she called home. I barely paid her any mind as I dove to Rakta's side, quickly healing as much as I could with a few potions on hand, but there wasn't anything to do about his self-amputation.

The arm was just gone, not even a scorch on the stone to remind the world that something important had once burned in that very spot.

Just like Shawn.

I had to compartmentalize. They were things I could do, things I couldn't. All that mattered now was making sure Rakta woke up safe and sound and able to still be a father to his children who needed him.

It took all my strength to force myself to stop staring at where I'd watched Shawn burn out of existence. There were people who were still alive and needed me, needed Penelope Iriend.

I settled into the chair of the tavern bar as easily as the weight of all my equipment would allow. Mother hadn't thought it was proper for me to go without a guard, but that would have, very obviously, defeated the purpose of why I'd come to the capital in the first place.

The Continental Adventurers of Derra, the worldwide organization that cared not for class or creed, but rather the willingness to put their lives on the line for money and other rewards!

It was akin to a mercenary group, although far larger with a more impressive set of rules and regulations, all of which would leave me ample time and liquid resources to invest into my own projects.

Such as the Self-Wielding Bender Hammer v5, a large mallet that could bend and smack people of its own accord, saving its wielder time and energy! There had been some issues with v3 and v4, a hard-to-get-out malfunction that seemed eager to bonk the wielder on the head.

I, well, was not bringing the Whomper v4 in to help me with the practical tests I'd heard were involved in getting registered with CAD.

And I doubted they'd be impressed by a prospective member that couldn't even make it to the capital by themselves! I would have been laughed out of there as soon as my butler told them to properly address me as Lady Iriend!

"Ha," I breathed out. "I am really tired though. Would have been nice to have some help getting everything moved."

There was still so much equipment . . . but I couldn't wait to purchase even more after I did a few missions for CAD. All that sil, free from House Iriend's influence, would be delicious.

"Excuse me, miss." An unfamiliar voice kicked me out of my reverie before I turned to look up at a somewhat strangely dressed, but overall rather handsome redheaded gentleman.

I looked around, wondering if he was talking to me. "Uh, yes?"

"Sorry to bother you, but, well, my name is Shawn Hanchett," he said, smiling in a way that really made his dimples pop, making him look even cuter. "Forgive me if I'm, uh, prying a little, but do you still need help moving stuff?"

I blinked before looking him up and down and smiling. "Penelope Iriend, and yes, I would love some help."

It was the first anniversary of the battle with Zactrik within the throne room of the palace, and Rakta had yet to wake up, but that was honestly the least of my current problems.

And yet, my mind kept going back to it. Rakta had yet to wake up. He was physically healthy, even his amputated arm having been properly doctored with little issue, but his mind . . .

Doh had said that his mind was fractured. Going inside his mind was dangerous, although she assured everyone that she'd be alright. I wasn't so sure, but what could I say on the matter? How could I tell an expert what was and wasn't dangerous in their field?

Wasn't it worth the risk, if it even existed, to bring my friend back? To bring those kids their father back? I'd originally visited them often, but . . .

There was Mortum in his mindscape, according to the memory magician. Or, at least, a darkness that kept the parts of his mind fractured and made it impossible for her to actually change anything, as frustrating as that was.

Daka apparently wasn't taking the fact that Doh was in her father's mind very well, but I was sure she'd learn to deal with it. There was more important shit to be stressed about than Daka's squeamishness about mind stuff.

Like the fact that until Winfred came of age, Queen Tracy Certimov was the one behind the reins, and I had to be there for her because I'd fucking promised. Ulric was around, too, somewhere, but there was shit going on that he couldn't help with, not unless I screwed up.

There was a war brewing, the houses were mad at one another, decrying the king's death as an assassination by CAD, by a rival house, or some other reason. I was sure Zactrik was behind it, but it could also very well be just the general insanity of nobility.

There was also a rumor that the Warlock King was actually a member of House Velbrun, which Queen Certimov had confirmed, sending a massive blow to the house.

Best rumor I ever fucking started. If a war was going to break out, I wanted to make sure that House of bloodsuckers didn't get a single drop of support.

And here I was, getting more tired every day, feeling the weight of my body sagging more and more. Shawn would have said something charming about the beauty of aging. Rakta would have told me a story about an ancient queen who spoke to the stars in regard to her trouble with age.

I didn't need charm or a story though. I just needed them to be here. I didn't have them though. I had a queen who, despite saying otherwise, absolutely laid the blame on her husband's killer getting away at my feet, at Ulric's feet.

Maybe she was right to do that. Maybe there was more that we could have done.

Zactrik had said a year ago that he was going to burn this nation to the ground, rain hellfire down upon it, but after near sleepless weeks and nightmares that were only organized by the inventing I did between them, I was beginning to almost look forward to it.

* * *

"How are you feeling, Penelope?" Rakta asked me as the clamor of the crowd around us gave a certain kind of privacy that I called a curtain of noise.

Actually, that might be a good idea for a device. I'd have to note that one down just in case I was not very drunk after this whole mess is over.

"I'm . . ." I thought about how to answer that question. "I'm doing about as fine as I thought I would be. It's a big day for Shawn, and I'm not going to do anything to ruin it for him."

And letting him realize how much of an issue I had would absolutely ruin it for him. He wouldn't cancel the wedding entirely, but it'd definitely just be a general downer, as Shawn would put it, for the rest of the night and maybe even beyond that.

Rakta nodded, taking me by my arm in the typical noble fashion and leading me over toward one of the corners of the grand ballroom. "I always imagined Shawn would be more for a smaller venue."

"Marrying the princess is a big deal." I successfully resisted the urge to roll my eyes. "My mother is probably around here somewhere. Can't imagine any nobility would have missed this event."

They could still worry about stuff like that while I was stuck working on a thousand different projects to figure out what Zactrik's next move was. It truly was a curse sometimes to be competent.

Competent and weak to requests from redheads. Not that I needed Shawn to ask me to help protect the empire from the threat that was Zactrik's incessant need to constantly escalate the shit that he meddled with, from local bandits to a small attempt at a coup in House Kire's land.

"Let me know if you ever wish to get a breath of fresh air," Rakta said, motioning toward one of the doors. "I've been wanting to take a walk myself. I've been told that Tracy has recently done some redecorating."

I gave him a nod but generally ignored the offer. I was appreciative, really, but walks never calmed my mind. I needed something to work on, something I could fix.

And yet, the biggest problem I had right in front of me wasn't some machine I could take apart and put together again.

Prosthetics were interesting. The research and development of how to replace one's body parts when they were stripped from you in the line of duty.

I had first looked into them thinking that Rakta, whenever he awoke, would certainly need one, but as I became more and more involved, I realized that I was finding something new for my mind to gnaw at.

The logic I held lay in one simple rational thought: if there existed an improved and upgraded version of your arm or your leg, why would you wait for them to fall off in a dangerous location?

My knees were getting bad, but if I were to replace them . . . I felt like the thought was ticking in my head, like that of a clock. A sound I heard often these days, a sound that meant I was probably either on the brink of greatness or insanity.

No sight or sound of Zactrik had been seen or heard in the last four years, and as Winfred grew into his role as prince of the empire, the impending doom of a civil war had finally become simple whispers and rumors once more. A pity, somewhat, seeing as House Velbrun's influence had waned considerably.

Queen Certimov had even carved some of their land away in the aftermath of all the empire's troubles, including Zactrik, originating from that house.

It'd all been donated to the devotees of the Depth of Death as an apology and compensation for years being heralded as a scapegoat for the troubles of the madman that was the Warlock King. And yet, I'd almost preferred his madness to Zactrik's. At least it had been a human insanity.

Strangely enough, regarding the silencing of the civil war, High Lord Dalton Tribus, as he liked to be referred to, unless in explicitly informal settings, had also had a hand in quieting such talk, although I wasn't sure how. I barely talked to anyone from my house anymore.

Regardless, Dalton's involvement was merely another rumor of the empire that Prince Winfred had been a little too slow in denying the entire veracity of. Furthermore, Queen Certimov was still far from my biggest fan, but she knew how much I did for this empire.

I was the mind behind every breakthrough, behind every innovation. No one matched up to the genius of Penelope Iriend, and no one thought to even try. I was dragging this empire into a new age even if I had to do it while it was kicking and screaming.

Zactrik thought that he had discovered some sort of perfected form? Something that could never be improved upon? Well, I would show him.

The human body had nothing on what I could come up with.

"You had your chance to burn this empire down, Zactrik." I grinned up at the stars as my machines began to whir. "But now we'll enter a new age without you."

And the first of my many airship designs flew through the sky, marking the first successful flight of what would revolutionize every facet of travel and trade within the empire.

FROM NOON TO DUSK
INTERLUDE:
HARRIET PILLOPS

As I did every early morning when work was light and Father had little reason for me to be at the shop, I tiptoed my way through the public market square, down past where the bakery was, picking up a fresh pastry, before approaching the outer training court.

And there he was. With his chiseled physique and dedication to his craft, Rakta was just an amazing specimen to behold . . . from afar. Usually from afar.

I don't even know what I would do if I were up there close to him, talking to him, but it was nice to watch him train. I could forget about the stresses of life and just . . . relax.

"Who are you?" The voice was firm and accusatory.

I turned around and felt my heart drop into my stomach as a beautiful, silver-haired noble-looking woman approached me as if I had done something wrong.

"Oh, uh." I looked around. "I'm, well, not really anyone . . ."

The woman raised an eyebrow. "Tell me your name and what your business is here other than ogling my friend."

"I wasn't." I swallowed, looking back toward Rakta's rippling back. "Okay, uh, I was, but it isn't . . . um, I was just . . . I'm not gonna do anything . . . My name is . . . Harriet."

"I know you aren't." The lady was suddenly very close to me. "So feel free to look, but don't let me catch you touching. Do you understand?"

And with that, having firmly kicked my heart up into my throat, the woman passed me by and began to sway her way toward Rakta, the muscular man finally looking up from his training, but not for me.

He had eyes only for her.

Getting labeled an enemy of the entire Certillian Empire and a criminal in all CAD-affiliated nations was, to be very honest, not what my intentions were when I joined Zactrik's organization.

Days after I had barely escaped getting killed by Rakta, I'd been informed that Rakta was now in a coma until Zactrik cured him or someone else figured out how to cure a sacrilege, and Zactrik had been poisoned by something that was actually hurting him.

"Anything else?" I glanced up at my aide, a half-minotaur man that shook his head silently. I motioned for him to leave and get on with the rest of his duties.

If Zactrik was out of action, well, I wasn't sure where any of this went. This organization, this multination plan, my own plan to seduce Rakta... Although that one had set sail at this point. Perhaps before I had to tip my hand to get Zactrik involved in the surgery like he'd wanted, there was a chance, but...

No, he'd definitely try to kill me if he saw me.

"Oh, Rakta," I said, frowning as I laid down on my desk. "Why does loving you have to be this difficult? Why did you have to fall into that woman's poisonous clutches?"

Lydia Velbrun, ugh, the worst person I'd ever met. Unkind, not a hint of generosity, and worse, really pretty! Like, dangerously pretty. The kind of pretty that I really couldn't compete with, and she always made sure I knew it.

Sighing, I felt my physical form deflate as Zactrik's little gift for me expressed itself. The genes of a chemisctory slime, a semi-intelligent ooze monster that could absorb and recreate alchemical reagents, usually for the purpose of self-defense or melting prey.

Zactrik had told me before the surgery that it would give me certain advantages. He had not stressed, in my opinion, how violent or torturous the surgery would be. I barely remembered any of it, but I had ... nightmares.

Still, producing certain reagents was good for influencing people, and supercharging my acidity was effective. Unfortunately, I'd been feeling the pain of Rakta's technique for days now, and the non-Zactrik physician at this cave base, well, he wasn't sure the pain would ever go away.

I'd been fried very effectively.

Trying to lie and build a relationship on deceit hadn't worked out for me. Instead of managing to kill Lydia's spawn and save Rakta to have him all for myself, I was now cursed with the knowledge that he was out there, in a coma.

And I still wasn't even sure how Zactrik had managed to get past all those defenses to the procedure chamber without being noticed, or rather, what exactly had seen through his big trick that he'd been so confident in.

Maybe if I worked hard enough, Zactrik would wake Rakta up for me? There was word floating around that we were shifting our focus from the empire to somewhere new, but I was sure I could still be useful.

"N-no, Father," I stuttered, frowning as I made an embarrassment of myself again. Dad had asked me some simple financial advice, to show me off to some of his friends, knowing I was . . .

I don't like talking in front of people. I don't like the way their eyes mock me as I make an honest attempt at helping, each of them expecting failure rather than any true advice. They didn't think I could do it, and it was like a self-fulfilling prophecy.

"Ah." Isaac Pillops shook his head, an amused smile on his face, before turning to his friends. "You'll have to forgive my daughter. She's very private about her intelligence. I'm sure she'll finally share some insights once we've all left the room."

They all got a bit of a chuckle at my father's joke, never noticing for a second how I glared at them when their attentions were turned.

I hated it when he did this, I don't know why he insisted on making me the fool of his jokes. I'd been trying to talk to him about some new business opportunities beyond the empire, but he said he'd never let me leave to pursue them, saying it was far too dangerous.

Ah, if only I had Rakta to protect me. The idle thought made me smile, but was besmirched by the memory that he was now a Lord Velbrun, that his children with Lydia were growing up . . . like an infection.

That wasn't a nice thing to think.

I was just frustrated that my father was plaguing me with this abhorrent mockery at a gala I'd had no interest in participating in, not when I had so much work left to do. There was no worth in the first impressions that he touted as important if my father was going to relentlessly sabotage my career with his introductions.

"So, Isaac." One of Father's friends looked away from me after clearing his voice of amusement. "I heard you had someone interesting reach out to you recently, but you declined."

Father narrowed his gaze, shaking his head. "I promise you that individual is not even half as interesting as he makes himself out to be."

"Ah, are we speaking of that little whisper that's been getting around?" one of the other unimportant merchants questioned, inciting my curiosity quite so.

"Cease." My father was no king, but he knew how to put an edge to his voice with Vitae as he gave each and everyone around him, besides myself, a fierce look. "There will be no more talk about this. If you have information, the only one you share it with should be one of our empire's finest or King Certimov himself. Do you understand?"

That quelled the interest in all but me as I realized that my father likely hadn't even considered I was still here, paying attention. Who exactly were they all talking about?

And yet, as I tried to meet the gaze of each and every merchant, trying to find someone who would sate my curiosity, I found not one person who I thought would go against my father's words.

It seemed I would have to do this myself.

I did not know why Father thought of me as incapable of leaving the empire on business, but if that were the case, I would simply need to find business elsewhere.

Business that he wasn't capable enough to pursue himself.

Out of all the spells that I had mastered, the **False Persona** spell was one of my favorites. The shell personality, effectively an outward-facing entity that had select memories and a personality that I could map out and alter, made it an almost impenetrable disguise on a behavioral level.

And the best part? I got to sit back and watch from a corner in my own head, watching as this shell that I created did all the difficult parts of playing the shy merchant that I never wanted to be again.

"U-uh, well, I . . ." The shell looked at the various dumb crooks that thought her an easy mark because, at the moment, she pretty much was. "Well, uh, I'm trying to find—"

I pressed a little, sending out the code phrase that I'd been given to hand over to the first motley crew that tried to play hardball with me.

"—A nice, um, a nice flagon of tea on a misty morning."

The crooks suddenly paused, each of them giving another a look, before shrugging and motioning me to follow. I was disguised at the moment, Harriet Pillops being wanted everywhere CAD had influence, but that didn't mean I couldn't still do a few transactions under some new identities.

While my old contacts had pretty much dried up when I was publicly outed as a criminal—in relation to the king's death, no less—I wasn't entirely starting from scratch.

In the constantly drenched city of Rainwater, on the edge of the Mana Wastes' border with Prayers, there were plenty who knew my money was good and didn't mind the law's interest in me.

It was strange having so many of my assets stripped from me, like a hole opening up underneath me, but this was just one more step to take. One more life to live in order to get what I wanted.

Zactrik needed a presence within the city, and I'd apparently impressed him with my ability to keep up a facade for so long. Somewhat frustrating, as it'd been a year since the palace attack and it was still slow going, with little update on Zactrik's state or whereabouts.

The poison that had been used on him, the golden-speckled rose, was one of the deadliest on Derra. I wasn't sure how they managed to get so much of it in such a short span of time, but it'd been an issue.

A part of me wondered how long Zactrik's recovery would take, but the other part of me was simply thankful that I had ample time to expand the treasury and influence for him.

As I began to be led up toward the leadership for this small little band of ruffians and ne'er-do-wells, I supposed that I truly was no mere merchant anymore, but something far greater.

I was a woman on a mission to save the man she loved.

Sneaking out to the closest town to Cerula to meet the strange and elusive business contact shouldn't have been difficult. They had been cryptic, but overall quite clear in their instructions.

And yet, here I was, dully considering the mistakes I'd made, the life I had yet to live as I dangled in the web of a giant spider, a venomous one by the looks of it.

I tried to keep my breathing steady, tried not to speed up the inevitable, but there was little to do but pray to the Great Beyond. I didn't want to die. I never wanted to ever die.

The large arachnid toyed with me, slowly beginning to raise up higher and higher off the ground, its horrid legs beginning to wrap me in layers upon layers of its thick, adhesive webbing.

Its horrid eyes, I could see my own face in its horrid eyes, and I was struck by how scared I looked, how weak I was. Rakta would never have been this weak. Lydia wouldn't have been this weak.

I was about to die, and no one would mourn me. Father would find someone worthier of inheriting his business, my death would barely make Rakta pause, and . . . and . . .

No one would ever remember Harriet Pillops. Perhaps that was for the best.

And then, a voice broke the thick fog of despair and terror that had clouded every survival instinct I'd had.

"Seems like you have found yourself in some trouble," a smooth, polite voice began to roll through me. "Do you need help?"

I'd never started screaming for help faster in my life, never wanting anything more than to be helped, than to be saved!

And suddenly the spider was dead, there was blood everywhere, and Zactrik Velbrun introduced himself and his plan to save the world.

Spend enough time shaking hands with people with mind-altering chemicals greasing your palms and you can really move up in the world over eight years. Not that I was truly surprised.

The Diving Bells, my little criminal organization within Rainwater, had clawed its way up from the bottom of the underground hierarchy and now sat decently among some of the most feared in the Mana Wastes. Not that Zactrik had placed me here to simply grow my reputation . . .

I'd thrown away the need for a shell personality at this point. Everyone who knew me for the sake of the business knew how I was, knew that I was confident and in charge. I didn't need to hide behind the shy little Harriet Pillops that didn't know how to stake a claim on her man.

Not anymore. These days, I had my pick of partners. From the most beautiful to the most conservative, all found themselves flocking to me and my power.

And yet, I was always waiting, always keeping an eye out for a sign. Zactrik had stayed very quiet, letting the rumors of a civil war back in the Certillian Empire pass by without even a hint of upsetting the status quo from my mysterious boss.

The last I had heard of Zactrik's big plan, he was getting agents in position within the Mana Wastes, but that's all I'd heard from my contacts within the group. If he was feeling better, he certainly hadn't made it clear to me or any that I spoke to.

"Not that it matters too much," I said, going over some specific reports that my cute little scribes had delivered early in the morning. "The underwater excavation is going swimmingly."

It'd take years, but the underwater chambers of Rainwater's most highly kept historical secrets would be unearthed, and Zactrik would be able to find . . . whatever he was looking for.

Sure, there were those who fought my excavation, members of CAD giving me trouble, and general citizenry and leadership against my push below, but . . . Well, those were handled easily.

And yet, it was alright. I did all that I did out of love, out of the knowledge that every life sacrificed, even my own dear father, was just one more step toward Zactrik restoring Rakta to his sanity and the saving of the world.

"Truly," I said, swishing around some wine, "it feels good to be a hero."

FROM NOON TO DUSK
INTERLUDE:
MACY BOOKER

*I*t's good to meet you, Macy." The way she said it was so amazing, I wasn't even really sure I understood what she was trying to say, but she seemed really nice. "I'm Natakia, and I think we're going to be friends."

It was the first time I agreed with her.

When Natakia returned from the palace, I already knew what had happened. I hugged her, trying to give her even a modicum of comfort, but she was distant in her mourning.

Not that her dad was dead, Mom had told me, he just needed to be put back together. He was just sleeping until that happened.

Her siblings were the same, but different. Daka had gotten off the carriage they'd taken to Gelvurt crying, and I'd rarely seen her not crying since. Dalton was distant, but it felt more responsible.

Like he was going to take care of things.

I supposed that was a good thing, although Mom said that with Natakia's dad in a big sleep, a lot of his power was actually passed down to Dalton, so I guess that made sense that he'd be responsible.

And now it was a few weeks after Natakia had returned, and she still wasn't feeling well, barely talking to me and only eating when Mom or I brought her the food.

"Natakia," I said as I came into the room, "I have dinner."

I'd had to speak more recently, which was difficult to do with how dizzy I got sometimes, but Mom said that it would pass and I just needed to keep up with my magic lessons. At least I wasn't vomiting anymore. That hadn't been fun and made me feel . . . weird.

"Mm." A bundle of Natakia was hiding under her sheets today. It was usually either I found her like that or standing in front of her room's open window. I wasn't sure what she was looking for when she stared out like that, but it always made me uneasy.

I came in, setting the food down, and spoke gently. "You need to get out of bed, Natakia. It isn't right to eat in bed."

After a moment, my best friend unfurled herself from the blankets that she had been cocooned in, but she made no effort to get out of the bed. A familiar compromise, but one that I would press on every time, just to see the day my friend got up and out of bed once more.

"It's roast chicken," I said, trying to smile excitedly at the idea, trying to talk like Mom did sometimes. "Zao spiced it just the way you like."

And with that, I began to slowly help her eat her food, speaking about all the beautiful things I had seen throughout the day leading up to this, more talking than I ever thought I'd do. It was hard, knowing what to say and having the confidence to say it at all.

I liked it when Natakia spoke for the both of us. She always understood me regardless of how little I spoke, our special connection, and I was so painfully aware of stares, not to mention the way some of the other girls at school would whisper about me without Natakia being there.

Natakia was like the sun chasing all the shadows cloying at me away, and it was always quite dim when she wasn't around.

The academy was really amazing, though, and there was even talk of it getting bigger in the next few years with the land belonging to the new house that Dalton was kinda in charge of. I hadn't seen him since he had returned, apparently either being out of the keep to speak with important people or secluding himself in his own room.

"Alright, Natakia," I said, finishing up the meal. "Thanks for talking with me. I'll come back tomorrow, alright? Are you going to go to magic lessons?"

A tutor had shown up, prepaid for months by Rakta before his mind broke, and I wasn't sure how long he was going to stay, but Natakia hadn't been going to classes. Neither had Daka, but that made sense. I don't think Daka used Mana.

Dalton went to the classes though. I know because I sometimes sat in there with him when Mom was too busy to teach me magic herself. Usually because she was trying to fix Natakia's dad.

When Natakia failed to give a response, I smiled and gave her a hug. "I'm here for you, Natakia, okay? I won't ever leave you again. I promise."

And with the slow, deliberate movements of an easily spooked cat, Natakia slowly hugged me back, the room feeling a tiny bit less dark with her responding to me. I wasn't sure where she was right now, in that head of hers, but I . . .

I hoped she'd come back to me eventually.

"Macy, how do I look in this?" She looked at me inquisitively, but I simply shrugged. "I really would like you to give more of an opinion on this. I'm sure you have one."

It was the first time I wanted her to hear me.

"And then Daka left," I said, sort of making a hand gesture in the air like a paper in the wind. "Probably sometime in the night. It was a few months ago, but there was a big ruckus trying to find her, and we really haven't had a chance to talk about it since."

I looked over at my conversation partner, but he was still asleep, no surprise there. It was three years since Rakta had been hurt by Zactrik, which I understood better now, but no change or improvement had been made.

"My dad went to go find her because, you know, he's got a better chance of catching up to her," I explained, "but there was no hide or hair. From what they know, she probably crossed the border. Do you know where she might've gone?"

I waited for a few moments before nodding. I wasn't going to get any-thing from Rakta today. I mean, I expected no less, but with Mom gone on some expedition in the Mana Wastes to learn more about memory magic, I was in charge of keeping an eye on his mind. It was my job to not give up on changes.

Not that I went inside there much. It was always the same dark, inky blackness that threatened to look back at me if I stared at it too long. Like something that didn't have eyes, but saw all the same.

"Natakia is doing better now, but she doesn't really tell me much anymore." That was kind of a sad thing to admit, but it was true. She'd become very private. "She has a new friend, some Velbrun that she talks about all the time. Esmeralda? It sounds familiar, but I haven't taken the moment to explore my mind palace about it just yet."

I liked to explore my mind palace in regard to things that made me happy. Like moments I shared with Mom, Dad, and Natakia when she actually, well, spoke to me about things. The Rose Gala hadn't ended well, but I still enjoyed seeing my friend in her natural environment for the first few moments . . .

And she looked happy these days, though, so really wasn't that what mattered? And she was eating, too, which was nice. Zao had pressed her about maintaining a healthy diet for her lifestyle, but I wasn't sure what had convinced her.

She did have a trip to the Velbruns planned pretty soon, signed off on by her brother and everything. I had been hoping she'd take me, but I hadn't been invited yet, and with Mom gone and someone needing to look after Rakta, well, maybe it was for the best.

"Oh yeah," I said, snapping my fingers and furiously trying to distract myself. "And Dalton is doing a great job, I think. I mean, there are some unhappy people in the streets talking about wages, but he showed me the treasury once, and we have a lot of money now. Well, not *we* like me, but *we* as in, you know . . ."

I made another gesture to get the point across, an effort wasted on my inattentive audience. Mom made it look so easy to talk to people, but I really could only pull off this energy between Rakta and Dalton, when he had time for any kind of chat.

Sighing, I looked around the room that had barely changed since I'd begun spending my lessons in here with Mom. "I don't know how she does it, spending all her time here trying to fix you. Dad's starting to question it, too, says there are, well, not better things to do, but well, there's been no change in three years. That's . . ."

I didn't finish that sentence. Dalton had made it very clear that his father would be treated with the best medical care and attention possible and had given Mom a lot of money to find solutions. I wasn't sure or even really knew what the alternative to waiting for Rakta to wake up would be, but it certainly wasn't on the table.

"Maybe it's a bit easier said than done, but I think we should just find and kill this Zactrik guy." I kicked my feet back and forth for a bit. "Well, that's everything. I'll talk to you tomorrow, Rakta."

And like clockwork, I went to wish my father a good night and head off to bed, made my nightly attempt to strike up a conversation with Natakia, and maybe, just maybe, she'd finally take the opportunity to invite me to go with her.

"What do you mean you're leaving?" She was tearing up, her eyes wet. "What am I going to do without you here?"

I was very dizzy at the time, but I knew it was the last time I ever wanted to leave her.

"Good morning, Rakta!" I gave a little trill of a whistle that opened up the magical curtains of the room. Self-cleaning and self-opening, very popular and very easily attained in Gelvurt nowadays.

I began to clean up around the room, doing my daily ritual as I tried to make sure that none of the dust bunnies that accumulated over the night wouldn't come out to bite. I giggled a little to myself.

Carefully, I dusted each of the portraits and paintings in the room, the smiling faces of Rakta's children, although only Dalton had ones that were relatively recent. Natakia had sent a portrait of herself to the keep about two years ago to celebrate her coming of age.

Also, well, to announce that she had renounced the Tribus name and was returning to her Velbrun roots. Dalton had been very unhappy about all of that.

And no one had heard anything about Daka since she'd up and left. I was still super worried about her, but, well, Dalton had stopped paying for search parties years ago. Something about his sister being a lost cause and other mean things I wasn't willing to think about.

"It's been a . . . strange eight years, don't you think so, Rakta?" I said, looking over at the comatose man that I had just naturally become the caretaker of since Mom never returned from her trip. "When Mom comes back and wakes you up with some crazy magic, it'll feel weird to have all these conversations with you again."

I was alone. I was allowed to fantasize a little bit. Dad certainly wasn't very hopeful, but he'd been caught between trying to find Mom or staying with me and making sure I grew up with a parent.

Honestly, it might have been better for him to go off and try. It really feels like he lost something just . . . giving up on Mom for my sake. And didn't that make me feel amazing, him giving up on Mom all for my sake, just so I'd be able to grow up with at least one parent.

"Oh," I said, remembering a little nugget of interest, "you're not going to believe this! Dalton just opened up a museum with a whole bunch of your stuff!"

It was pretty impressive. The Tribus Museum had a lot of artifacts collected from Rakta's past. That was actually where his weapon, Crow, was being held on display. It also had a lot of testimonies from those that Rakta had saved in the past, which really painted Rakta like the hero I grew up hearing about.

"Yeah, I accidentally made a joke about putting you in there, and Dalton almost fired me, which would have been really awkward because I don't know what I'd do if I weren't here, ha ha." I laughed like it was a joke, but it really wasn't.

No close friends, nothing. I mean, I sometimes joked around Dalton, but he was always very serious-minded, and Natakia had stopped responding to my letters years ago, and no one seemed to like me because there was this weird rumor that I was going around kissing boys as their girlfriends, and . . . and maybe that was something Mom would have done, but I . . .

I sat down beside Rakta and just let myself cry a little bit, just a teeny tiny little bit. I missed Mom. I missed Natakia. I missed when everything was so simple and I didn't have to cast magic on myself every night just so I wouldn't forget my name and shit. I hated how often I used my magic just to remember all the people I'd lost for no reason . . .

"This"—I wiped my nose with my sleeve, pointing at the sleeping man—"is all your fault. If you'd just not gotten hurt, not gotten put to sleep, whatever, then it would have all worked out. Everyone would be happy. Nothing would be bad. I'd still have my . . . my best friend."

I could cry a little bit more; it was fine. Who was going to judge me, the comatose father of both my super-distant best friend and my meticulous boss? The dust bunnies?

"Fuck me." I giggled hysterically. "I'm such a mess."

Here I was, blaming a mindless slab of meat for all my problems when he'd given up everything just to protect us, literally risking his life being a hero! What the hell was wrong with me!?

"It's alright, Doh," an unfamiliar voice interrupted me, making me lose my breath like I'd been punched. "I'm okay. I'm awake. You don't have to cry."

I looked up and stared straight into the eyes of the man who had been asleep for eight years, tears beginning to flow even more. "Oh, oh fuck."

He hadn't moved an inch out of the bed, only turning his head slightly to see me as his eyes gazed into my own, and I just started sobbing at how strong he was, how alive he was.

Rakta Tribus was back, and the first thing he saw was me crying like a little girl.

ABOUT THE AUTHOR

Payton Fletcher is the author of My Children from Another World, a slice-of-life reverse-Isekai trilogy, as well as a small-town journalist. Also known as _Glasses, Fletcher first fell for the stories of his great-grandfather and the rest of his family. When he became a journalist and began to hear even more people's stories, he decided to finally put his own ideas down on paper for the world to read. In addition to writing, he spends his time walking around his downtown area, researching new ideas, reading new books, and trying to put his glasses back together whenever they fall apart. Fletcher lives in southern Georgia.

Podium

DISCOVER
STORIES UNBOUND

PodiumAudio.com